Golden Magic

The Path of Dragons, Book 3

Pedro Urvi

COMMUNITY:
Mail: pedrourvi@hotmail.com
Facebook: https://www.facebook.com/PedroUrviAuthor/
My Website: https://pedrourvi.com
Twitter: https://twitter.com/PedroUrvi

Translation by:
Christy Cox

Edited by:
Mallory Bingham

DEDICATION

This saga is dedicated to all my unconditional readers. Thank you so much for all the support.

.

Other Series by Pedro Urvi

THE SECRET OF THE GOLDEN GODS

A world ruled by merciless Gods. An enslaved people. A young slave-hunter at the service of the Gods. Will he be able to save his sister when they take her?

This series takes place three thousand years before the events of Path of the Ranger Series.

Different protagonists, same world, one destiny.

PATH OF THE RANGER

A kingdom in danger, a great betrayal, a boy seeking to redeem his father's honor. Will he succeed in exonerating him and saving the realm from an enemy in the shadows before it is too late for the whole North?

The beginning of the legendary story of the Snow Panthers of the Norghanian Rangers.

THE ILENIAN ENIGMA

A powerful evil. A deadly destiny. Will a young warrior fulfill his calling or doom millions of lives?

This series takes place after the events of Path of the Ranger Series. It has different protagonists, but one of the Snow Panthers joins the adventure in the second book. He is a secondary character in this series, but he plays an important role, and he is alone...

SERIES READING ORDER

This is the reading order, top to bottom, following the main story of this fantasy universe. All series are related and tell a part of the overall epic story.

"I can't believe we're in this situation again," Nahia shook her head hard and kicked a pebble that rolled along the path they were treading. She did not bother hiding how unhappy she was, and it showed a league away.

"I was already expecting it… this is how our dear despots play us," Daphne commented as she adjusted the shield she was carrying on her back.

"We begin the third year at the academy and, of course, it couldn't start any other way than facing a deadly test," said Lily, raising her hands in the air and blowing the air out of her lungs in an expression of her frustration.

"I believe our lords want to measure the advances we've made in our first two years of training," Aiden pointed out as he watched the surroundings with a hand on the pommel of his sword and the other on his dagger. He walked with his chin high, as if nothing could defeat him.

"We've already more than proved it during the last two years!" Daphne protested, clenching her hands into fists.

"More than proved it. Especially in the war against Drameia we've just returned from. We're alive by a hair's breadth," Lily added, making a face of disbelief.

"Finding myself back in this situation is something that upsets me very much. It's neither fair nor necessary," Ivo said with a deep sigh, and then he shook his head. His stride was almost twice that of Daphne's, and he shortened it so they could all march at the same pace.

"Dragons are as brutal as they are methodical, especially in training and understanding their Path. We'll have to face this test and overcome it, since it's required to start the third year," Taika said in his soft, silky voice as he set their marching pace.

"It's clear to everyone that they're ruthless blockheads," Daphne stated.

"You'd better lower your voice, they're watching us," Aiden warned her. "They won't tolerate the least amount of contempt in their presence."

They all gazed up unobtrusively. The six dragons, the squadron leaders, were flying over the area. They did so in circles, separated, each over the route their squadron was following.

Nahia saw that Irakas-Gorri-Gaizt was right above them, about two hundred paces high. Close enough to burn them all or plunge down with its claws forward, tearing them to pieces in a moment. She guessed it was far enough away not to hear them, but even so, she was not altogether at ease.

She looked ahead, following the path, and thought that the morning had begun very strangely. Not only that, it was getting more and more complicated by the moment. They had been forced to line up in the bailey of the Academy at first light. It was the first lineup of the year after the graduation ceremony of their second year, so everyone had assumed the third year was beginning. They were wrong. She remembered that the only good thing about the graduation ceremony had been that she was able to see that Logan and Ana had returned from the war mission in Tremia alive. That had not been the case for everyone; several squads had suffered casualties, resulting in not just wounded, but also dead. Colonel Lehen-Gorri-Gogor had delivered his usual speech about how fortunate they were to be able to graduate from the second year at the illustrious martial academy of Drakoros and the great honor this meant. Nahia had forced herself to swallow the acid rage crawling up her stomach toward her mouth at hearing all those lies from the leader of the Academy. The dragons could take their glorious Path and throw themselves with it to the bottom of the oceans and drown so they would never have to see another dragon again. Several whole worlds would be grateful for it: countless souls. Unfortunately, that was not going to happen. They would have to be pushed, with their snouts and claws tied, and a heavy weight around their necks.

The graduation badge award, which the Colonel presided over, left Nahia astonished once again. Not the ceremony, but the six Dragon Riders who came down from the sky on the backs of their great dragons to give them the second-year silver badge. It was like the first-year one, but with a different dragon and the number two engraved on it. Nahia still could not believe there might be slaves from the different races who rode powerful dragons. It was beyond her understanding. Watching it left her speechless, unable to fathom the reason. Something she did notice was that those Dragon Riders were not the same ones who had handed them the badges the year before. That meant there were at least a dozen riders, most likely more. The reason for their existence escaped her, but she would find the answer. She needed to understand how they could exist. Perhaps there was something that might be useful in their search for freedom.

Lining up that morning before Irakas-Gorri-Gaizt in the bailey, Nahia had experienced a funny feeling, a sense of something not being entirely right. She had thought it was only her fears manifesting at the beginning of the third year. She had been mistaken. At an order from their leaders, they had set out in formation. And here was where things had started going awry. To everyone's great surprise, the leaders had led them outside the Academy. They had exited through the north gate.

Once outside the Academy, Irakas-Gorri-Gaizt had taken to the air, and from it informed them with a direct order, accompanied by a feeling of severity, that the third-year test was commencing. Nahia's fears, and also those of her comrades, were confirmed.

Hence the bad mood and concern all of them felt at that moment, Well, with the exception of Aiden, naturally. Everything the dragons ordered was okay for the Drakonid. Or at least, that was what he said, although he did not always behave as if it were so.

"We'd better keep going in silence for a while, and without protesting, in case something reaches their ears," Taika said, watching the dragons circling up high, unobtrusively.

"Yeah, better be prudent. Things are going to get ugly," Ivo predicted, sighing sadly.

"Yeah, we'd better be, I agree. Although it makes me very angry not to be able to complain," said Daphne.

"Oh, go ahead and complain, but under your breath," Lily said, smiling.

Nahia just had to smile at that.

The three squads of the Red Squadron marched as one: the Igneous Squad on the left, the Ardent in the middle, and the Searing on the right. Nahia had always wondered what was behind that gate, north of the Academy. Now she knew. They were seeing it, and it was something unbelievable. They had just climbed a small hill covered in grass that looked out on an immense lake of blue water. The surface reflected the sky and the few clouds in it. It was so large you could not see the other shore from the one they were standing on.

This is Lake of the Sky. Do not stray, and maintain formation and pace at all times, they received Irakas-Gorri-Gaizt's order from the heights, together with a feeling that it would not tolerate mistakes.

Nahia was awed by the beauty of the lake. She understood the reason for the name, since it reflected the sky with total clarity. They continued bordering the great expanse of blue water, and it turned out to be a very pleasant walk. This place transmitted quietness, peace, serenity, things that did not exist in Drakoros. They went on, maintaining the pace since their leaders were flying over them, but they had a small margin of freedom which they were all enjoying.

"I want to go to the shore and see my reflection in the water," Lily had said, making a move to break from the formation.

"Don't you dare," Aiden warned her, jabbing his thumb upward.

"I only want to see myself mirrored. I bet I look amazing and radiate irresistible magnetism in this environment."

"You do and you are radiant, but Aiden's right, don't break formation or Irakas-Gorri-Gaizt will make you pay," Taika warned her.

Lily waved in frustration and kept her place in the formation without missing a beat.

"Let's enjoy this wonderful landscape nature is offering us," Ivo said.

"And this warm summer breeze loaded with fragrances," Taika added, filling his lungs.

"If those dragons were further away, this would be a walk to remember," Daphne commented, glancing back.

"They're far enough for us to enjoy ourselves a little," Lily told him, smiling, and tossed her jet-black mane in the breeze.

Nahia also shook out her blonde hair and filled her lungs with the fragrances of summer while her blue eyes lost themselves in the water of the lake. It took them several hours to go around the great expanse of water, and they all enjoyed the environment and the walk. It was a moment they would remember for a long time.

After leaving behind the great lake, they had marched on for several more hours until they arrived at a large forest of oak trees.

Cross the forest. In single-file formation and without changing the pace. If you slow down, I swear you will regret it, Irakas-Gorri-Gaizt ordered them.

The Searing Squad stepped back and the Ardent took the lead, leaving the Igneous in the middle. They entered the forest and they noticed that the terrain was flat and thick with vegetation. Moving forward was not easy, so they enjoyed the surroundings a little. Being in the middle of an oak wood was commonplace for peasants, but since they could not leave the Academy, it was a true gift. Nahia was enjoying the walk immensely. Being in nature once again, inside a beautiful forest with hundred-year-old oaks, breathing the smells of nature of the forest, listening to the birds, seeing squirrels, filled her soul with some joy.

"This place is wonderful," Ivo said, opening his arms as if he wanted to embrace the whole forest.

"It's only a forest, what's so wonderful about that?" Aiden contradicted him with a blank look in his Drakonid face.

"Forests are magnificent places, full of flowers and fauna, full of life," Taika corrected him.

"I'm not saying they're not good places for hunting and finding mushrooms and roots, but from there to wonderful or fantastic..." Aiden shook his head.

"You are a granite-head and don't see the beauty of this place. For my people, forests are sacred," Daphne told him.

"For mine, it's a habitat to hunt and live in," Taika told him.

"For mine they're only forests," Aiden said with a shrug.

Nahia and Lily looked at one another. For them forests were not as important as for Daphne and Taika, but they did appreciate the beauty and everything they offered.

"Today they're offering us a bit of freedom," Nahia said, looking up. No dragons could be seen since the tops of the trees covered them.

"Very true. Today, for the time it'll take us to cross this forest, we'll be free," Lily said.

"Something we must enjoy and value," Ivo said.

"Don't slow down the pace, remember our orders," Aiden warned them, intent on keeping them going.

The hours it took them to cross the oak wood provided them with an illusory sensation of freedom. They felt alone in the middle of a landscape of green and brown hues filled with life. Nature entered them through every pore. Although they all knew the feeling of freedom was not real, they enjoyed it all the same. Sadly, any illusion, no matter how nice and pleasant it might be, always came to an end, being in itself ephemeral. And so it was. They reached the end of the forest and their free walk. As they came out onto a clearing covered in tall grass, they saw the dragons again, flying over them, not too high up. The freezing shower of reality that accompanied that vision hit them, reminding them they were nothing but slaves doomed to fight and die for the dragon lords.

We move north. Keep the same pace. They received Irakas-Gorri-Gaizt's order as it passed over their heads, the air it created messing with their hair. It seemed to want to remind them who was in command here. Who was the lord and master.

Night began to fall while they traveled in silence along the plains, covered with a soft green carpet. Nahia enjoyed the feeling of walking on earth and grass. It was so different from stepping on the stone-paved floors of the Academy. It reminded her of when she used to go gathering medicinal plants with her grandmother. How distant it all seemed now. It had only been two years since the last time she had experienced the pleasure of walking in the countryside with her grandmother, but to her it seemed like two decades.

When night fell, they received a new message from Irakas-Gorri-Gaizt as an unappealable order.

You will keep going forward to the north in formation. There will not be rest for anyone. Maintain the pace at all times. Adjust your eyes to the dark and don't slow down. If you need water, drink from the water skins you're carrying but without pause.

Nahia looked at her comrades with horror. It was going to make them march all night, after marching all day. Lily blew the air out of her lungs loudly and all her sensuous beauty left her, only to be replaced by unrest. Daphne growled and muttered curses in the language of the Fatum, which erased the natural beauty of her face. Ivo simply heaved a deep sigh; his beastly Tauruk face did not lose its tranquil look. Taika did not react in any way to the announcement. He was looking to both sides with narrowed eyes, scrutinizing the night. Aiden stiffened as if they had tied a broom stick to his back and looked ahead with eyes that radiated the confidence he felt that he was going to make it.

The night march turned out to be not only tough, but complicated. The terrain was flat, and because there was a summer moon in the crescent third, they were able to make out where they set their feet. But they had to cross two more forests, one of beeches and the other of linden tress, as well as three relatively deep rivers, which became quite arduous, particularly since they could not slacken the pace. While they crossed the rivers, Irakas-Gorri-Gaizt appeared above them to make sure they did so quickly, despite the currents of two of them being quite strong.

It's nothing but a river! No slowing down, keep up the pace!

A river with a strong current and at night, Nahia thought as she lost her step and the current took her. Luckily, Aiden was marching behind her and realized what happened. He grabbed her arm hard and prevented her from being dragged off by the river.

"Thank you… Aiden," she said gratefully, swallowing water.

"You're welcome. Regain your footing and keep going so you don't slow us down too much."

Nahia regained her footing and kept her balance. She went on, relieved.

She was not the only one to have trouble. The water reached Daphne's nose and she also lost her footing. Ivo grabbed her and carried her on his hip, holding her fast with his right arm. He carried her at his waist as if she were a little kid.

"You're… a great… beast…" Daphne reminded him, also swallowing quite a lot of water.

"I'm Ivo," he replied and smiled nonchalantly.

Before dawn, tiredness began to take its toll in the squads. Nahia felt exhausted, and she realized that Lily and Daphne were too. Even the imposing Ivo was walking more slowly now. The Ardent and Searing Squads were also having difficulties keeping up the pace because they were so tired. Nahia wondered whether the dragon leaders had been flying all night. She doubted it. Most likely they had stopped to rest. No matter how powerful and strong they were, it was an effort for them to travel through the sky, they could not be immune to tiredness. As Ivo would say, all creatures of nature had to follow the rules. None could avoid growing tired when making an effort. She looked up at the sky and did not see them, which confirmed her thought.

With dawn, the leaders reappeared in the clear sky with their enormous wings circling over their squadrons. Irakas-Gorri-Gaizt plunged down fast and glided over them.

Stop at the hill, it ordered them.

They had all been looking up at the sky when they saw their leaders appear and had not noticed the hill. They reached the top and watched. To the north, there rose a huge mountain with a single snowcapped peak.

They had arrived at the place of the test.

Chapter 2

Nahia was staring at the great mountain. She had no doubt that the majestic, imperturbable rocky formation was where the third-year test was going to take place. The very high mountain seemed to penetrate the sky itself, with its snow-capped peak. In itself, it represented a challenge.

"That mountain's going to give us trouble," Daphne predicted, wrinkling her nose as she contemplated it.

"Apart from the fact that we're exhausted," said Lily, who adjusted her supplies satchel on her back beside her shield.

Nahia nodded. She felt the same way. This time it was not a feeling, it was what she was seeing. In front of it, they were mere ants.

"What's worse still is that I doubt we'll be allowed to rest."

"The dragons will not give us pause, no," Taika agreed.

"It's the best way to strengthen our body and spirit," Aiden said.

"I'll strengthen that rock-head of yours, with a pick!" Daphne shouted at him.

"And I'll help with a hammer and chisel," Lily added.

Move on to the base of the mountain, came Irakas-Gorri-Gaizt's order.

They obeyed at once. The closer they came to the great mountain, the more impressive it seemed to them. They were able to make out levels of rock and caves on the skirt and in the upper levels. There were steep slopes, some almost perpendicular which seemed hand-carved. Once they reached the base, they had to go around large rocks that had fallen from the mountain to its base.

They stopped, restless, awaiting orders, which did not take long to come.

Igneous Squad, maintain position without breaking formation. Ardent Squad, go a thousand paces to the west. Searing Squad, a thousand paces to the east. Facing the mountain, Irakas-Gorri-Gaizt messaged, along with a feeling of great urgency.

Both squads moved fast to obey the orders and soon vanished among the great rocks.

For a long moment they did not receive any more orders and

were able to rest, although not much, since they had to maintain their positions and stay on their feet. At least they were no longer marching, and this they were all grateful for. Nahia guessed that if their squad had been ordered to spread out, the others would have received the same order. What were the dragons up to? She did not know, of course, but it would be nothing good, she was sure.

"Can you see the other squads?" Lily asked as she looked around, shading her eyes with her hand. The summer sun was quite intense that day, and at this height amid the clouds it always affected the eyes.

"I can't see them, but my sense of smell is picking them up," said Taika, tapping the side of his nose with a nail from his right claw.

"I can't see them with all these large rocks around us," Daphne said as she strained her neck to try and see beyond them; something impossible for her, since she was the smallest of the group.

"What I can't believe is that we're being forced to take part in this test. Both squads have two members in the infirmary," Nahia said, upset.

"True. They returned badly wounded from the war and haven't recovered yet," Lily said, shaking her head. "Luckily they haven't died, at least not yet…"

"The fact that a squad has wounded members or casualties doesn't excuse them from participating in the regulatory training," Aiden said as if it were a sin even to think about it.

"If they have people in the infirmary, they should not be taking part in a deadly test," Ivo said," And we know from past experience that the beginning-of-the-year tests are just that."

"They have less possibilities of survival. The more people in the squad, the better the odds of coming out alive," Taika said.

"The fact that they have less possibilities will make them strive harder and have a better result in the test. It's a disadvantage, yes, but it will strengthen them," Aiden stated and made a face that meant he did not see it as an excuse not to participate.

"Forcing them in these conditions is the work of heartless sadists, rock-head," Daphne told him.

"Which is what our lords are, granite-head," Lily added.

Aiden made a face that meant he did not care what they said.

"I'm right, so I'd rather not listen to your comments against me or our dragon lords," he replied and mimicked covering his ears.

"You're more obnoxious every day," Daphne chided him, jabbing her finger at him.

"I've told you what I think, which is what our lords think. Continuing this argument gets us nowhere."

"As it could be no other way," Daphne rolled her eyes.

"We're going to take you to a cliff," Lily threatened him.

Aiden turned his back on them and looked up at the sky where the dragon leaders were flying.

Nahia was trying to glimpse her squadron comrades among the great rocks, but without any luck. She wondered how those large boulders, part of the mountain, could have fallen all the way down.

"At least our squadron hasn't had casualties. Others haven't been so lucky," Taika commented.

"It's a disgrace, what's happened at the end of the second-year test. There are several squads that have suffered casualties in the war against Drameia. It's devastating. Dying that way in a test... without any need... it's capital cruelty," Ivo sighed deeply and shook his head.

"It's unpardonable to make those squads take part in this beginning-of-year test. Beastly, without scruples," said Nahia, who could not believe they were forced to take part anyway. Well, she did believe it, because something like this was expected from the dragons, creatures of brutality that lacked both pity and empathy.

They all looked at Aiden, waiting for his comment in favor of the dragons, but the Drakonid looked up at the white tip of the mountain and said nothing.

They stood waiting and still for a good while. They did not know why or what was awaiting them. The passing of time only made them more nervous. From the south, two enormous dragons came flying. They passed over their heads and headed up to the peak of the mountain. They were unmistakable, even flying up high. But to remove the last vestiges of doubt, they passed over the squadrons in a low flight to then soar to the mountain peak. It was Colonel Lehen-Gorri-Gogor and Commander Bigaen-Zuri-Indar.

"The judges are here..." Lily said, disheartened.

"Now the suffering begins..." said Daphne, frowning.

"That's what I'm afraid of." Nahia was watching the circular flight of the two enormous dragons over the white peak.

"Let's stay united and we'll make it," Taika tried to cheer them.

"He's right. Only thus will we manage to overcome the

adversities that face us," Ivo added, looking at the mountain with narrowed eyes.

"I don't know why you're so worried. We'll win any test our lords challenge us with. That's our duty, and we'll fulfill it with honor," Aiden stated.

Daphne and Lily looked at one another and shook their heads.

"You're hopeless," Daphne said.

"I don't care. I'm perfectly happy the way I am," Aiden said, very sure of himself.

Prepare to start the third-year test, Irakas-Gorri-Gaizt's order reached them. They raised their gaze and saw their leader flying in circles above the squadrons' position. They also made out the other leaders making the same flight, so they guessed where the other squadrons were located—all separated, but all facing the great mountain from the southern side.

"Let's be careful and watch out," Taika advised them.

"We'd better," Daphne added.

The test is simple. You have half the night to reach the peak of the Mountain of the Past. Those who don't make it will be expelled. It's that simple. The message came with a feeling that it expected nothing less of them. Yet, Nahia detected something else, something that made her think there was something more to it.

"A test of climbing and resilience, piece of cake," Aiden said, already puffing up.

"I'm not good at climbing and resilience," Daphne told him.

"I don't understand why they always give us physical tests, I'm so good at the emotional ones," Lily joked with a grin.

"The dragons don't care about your emotions," Daphne said. "Or the others."

"I think they're not telling us the whole truth…" Nahia predicted. "I don't believe the test is going to be that easy."

"It wouldn't surprise me in the least. Honesty isn't a characteristic of dragons," Ivo commented with a shrug.

"It's a test. There will be hidden difficulties. We should expect that, so let's all be very watchful," Taika warned them.

"As it should be. A test has to be difficult and demanding," Aiden added.

"I swear I'm going to pick up one of these giant rocks and smash your marble-head with it," Daphne threatened him.

Start the test. You must be the first to arrive, before the other squads. Victory must be for the Red Squadron. Strive for it and win the test. Let nothing stop you until you reach the top. Absolutely nothing. Bring me the glory of victory. Let the rest of the squadrons know that the Red Squadron is the best. Go! Now! It gave the three Red Squads the order to start.

Nahia looked at the red dragon above her head and then at the great mountain in front of them that seemed to rise like an insurmountable obstacle. She did not have time to think about anything else, because Aiden shot out toward the mountain.

"Hurry up! We have to be the first to reach that summit!" he shouted at them.

"I think it'd be best if we throw him down once we reach the top," Lily told Daphne.

"I totally agree. We'll do that," Daphne nodded.

"Come on, let's follow him," Taika waved at them. "Whether we like it or not, we have to climb that mountain and try to be first."

The others nodded and followed Taika, who ran after Aiden. The Drakonid was already climbing one of the sides of the colossal mountain of rock.

They began the climb, and they soon found out that the mountain was as imposing as it looked. Aiden set a demanding pace, which he had to decrease quickly because of the steepness of the slopes and the difficulty of the climb. They went in single file, with Aiden leading and Taika close behind. Then came Lily, Nahia, and Daphne. Ivo brought up the rear. He had trouble climbing because of his hoof-like feet.

Nahia was going up, leaning forward. The climb was going to be long, tough, and complicated. They were not only tired from a day and a night of steady marching, but all the gear they carried was heavy and it hampered their every step. If it were up to her, she would throw her backpack, shield, sword, and dagger down the mountain. She would only keep her Learning Sphere, which was light. Unfortunately, doing so was absolutely forbidden. If they lost any part of their equipment, their leader would roast them alive.

The climb became more and more difficult as they went higher. That majestic mountain seemed to be telling them it was not a good idea to try and scale its heights. Nahia agreed. Unfortunately, the dragons flying above them did not think the same way; each leader was flying over their squadron as they went up the mountain scattered about. Nahia could now see the Ardent and Searing Squads climbing left and right of her position, keeping the thousand paces of separation. The mountain was so immense and wide that all the squads had plenty of space on the south side.

Tiredness became evident when they began to climb the practically vertical wall they had reached. From there on, they not only had to go up the mountain, but climb up the nearly vertical rock slope as well. Not just them, but all the other squads too. The mountain did not want them to keep walking up its slopes.

Keep going! To the top of the mountain! Crown the summit! Irakas-Gorri-Gaizt's order reached them as it watched, flying above them. It came with a feeling of great urgency.

They looked at the rock wall with apprehension. It was not going to be easy to climb that way.

"I'll go first. Follow me," Aiden said with his usual confidence. He began to climb the rock, but not without difficulties.

Taika followed him and the Felidae did climb well, a lot better than the Drakonid, but he did not overtake him, letting him lead the climb instead. Lily followed Taika, and Daphne went up after the Scarlatum. They both had trouble and went very slowly.

"Please, you go first," Ivo told Nahia, who nodded and did so.

Suddenly, there was a strange noise, like the sound of a rock snapping. This was followed by another, like a rock was sliding.

They stopped and looked up, which was where the noise was coming from.

"What the….?" Daphne started to ask.

At that moment, there was a landslide.

"Watch out, rocks!" Aiden warned.

"Flatten yourself against the mountain!" Taika shouted.

They all flattened themselves as much as they could against the rock of the slope. Huge boulders fell, brushing their heads and backs. Nahia looked up and saw the landslide. She knew that if it hit them, it would mean their end. Whether from the initial blow of the rocks or the fall off the mountain from that height and the crash against the ground, it would kill them. Then dirt and bits of rock got in her eyes and she had to shut them.

"Don't let them hit you!" Lily shouted. Although there was not much they could do to stop being hit.

"Pebbles! Watch your eyes!" Nahia warned them.

"Cover your head!" Daphne cried.

Ivo was unlucky, and a piece of sizeable rock hit him on the head. "Ouch!" he growled.

Lily looked down and saw. "Hold on tight!" she shouted at Ivo.

The Tauruk tilted his head, which was bleeding. He was half dizzy from the blow.

"I'll go and help him," Taika said, and with his cat agility he went down the slope at tremendous speed. He reached Ivo's side and pushed him with one paw against the wall of rock while he held on with the other one.

"Thank you… I'm… better…" Ivo muttered, trying to recover and not fall off the wall.

"Let's wait a little," said Daphne as she watched Ivo, realizing the Tauruk was still suffering.

"Breathe deeply, it'll help you clear your head," Taika advised him as he continued holding him just in case.

They waited until Ivo began to recover with deep breaths. His head was still bleeding, but he no longer felt dizzy.

"We can go on. I'm fine now. I have plenty of extra blood, don't worry," he said, wiping the blood that was getting into his eyes with his forearm.

"I have to tend to that wound," said Daphne.

"We can do that once we reach one of the caves above," said Aiden, who had already noticed two which he was pointing at.

"Yeah, this is no place for healing," Daphne had to agree with him.

"Let's keep going, there's not much farther to the first cave," Lily cheered them.

They continued the climb carefully. Taika was watchful that Ivo did not faint or make a bad handhold because of the blow. Daphne and Nahia were also alert; even if there was not much they could do, they had enough to deal with not falling off the rock wall themselves. Luckily, they found a couple of narrow natural ledges where they were able to rest for a moment. They led Ivo up to them, and from there to the first cave they could climb without any more mishaps. Aiden gave them a hand and helped get the Tauruk up, followed by Taika. They all reached the wide ledge where the cave was. They sat down to rest amid snorts and sighs of relief for leaving the vertical rock wall, albeit briefly.

"That was a serious blow," Ivo said, putting his hand to his head.

Nahia wrinkled her nose and looked upward. The practically vertical slope went on to the frozen peak, which seemed unattainable. They did not see more rocks falling or the reason for the landslide.

"We escaped by a hair's breadth. Thank goodness…"

Daphne stood up to tend to Ivo's wound.

"Don't worry, your head is harder than the rock that hit you. You'll survive."

"My head's hard to protect my restless mind," Ivo said, smiling at her. He did not seem to be concerned about the wound.

"That must be it," Daphne replied, smiling back. She pressed her hands on either side of the cut, called on her inner dragon, took elemental light energy, and transformed it into healing energy. She sent it through her hands and applied it to the wound. Healing was a complex process and difficult to master. Daphne complained about it all the time, but then, when she had the chance to use it and help her friends, her face changed. Her usually sullen look turned to pure joy, at least for a while.

"She's going to leave you more handsome than before, you'll see," Lily said mischievously.

"It'll be difficult to make me handsomer. I'm a Tauruk with a beastly face, there's nothing handsome about me."

"Don't lose hope, with time I bet Daphne will be capable of working a miracle with her magic."

"Not even with all the time in the world," Daphne said as she continued healing the wound. It was no longer bleeding and the cut was closing,

Taika bent down and felt the rocky floor. He made a funny face.

"Is something wrong?" Nahia, who had noticed, asked.

"Don't you hear?" he asked and put his tiger's ear against the floor.

Aiden looked in every direction.

"I can't hear anything. I don't detect any danger either."

At that moment, from inside the cave came a beastly creature. It gave a tremendous roar, similar to a dragon's, and showed fearsome teeth and a maw with which it intended to devour them.

Chapter 3

Nahia nearly fell backward and off the mountain from the fright. She waved her arms to keep her balance and managed to recover, but only just. Lily was not that lucky, and after jumping back she began to lean over the ledge. She was going to topple down the mountain and let out a little yelp that did not even leave her throat, but Ivo grabbed her right arm from the floor and prevented her from falling. Daphne cried out in surprise; not because of the monster, but because she believed Lily was going to plunge into the void.

They turned toward the creature. Nahia did not know what it was, but one thing was undisputable: it looked like a dragon without wings. It had a dragon's body and head but it was much smaller, about twenty feet long. It stood twelve feet tall and about nine wide. Its whole body was covered with brownish scales, its eyes and its teeth were those of a dragon. She noticed it had streaks of red scales that went all along its back.

"Watch out, it's a drake!" Aiden cried, and he swiftly unsheathed his sword with one hand and grabbed his shield with the other.

Nahia had no idea what a drake was, but judging from Aiden's cry and how quickly he had prepared to defend himself, she guessed it was nothing good. Besides, any creature that resembled a dragon was most likely dangerous. She was not wrong. The beast came forward on its four legs to attack Aiden. It delivered a horrific bite with a jaw full of fearsome teeth. Aiden protected himself with the shield. The next attack from the monster was an onrush. The drake knocked him down with a terrible blow against the shield and Aiden himself, who was thrown backward. If it had pushed him a bit harder, the Drakonid would have toppled down the mountain.

"We have to get rid of it!" Taika cried, running to help Aiden. With a great feline leap, he got onto the beast's side and delivered a cut with his sword, followed by a thrust.

Nahia thought he had the beast. Taika's attack had been swift and accurate. No doubt he had killed it, or at least seriously wounded the monster. But she was entirely wrong. The drake roared and turned to Taika. It was not even wounded. The tiger's sword had not pierced the scales that covered the monster's body.

"It has dragon scales! Steel doesn't pierce it!" Taika cried, warning the others.

The drake delivered a claw strike with its left front leg and Taika covered himself with the shield. Meanwhile, Aiden was recovering, getting back to his feet in a defensive position behind his shield.

Lily and Daphne were already prepared to fight when two more drakes came from the back of the cave, roaring threateningly.

"Two more! This is getting ugly!" Nahia warned as she advanced toward them with Daphne and Lily, forming a defensive line behind their shields.

"Sheath your swords, use magic!" Nahia told her comrades.

"Right. Let's see how they fend against magic," Daphne replied.

"I hope very badly… because they're terrifying," Lily said wishfully with a horrified face.

The two drakes approached them with heavy steps. Their muscular torsos and legs were impressive. Each one's tail also looked very powerful. Nahia was unnerved by the beasts' claws and teeth, which had to be somehow related to dragons. They looked like lesser terrestrial relatives.

Ivo stood beside them.

"I'll deal with the last little dragon," he told them.

"Are you sure you can fight in your current state?" Lily asked him in a worried tone.

"Yeah, don't worry. Daphne healed my cut and I don't feel dizzy. Don't worry about me," he said and walked determinedly toward the monster, sword and shield in hand.

"He's tough and strong, don't worry about him."

"It's hard not to worry in this situation. These drakes look like very bad news," Nahia said.

"So, let's finish them off and be done with it," Daphne replied, wrinkling her nose and staring fiercely at the beast coming to attack them.

"These must be cousins of yours, Aiden," Lily told him as she dodged a bite to her head and threw her Elemental Ice Claw at the beast's right leg.

"Tell them that since they're family, they should get along with us," Daphne said to Aiden as she used her Elemental Light Breath to momentarily blind the drake attacking her, seeking to bite her leg off.

Aiden had been knocked down by a tail blow from the beast he was fighting and was breathless, trying to recover.

"Very… funny…" he muttered under his breath.

Taika was protecting Aiden, trying to strike the drake's eyes with his sword. He delivered lightning strokes and shifted immediately to avoid a claw or the monster's jaws. The drakes were enormous and powerful, but not swift or nimble. Taika had already noticed and was taking advantage of it. Suddenly, the drake he was attacking opened its mouth, and instead of trying to bite him, it aimed its maw at Taika for a moment. The drake's eyes shone with a red flash and Taika had a very bad feeling. He lunged to one side, and a moment later a burst of flames came out of the monster's mouth.

"Watch out, fire breath!" Aiden warned, already standing.

Taika summersaulted to get away from the flames. He was agile and fast enough that the fire could not touch him. The drake tried to burn him by prolonging its fiery breath and following Taika as he tumbled, directing its igneous stream at his body. Taika lunged to the side again and summersaulted, escaping the fire that sought to incinerate him.

Nahia saw it out of the corner of her eye and warned the others.

"They have fire breath! Watch out!"

Lily, Daphne, and Ivo turned to look at Nahia and then Taika, realizing what was up. They stepped back and reconsidered their attacks.

"That's all we needed! The little wingless dragons are actually dragons that don't fly," Daphne complained.

"Strong, sharp teeth and claws, powerful body and tail, fire breath… yeah, I'd say they're truly wingless dragons," Lily agreed as she prepared her Elemental Ice Breath to attack the drake staring at her with a murderous intent.

"Be careful!" Nahia warned them, seeing the drake opening its mouth.

Daphne realized it was going to throw fire. "Watch out, fire incoming!"

"I'll deal with it," said Lily, and she stood in front of the drake's open jaws. Just when the fire started to leave the monster's maw, Lily called on her Elemental Ice Breath. An icy jet launched toward the drake's maw. Both Elemental Breaths met half way. The fire crashed against Lily's icy water. There was a struggle of elemental forces: fire against water.

The drake's eyes shone with a red gleam as it wrestled with Lily; she delivered her freezing stream, putting out her opponent's fire.

"Well done, Lily!" Daphne cheered her and ran to help her.

"The two of us can defeat this monster!" she replied to Daphne and kept delivering a powerful stream of water so cold it was almost ice. When it met the intense jet of fire, steam formed that climbed up to the sky.

"Don't worry! I'm at your side. Watch your eyes, I'm going to attack," Daphne told Lily, and she attacked the drake with her Elemental Light Breath. When this crashed against the fire, there was a burst of intense light that stunned the drake.

Nahia saw that her comrades were managing to hold back their drake, but Ivo was having some trouble. The monster he was fighting had hit him with its tail and front claws and had forced him to retreat. Now it was going to launch its fiery breath at him. Nahia doubted Ivo would be able to use his magic in the situation and state he was in, besides the fact that he struggled to use his magic normally. She ran to help him, and as she did, she summoned her Elemental Fire Breath.

"Move back, Ivo!" she called as she arrived at his back.

Ivo turned his head and saw her coming. He stepped aside, and even as clumsy as he was, it was enough for Nahia to lunge into a full attack. Her Elemental Breath left her mouth as the drake let out its own. Both breaths met and there was a crash of fire. The burst of flames when both breaths collided made Nahia almost tumble backward. She managed to stand firm in a defensive stance.

The drake shook its head. It had not liked Nahia's attack at all, but it did not cower. It moved toward her. It did not seem to mind that Nahia also had Elemental Fire Breath. It moved slowly toward her and launched the stream of fire at her, trying to reach her body. Nahia did not flinch and used her Elemental Fire Breath again. The flames that came out of her mouth bore a resemblance to those of the drake, which had to stop its advance. The monster's flames could not endure its opponent's. Nahia realized her skill was going to run out and stopped her flame, gathering more energy from within herself and channeling it toward the Elemental Fire Breath to keep it alive. She noticed the drake looked unsure, and this encouraged her. She sent even more energy to her breath and the flame increased, almost doubling in intensity. The drake saw that its flame was consumed by Nahia's and started to retreat slowly, with unsteady steps. Nahia noted that her fire was more powerful than the drake's, and she moved toward it. If she managed to hit it, the creature would most likely burn.

Suddenly, Ivo used a fighting strategy which only a Tauruk-Kapro could think of. He threw his steel shield with all his strength at the open mouth of the drake. The shield flew parallel to the floor at great speed. He threw it with such strength that there was a dreadful sound of teeth breaking on impact. The drake roared in pain and shut its jaws while bits of teeth fell to the floor. Nahia had not been expecting such a maneuver, and for a moment, she was a stunned as the drake.

"They don't have scales to protect them there," Ivo said nonchalantly.

Nahia recovered from her surprise and went on with her attack. She took two steps forward and reached the drake's head and part of its torso with her Elemental Fire Breath. She did not know whether this creature would have magic defenses, but since it was similar to a dragon, she guessed it would. The drake's scales flashed with a strong silver glow, which Nahia took as a defense. She sent more energy to her breath to try and destroy its defensive magic. The drake kept backing up, roaring with rage. Nahia kept coming at it, sending a tremendous stream of fire at her enemy.

Suddenly, from underneath the drake and emerging from the floor, four creepers appeared, which went up and curled around them. The drake looked down at the floor, not understanding. A moment later, they had it imprisoned. The monster pulled with all its might to free its legs, but the number of creepers was increasing every moment, climbing up its legs, thicker and coiling more as if they had a life of their own.

Nahia knew this could only come from one place. She looked askance at Ivo and saw him with his arms spread open, summoning. These were his creepers, formed from Druid magic. She had to use the advantage her comrade had given her, so she stepped forward and directed her Elemental Fire Breath only at the monster's head to avoid hitting and burning the creepers restraining the drake. The flames hit the drake's head and it roared desperately, its defenses flashing silver once more, but they soon faded. Nahia intensified her attack and the drake's head caught on fire. She sent more energy and a tremendous burst of flame enveloped it. The beast fell to one side, dead, its legs still imprisoned. Nahia felt it was a terrible way to die, but at least it had been quick. The drake would have killed her or Ivo if it could, and without any consideration.

"That was very good, Ivo. You're formidable," Nahia said to her comrade.

"I am Ivo," he replied with a shrug. Then he went up to the beast and retrieved his shield.

Lily and Daphne combined their Elemental Breaths and created an effect the drake could not cope with: stunning and then freezing it. It defended itself with its fire breath until it finally could not hold up any more. The two Dragon Witches were more powerful than the drake. It tried to run for its life, but Daphne realized its intent and blinded it again. Lily did not give it a chance to recover; she froze its head and half its torso, its defenses depleted. The beast was left standing, blind and half frozen.

"Is it dead?" Daphne asked Lily.

"I don't know, but I'd say yes. Just a moment ago its magical defense dropped. Or at least it didn't glow silver anymore."

"Yeah, without magical defense it must be dead." Daphne nodded.

Taika and Aiden were also trying to finish off the drake they were fighting. They were taking a slightly different approach. Taka had climbed onto the back of the monster, and after reaching the head he had plunged his knife in both eyes, blinding it. The beast was trying to throw him off by shaking its whole body and tail, but Taika was not falling off. He was holding onto the monster using his darkness magic. The dark tentacles he had created were around the beast's neck, and Taika was holding on with all his might.

Aiden had delivered several thrusts of his sword into the monster's maw when it tried to defend itself with its fiery breath. Blinded, it could not see where the Drakonid was attacking from. Since he could not finish off the monster, Aiden had created a ball of storm he was now going to throw into the monster's maw. However, the drake had closed its jaws so the sword would stop bothering it.

"Make it open its mouth!" he shouted at Taika.

"I'm trying!" the tiger said from the drake's back, and he pulled the tentacles around the beast's neck with all his might. He kept pulling hard and the drake seemed to choke. It had no choice but to open its mouth. Aiden was waiting for this moment. He threw the stormy ball right down its maw. There was an explosion followed by lightning, which gravely wounded the monster. It roared with pain, and Aiden seized the moment to finish it off by plunging his sword deep into its maw to the back of its throat.

A moment later, the three drakes lay dead in front of the Igneous Squad. Everything fell silent, and the tension evaporated while they looked at the bodies and into the cave.

"Are there any more?" Nahia asked with a nod to the mouth of the cave where the three creatures had emerged.

"I hope not!" Lily said, watching the cave with narrowed eyes.

Taika jumped off the back of the dead drake and went over to the entrance of the cave with his feline walk. He looked inside for a while. The others watched without moving, as if a stray sound or movement might bring out three more monsters to attack them.

They waited for a long moment, but nothing happened.

"I don't detect any more creatures inside," Taika reported.

Suddenly, they heard a shout from the east. They turned toward it. It was a human cry, of battle.

Taika hastened out to a ledge so he could see what was happening.

"It's the Searing Squad. They're in trouble."

Nahia ran to his side to see.

"They're fighting against three drakes, but there's only four of them. They have to be having serious problems," Taika said.

"We have to go and help them!" Nahia cried as she motioned for her companions to follow her along the ridge to the east.

"No! We have to keep climbing. The order is to reach the peak first. We don't have to help other squads," Aiden corrected her in a dry, determined tone. He pointed at the summit.

"Could you be more of a marble-head? Of course we're going to help them!" Daphne yelled at him and motioned for Nahia to go and that she would follow.

"Only a Drakonid rock-head would say something like that when their comrades are in need," Lily shook her head and followed Nahia and Daphne.

"We have orders, we can't disobey them. We have to keep climbing," Aiden made a face of disbelief at their refusal to keep climbing.

Ivo reached him and put a beastly hand on his shoulder.

"We'll fulfill the order, don't you worry, but first we're going to help our comrades. It's the right thing to do. Deep down you know it too," he told him in a deep tone and walked to the ridge.

Aiden looked at Taika, but he gave him a regretful shrug and followed after the girls with steady, fast, balanced strides, as if he were walking along a wide road instead of a narrow, dangerous ridge.

Chapter 4

Nahia, Daphne, and Lily advanced with difficulty toward the east along a ridge on the side of the mountain. The ledge they were following was very narrow; if they became distracted or took a wrong step, they would fall to their deaths. They had to step sideways in the final stretch with their bodies flattened against the rock. Luckily, the entrance to the cave where the Ardent Squad was fighting was wide. Nahia leapt over a void in the ledge and then dropped down onto the cave ledge. Daphne and Lily followed close behind her.

As she straightened up and covered behind her shield, Nahia assessed the current situation. She did not want to run headlong into a dangerous fight—that was never a good strategy. Cordelius was fighting a drake at the mouth of the cave. The drake was trying to incinerate him with its fiery breath and the big Kapro was defending himself as best he could while he tried to kill the creature. Brendan, the blond human, was fighting a different drake. This was a fight of magic power: Brendan's Elemental Fire Breath against the drake's fire breath.

Lara, the black panther, was using a similar strategy to Taika's and had climbed onto the back of the drake she was fighting, which tried to throw her off amid roars and frantic shaking. Draider, the Drakonid boy on the Ardent Squad, was on the floor, and part of his body was on fire.

"I'll help him!" Daphne cried and ran over to Daider.

"Lily, come with me, we'll help Cordelius," Nahia told her, guessing that for now Brendan was holding his own.

"Good. I'm coming." Lily narrowed her eyes with determination.

Right then, Taika dropped beside her after leaping off the ledge.

"Go, I'll help Lara," the tiger said.

An instant later, they were all running to help their squadron comrades. Ivo had not arrived yet but was approaching warily along the ridge. This type of climb was very complicated for the great Kapro. Aiden had not yet moved from where he was and had his arms crossed over his chest while he shook his head angrily.

Nahia and Lily reached Cordelius, who was avoiding the drake's fiery breath with clumsy movements. His cloak was on the floor, burnt to a crisp.

"We have to use magic against them," Lily warned him.

"I thought so, but magic isn't my forte," Cordelius replied and showed her his sword and shield. He was running around the drake, which was trying to get him with its breath.

"Don't worry, we'll help you," Nahia reassured him.

"Thank you!" Cordelius kept circling the beast, because if he stopped it was going to hit him with its fiery breath. Luckily, the monster was even clumsier than the Kapro.

Nahia thought that if they were not in danger of death, the scene would be quite comical with the great Kapro running in circles around the small wingless dragon as it tried to roast him.

"I'm going to use my Elemental Ice Breath against its fiery one," Lily warned Nahia.

"Good, distract it and I'll attack with my magic."

"Consider it done," Lily nodded and opened her mouth to launch her Elemental Ice Breath. It hit the drake's body and it turned to her, giving up on chasing Cordelius. Both breaths, fire and ice, met, and the struggle of power between the two elemental magics began. Lily stood firm with her knees flexed and her head slightly forward. She withstood the first impact pretty well.

Nahia took advantage of the fact that Lily had all of the drake's attention to use her magic against the creature. She called on her Elemental Fire Claw and a large fiery dragon claw enveloped her right hand. Covering herself with her shield, she approached the monster as it fought against Lily. Before the drake could attack her, she leapt forward and clawed its left leg. She did not know whether she would be able to pierce the magical defenses of the drake, but she had to try. There was a silver flash when the Elemental Fire Claw hit its leg. The drake did not seem to feel anything; it did not flinch and kept trying to kill Lily, who was holding up like a powerful sorceress emerging from an iceberg.

In the middle, Taika reached the drake Lara was on top of. With a swift, powerful leap, he too climbed onto the creature's back, which roared in rage.

"Thanks for the help," Lara said as she held onto the drake's crest that went down its back and tail.

"We have to help one another," Taika replied and concentrated on calling on his darkness magic.

The drake was shaking itself hard but could not throw them off. It could not attack them with its fiery breath either, since its neck was not very long and it could not twist it to aim at them. The fire attacks went to the right and left of Taika and Lara, who stayed in the middle of the drake's back halfway up. In order to reach them it would have to break its neck, which would kill it anyway.

"I can't manage to pierce its scales... luckily they don't know how to roll over and up here it can't reach me... with its maw or claws," Lara told him, speaking haltingly from the effort of the fight against the creature.

Taika created dark tentacles and let them coil around the creature's neck before replying.

"That's good, or else it would squash us. It doesn't look very nimble."

"No, it's not... but strong and dangerous? Very. Besides, it must weigh as much as a house."

"You have to use your magic to kill it," Taika told her.

"Alright, I'll try," said Lara.

Using all his strength, Taika pulled on his tentacles, trying to strangle the monster. The more he pulled, the more the creature resisted, moving its head from side to side, roaring furiously. Suddenly, Lara managed to conjure her Elemental Air Maw and delivered a terrible bite on the drake's neck, one charged with storm lightning. When she bit down, the lightning discharged onto the drake's nape. Its defensive magic activated and a silver flash defended it from the magical attack.

"It didn't pierce it," Lara said ruefully.

"Keep trying, you'll get it," Taika said as he pulled on his black appendages with all his might.

Ivo reached Brendan as he kept aiming his fiery breath at the drake. He was not losing, but he was not winning either. They were both sending their breaths at full magical tilt, which was consuming the inner energy of both. Whoever exhausted their magic first, beast or human, would die.

"Help is here," Ivo told Brendan, who was sweating profusely. It was not from the heat of the fire but from the tremendous effort he was making. He did not answer, he simply could not. He glanced at Ivo out of the corner of his eye, and Ivo understood that Brendan had seen him and knew he had come to help. He stood right behind Brendan and crouched so his head would not be exposed above the human's, since he was a lot taller than the human. Calmly, he began to call upon his Druid magic and combined it with his elemental earth magic. After a long moment, from under the drake's right leg, the earth shifted, as if something was sprouting from it. Before the drake realized what was going on, half a dozen strong, sharp stone stakes emerged from the ground and buried into its claw. It raised its leg immediately, shook it, and started to retreat. They had wounded it.

"As I thought—it doesn't have scales on the bottom of its claws," Ivo muttered, satisfied.

Brendan intensified the attack when he saw the beast retreating and motioned for Ivo to go with him.

Aiden arrived with a leap at the site of the fighting and ran to Daphne, who was tending to Draider's burns.

"How is he?"

"Well, you finally decided to join us. What an honor," Daphne replied in a huff.

"I'm not going to let any of my people die without helping them."

"Half his body is burnt. The scales we all wear have protected him enough, but even so he has deep burns, some on his face. I won't be able to heal them all. They'll leave scars, I'm sorry."

"A Drakonid doesn't care about that. Physical beauty has no value for us," Aiden told her, waving the matter aside.

"Of course it does," Daphne retorted. In her culture, beauty was everything.

"On the contrary... it'll show my courage in the battle..." Draider said proudly.

"You're all a bunch of granite-heads." Daphne shook her head and continued sending healing energy to Draider's burns.

"We should move him back. That drake is too close for comfort," Aiden told the Fatum.

Daphne raised her head and saw the drake with Lara and Taika on its back, lurching from side to side, desperate and furious, raging as it tried to shake them off.

"Yeah, let's retreat before it crushes us," Daphne agreed.

"Finish healing him, I'll protect you." Aiden stood in front of them with his shield and sword in hand in a defensive stance.

Daphne sighed. Now she could heal him better, with some peace. Healing magic and battle did not get along well, at least as far as she was concerned. She did not know whether this was the same with other healers, but she assumed it would be similar. In order to heal she needed concentration, and for this, peace and quiet. The middle of combat was no suitable place to heal anyone, and yet, she had the feeling it was precisely where she would have to use her healing magic. She was a Dragon Witch and her skills would be used in battle, not in the comfort of an infirmary. This discovery left her cold. She would have to talk to Nahia and Lily to see how she could improve her healing in less hostile environments. Yes, she would have to do that.

Meanwhile, on the eastern side, Nahia delivered another blow with her Elemental Fire Claw, determined to see how far the magical defenses of the beast held up. Another silver flash told her the magical defenses of the creature were resisting. That was not good. She sent more energy to her claw so it would be more powerful and deliver a stronger blow. She waited for the right moment and delivered a third attack to the same leg. The creature did feel this one. The drake turned toward Nahia while its leg oozed reddish-black blood. Lily did not miss the chance and she advanced with her Elemental Ice Breath, hitting the beast on its right side. Nahia blocked the drake's breath with her shield and withdrew, quickly stepping back without turning from the monster's face or breaking her cover.

Cordelius finally managed to summon an Elemental Claw and attacked the drake on the right back leg with powerful blows. The creature roared in pain, which made its fiery breath die out. Nahia stopped retreating; it was the moment to attack, they had the beast wounded.

"All at once!" she shouted at Lily and Cordelius.

And the three attacked at the same time. Nahia and Cordelius went for the legs with their Elemental Claws and Lily for the head with her Elemental Ice Breath. The drake seemed to hesitate for a moment, seeing the three of them advancing on it together. It decided that the most dangerous enemy was Lily with her Elemental Ice Breath and attacked her again with its own fiery one. Lily withstood the attack and made a sign with her right hand for them to attack now that the drake was focused on her. Nahia and Cordelius launched their attacks, delivering claw blows to the legs, her claw striking the front ones and his, the back. The drake roared again in pain, its fiery breath dying down. Lily's icy breath reached its head and froze it completely. A moment later it fell to the floor, dead.

Lara managed to pierce the drake's magic defenses after half a dozen consecutive attacks. Her Elemental Air Maw penetrated and the discharge entered the back of the monster's neck. It roared in agony.

"I did it!" she cried, victorious.

"Finish it. I'm not able to strangle it," Taika said. Although he pulled on his tentacles coiled around its neck with all his strength, he could not asphyxiate the beast. He was standing on the scaly back pulling with his whole body, and although the drake's head was bent back, he could not succeed. At least he was holding onto the monster and it could not shake him off.

"I'll do it," Lara said and delivered another half-dozen bites of storm with her Elemental Air Maw, which struck the back of its neck. The black panther's magic not only managed to wound the drake as if it were a sharp claw buried in it, but the elemental magic discharges increased the power of the attack. The monster died, its neck burst. It collapsed, and Lana and Taika jumped down nimbly before it touched the floor.

There was only one drake left standing. It was wounded and defending the entrance of the cave. Brendan did not cease to attack it using his Elemental Fire Breath. The drake was having a lot of trouble defending itself, since Ivo had wounded two of its legs with sharp, rocky stakes. It was defending itself using its fiery breath.

"Perhaps if we let it go it'll leave," Ivo said to Brendan. The big Tauruk was crouched behind the human, preparing another attack that did not finish manifesting.

The human boy shrugged without ceasing his attacks. He could not speak or move his head or his attack would lose effect. Ivo interpreted his shrug as a "You really think so?"

"We lose nothing for trying. Let's step back. You keep up that breath, and let's see what it does."

Brendan made an affirmative gesture with his right hand.

Ivo took two steps back and Brendan took one. The drake did not move. Ivo took two more steps back and Brendan took another. The drake did not move this time either. Brendan stopped using his Elemental Fire Breath once the drake was out of reach and the drake did the same. For a tense moment, they watched each other. It appeared that Ivo was right; it might not be necessary to keep fighting. The drake then looked up at the sky, roared, and then it attacked, limping on two legs.

Brendan called on his Elemental Fire Breath once again. The drake was about to do the same, but sharp stone spikes and stakes emerged from the ground and buried into its back legs. It lost its balance and fell on its face. Ivo had been conjuring during the impasse. Brendan took advantage of the moment and advanced toward the drake, catching it in the head with his burst of fire. The drake's magical defense withheld. But the beast could not get back onto its four injured legs. It tried and fell again. Brendan kept up the attack and the monster's defenses finally gave out. It opened its mouth to use its breath, but it was already too late. Brendan had defeated it. Its head burnt to a crisp and it died with a roar of agony.

Brendan stopped sending his Elemental Fire Breath. He sighed and turned to Ivo.

"I'm sorry."

"We tried," Ivo said resignedly. He looked up at the sky and saw their leader watching them. The drake had not wanted to disobey its winged masters and had preferred to die.

The two squads gathered around Draider who, although he had parts of his body and face burnt, did not seem to feel any pain.

"How are you?" Brendan asked him.

"I've been scorched, but I'll survive," the Drakonid replied.

"Will you be able to go on?" Lara asked, and there was concern in her tone.

"I think so." Draider stood up with Daphne's help.

"He's been lucky. The burns will leave ugly scars, but there were no serious injuries," she explained.

"He's strong, he'll survive," Cordelius said, putting his big hand on the Drakonid's shoulder.

"Ouch!" Draider shrank back from the touch with a grimace of pain. "Better put your hand on the other, this one's scorched."

"Oops, sorry," Cordelius's eyes opened wide and he changed his hand to the other shoulder.

"They'll hurt a lot until they finish healing. He needs time and a more skilled healer," Daphne said, opening her arms wide to express she had done everything she could.

"You've done a great job. We really appreciate it." Brendan told her.

"Thank goodness you came to help," Lara said gratefully.

"It's the least we could do," Nahia said. "We have to help each other, always."

"You're right. The Academy encourages competitiveness among all of us, it shouldn't be that way," Brendan said.

"There are things that shouldn't be like they are, at the Academy and in our world," Ivo agreed.

"Like making you do this test with only four members in your squad, for instance," said Lily, shaking her head.

"We're tough and strong, we'll do it," Cordelius said, more to encourage his comrades rather than out of faith in himself.

"You have to, that's true, but it doesn't make it right," said Nahia. "There are many things that aren't right, and you all know that. We can't keep letting them do this to us. To us and all of Kraido. We have to do something, it's our duty."

There was silence for a moment. They all understood what Nahia meant.

"We don't have time for any of that now," said Aiden. This conversation upset him greatly. "We have to keep climbing."

"Don't worry, I'll reach the summit," Draider assured them. He did not want to talk about that either.

"Thanks again for the help," Lara told them, looking each one in the eye.

"You're welcome," Daphne replied.

"If the situation is reversed, help us," Lily said.

"You can count on that, you have my word as a Kapro," Cordelius promised with a hard nod.

"We'll help you," Lara promised.

"As for what you said, Nahia, you're right. We'll talk at the Academy," Brendan said, looking intensely at her.

"Whenever you want," Nahia accepted.

As if it had been listening, they received an order from the heights.

Igneous Squad, return to your position and climb from there. You were not told to help any other squads. Ardent Squad, keep climbing at once. The order came with a feeling of frustration and rage. Irakas-Gorri-Gaizt was clearly displeased with what had taken place there.

Chapter 5

They helped one another climb up a side of the rocky wall on the east side of the cave and then along the upper ridge until they reached the cave where they had defeated the drakes. The way was not easy and they took risks at a couple of spots, but they could not disobey their leader.

"We have to keep climbing from here," Aiden pointed at the spot.

"Start making your way up," Taika told him, "we'll follow you."

Aiden looked for the best place to climb, and a moment later he was already on the path.

"Let's keep going, Irakas-Gorri-Gaizt is watching us." Taika warned them, gazing up unobtrusively.

"Yeah, let's move on before it suffers a rage attack," Lily said as she started to climb.

Ivo brought the rear.

"This climbing thing is not something we Tauruk-Kapro love. We were not made for this purpose. I'd better climb up last so I'm not in anybody's way."

"Cheer up, Ivo, we'll all get there," Nahia reassured him.

Ivo sighed and started climbing the wall with difficulty.

The way up from the lower caves was slow and dangerous. They were tired, the slope was getting steeper all the time and more difficult to climb, and if they got distracted, they would not survive the fall. An additional factor whose impact they had initially forgotten took the forefront once again: it was the height, the tremendous height they were at. They had adapted to living at such heights in that realm, after suffering from them the whole first year. Since they were acclimated, they had forgotten they were among the clouds, and climbing the mountain meant going even higher. They were not only among the clouds, but on a mountain above them. The pressure of the air was so thin at that height that it punished their lungs, and it was difficult to simply breathe. Making an effort like climbing the mountain increased this difficulty.

Nahia tried to fill her lungs, but it was not easy. It was as if she filled them but only a bit of air went in, or that was what it seemed like to her. As if it hurt to breathe the air up here. It was so thin that you had to breathe three times more than usual. Her lungs hurt and it was hard to even inhale. She took a step and had to constantly stop to breathe. It was torture. She watched her comrades climbing; they were all suffering from the same torture as she was. The height affected them all equally, but she noticed that the three girls had less trouble than the boys since they had larger bodies, especially Ivo.

With a lot of effort and suffering, they reached the upper-level caves and found a relatively wide ledge. Taika and Aiden took a look around the caves. They were shaped like stars and the whole mountainside was full of them, as if a hundred stars had crashed against the mountain and penetrated the rock. The size of each opening was no bigger than Daphne.

"A drake couldn't fit in here," Aiden said, looking inside the lower ones.

Taika had gone up to the third line of caves and looked inside several ones, moving with his usual feline agility.

"I can't detect any danger, but it's too dark to see the back of these caves," he said, leaping down.

"They're small… if an enemy comes out… it won't be much of a problem," Ivo said. He had just arrived and was kneeling on the edge of the ledge.

Lily and Nahia stepped over to help him so he would not fall back and off the mountain.

"Come on, big guy, drag that mass of a body of yours inside," Lily said, pulling his arm with all her might.

"It's like trying to move an ox," Nahia complained as she did the same.

"Instead of going to the gym, we could just lift Ivo every evening," Daphne joked, collapsing on the floor, dead tired.

"Good idea. I bet we'd end up crushed," Nahia said, grinning.

"Are you feeling all right?" Taika asked Daphne. "You're looking very pale."

"Yeah… it's just my healing… it leaves me exhausted."

"It tires you?" Ivo asked from the floor where he was lying on his stomach. By the way he asked, he was really interested.

"Yeah… it's as if I made… a physical effort. It's not, because it's magic, but it drains me."

"That's interesting… I wonder if that will also happen to me with certain Druid skills."

"You'd better find out soon, because if that's the case, using those skills puts you in danger on the battlefield," Aiden told them.

"For once… the granite-head is right," Daphne agreed.

"I'm always right. Whether you admit it or not is a different matter altogether," Aiden said, sure of himself as he folded his arms. Then he looked up.

"And then he wonders why we call him rock-head," Lily said casually from where she was sitting on the floor, shaking her head.

"There's not much left," Taika said. "One last effort for what remains of the climb and we'll finish the test."

"I'm already feeling cold." Daphne rubbed her arms.

"It's due to the height and how close we are to the summit," Taika said, pointing at it. They were very close to the start of the white peak. They could see the snow and ice that covered it, it seemed to be within reach.

"Yeahhh, we're almost there," Ivo said to cheer himself up. He remained lying on the floor.

Nahia looked at the summit. The feeling that it was so close cheered her up. She was aware it was not really that close, nor would it be easy to reach, but she could not help stretching her arm as if to touch it and smile. They were almost there and would survive the initial test of the third year. She blew the air out of her lungs, relieved.

A sound like a muffled murmur reached them.

"What's that sound?" Daphne asked, raising an eyebrow.

Taika and Aiden listened attentively.

"It sounds like the breeze rustling through the leaves, but there isn't any…" Lily commented blankly.

"Rather than wind… it sounds like fluttering wings," said Ivo.

"Lots of fluttering wings," Taika said, turning toward the wall of rock behind them.

Suddenly, dozens of flying creatures came out of the star-shaped caves.

"Bats?" said Nahia when she saw them.

"Aren't they too big to be bats?" asked Lily.

Nahia realized they were at least three times the size of a bat. A couple made a low pass at her head and she was able to see them better. No, they were not bats. They had the body of a reptile, although their wings were similar to a bat's. They seemed to be a mix between an alligator and a bat. Their bodies were covered in green scales but unlike alligators, their limbs were shaped as claws. They were not very big, but they looked mean.

"They're tiny little dragons," said Ivo, getting up to see them better.

About a hundred came out of the cave and flew around them in circles, going up and down everywhere and making shrill noises.

"Why are they flying around us?" Daphne asked, also standing.

"They must think we're intruders," Aiden reasoned, swatting a couple of them that flew too close to his head with his hands.

"Are they baby-somethings?" Nahia asked.

Taika also waved away several flying too close to his head.

"They're not babies. I'd say they're adults."

"Well, they don't look dangerous. They must be some species we don't know about," said Ivo, watching them with great interest.

"Aiden, don't you know what they are?" Nahia asked.

The Drakonid shook his head.

"I'm afraid I have no idea what these flying creatures are."

As they watched them, the shrill roars of the flying reptiles became more intense as well as their passes over the heads of the group. They started brushing against heads and bodies.

"Maybe we'd better move, I don't like their attitude," said Daphne.

"Yeah, they don't seem to like our presence here," Lily added.

They took a couple of steps back, and suddenly one of the creatures attacked Ivo's face.

"What do you think you're doing, little one?" the Tauruk, asked puzzled by the attack.

A second one attacked Aiden, also in the face.

"Shoo, vermin!" he cried angrily.

Nahia noticed they were both bleeding.

"Watch out, they've made you bleed," as she finished the warning, two of the creatures attacked her. Nahia bowed her head to cover her face and felt claws and teeth bury into her scalp. These creatures had wickedly sharp claws and teeth.

"Defend yourselves!" Daphne cried, covering her face with the shield.

Aiden and Taika were already defending themselves with sword and shield. They hid behind their shields while delivering sword thrusts up and down. They managed to bring down several of the creatures, but the creatures attacked from all directions.

"Careful with the sword strikes or we'll hurt each other!" Nahia warned, barely able to see anything amid all the creatures flying above them in unpredictable patterns before attacking them. The shrill roars were now so intense that it hurt to hear them. Besides, they confused the mind, making it difficult to think.

"Blasted beasts! They've scratched my face! My face!" Lily was yelling furiously. She delivered sword strikes here and there. She was bleeding from several head wounds, one on her right cheek.

"Shield your eyes! They're attacking my eyes!" cried Ivo as he delivered back-strokes with his shield, hitting the attacking creatures.

The situation became chaotic. The tiny dragons attacked them from every direction. They were swift, their attacks were lacerating, and there were countless creatures fluttering aggressively everywhere. They soon found themselves overwhelmed.

Suddenly, more flying creatures came out of the caves. These were similar to the ones already attacking them but not identical. Nahia noticed they had red backs, unlike the ones attacking them which were all green. She did not like this; she had a bad feeling about their arrival. One which came true almost as fast as she thought it. One of the creatures opened its mouth, and instead of biting it launched a small flame.

"Watch out, they have fire breath!" Nahia warned her comrades.

"Little devils!" Daphne cried as she covered herself behind her shield, avoiding the red creatures' attacks.

"Guard your face and head!" Taika warned them as he continued bringing down creatures with his sword. Beside him Aiden struck right and left, knocking down creatures. The problem was, more kept coming from the caves. The situation, already chaotic, was becoming impossible. There were flames all over, and although they were not very big, they were quite intense. The flying red-backed creatures were attacking their faces with their fiery breaths, and a distraction might cost them a terrible burn or the loss of an eye.

"We have to get out of here!" Lily cried when a flame burnt part of her hair and her right ear.

Nahia's cloak was burning, and she had to take it off and throw it on the floor while she defended herself from other attacks behind her shield.

"Let's retreat to the west side of the ridge!" Taika said.

"Come on! In an orderly fashion!" Nahia shouted as she began to retreat.

They all went backwards with their shields in front of them for cover. The swarm of creatures never ceased attacking them with claws, teeth, and fire. For every one they killed, two more came out of the caves, some green and some with red backs.

"How are we going to climb?" Daphne asked, seeing that the tiny dragons had not stopped attacking.

"We need to use our Elemental Breaths to distract them!" said Taika.

Nahia understood the stratagem.

"Lily, Daphne, and I will distract them with our breaths while the rest of you escape to the summit!"

"Are you sure?" Ivo asked in a worried tone.

"I don't think your breaths will work in this situation," Nahia told them.

Ivo looked at the hundred-odd creatures and nodded. "Fine."

"Come on, Elemental Breaths!" Nahia cried, and she concentrated on summoning hers. She hid behind her shield while fire and claws hit it. Beside her, Lily and Daphne were doing the same. Ivo, Taika, and Aiden protected them from the creatures attacking from above. Luckily, the red-backed creatures had very short range with their fire breath.

Nahia was the first one to produce her Elemental Fire Breath, and she maximized it using the lessons learned from her Sorceress Talent classes. She gathered a great amount of energy from her inner dragon and turned it into fire. She moved the shield slightly away and opened her mouth, letting out a tremendous flame, both in power and reach. Her fiery breath was three times as big and powerful as a regular Elemental Breath. Over thirty creatures fell, incinerated, to the ground. Nahia maintained the breath to reach any creature entering her range, since they flew erratically. They went up, down, and turned without any apparent sense or reason.

Lily released her Elemental Ice Breath and a dozen creatures fell to the ground, frozen to death in mid-flight. Her breath did not compare in power or reach to Nahia's, but even though Lily was not a Sorceress it was still very powerful.

"Eyes!" Daphne warned them an instant before releasing her Elemental Light Breath, creating light so intense she blinded another fifteen creatures that flew off in every direction, bumping into the wall of rock, falling down the mountain, and crashing against the ground.

The three kept up their breaths and sought to reach the rest of the creatures that had survived the initial attack.

"Ivo, start climbing!" Taika said.

The great Tauruk turned to face the wall of rock. He hesitated. He did not want to leave his comrades.

"Climb, Ivo!" Aiden urged him.

The beastly giant did not move.

Ivo looked at his comrades and saw them fighting. He also noticed that more winged creatures were coming out of the caves. He was about to go and help them instead of climbing.

"Go up, Ivo, quickly!" Taika yelled at him when he realized his comrade was having doubts.

"Fine… fine…" Ivo said resignedly and started climbing, albeit feeling quite unsure.

Aiden and Taika covered the girls' backs for a moment longer, and when they saw the situation was a little more under control they started up. They had to escape as fast as they could, because more creatures kept coming out of the caves like furious giant wasps. And the furious onslaught did not seem about to abate.

Chapter 6

Nahia kept sending her Elemental Breath of Fire against the creatures, which kept coming and attacking. She touched Daphne's shoulder and jabbed her thumb at her to retreat and leave.

Daphne viewed the situation for a moment, and after wrinkling her nose doubtfully, she stopped blinding the creatures with her Elemental Breath of Light.

"Fine, I'm leaving. Be careful and walk fast," she warned them and followed Taika and the others upward.

Now only Nahia and Lily remained in charge of the situation. They were proving to be a successful distraction. The creatures were not following the rest of the squad as they went up, content to continue attacking the two of them. The problem was that they kept coming out of the caves, as if thousands of the little beasts remained inside.

Nahia touched Lily's shoulder and motioned for her to retreat. She had just brought down thirty more creatures and it was the right moment. Lily looked at her out of the corner of her eye hesitantly. Nahia insisted and repeated the motion. The Scarlatum still hesitated a moment longer. She was frowning, a clear sign that she was very worried. If there was something Lily seriously hated, it was frowning, since the marks might stay forever and ruin her beautiful crimson face. And there was little else Lily valued as much as her beauty and personal magnetism, if anything.

She finally made the decision and began to retreat without ceasing her Elemental Breath of Ice. She was very careful not to hit Nahia with it as Nahia continued attacking with her Elemental Breath of Fire. She reached the spot where their comrades had climbed up and stopped throwing her breath. She glanced at Nahia one last time and frowned again. Nahia, who felt her at her back, waved her on again. Lily muttered a protest, shook her head, and started climbing as fast as she could.

Now it was only Nahia in front of the creatures. She was still launching her Elemental Breath of Fire but was beginning to have a funny feeling, something like a warning from her subconscious that she would not be able to keep it up much longer. She was using a lot of inner energy to sustain her fiery breath, but if she stopped the flying creatures would lunge at her all at once and kill her. She had to think through how to get out of this mess alive. Out of the corner of her eye, she saw Lily already halfway up the wall. She knew she needed to gain time in order to do the same, but nothing came to mind. She was too focused on finishing off all the creatures that swarmed at her, moving her head up and down and side to side as she directed her breath. Her neck and mouth hurt from the continual effort.

Suddenly, something fell from above. She could not see it well since she was so concentrated on killing the creatures. She had the impression that it might be an elemental ball. It hit the ground in front of her and burst. Everything went dark around her. She understood at once. It was Taika. He had dropped a ball of darkness to help her escape. That was the opening she needed. She thanked the heavens for having such intelligent and skillful comrades. The kind who did not leave their friends behind, which was even worthier and more creditable. The idea Taika had given her grew strong in her mind. She knew how to get out of there. She maintained her Elemental Breath of Fire, although she could see nothing ahead of her, and began to summon a ball of fire. She had never tried anything like this: maintaining a skill while summoning a second one. She felt like she was going against nature, that she should only summon one skill at a time. But if she wanted to get out of there, she needed two, so she concentrated on succeeding.

A second ball dropped, and when it burst the blackness became even deeper. It was as if a fog, black as a moonless night, had risen in front of her. She could see to her sides and behind her, but in front was a wall of absolute darkness. The creatures came in and out of the darkness, confused and disoriented. She continued summoning her ball of fire while simultaneously launching her fiery breath. She did not feel like she could do it, but she had to try it now that she had a moment, thanks to the confusion Taika's darkness spheres had caused.

She concentrated as hard as she could, given the circumstances, and suddenly in her right hand the sphere of fire she had been summoning appeared. She could not believe it—she had done it! Her Elemental Breath of Fire was still in effect and she had the ball of fire in her hand. But something odd happened; her breath began to go out. For an instant she was confused, unsure of what was going on, so she tried to calm down and think. She quickly discovered the reason: she was sending her inner energy to the ball and not to her breath. Here was a problem she had never faced before: how to divide her flow of inner energy. It was always one stream, but now she needed two in order to maintain the two skills she had summoned. She concentrated on the flow but two of the creatures crashed against her blindly, one striking her chest and the other against her leg. This distracted her. Within the darkness the creatures flew in every direction erratically, bumping into one another. The dangerous ones were those that left the blackness, those she had to bring down, although luckily there were less of them.

She took a step back and tried to concentrate again on her stream of inner energy. Her Elemental Breath of Fire was going out, and if it did that would be a disaster. She had to send more energy to it, so she focused on splitting the stream with all her might and then visualized in her mind the two skills: the breath and the fireball. She had to split the flow and make it reach the two. She imagined a big river that reached a large boulder in the middle, one that could not be carried away, forcing the stream to branch into two paths. She thought it was a good mental image of what she wanted to achieve.

Suddenly, there was a silver flash and her breath revived. It went from being faint and weak to projecting fire once again with great force. Several creatures lunging at her died, incinerated among shrill cries. The flow of inner energy was now split: one part fed her breath skill and another her fireball. Nahia could not believe she had done it. She was delighted. But the joy of her success vanished when three creatures attacked her, emerging from the blackness.

She took two steps back and incinerated the attackers with her Elemental Breath of Fire. She calculated how much energy she had already sent to the fireball and thought it was enough for what she wanted to do. In any case, she had no more time. Another hundred creatures would soon come out of the darkness, and that would be her end. She took one more step back and threw her ball of fire into the middle of the blackness in front of her. There was a tremendous explosion, which struck all the creatures inside of it. They died in an instant from the terrible explosion and the flame that spread around the point of impact on the ground. A huge flame rose to the sky, and

Nahia herself fell backwards from the strength of the burst.

"Wow… what an explosion…" she muttered from the ground. It had been a lot larger than she had calculated. No doubt her Sorceress lessons from the year before were bearing fruit. She watched the blackness, which was now a cloud of tall flames.

"Nahia, come up!" she heard Daphne's urgent voice.

She did not need to be told again. Her mind urged her to get out of there at full speed, assuring her she now had a chance to escape and she must take it. And she did. She got up from the ground as fast as a cat and began to climb the wall, aware that more flying creatures would come out of the caves and seek to kill her. Behind her, she could hear the screams of the creatures that met a fiery demise in the midst of the darkness that still persisted. She found it odd that her fire did not consume Taika's darkness before realizing that in order to destroy Taika's darkness they needed Daphne's light. Only that would destroy it.

Nahia climbed faster than she ever had before. She had outsmarted the flying creatures, and this was her chance. The only problem was that she was out of breath from the height. Her mind wanted to climb like lightning, but her lungs refused to let her body take more than small steps. It was very difficult to breathe on that wall. The height was becoming a problem that might kill them, directly or indirectly, as was now the case. She was a little higher up the mountain, but not enough to escape. If she did not go further up, she was going to get caught. She filled her lungs several times and tried to get away, climbing, but unfortunately not as fast as she would have liked.

Suddenly, two more balls dropped to the ground, one of ice and the other of storm. They exploded, one on either side of the blackness, and discharged devastating ice and lightning. Nahia saw the explosions and several creatures dropping dead. How grateful she was for the help! She smiled and filled her lungs again with difficulty, but she managed. Her comrades were covering her escape, and this encouraged her to keep climbing, no matter how hard it was to breathe. She now climbed with a little more hope because of her friends' help. Even so, it was hard to reach her comrades, not only because of the high altitude, but because the wall of rock was now covered with snow and ice. They now had to be even more careful to not slip and fall.

"You finally made it," Lily said with a sigh of relief.

Nahia's hands reached the ledge where her comrades were waiting. Ivo gave her his own huge hand and Nahia took it gratefully. The strong Tauruk lifted her as if she were a rag doll and gently deposited her on the snow-dusted, frost-covered ground.

"That thing…. below… was interesting…." Nahia muttered as she tried to catch her breath.

"You don't say. The bad kind of interesting," Daphne said, wrinkling her nose as she did when she did not like something.

"My face is all scratched and my hands and hair are burnt, I'm so angry! It's a catastrophe!" Lily moaned.

"We all have cuts and burns, but they're not serious," Aiden waved it aside. "They're the marks of a warrior. You ought to be proud."

"They're not important to you, you're uglier than a nightmare! For me it's very serious!" Lily exploded.

"Take it easy, I'll heal those cuts on your face. There will be no trace, not even the tiniest scar, I think…" Daphne told her.

"You think? What do you mean 'you think'? There can be no scars anywhere on my body!" Lily raised her hands and waved them, beside herself.

"A scar is horrifying to a Scarlatum, the worst thing that could happen to them," Ivo told them. "They live for their beauty and charm."

"I'm beginning to see that," Nahia said, lying on the snowy ground. She was cold. The temperature was very low up here. She had not realized when she was climbing as fast as she could, and of course had felt warm from the exercise, but now that she was resting, she felt it.

"It's very sad," Aiden said. "What superficial values."

"Shut up, you're uglier than a chasm!" Daphne snapped as she laid her hands on Lily's face.

While Daphne strove to heal Lily's wounds and not leave any scars, the others rested.

"We can't stay here much longer," Aiden said. "We have to keep climbing to the top."

Nahia agreed. Besides, she was freezing. She had sweated during the climb, and now that sweat was freezing on her skin at such glacial temperatures.

"There you go. I can't do anything about the hair. That will have to grow back on its own," Daphne told her.

"I'm worried, terribly worried. I need a mirror." Lily was beside herself.

"Don't worry, I swear you're beautiful," Ivo told her.

"Sure, you'd say anything to humor me."

"I'm Ivo," the great Tauruk shrugged.

"We have to keep going. We're almost there and the temperature is too low, we could get sick," Taika told them.

"Fine!" Lily protested furiously.

Nahia had never seen Lily in such a state. It was true that their personal beauty and physical appearance were all important to the Scarlatum.

Aiden took the lead and began the last stage of the climb. The others refused Daphne's care until the test was over. They all had cuts and burns on different parts of their bodies, but they were not serious and each of them was determined to keep going.

The final stretch was tough and freezing. The snow covered the whole summit of the large mountain. They soon found out it was not only snow, but also ice and frost.

"Be careful. It's very slippery," Aiden warned from the lead.

They went up slowly. They had to secure every step, since they were treading on ice on the rocky ground and the slope, albeit not as steep as before. If they lost their grip with either their hands or feet, it would send them to their death all the same. The worst thing was that they were climbing without gloves. They had not been given any. Most likely on purpose, to make the last stretch of the climb even harder. Nahia's hands froze at the first frozen ramps. She tried to go on, but the time came when she could not feel them and they were almost unresponsive. She could not grasp the rocks. They had to climb at a crouch and hold on, since the final slope to the peak was quite steep.

"I can't feel my hands!" she warned her comrades.

"Me neither!" Lily replied.

"Same here." Daphne was trying to warm her right hand with her breath, but there was barely any warmth coming from it.

"Use your cloaks. Cut them with your daggers and wrap your hands in the strips," Taika told them.

Ivo nodded. "That's a very good idea."

"Be careful when you do, don't lose your balance," Taika warned.

Cutting up the cloaks was more difficult than they thought. They had to use the daggers precisely and cut where there were no scales. It took them a long time, but they finally did it. They wrapped their hands in the cloak strips and tried to reach the summit. Nahia was tempted to use her Elemental Breath of Fire on her hands, but that would be crazy, since she would burn them. One of the main things they had to be wary of when using their magic was not hurting themselves or others. That freezing cold gave her crazy thoughts. She did her best to dismiss such notions and try to rationalize her ideas.

They were almost at the top and could see the summit clearly. Wrapping their hands helped with the cold, but it made it more difficult to maintain a good grip. They had to concentrate more to hold on properly and keep going.

Suddenly, Nahia heard a scream. She looked right and saw someone falling down the mountain. She held her breath. Whoever it was managed to hold on at the last moment and stayed still, lying there. Based on the distance it wasn't a member of their squad; it must be one of the Searing Squad's members. She could not see their face, since it was buried in the snow. She waited a moment and then saw someone going down to help. She did recognize this one: it was Beck, the Fatum from the Searing Squad.

"Trouble!" Nahia warned her group and pointed at the two members of the other squad.

Her comrades, forming a long climbing line upward, looked to where she was pointing.

"It's the Searing Squad," Daphne recognized them.

"One of them seems to be in trouble," Ivo said.

"We must reach the summit, we're almost there," Aiden said.

"What if they fall down?" Lily asked.

"They have to reach the summit by themselves. Like us," Aiden insisted and pointed upward.

Nahia sighed deeply. She was exhausted and her hands were not really responding. But she could not leave them there without trying to aid them. She took a deep breath of the icy air and made her decision.

"I'm going to help them!" she told her comrades.

"I'm coming too!" Daphne said.

"No! We must finish the test!" Aiden yelled angrily.

Nahia ignored him and began to move to the right instead of climbing further up. With each side movement, she felt her hands killing her. A little further up, Daphne was also moving to the right like her. They were not going to leave their squadron comrades to their fate. No matter how much it upset their red leader.

Chapter 7

They reached their squad comrades. They were on the north side of a large boulder, leaning against it to keep from falling.

"How are you, Beck?" Nahia asked, recognizing the Fatum boy. He had received a hard blow against the boulder they were leaning on.

"Frozen… to… the bone…" he said, teeth chattering.

"He slipped. We were almost at the top," Logar said regretfully. His lion mane had frost on it.

"Well, at least he didn't get himself killed." Nahia looked down and made a face that meant it might have been much worse.

"I'm not sure, I… hurt… my back…" Beck tried to say, but it came out haltingly between the blow and the cold.

"You were very lucky to strike this boulder. It stopped your fall downhill," Logar told him. "I was afraid we'd lost you."

Beck nodded with his eyes closed.

Daphne arrived just then.

"Injuries?" she asked.

"He has several cuts on his hands from the flying creatures," Logar explained. "That's why he lost his grip."

"And a strong blow to his back, I think," Nahia ventured.

"I can heal those injuries," Daphne said, crouching beside Beck. "Cuts and blows, if they're not too bad, I can handle. Take it easy," Daphne said, trying to ease him.

"That would be fantastic. We're almost there…" Logar shook his head, saddened.

"Thank you… thank you… so much…" Beck managed to say to Daphne. He could not stop trembling.

"Don't thank me. It was Nahia who decided we had to help you. I only followed her in case she got into trouble."

"Thank you, Nahia, honestly," Logar said gratefully.

"Don't mention it. I don't leave a comrade behind."

"You… are… amazing…" Beck said with a look of pain, teeth chattering.

"Try not to tremble so much," Daphne told him as she held his hands in hers and tried to heal his injuries.

"I'm… trying…"

"Try harder," Nahia said.

Logar held Beck's arms and stopped the trembling.

"Thanks, that helps a lot," Daphne told him, and she hastened to heal the cuts.

Nahia watched her friend work and thought it was wonderful what Daphne could already do with her Healer Talent. Nahia was envious. She would have liked to be a Healer instead of a Sorceress, but nothing had ended up as she hoped at the Academy. Beck's wounds began to close, but he looked worse. It was the cold.

"Beck is freezing. Even if Daphne heals his injuries, he won't be able to climb," she told Logar.

"He must," the lion said.

"The rest of the squad?" Nahia asked him.

"At the summit. We were nearly at the very top, they can't come down. They wouldn't be able to climb back up. They're as frozen and tired as Beck. I still have some strength."

"You're brave. It does you credit that you came down for him," Daphne told him.

"I couldn't leave him down here like that…" Logar shook his head.

Nahia nodded and looked into his eyes. They both knew that if they left him there, he would die. The dragons would never help. They would let him freeze and die where he was. Thus, ruthless was the Path.

Daphne spent a long time healing Beck's body's injuries, and when she finished she turned to Nahia.

"I can't do anything else. The cuts are closed and the bruises are treated, but he's never going to be able to climb like that. His limbs are practically frozen."

"We have to save him. Maybe I can carry him," Logar suggested.

"You're a brave lion, but that's crazy. You'd both fall down the mountain," Nahia told him.

"It's a hard enough climb already; carrying someone else is a death sentence," Daphne joined Nahia, determined to make sure the lion dismissed the idea.

"We have to warm him up. I can make a fire…" Nahia was trying to find a way to help him.

"Good, we could start there," Daphne said encouragingly.

"Fine." Nahia called upon her Elemental Breath of Fire, but completely opposite to how a Sorceress would. She kept it small and weak. She had never tried anything like that, and the end result was mini-fire breath. She projected it in front of her comrades. The three gathered close to the flame and put their hands to it to warm up.

"This… is… very good," Beck told her.

"You'll have to keep it up for a while so he warms up," Logar said.

Nahia made an affirmative sign with her right hand. In so doing, she realized that if she put her hands under the fire, she would also warm up. She only had to make sure not to touch the flame.

For a long while, they warmed up with Nahia's small fire, and at last they all managed to warm up. Beck was still feeling the cold, but his limbs were responding again and he had some color to his face.

"I think we'll be able to finish," Logar said, looking up toward the summit.

Nahia stopped sending her Elemental Breath.

"Are you sure?" she asked.

"Yeah, I feel a thousand times better," Beck said.

Nahia was delighted.

"Let's all finish this stupid test," said Daphne.

"Yeah, before these accursed beasts kill us," Nahia replied, looking up at the sky where Irakas-Gorri-Gaizt was watching them, flying in circles like a colossal red vulture.

"Thank you, Nahia and Daphne, really. You saved my life," Beck thanked them again, smiling sincerely.

"Yes, thank you very much, both of you," Logar joined him.

"Let's show those monsters that they can't do anything to us. Let's finish this test," Nahia said, enraged.

She was not expecting the two squad members to join her in cursing the dragons, no one ever dared. It was to be expected. But she was wrong.

"Let's show those soulless monsters they can't do anything to us," said Logar.

"They won't kill me today, heartless beasts," Beck joined him.

Nahia was very surprised to hear them. She saw rage and hatred in both their eyes, and this gave her hope. The more people in the Academy who felt this way, the higher chance they had of obtaining freedom someday.

"We'll see you at the summit, victorious," Nahia told them.

Logar and Beck began to climb the way they had come down. Nahia and Daphne went northwest. The rest of their squad was waiting for them a little further up. They went up carefully, but now that their hands and feet responded, it was much easier to travel the distance that separated them. They reached Lily.

"Everything all right?" the Scarlatum asked them.

"Yeah, everything's fine. Let's keep going," Nahia replied,

"Granite-head is already at the top," Lily told them.

"I expected no less," Daphne said.

They went up the last ramps and reached the peak. Five steps away from the summit, Aiden was waiting for them.

"It took you quite a while. I've been waiting a long time," he said, bad-humored.

"It took us what it took us," Daphne replied, wrinkling her nose.

"You should've waited," Lily said to Aiden, looking angry.

"And what do you think I'm doing?"

"You're only waiting because you're not allowed to finish without the whole squad," Lily accused him.

"As it should be. We're a squad, and we must arrive at the goal as a squad," Aiden admitted.

"Let's finish and not argue now," Taika told them.

They all nodded and reached the summit, where they found the banners of all the squadrons stuck in the snow. They took theirs and raised it, victorious. On the other side of the peak rested those who had already arrived. Among them was Logan's squad. Nahia saw him and was very happy. She sighed in relief. They had made it without casualties, and besides, Logan was there, as handsome and strong as ever, albeit somewhat exhausted. His usual reserved look appeared gray, without light. No doubt because of the effort. Everyone at the top of the mountain looked worn out.

Igneous Squad, you have completed the test, although in a shameful manner. Return the banner to its place and rest behind the peak with the others. I am very disappointed and furious with the behavior you have shown. That will be addressed later.

Nahia watched the arrival of the squads while she thought about the message of their leader. No doubt he was furious because they had helped the other squads. A short while later, the Searing Squad arrived. Logar and Beck had made it to the top. Nahia could not care less about the punishment Irakas-Gorri-Gaizt might give them for helping the other squads. It had been worth it. It would always be worth it.

They had to wait quite a long time until the last squad reached the summit. The cold, cutting wind at the top of the mountain; the icy temperature; and the tremendous height they were at pressed on their lungs, preventing them from breathing normally. It was an additional punishment they did not need, and yet, Nahia knew this was precisely what the dragons wanted, that they suffer until the last moment.

On your feet, Red Squadron, Irakas-Gorri-Gaizt's order reached them.

Nahia and her comrades stood up at once, and as they did, they saw that the rest of the members of the other squadrons did so too.

The six squadron leaders came down from the sky where they had been following the test. They landed along the southern rim of the summit, straightening up and roaring, almost in unison. A moment later, the two great dragons that had been flying in circles around the summit came down and landed on the tip of the peak of the great mountain, like royal eagles controlling their domain.

This year, the beginning test of the third year has fulfilled the expectations I had. Most of the squads have done well enough. A couple have gravely disappointed me. Their leaders will make sure they amend the behavior of those squads at once, since it is unacceptable. They will do so with the suitable punishments, of course, as it must be. They received the powerful message from Colonel Lehen-Gorri-Gogor, the dragon responsible for the Drakoros Academy.

Nahia exchanged glances with Lily and Daphne. The three knew that their squad would be one of those punished. Aiden also knew it because he snorted hard, enraged, and the snort was directed at Nahia's nape. She was wondering which other squad would be punished.

The test is over. You will come down the north side and then return to the Academy by the same route you followed to get here. Each squadron will take care of their injured and dead, they received the Colonel's and Commander Bigaen-Zuri-Indar's order.

Nahia realized then that there had been casualties in the test. She had been so immersed in everything going on and felt so exhausted, she had not had time to give it a thought. She wondered how many and from which squadrons. She felt the flame of rage light up in her stomach. She tried to control it. The colonel and commander were right there, a few paces away from her. If she said or did anything to upset them, Irakas-Gorri-Gaizt would kill her right there for the dishonor she caused.

Go now and return to the Academy. The third year awaits you, and it is one you will remember for the rest of your short lives. It will be a complicated year. You have much to learn and improve before you graduate. It is your last year here. Do your best, do it well, and you will manage to graduate as Dragon Warlocks and Witches. An honor few achieve. Fail, and you know what awaits you, the Colonel messaged to them, along with a feeling that it expected them all to try their best.

Nahia took a deep breath. They only had one year left and they would leave that academy of horrors. The problem was going to be surviving the whole year. She had already guessed it would be more difficult than the previous years, and those had been torture.

One last note before you start the journey back. This year we have the added incentive of the war in Drameia. No doubt it will influence the course of the academic year. You must also know that among those who manage to graduate, the best might be chosen to serve as Dragon Riders, a very special honor which a privileged few will be able to enjoy. I trust that will encourage you to strive beyond the best of your abilities. That is what is needed to be the best. Do so, and you might enjoy that honor. This time the message came with a feeling of doubt that anyone would succeed.

Nahia felt rage that it underestimated them and thought that she would succeed, if nothing else to prove to that ruthless and conceited dragon that it was wrong. Then she thought that she would have to ride a dragon and she dismissed the idea at once. She did not want to be a Dragon Rider—nothing was further from her wishes. At that moment, she only wanted to get out of there. Riding a dragon was the last thing she wanted. Besides, she did not understand why the dragons wanted riders at all. It seemed like a contradiction. The dragons did not need to carry Dragon Warlocks on their backs. Why? She could not understand it and did not want to, either.

Squadrons, march back to the Academy. Take your wounded and dead. Squadron leaders, lead them, the Commander ordered. The leaders bowed their heads, and a moment later the Colonel and Commander took off. Watching them fly away, so huge and powerful, Nahia had to admit, much to her chagrin, that they were awesome creatures.

Also, hateful and dangerous. She wondered whether one day she and her friends would be able to finish them off. She wanted to think they could. Lasgol had shown her undeniable proof that they were not indestructible. Perhaps it would be much harder to kill dragons as powerful as those, but it had to be possible. They would do it.

Nahia looked at her comrades and made a cheerful sign.

They started back to the Academy.

Chapter 8

For the first time ever—she never believed it could happen—Nahia was glad to enter the Drakoros Academy, to cross the high walls guarded by young dragons and get to the barracks. Her and all her comrades. They arrived broken from the third-year beginning test. They went straight to their beds. They did not even have the strength to talk. Breathing and moving their legs was already a colossal effort. If reaching the summit of the mountain for the test had been death, returning to the Academy had been nothing less. They had been in high spirits when they started back down the mountain, but they had not counted on the fact that they were exhausted and the Academy was far away.

Once they reached the foot of the mountain, they realized that a long journey awaited them and their battered bodies were exhausted. Each squad began to have members who fainted and fell on the spot. Things became so bad that the leaders had allowed them to stop for a three-hour nap near a beech forest. This frugal rest had saved them from staying where they were, but it had not restored their worn-out strength. Not even close. They needed to sleep at least one whole day and night in order to recover, something which, of course, the dragons did not allow. They had to go on, and thus they arrived at the Academy at dawn after marching again for a day and a night.

Nahia had hoped the dragons would let them rest after such a tremendous test. She shut her eyes in her cot, and as her eyes closed, she wished to sleep for a whole season. Unfortunately, in Drakoros, wishful thinking never amounted to anything. With the first light of the following day, the roars of the squadron leaders woke them all up.

"No, no, no!" Daphne shouted, lying on her face in her cot, refusing to wake up to the call to line up.

"I'm dead, I don't have the strength to move," Lily protested without moving from the cot where she was sleeping on her back without opening her eyes.

"They're calling all the third-years," Taika informed them as he looked out of the widow." The six leaders are in the bailey."

"Our leader is already waiting for us. We need to hurry up!" Aiden was dressing as fast as he could. "We've overslept!" he cried, concerned.

Ivo yawned, opening his mouth as wide as it would go. He began to rub his eyes without getting up.

"The mind needs rest, just like the body. To deprive us of rest only impairs our physical and mental faculties. I don't see the meaning behind this…" the Tauruk said with his usual calm.

"It makes sense to them. They only think about torturing us!" Lily exploded. "I need my beauty sleep! I'm getting older by the moment!"

"They're not going to give us any rest. You know it," Daphne told her as she sat up in her cot with slow movements, without any strength. She had one eye open and the other closed and was already wrinkling her nose.

Nahia was so worn out she had only managed to roll onto her side in bed. She knew she had to get up, but her body refused to. It was as if all the strength had been sucked out of her. Blood ran through her veins, but it carried no vigor.

"We'd better go down to line up, or we'll be in trouble," Taika told them as he stretched to loosen up his cramped muscles.

"My hands and feet hurt like a nightmare," Nahia said once she managed to stand up with difficulty.

"I can beat that. Besides my hands and feet, my arms and legs hurt too," Lily told her as she got up with grunts of pain.

"Even my head hurts. And don't even get me started on my lungs," Daphne said as she tried to clear her head and open her other eye.

"As far as your lungs go, it's logical because of the effort and height. I think we're all hurting the same," Ivo said, breathing through the nose and filling his own lungs. He made a pained face. "As far as your head goes, that's a bit irregular."

"Yeah, my lungs are also sore," Nahia said, nodding and pressing on them to see whether they hurt. She grunted. They did hurt, it would be better not to press.

"The headache might be from the combination of physical and magical exhaustion," Taika ventured.

Daphne, both eyes open by now and getting ready, nodded.

"Yeah, there was much of both."

64

"Hurry up, we have to go line up," Aiden insisted as he gestured at them from the doorway.

"We're all ready, granite-head," Lily replied as she massaged her face.

Tired, sore, and sleepy, they finished getting ready as fast as their battered bodies and minds allowed and went down to the bailey to line up. And of course, there was Irakas-Gorri-Gaizt waiting by their banner of fire. It had changed places and was now at the north side of the square, near where it ended, the entrance to the castle at its back. Seeing it there waiting for them, Nahia guessed that since it was their third-year, they were advancing their position toward the castle. Maybe that was not actually the case; she had no way of knowing. But she did know that simply seeing their leader made her skin crawl.

They arrived in front of the banner and quickly lined up with heads bowed. Nahia saw the Ardent and Searing Squads lining up on their right and left. Several members glanced at them in greeting, as well as acknowledgement.

On your knees, Squadron! Irakas-Gorri-Gaizt's message reached them so strongly that their heads hurt as if they had been pierced with a hot iron right in the middle of their forehead. A feeling of fury accompanied the message.

"Ouch!" Daphne uttered under her breath. Nahia shut her eyes hard to bear the pain. Their leader was in a terrible mood.

Once again you dishonor me! The Commander and the Colonel have lectured me. You have put me to shame before the other leaders and my superiors! This is unacceptable! Your behavior is inadmissible! The mental messages reached them with such force and fury that they were all forced to throw their heads back. Several put their hands to their heads, trying to stop it. The pain increased, as if with every cry another nail was buried in their forehead, piercing the center of their minds.

Nahia had already expected the first meeting with their leader to be along these lines. Their leader did not care that they had finished the test absolutely broken and exhausted and that the rest they had been granted was not enough. Now they had to face the fury of the great red dragon. Daphne and Lily looked resigned, like Nahia. They already knew the wrath of Irakas-Gorri-Gaizt would fall upon them like the weight of the mountain they had just climbed. They were not going to escape their leader's wrath. Taika made a pacifying gesture with his hands. It was best not to show any feeling and endure the hurricane like stone statues.

As they were on their way to line-up, Aiden had already told them off for their behavior during the test. He was sure they were going to be punished severely. He blamed them for whatever might happen and, despite Lily's and Daphne's protests, he made his opinion known. Ivo took it with his usual calm. Whatever had to be would be. And here they were waiting for whatever was about to befall them. Not only them, the Ardent and Searing Squads too. They had apparently also not behaved like they should have during the test either. Nahia did not care what their leader or the other dragons thought. What was important was that everyone in the Red Squadron had survived the test. The rest did not matter. Unfortunately, Irakas-Gorri-Gaizt was not of the same opinion, but of course, the red dragon cared less about their survival than looking good before the leaders of the Academy.

The disappointment I have suffered from this Third-Year Beginning Test has been monumental! When have I ordered the Igneous Squad to help the Ardent Squad? When have I ordered the Igneous Squad to help the Searing Squad? Never! Now the message exploded in everyone's mind as if it were attacking them with its thoughts, and they all held their heads from the intense pain they suffered.

Nahia bent over, trying to bear the sharp pain. It was as if something had burst in her mind. She bore the harm and saw her comrades in the same situation. Irakas-Gorri-Gaizt was really furious. Nahia did not understand why. So what if they helped their comrades? It was the right thing to do. And even if the dragon did not accept it, the whole squadron was intact. That was a real triumph. Why did it not see that? The reason surfaced in her mind a moment later, the pain delaying her thoughts. Because it was a dragon, that was why. Only a dragon would be outraged by one squad helping another in their own squadron. Where was the fault in that if they managed to finish the test alive? Just thinking about what would happen to them if they had helped another squadron filled her with dread. Irakas-Gorri-Gaizt would be roasting them right now. If it did not accept that they had helped squads from their own squadron, it would definitely hate them helping a rival one.

The order was to finish the test as fast as possible! Each squad had to try and reach the summit first. I ordered it explicitly. In a test of speed, you do not stop for anything! Nothing at all! The messages were filled with rage, causing intense pain to the whole squadron. No one was spared.

Nahia knew that in Irakas-Gorri-Gaizt's eyes they were nothing, and it was proving that again. It did not approve of what they had done because they had shown themselves superior. For this dragon and all others, they were only slaves from inferior races that had no value and whose death was something completely acceptable and normal. If she had Lasgol's bow in her hands, she would try to kill that soulless being. She would pierce its black heart. She would likely fail, but she would die trying. She would die happy. She reminisced on such thoughts in the midst of the pain she was feeling and realized that if she died like that, she would achieve nothing. Sacrificing herself without reason was not good for reaching any goal. No, that was not the way to achieve freedom. She would save herself, to fight and defeat the dragons, now that they knew there was a way of doing it.

You have shamed and dishonored me before the Colonel and the Commander. For this, you will all be punished. Each and every person, without exception. You will go to the dungeons to work for the whole season. But I will be fair. Not all of you will suffer the same punishment. The two repeaters who have already been to the dungeons will have a more severe punishment, because they deserve it. Thus, you will learn your lesson. If any of you do not survive, I am sure it will be an incentive for all of you in the future. Orders are carried out, not interpreted.

The announcement left everyone worried. They had not been expecting such a punishment, or that Irakas-Gorri-Gaizt would punish the whole squadron. It was disturbing, and it showed how furious it really was. If the punishment itself was bad, the fact that the whole squadron would be barely sleeping for an entire season was going to be disastrous, especially in the squadron formation training. There was nothing worse than exhaustion. When there were only one or two people punished, they could pretend, but with the whole squadron punished it was going to be terrible. Their poor performance might bring on further punishments.

Nahia thought they were beginning their third year in the worst way possible. This was going to be a calamitous year: she could foresee it. Not only her, but Daphne and Lily clearly also knew they were going to have to bear this last year. Nahia realized that Taika, Aiden, Ivo, and Lily would go to the second underground level of the dungeon for the first time, not good at all. She was worried. It was also troubling that Daphne would be going to the third underground level with her. She would have to prep her to survive the underground world. Her concern was growing, despite the fact that she could barely think with the headache she had.

Irakas-Gorri-Gaizt let out a long, sustained roar, as if letting all its rage and anger leave its body.

Nahia seized the moment to glance around unobtrusively to find Ana and Logan. She found them in their squadrons, and this cheered her up. Seeing them always raised her spirits. It made her feel less alone and vulnerable, more accompanied. Although, really, in the Academy they were all left alone to undergo the horror represented by the dragons. But Nahia's heart rejoiced from seeing them. They were her friends. They had started this horrible adventure together, and so far, they were still alive. She thought about poor Maika, who had died at the end of the first year. He heart shrunk at the memory. One day they would get justice for her and the thousands and thousands like her who had died unjustly and improperly under the oppressive claws of the dragons. As she looked at them, she realized that both their friends' squadrons were missing a whole squad each. That was terrible. Twelve unjust deaths added to the endless list of victims killed by the dragons.

The third year begins. This is the last year in the Academy. Irakas-Gorri-Gaizt grew a little calmer and its message did not hammer their minds. The looks of pain gradually subsided from the faces of all in the squadron. The looks of concern remained. Their worries would not vanish so easily. *The squads and squadrons will be reorganized according to the casualties they have suffered during the first two years of training. You will notice some squads have disappeared. Since they had few members, these have been sent to other squads which also had members missing to complete them. What does remain is the fact that any squadron must have at least one squad so it does not disappear. This has made some members move from one squad to another so the six squadrons live on. Luckily, this is not the case with the Red Squadron. There are four members missing, two from the Searing and two from the Ardent, but I trust they will recover. If they do not, there will be no more substitutions this year. There is no one available after the reorganization.*

Nahia was processing the message and trying to calm the flame that had awoken in her stomach. Her rage wanted to burst into a fire and incinerate that inhumane dragon and all the others. They were talking about the deaths they had caused as if they were only numbers. Worse than that, they were nothing more than vacancies to them, gaps in squads and squadrons.

Now, break ranks and find your sleeping quarters in the third-year barracks. There is plenty of space. Afterward, go to Administration and get your third-year clothes. Once you have them, you may go and have lunch. Go, and remember that tonight you begin your punishment after dinner, it ended on a calmer note, without affecting their minds and causing pain, which they were all grateful for.

They left immediately, not only because they had to follow an order without delay or hesitation, but to avoid another message loaded with intense pain. They did not speak, they simply fled the square. They went to the third-year barracks. There was indeed plenty of space, since it was as large as those from their first and second years but the number of pupils had reduced significantly. They got themselves a room upstairs with a view of the square. Aiden was not pleased because he wanted one closer to the door. But that one had no views since it was downstairs and the girls did not want it. In the end they had insisted stubbornly, and the Drakonid, knowing he would lose the argument in the end, had yielded. They divided the room like they had the previous years and all occupied the same beds and closets. There was not much difference between this barrack and those of first- and second-, with the exception that it appeared empty, with many people missing. Nahia looked down the long corridor outside their room and the stairs and felt they transmitted loneliness.

This feeling was repeated in the dining hall. They were all sitting at their new table, close to the entrance, looking around. They were trying to get used to the new setting.

"Well, it's strange to be sitting here," Ivo commented, looking at the door where the first-year squads were entering.

"Strange? Why do you say that?" Aiden's face was relaxed and a half-smile was on his lips. He seemed the most at ease.

"Because I didn't think we would get here," Ivo admitted, feeling the table and the long bench with his large hands.

Lily looked at him with wide eyes.

"That's a somewhat surprising statement coming from you, the reflective philosopher."

"I did not want to upset you, but if you study the situation, you'll reach the conclusion that almost no squad manages to reach the third year with all its members. We are an exception."

"You are absolutely right, my friend," Taika said, watching the other third-year squads sitting at their new tables.

"Yeah… many haven't made it," Lily said with a sad face.

"Too many," Daphne said, shaking her head.

"I was sure I would get to this table," Aiden said as if the opposite was not even a possibility.

"You're always so sure of yourself, but not so of others," Daphne said accusingly.

"Because I'll make it, and you, well…"

"We'll make it, same as you!" Lily finished the sentence for him in an angry tone.

"I hope so," Aiden made a gesture with his hands, meaning that it remained to be seen.

"Is there any other adverse conclusion you've reached and that you're keeping to yourself to avoid upsetting us?" Lily asked Ivo, raising her eyebrow.

"Yes. I've made some educated guesses," Ivo confirmed.

"So, are you going to tell us?" Daphne asked in a tone that indicated he ought to.

"I'd rather not create unrest and nervousness unless it's necessary."

"But it might be something important we should know about," Nahia told him with a questioning look.

"Don't worry, if it's important I'll let you know in due time."

"You're mean…" Daphne protested.

"I'm Ivo," the great Tauruk shrugged.

They kept eating while they watched what went on around them.

"I still think they should give us different clothes each year," Lily commented, looking down at her black sleeves with silver scales.

"They are different. They have a different dragon and the number 3 on the cloak," Aiden corrected her.

"I mean the color. This black is horribly dull," Lily replied, making a disappointed face.

"It's suitable for combat, especially if it takes place at night," Taika explained.

"I'm not arguing against that, but a strong orange or a bright red are much livelier," Lily posed in her imagined colors.

"And more prone to getting attacked," Taika said.

"It's good to be wary…" Nahia told her.

"You take the joy out of everything," Lily protested as she waved her hand, dropping the subject.

"There are so few of us left..." Nahia commented as she compared the first-year tables, which were full, with the second-year ones, who had already lost a good number of their members. The third-year tables were the starkest, a lot of people missing. Too many people.

"It's horrible," Lily commented without her usual good mood.

"I'm terribly sorry for the first-year newbies," Daphne said. "Look at their frightened faces. How many will get to the third-year tables?"

"Less than half," Taika answered, having done the math already.

"What useless slaughter... what an abomination." Nahia was shaking her head, unhappy and feeling hopeless.

"We're still alive, which is what matters. We can be happy," Aiden said, trying to cheer up the group, but that was not really his thing.

"Don't be such a granite-head. Think about all those who have died instead of yourself for once," Daphne told him.

Aiden thought about it for a moment. He nodded and said no more.

"The sad thing is that we'll still have some casualties this third year," Ivo told them.

"We must tread very carefully," Taika warned them. The tiger's eyes were dull with worry.

"Starting tonight in the dungeons," Daphne added.

"Yeah, that's going to be dangerous, for all of us..." said Lily.

"Don't worry, I'll help you," Nahia said as she realized that Taika was absolutely right. "I'll tell you how things work down there and what we have to do to survive. It's a different world, with its own rules. It's dangerous. You must be very careful."

"Just hearing the words 'dungeon' and 'underground' give me the willies. What a loathsome place," Lily said.

"Wait until you see who inhabits it and what it guards. You're going to love them, they're super sociable," Daphne said sarcastically.

Lily looked at Nahia.

"There are pretty loathsome creatures down there, yup," Nahia confirmed.

"Just what I need," Lily moaned. "Besides, it'll be very damp and the air will be rancid down there, my hair will be ruined."

"I don't think your hair is what you should worry about in the dungeons," Ivo told her.

"Listen to me carefully and I'll tell you everything you need to know. Remember it, you'll need it," Nahia said, and she told them everything she knew and had experienced in that underworld. While she did, she was thinking that her comrades had to survive, no matter what. A feeling of fear for their lives overcame her when she realized she would not be able to help them at every turn. This left her with a bad feeling inside, one she could not get rid of.

Chapter 9

They headed to the first class of the third year after stopping at the Square of the Path, behind the castle, to ask the Exarbor of Studies beside the fountain. They found the Exarbor with the red breastplate to one side of the fountain. As usual, they had changed positions, and the first day at the fountain was always an anthill with all the squads looking for their classes. It took them a while to reach him and get the information. Nahia still thought those Exarbor toyed with them in a strange game of confusion which amused them for some reason. Once they finally spoke to him, they were informed that they had Third-Year Dragon Magic in the Arcane Arts building, Olpiom classroom. This last part left them a bit confused.

They arrived at the great round building, featuring a garden with gold- and silver-leafed trees, large fountains in the middle, and the huge white sphere on the flat roof. Every time Nahia saw both the garden and the large white ball, she thought there was magic in them. She was certain. They met several squads which, like them, were coming to find their classrooms. They greeted each other and set to work quickly. They could not be late, least of all on the first day.

"What was the name the Exarbor of Studies told us?" Lily asked, looking at the plate above one of the classroom doors.

"He said O-L-P-I-O-M," Daphne replied, spelling it out.

"Strange name," Aiden commented, scratching his scaly head with one curved nail.

"From the little the Exarbor of Studies said, it's the name of one of the worlds," Taika said.

"Yeah… but it's strange… he said the names of the rooms are the names of worlds, but he didn't tell us anything about them," Ivo commented, reflecting on it.

"Worlds conquered by the dragons I'm sure," Nahia guessed.

"Most likely," Aiden nodded. "Our lords show their power and glory by naming the classrooms after conquered worlds."

"And you show your rock-filled head by uttering nonsense like that," Daphne replied, wrinkling her nose.

"Why is that nonsense?" Aiden asked blankly.

"Because if they are conquered worlds, they will have killed thousands during those conquests, you granite-head," Lily snapped.

"Every conquest has its price…" Aiden began to say, but seeing the looks of hate Daphne, Lily, and Nahia were sending his way, he shut his mouth and looked away.

"This room is called Saurion, it's not ours," Ivo said, pointing at the name on the plate.

"True, let's keep looking."

Taika moved with his cat-like agility and speed to the second door on his left.

"This is Drameia…" he said.

"Drameia is Tremia. They can't have conquered it already, could they?" Nahia asked with a feeling of great unrest in her heart.

"From what we saw there, they were far from conquering Norghana. No idea how they'll be doing in other kingdoms, but if there are two or three others as resistant as them, I doubt they have," Daphne reasoned.

"It's too soon for them to have conquered it entirely," said Lily with assurance on her face.

Nahia looked at Taika for his opinion.

"It's too soon for a full victory. They might have conquered some kingdoms, but not the whole continent-world," said the white tiger.

Nahia let the air out of her lungs in a long, relieved breath.

"Most likely the dragons consider it conquered even when it hasn't been yet," Ivo sad.

"Because they're conceited bullies," Lily said, slightly louder than she should.

"Shhhhhh!" Aiden warned her, gesturing toward the classrooms.

Lily raised her hands. "Sorry, I couldn't help it."

Another squad passed them, seeking their own room, and they were all silent for a moment.

Nahia lowered her voice before addressing the others.

"Lily is right. Now, let's look for our classroom. We'll find out the meaning of those names later."

Taika nodded and headed to the next door.

They had to pass two more doors before they reached theirs.

"Here it is: Olpiom," Taika said.

"Let's see what this year's magic class brings us," said Daphne before going in.

"It'll be great, you'll see," Lily said, loaded with irony.

"Oh yes, so great," Daphne said with a deep sigh.

They went into the room, which was even larger than the second-year one, a room that had already been huge. Nahia guessed why the third-year classrooms were larger: there were fewer squads, so they needed fewer classrooms. She shook her head, upset. At the far end of the room they saw the dragon that taught the magic class. It was a crystal dragon. It was huge, definitely a female and close to nine hundred years old, judging from its size and look. It was strong and muscular, but less than a male. Its face, eyes, and snout, on the other hand, were more delicate and refined than a male's.

Nahia watched it unobtrusively, keeping her head down. She looked at it again and doubted her approximation of its age, since its scales shone as if covered with crystal. It was very difficult to establish its age based on physical appearance alone. The flashes it gave off when it moved its body confused her. It shifted its wings to gather them at its sides and then stretched its head to look at them all.

Nahia felt as if the crystal dragoness was studying them. She looked to her right unobtrusively, and it was then that she realized there was another squad in the room. It was the Hurricane Squad from the White Squadron. She recognized Markus, the strong and nimble human who used to train with Logan. He noticed her looking at him and greeted her with his eyes. Nahia returned the greeting by looking up and then back down. Markus had long, light-brown hair that fell down to his shoulders, and his eyes were also light brown.

She studied the rest of the squad. With him was a pretty, delicate Fatum, a Kapro almost as large as Ivo who looked more brutal, a male Scarlatum who smiled a lot, a very picturesque Felidae jaguar, and a female Drakonid who did not look friendly at all. Nahia only knew them by sight and she was ashamed she did not remember their names. That should not happen. No matter how little contact they had with the other squads, they should know everyone's names. Especially those who had died in this hateful place. They should remember them; it was the least they could do for the fallen comrades. She clenched her fists and promised herself to make the effort to know everyone who remained in the squads. She had to get to know them all, and if anyone else fell—which would likely happen—she would remember. She also promised herself to persuade her squad mates, at least, to make the same effort. It was terrible to realize how insensitive this place of pain and blood was making them.

The great crystal dragoness roared and they all knew it was time to start the class.

I will introduce myself. I am Buru-Beira-Gogoa, and I will be your new teacher of advanced magic for this year. Today begins a new year for you, where much is expected of your skills and effort. This is the last year of training and therefore the most demanding. Also, being at war, we must speed up training. Therefore there will be no Learning Pearls, Spheres, or Orbs. From now on all magic will be performed without outside help. On the other hand, it is also the one you will get the most out of. You will start today by learning one of the most singular disciplines of dragon magic, one that is as powerful as it is fearsome. One that is very difficult to master but which provides a power without paragon over the enemy. It is the envy of all those with the talent for magic.

Nahia wondered what it might be, since their elemental magic was already powerful, or so it seemed to her. Lily gave her a look of doubt mixed with interest. Daphne was already frowning. She did not like the sound of that. Nahia gave them a look meant to transmit calm, but she was not successful. She was not at all easy, and her friends felt it. Not only was she restless, she was also intrigued, which surprised her. As a rule, she was always fearful, not looking forward to finding out more about the matter.

This new discipline has nothing to do with the elemental magic you have been studying and developing so far. It is more powerful and at the same time harder to master. That is why not all of you will do so. It is not within everyone's reach; only the best among you will achieve its full mastery.

Now they were all very worried. If not all of them were going to make it, did this mean whoever did not succeed would die? Nahia refused to believe they would be killed for not succeeding. They had come this far, after two terrible years of painful effort and deadly danger; they could not kill them now at the very beginning of the third year. She thought about the beginning-of-the-year's test and realized they would be killed without a doubt.

Dragon magic has three main disciplines. One you have been studying for a long time and have already mastered: Elemental Dragon Magic. The second one, which you will start learning now, is Mental Dragon Magic. The third, Special Dragon Magic, is forbidden to you. Only dragons can perform it.

Although she did not fully understand, somehow Nahia knew this made sense. Elemental Dragon Magic was what they were already using. Mental Dragon Magic had to be what the dragons used to send messages to their minds. She wondered whether the feelings which sometimes accompanied the messages were a part of this magic discipline. Most likely, especially because they came when the dragons were furious. These emotions seemed to be part of the message itself, or so she thought.

Daphne pointed at her own head with her finger unobtrusively, frowned, and closed her eyes hard for an instant. She was thinking the same thing.

Nahia had no doubt about what Special Dragon Magic was. She was sure it was what allowed the dragons to create the portals above the Pearls to travel long distances through them. They were able to change their spatial situation when they traveled from one Pearl to another through a portal. She also understood why she and her companions were forbidden from learning this magic discipline. If the slaves learned how to open portals, they would have a way to escape. It was an escape route, and this the dragons would never allow.

A long, silent sigh left Nahia's mouth. At that moment, she wanted more than anything else to be able to use Special Dragon Magic and open portals. That would give them a chance, not only of escaping, but of going and seeing other peoples and races,--enemies of the dragons—and uniting them all against their overlords. Indeed, she longed for this knowledge. She remembered during her last encounter with Lasgol and Camu that they had told her that the creature could open portals and travel through them to any of the Pearls in Tremia. The dragons were not going to teach her how to do this, but perhaps Camu could. The question was whether she could learn if Camu offered to teach her. She was not sure she was capable of learning—she was just a human. But if the dragons forbade them from learning this magic, it had to be for some reason. Otherwise, they would simply tell them they were not powerful enough to use it and would treat them as the inferior beings they believed them to be.

You must all at least recognize and learn Mental Dragon Magic, so you can defend yourselves from it. Those who can also master and use it will have a new power, one like no other. Mental power is a lot more powerful than you might imagine, as you will soon find out. Those of you who achieve it will not only be more powerful, but will have the recognition of your peers and the approval of their dragon leaders.

Lily looked very impressed, Daphne as if she did not believe a single word. Taika looked thoughtful and watched with narrowed eyes. Ivo appeared relaxed, as if all this had nothing to do with him. He seemed to have already decided he was not going to be good at this type of magic. Nahia could not see Aiden's face, but she was sure it would be one of absolute satisfaction. The Drakonid was surely confident he would successfully master this new powerful magical discipline.

I see in your eyes, doubts and uncertainty. I believe a demonstration will clear things up for you. It is always better to experience and feel something, rather than only receive an explanation, no matter how elaborate it might be, Buru-Beira-Gogoa messaged them, and Nahia swore its mouth twisted into an evil smile.

Before they could assimilate what the dragoness wanted to tell them, they all felt a new message reaching them, one unlike the others. Instead of sending a message, this one came loaded with something very different: pain. They all felt a sharp sting in their minds. Nahia realized that this pain was not like others that had accompanied the mental messages. When the dragons were angry, their messages came with a feeling that hurt them. When they were furious, that feeling was even stronger. But this was slightly different. There was no mental message. The dragoness had sent them pain in a direct manner. Not only that, it was more localized, sharper than what they had felt up until now.

The pain you are feeling now is only a small sample of what you can get to do with this power. Mental Dragon Magic can cause pain to other minds, especially inferior ones. I will show you how much more you can do once you master this powerful magic. What is coming is nothing more than another little demonstration.

Suddenly, they all felt the intensity of the pain triple. They put their hands to their heads, trying in vain to endure the tremendous suffering. Several fell to their knees.

As you can see, I have you under my control and domain. Right now, you are no longer potential Dragon Warlocks, you are simple puppets, incapable of defending themselves or even thinking. But, this is nothing compared to what you can achieve with this power I am now using against you. A power that all dragons have, and which the most powerful are capable of taking to unthinkable extremes, especially for you, the inferior races. Your imagination cannot even dream of something so powerful.

Nahia was struggling against the pain. She wanted to get rid of it, eradicate it from her mind. The dragon was using some kind of skill on them, and they could do nothing to prevent it.

Now, to finish showing you the power of this magic, I will make you all drop to the floor, useless.

Nahia wanted to shout *no!*, but she had no time. An insufferable pain burst in her mind as if a ball of fire had exploded in it. She fell to her knees, unable to bear such agony. Her comrades fell just like her. None were able to bear the punishment. The pain was too strong, the suffering unbearable.

I will end the demonstration with all of you prostrated before the power of dragons, as it should be.

The pain intensified again in everyone's mind, even more intense. Their anguish was such that Nahia fell on the floor. And with her, all the others; not one of them remained standing. None of them were able to cope with the pain the dragon was inflicting on them. It was too intense, an agony directed straight at their minds. There was no escaping it. Usually when someone suffered an injury, the pain traveled from the wound to the mind. In this case, there was no journey—it happened directly in their own mind and it was much worse, much more powerful. There was nothing they could do. They were all rendered useless, lying on the floor with their heads in their hands, unable to think or act. Dominated by unbearable pain.

It is not a pleasant experience, I know. But this way you will understand what I am trying to transmit to you perfectly. Very often pain is the best teacher, in magic and in many other walks of life. It teaches us lessons of great value that are not forgotten with the passing of time. I can assure you that you will remember today's lesson for the rest of your lives.

Just when Nahia thought her mind was going to burst with insufferable pain, it vanished completely in an instant just as it had come, without warning, in the blink of an eye. For a long moment, they all remained sprawled out on the floor, unable to get up. They could not do anything, even think, as if their minds could not work from the tremendous punishment they had suffered. And since the mind did not work, neither did the body. If their heart beat and they breathed, it was subconsciously, not because their mind ordered it. If a pack of ferocious beasts were to come in now and devour them, there would be nothing they could do to defend themselves.

I think the demonstration has been more than satisfactory. For me, without a doubt, for you not so much, but now you understand the power I am speaking of. I will give you a moment longer so that you can recover before we continue with class.

Nahia felt like dragging herself out of the room, but her hands and legs did not respond. She looked at her comrades through aching eyes. Their faces also showed extreme pain. They were all as bad off as she was. They had a moment more to recover, and it seemed to Nahia like a sigh.

Everyone, on your feet. Do not make me use my power for real.

At the sound of the threat, they all did their best to get up. Each of them was in bad shape. Nahia thought that if the dragoness used her power "for real," the pain would actually kill them. The idea that a dragon might use its mental magic to kill them with unequalled mental agony made her so sick she could barely stand. If she had thought dragons were powerful before, she was now finding out they were even more terrible. She began to lose hope of being able to fight them. She had to make great effort to not crumble; there had to be a way, and she would find it.

Now, close your eyes.

They all did as they were told, but they did not manage to calm down; rather the opposite. When they shut their eyes before the great dragoness, their fears rocketed. What was it going to do to them? They all feared worse pain and suffering. Nahia prepared for it, but nothing happened, at least nothing painful. Nahia was very surprised, just like her comrades.

I am going to make out the mental aura of each of you and then send it to your minds so you can perceive it. Concentrate on detecting it.

Nahia could only see darkness and, beyond that, fear. But then she felt powerful magic. The hair at the back of her neck curled and she knew the dragoness was using magic. She half-opened one eye and glimpsed the dragoness shining an intense silver. She shut her eye again. She did not want to get into any more trouble, least of all after receiving a sample of the pain the dragoness could inflict on them.

Suddenly, she felt several bright dots appear beside her. She could detect them in her mind as if they were lights given off by the flame of a candle. She tried to see them, but they were weak and seemed to sway in the wind. She felt them very close by however. She did not know how she could tell they were close, but that was how she felt.

Based on their proximity, she guessed it was her comrades. It gave her a most singular feeling.

Concentrate on the dots of light you notice in your minds. Now you only detect a weak brightness, but that must change. You must come to perceive the full mental aura of those around you. That is what we will work on first. My assistant of advanced magic, Exarbor Membor, will pair you up so you may begin the exercise.

The Exarbor came out from behind the dragoness and came closer. He first addressed the Igneous Squad.

"Human with Felidae… Fatum with Tauruk… Scarlatum with Drakonid…" the Exarbor paired them up, pointing a twiggy finger at each one of them. "Stand… one in front of the other…"

He left them like that and went to pair up the other squad. They waited until everyone was in position.

When I tell you, close your eyes and concentrate on the point of light in front of you. I will help you to identify it. Once you see it in your mind, you must use your inner energy to study that point of light. If it changes and starts becoming a circular aura, you will be making progress. If you only manage to see the point of light and it does not change, you will be failing.

Nahia was watching Taika, who made a gesture she interpreted as not being sure he could do it. Nahia gave him a sign of encouragement and strength by clenching her fists and slightly raising them.

Begin the exercise. Whoever gets it will be rewarded. Whoever does not will be punished. It is that simple. The reward will be to avoid being punished, a mental attack similar to the ones you have already felt. I believe that will motivate you to make your best effort.

Taika swallowed, while Ivo looked resigned. They knew they were not going to succeed. Aiden tried to maintain his usual look of confidence, but did not fully manage. He had doubts, many doubts about being able to succeed, and it showed. Nahia, Lily, and Daphne were worried, but they were better with magic, they might do it.

"Total… concentration," Membor said.

Nahia concentrated by closing her eyes, and instantly she saw several points of light. She focused on the one in front of her. She had to see Taika's mental aura. Not only to avoid the punishment, which would be tremendously painful, but in order to help her comrades so they also succeeded and avoided the suffering.

A mind's aura is something every Dragon Warlock must be capable of perceiving. Your dragon magic will allow you to do just that. It is a privilege of the dragon blood that runs through your veins.

The point of light that Taika's mind represented blinked several times. Nahia focused on analyzing it. She summoned energy from her inner dragon, and once she had it, she sent it to the point of light. When the energy interacted with the point of light, it started to expand. This was a good sign. Nahia took courage and sent more energy to interact with the light, and gradually the light began to open and form a circle. Not only that, its color began to change. It was no longer a whitish light. Almost silver, it began to take on different colors and hues.

A few of you are doing well. I can see how you are achieving it. The others, most of you, are going to suffer in this class. Those of you finding success must get the mental aura to shine brightly.

Nahia noticed that Taika's mental aura barely shone. She could see the colors and the round shape, but they were dull. They were not shining, and this worried her. She was doing well, but not as well as she had thought.

They strove all day, until at the end of class Buru-Beira-Gogoa ordered them to stop the exercise.

The moment has come to pass my verdict on what you have managed today. Those who have done well enough, even if they have not succeeded in seeing the mental aura shine with total clarity, will not suffer. The rest, unfortunately, will.

They had no time to prepare. Suddenly, most of the class was on the floor in tremendous pain. Nahia was not one of them. She stayed on her feet, since she did not feel pain. She was expecting at least Daphne and Lily to avoid the punishment, but it was not so. Only she had managed to avoid the punishment out of her whole squad. She felt awful watching her comrades on the floor, unable to do anything to help them. She thought she ought to be suffering with her squad comrades, that it was not fair she did not suffer while the rest did. But after a moment, she realized her suffering would be gratuitous. She would not achieve anything. No one should suffer— not her or anyone else in that class—but unfortunately, she knew it would not be like that. She raised her gaze and saw that only Markus, on the other squad, was standing.

The class is over. Go. I advise you to head to the library and study Mental Dragon Magic. You'll need to.

Nahia tried to help her comrades get up, but they were so sore she had to wait a while to do so. The third year was going to be full of suffering; she could foresee it, and this only proved it.

Chapter 10

Nahia arrived at the door of the dungeon building with her squad comrades. They had not spoken on the way from the dining hall. Considering they had crossed nearly the whole Academy, the silence betrayed how nervous they were. They stopped at the door guarded by two black dragons, one standing on either side of the great doors leading into the building of dark rock. The two dragons eyed them briefly with their black eyes. Nahia was already used to them, but she saw Lily shivering.

"This fortress gives me the willies, surrounded by those high walls with those round pointed towers with spirals all around them," Lily admitted.

"I find the main building even stranger. It's also round, with a spiral from the base to the high tip," Taika commented as he watched the black fortress carefully.

"There are four dragons watching, one on each corner," Aiden said.

"Besides those two imposing black dragons at the door, you mean," Ivo added.

Aiden nodded.

"There are always two black dragons at the door, and then a red one, a blue one, a white one, and a brown one at the corners."

"I find it very odd that there is no crystal dragon," Taika commented.

"There is," Daphne corrected him.

"Where? I don't see it," Taika asked, narrowing his eyes to see better.

"It's in the main building, inside. If there's an escape attempt, it goes up to the top of the building and creates a great glow that lights up the whole area," Nahia explained.

"And it stays hidden?" Ivo asked.

"That's right," Daphne nodded.

"And how do you know?" Aiden asked blankly.

"If you come enough times, you discover the little secrets of this place," Nahia replied with a shrug.

"I'd rather never come." Lily shook herself with another shiver.

"Yeah, I agree with you. This place is dark… I don't like it, it disturbs my inner peace," Ivo said, frowning, which was rare for him.

They heard footsteps approaching and turned round. The Ardent and the Searing Squads arrived and joined them. They all looked restless.

"Greetings, Igneous Squad," said Brendan, the blond human from the Ardent Squad. He sounded worried.

"Greetings, Ardent Squad," Nahia said in return.

"Greetings from the Searing Squad," said Logar. The Felidae lion sounded uneasy, which was rare for him.

The other members of both squads exchanged brief greetings.

"I see you've recovered," Daphne told Beck, whose head was bandaged.

The Fatum half-smiled.

"Half-recovered. I ended up in the infirmary. The surgeon Exarbor who took care of me said I had been very well tended, so thank you again."

Daphne nodded. "It was nothing."

Along with Beck and Logar were the Tauruk, Valka, and the Drakonid, Lita, who nodded gratefully and respectfully at Daphne.

"How are your burns?" Daphne asked Draider, the Drakonid from the Ardent Squad.

"Well. They gave me some ointments I have to apply on the burnt areas, but it's nothing," he waved it aside.

"Now you look much tougher and more fearsome. Scars give character and show your worth," Aiden told him, and his tone was obviously sincere and serious, not designed to cheer him up.

Draider took a deep breath and lifted his chin.

"Those I receive in battle will be even more honorable."

"As it should be," Aiden nodded. "Our scars will be the proof of our valor and honor."

Daphne and Lily exchanged a look of disbelief at what the two Drakonid were saying. Nahia understood them—the truth was that Drakonid were a tad excessive with anything that had to do with fighting.

"What news of your comrades?" Nahia asked Logar.

"They're still at the infirmary. They'll recover, they just need more time," the Felidae lion said, and his fierce face showed concern.

"Well, look at the positive side. They're spared this punishment," Lily said, smiling, and jabbed her thumb at the dark fortress prison.

"That's true, good news mixed with the bad," Beck shrugged and smiled, resigned.

"Our two comrades also seem to be okay. They're going to live," Brendan announced, letting out a sigh of relief. "In two weeks, they'll be back with us."

"Or so they told us at the infirmary." Lara's panther eyes seemed to indicate she did not fully believe it.

"That's very good news, let's hope it comes true," Nahia said, wanting to remain optimistic.

"I hope so too," Brendan nodded. "We must all finish the third year."

"Indeed, let's hope so," Lara joined in, still looking skeptical.

"We will!" Cordelius, the huge Kapro, promised, clenching a massive fist.

"Of course we will!" Aiden said, making the same gesture as the Kapro.

"For now, we need to survive this punishment…" Brendan commented as he watched the black fortress.

"They say very bad things about this place." Logar seemed uneasy about what they would face inside.

"Have none of you been inside?" Nahia asked, indicating the door of the building.

"No, none of the Ardent Squad members," Brendan said. "We've done punishments cleaning the kitchens and latrines, but not this."

"We've been punished with rebuilding walls and towers, but not here either," Logar said.

"It appears our leader likes to send us here," Daphne said to Nahia.

"Yeah, particularly me," Nahia smiled resignedly.

"Is it as dangerous… and weird, as they say?" Lara asked.

"I don't know all the rumors, but some of those I've heard are quite accurate," Daphne replied.

The answer made them nervous. They looked worried and restless. Nahia realized she had to help them.

"Listen to me for a moment before we go in," she said.

"Of course," Brendan said.

"We're listening," Logar encouraged her.

The other members of both squads paid close attention.

"Gather around. I'll speak fast, since we don't have much time," she said and proceeded to tell them everything they should know about the place and more specifically about the first underground level, which was where they would be working. She did it as fast and with as many details as she could. She also tried to calm them, especially when she told them about the dangerous parts, like the Serpetuss. It was not good to enter the dungeons with fear eating at their hearts. They needed to do exactly the opposite—have courage.

"Let me do the talking and I'll make sure you don't have any problems."

"Thanks, Nahia," Brendan said, and he put his fist to his heart.

"Your help means a lot," said Logar, who showed his respect with a bow of his head.

"It's nothing. It's my duty to help you, since I know the place well. The most important thing is to not show weakness. Keep your heads up and courage in your hearts at all times. It's a dark, dangerous place, but you are strong and brave, full of light, and you will survive."

"Big words," Lara said.

"Words of experience, nothing else," Nahia replied, determined to help them. The last thing she wanted was for something to happen to them. "If you have any doubts after tonight, we'll clear them tomorrow before going in."

Cordelius nodded. "Very well."

"It will be tough, especially due to lack of sleep. You'll be very tired, but we'll all survive," Nahia promised.

"You can do it if you keep your mind focused on the task at hand and survive," Daphne told them.

"They speak from experience," Lily said, smiling.

The members of the three squads nodded, looking at one another.

"Everything will be fine," Nahia said after a moment.

"Let's go," Brendan said.

Nahia turned and approached the door. The others followed her. They waited for a long moment under the gaze of the two black dragons. This alone could make anyone nervous, but no-one moved. They bore the scrutiny and the situation.

At last, the door opened and a familiar figure appeared on the threshold.

Tarcel, the Dungeons Chief Tergnomus, slapped his forehead and then shook his head.

"My eyes deceive me. It can't be. You're not only back, but you come with not only your squad, but the whole squadron!"

"You know I can't stay away from your wonderful, cheerful company for long," Nahia joked.

"All of you have been punished?" Tarcel asked, eyes wide with disbelief.

"All of us, I'm afraid," Nahia nodded.

"This is preposterous. You're incredible," Tarcel was shaking his hands, all worked up.

"I swear that although I love to see you and your gang, this wasn't my decision."

"Of course it wasn't your decision, you've been punished again! I've told you a thousand times not to be punished here again!" he replied, disgruntled.

"This time I've brought my friends."

"Hello, Tarcel," Daphne greeted him.

The Tergnomus could not believe his eyes. He looked up at the night sky and started cursing in his own language.

"I told you to do your best to not be sent back here, least of all with your whole squad."

"I did try, but I failed," Nahia shrugged.

"I don't know why I bother. I was sure I would see you again," he told her in a resigned tone. Then his eyes shone. "You're a troublemaker, and you know what happens in this academy to people like you."

"Yes, I know," Nahia nodded.

"You can't say I haven't warned you. I've been telling you so ever since you first came. You won't make it to the end of the Path this way."

"It's a complicated Path…" Nahia made a face that implied it was not for lack of trying but that things had gone awry.

Tarcel was not impressed by Nahia's remorseful face.

"I'm extending this warning to all of you." He pointed first at Daphne and then the others. "Learn your lesson and make sure you never come back."

"We appreciate your concern for us," Daphne told him.

"No, you don't, but it doesn't matter. I'll sleep well at night when you are dead," Tarcel replied, disgruntled, and then he turned. "Follow me inside."

They went in and followed him to the Register Exarbor. They found him looking grim and imperturbable, writing something down in a large tome at his desk.

"I've brought a large group," Tarcel warned him.

The Exarbor did not flinch. He looked up from the tome at the new arrivals.

"Familiar faces… Nahia and Daphne… of the Igneous Squad… Red Squadron…" he recognized them the moment they stood in front of him.

"Hello again," Nahia said, and she realized she did not know his name. She decided to ask him. "I don't remember your name…."

"That is because… you have never asked me…"

"So, what is it?" Daphne asked him directly.

"I am Jaibor… Chief Exarbor… of the Dungeons' Register," he replied in a solemn tone, as if the position were one of such great importance that it required everyone to know it.

"I'd say it's nice to meet you, but given the situation…" Nahia made a gesture that implied this was not a pleasant occasion.

"It's… understandable," the Exarbor replied.

"You look the same," Daphne told him, and by the way she said it, it was not a compliment.

Jaibor, though, took it as a compliment and slightly moved his head, which had some faded leaves. He began to consult from two other tomes he had opened beside him without turning.

"Let's see… you have a whole season of punishment… the whole squadron… assigned by your leader," he said, and looking up, he gazed at each of them carefully. "Different punishments… I will start with the repeaters…"

"Yes, the ones who won't learn," Tarcel added.

The Exarbor did not pay attention to the Tergnomus' comment either.

"Nahia… underground level 3, feeding and cleaning tasks."

"Because I am a repeated offender, or because our leader decided such?"

"The punishment… has been assigned by the squadron leader… he will have considered your… recidivism."

Nahia sighed deeply. Although she already knew the place and had an ally in this underworld, she was not at ease. It was as if she had a premonition that something bad was going to happen to her there, in the deep.

"Daphne… underground level 2… feeding and cleaning tasks."

"Underground level 2? Shouldn't it be underground level 1?"

"I don't make… mistakes with punishments…. It's… the second underground level."

"Because it's my second offense?" Daphne raised both eyebrows.

"By your leader's… decision."

Daphne looked at Nahia who returned the glance with a nod, indicating it was most likely for being a repeated offender.

Jaibor looked at the others waiting behind Nahia and Daphne.

"The rest of the Igneous Squadron… Lily… Ivo… Taika… Aiden, underground level 1… cleaning tasks."

The four had been already expecting this. Thanks to all of Nahia's and Daphne's explanations, they were not so nervous. They already had a good idea of what awaited them.

"I expect you to clean properly. Apply yourselves well if you don't want any additional punishments," Tarcel said, disgruntled.

"There won't be. We'll apply ourselves to the best of our abilities, as we always do with any task we're given," Aiden said stiffly.

"Let's continue…" Jaibor said without ceremony.

"Yes, keep going." Tarcel seemed to calm down a little, his disgruntlement reduced, or at least as peaceful as a Tergnomus could be, which was not much.

"Members of the… Ardent Squad… Brendan… Cordelius… Lara… Draider… underground level 1… cleaning tasks."

The four looked at Nahia and Daphne with a certain restlessness in their eyes. The two dungeons veterans made a soothing gesture.

"Members of the… Searing Squad… Logar… Beck…Valka… Lita… underground level 1… cleaning tasks."

"The dungeons are going to be spotless and shiny with so much help," Tarcel said, and for a brief instant there was a smile on his face.

"You must… all report here… every evening… for one whole season… and I will write you down. If any of you can't… because of an accident… in or outside the dungeons… I will inform your leader…" Jaibor told them.

"You'd better not miss a single evening," Tarcel warned them. "The wrath of a leader is much worse than this punishment,"

Nahia had no doubt of that. What worried her was that something could happen to any of them in the dungeons. She hoped nothing bad occurred, but there was no certainty that anything would go well when it came to the strange and dangerous prisoners in that underworld.

Chapter 11

"Very well. You already know your punishment. Now, follow me. Form in groups of two by squad behind me. That way we'll have fewer problems," Tarcel said, sighing loudly and then muttering something in the Tergnomus language which none of them understood.

They did as he indicated and followed him. He led them across several halls toward one that was an anteroom with a heavy metal door that looked reinforced and well secured.

"Wait a moment, I'll bring you the bracelets," he said, leaving them for a moment. They were left alone in the great hall in front of the door.

"Is this the way to the lower levels?" Taika asked.

"Yes, it opens onto a wide staircase made of rock that goes down into the deep," Nahia explained.

"Deep? But there are only three underground levels, aren't there?" Brendan asked at Nahia's back.

"That's right, but between each underground level there's a huge distance. Or rather depth," Nahia turned and explained with her hands. "It's as if they excavated a hundred floors down with only three in use. The first one is regular height. We don't know about the second floor because we've never been there."

"We'll find out today," Daphne said with a shrug and a resigned look on her face.

"And the third underground level is as high as twenty floors or more," Nahia said. "It takes a while to get down there, but coming up? Don't get me started on that."

"Understood. Three underground levels, each different heights and at different depths," Logar summed up.

"That's right."

Tarcel came back with the bracelets.

"This is for you, underground level 3," he told Nahia, who took her bracelet and immediately put it on. She knew all too well what might happen if she did not wear it.

"This is for you, underground level 2," he told Daphne, who put it on.

"The rest of you, here. Take them and put them on. Never go down without them. The guardians have been restless for a while, and it's dangerous. That's why I'm giving them to you before going down. And don't you dare lose them. The dragons don't like having to charm new ones."

They all put on their bracelets. Tarcel made sure of it, and once he was ready, he took out a bunch of large keys, using one of them to open the door.

"Follow me. If you encounter a Serpetuss, one of the guardians, stay as still as statues. As long as you have the bracelet on, it won't do anything to you. Don't run. They see that as aggression and will attack you. In the time I've been here, I've seen all kinds of foolishness with the guardians, from running to quaking or even attacking them. They all end the same way: with one less pupil. You've been warned."

No one said anything, but they all understood. Nahia had warned them about all of this, but she was glad Tarcel had mentioned it.

They went down the dimly lit stairs to the first underground level. There, Tarcel opened the door with his keys and motioned for them to follow.

"I'll take you to Framus, who is in charge of this level. He will assign you a cleaning shift," Tarcel explained, and they went through several stone rooms until they reached one where several Tergnomus were busy.

Nahia recognized Framus and greeted him with a nod. "You brought me a whole squadron?" he asked Tarcel blankly.

"Almost. Two repeaters are going to the lower levels, but the rest will stay here with you."

"Well, today is my lucky day," he said and looked at the two other Tergnomus fixing tools. They nodded, but their faces did not show joy. Nahia was not surprised; the Tergnomus never even smiled. They were a bad-tempered race with very little patience. Although there were nobetter workers than them.

"That remains to be seen. Let me know how well they clean," Tarcel told them.

"They will clean energetically, and they'd better do it thoroughly," Framus said. "I trust I won't have to explain twice."

No one said anything. They all took the Tergnomus' warning to heart.

"I'll divide you by sectors. There's a lot to clean."

"I'd like to be assigned to Ufrem's sector," Lily said suddenly.

Framus looked at her blankly.

"And why is that?"

"It's where my comrades Nahia and Daphne have been. They've told me the best way to clean that sector," Lily replied. "I want to do as well as they did or even better. I believe I can do better," Lily said, smiling at the annoyed cleaning manager.

Framus looked a Nahia and Daphne, who nodded.

"First time I've been asked such a thing," Framus scratched his long nose.

"We're very competitive," Daphne said.

"I want to beat those two," Lily told him.

Framus shrugged.

"As you wish, but you'd better leave everything spotless."

"I will. Thank you," Lily gave him another one of her charming smiles.

"Anyone else have a special request?" Framus asked in a mixed tone of sarcasm and annoyance.

No one said anything.

"Good. I'll put you in groups of two and assign you to different sectors. This level is large and has a lot to clean."

"I'll let you work," Tarcel said to Framus and made a sign for Nahia and Daphne to follow him.

As they were leaving, Nahia looked at Lily and winked unobtrusively. Then she looked at Taika, Ivo, and Aiden and made an encouraging fist. As she went by the Ardent and Searing Squads, she did the same gesture. Daphne, who was right behind her, also made a cheering gesture.

They went to the stairs once again and started going down, following Tarcel. The steps were very poorly lit, and because they were black rock, they had to be careful where they stepped. Nahia already knew this world, but Daphne was just beginning to enter it, her nose already wrinkled. Nahia always felt like they were going down into the black depths of an abyss following those stairs, only dimly lit by a few torches.

Tarcel opened another door, this one a gate with metal bars on a landing in the middle of the stairs.

"This is getting more and more dismal by the moment... it's like going down into a world of damp darkness," Daphne commented.

Nahia looked at her and nodded.

"It's the dungeons, what did you expect?"

Daphne nodded in agreement to appease the Tergnomus.

They continued down, single file. They descended the equivalent of five floors and then reached the door to underground level 2. It was massive, made of reinforced steel and guarded by two torches, one on either side.

Nahia pointed her finger above the door. Daphne noticed and looked. She did not see anything odd and squinted. Suddenly, the shadows above the torches at the top of the door shifted. Daphne started back. She could not see what was there, but something had moved and scared her.

"Take it easy. It's just the Drobeltz, the watchers of the stairs."

"They're not visible," Daphne said, unable to see them.

"Of course not. They watch without being seen," Tarcel said, bringing out a tiny oil lamp he lit with one of the torches, which gave off a silver light. Daphne was horrified when she saw the creatures. There were two right above their heads.

"They're like giant black lizards," she said with a shiver as she saw the creatures' forked tongues.

"Don't lose your bracelet and don't run, or you'll never get past these stairs. They have very sharp teeth and they love meat. They're fantastic predators."

Daphne shivered again at this.

"Turn off the light, I'd rather not see them."

Tarcel nodded. He extinguished the light and opened the door that accessed underground level 2. They went in and found themselves in a wide, gray rock hall. Two oil lamps lit the place. A strong-looking Tergnomus was sitting on a work bench working on repairing some chains with a ring. Nahia was surprised by how strong his forearms and chest looked, a lot wider than Tarcel's, although he was the same as any other Tergnomus in height.

When he saw them, he left the chains to one side and looked at them.

"Tarcel, what a surprise, you bring me workers?" he asked in greeting.

"One worker, Portesus, for cleaning," Tarcel replied, pointing at

Daphne.

"Good, good. We're short of help at this level. I trust you'll clean properly," he told Daphne.

"I'll do well," she assured him.

"Portesus is in charge of the second underground level. He'll assign you your tasks."

Daphne nodded.

"What kind of prisoners are on this level?" she asked.

"Important prisoners," Portesus replied.

"Important? In what sense?" Nahia asked, interested by this.

"In what other sense? Important to the dragon lords," Tarcel said grumpily.

This interested Nahia even more.

"Dragons?" she asked to see what they said.

"There's not room to keep dragons here. Dragons are on the third, as you well know," Tarcel said.

"Then what's on this level?"

"Other kinds of beings," Portesus said.

"Beings like creatures? Or beings like us?" Nahia insisted, wanting to find out what kind of prisoners they kept there.

"You ask too much, pupil. That's bad. Very bad for the health," Portesus told her.

"She has very bad habits," Tarcel said, eying Nahia. "Whatever is or isn't prisoner here is none of your business."

Judging by the angry looks both Tergnomus were giving her, Nahia knew she could not keep asking.

"Dangerous?" Daphne asked to break the tension.

Portesus looked her down from head to toe.

"Yes, dangerous. You'll have to tread carefully. The cells here aren't like those on the first level, as you'll soon find out. The important thing is not to go near the prisoners. That's what you have to pay more attention to. If you don't go near them, everything will be fine."

"In any case, they're less dangerous than the ones in underground level 3, if that's any consolation," Tarcel told Daphne.

"It's not very comforting, actually."

"Then perhaps you'll learn the lesson this time and we won't see you again," Tarcel replied in an irritated tone.

"We're not here by choice," Daphne said, wrinkling her nose.

"Sure, but you are here nonetheless, which in the end is the same," Tarcel told her, also wrinkling his nose as he stared Daphne in the eye.

"Let's hope it's the last time you see us." Nahia meant it, but it did not sound very convincing.

"Something tells me that won't be the case," Tarcel said. "Come on, let's keep going. The third level is very deep, and time escapes us."

Nahia looked at Daphne when she went by her.

"Be careful, see you at the barracks."

"You too. Don't trust the dragons down there."

"Don't worry, I won't."

Tarcel went back to the stairs, and once Nahia was with him, he locked the door to the second level with his heavy keys.

"Let's keep going down."

Nahia followed Tarcel, who did not say anything else during what remained on the way down. All the Tergnomus had a cantankerous character, quick-tempered, although the first time Tarcel had not appeared very annoyed. Only on her subsequent visits had he begun to show signs of annoyance, and more every time. It bothered him that she was here again. As if he did not have enough trouble with the dragons already. For being so short, the Tergnomus went up and down the stairs with great ease.

They went farther and farther down into the midst of the darkness, because the deeper they went, the fewer lit torches there were. She found it strange that although she had been down here for a whole month the previous year, it seemed like the first time. Her mind seemed to have desperately tried to forget all the times she had been down to that dark, oppressing world. She was calm, although she knew she was deep under the earth and heading to see dragons and other creatures of the most dangerous, lethal kind. Not to mention they were surrounded by Drobeltz which followed them in the shadows.

They finally reached underground level 3. Nahia sighed. It had seemed like an eternity. She thought about the way back up and had to dismiss the idea. The way up was exhausting and took forever. Her mind had no trouble remembering this. She decided it was best not to think about it; she would face it when it was time to go back up.

"Brings back good memories, doesn't it?" Tarcel pointed at the door.

"The best," Nahia replied, making a face.

"It hasn't changed much since the last time you were here."

"I can imagine…" Nahia did not think the place could change, not with those dragons kept prisoner down there.

Tarcel opened the reinforced door and they went in. Nahia saw four Tergnomus working. She recognized them at once. She was once again surprised that they looked much stronger than Tarcel and the surface Tergnomus, and even stronger than Portesus on the second level. She reasoned that the most likely explanation to this was that the deeper you went into the dungeons, the more strength was required to do the work.

"Well, look at what they've sent us from the surface," the leader of the group greeted her, shaking his head.

"Hello again, Utrek," Nahia greeted him.

"You don't learn your lesson, do you?" he asked ironically.

"I simply like your company. I missed you," Nahia replied.

The four gave what might be considered a guffaw, although coming from a Tergnomus it was more like a growl of laughter.

"I like you. I hope you don't end up as food this time either."

"That's my wish too."

"I'm not happy to see you. You shouldn't be here again," Burgor said.

"Didn't you miss me a little?"

"Of course not. Besides, you're a troublemaker," the Tergnomus jabbed his finger at her.

"And here I thought you were fond of me."

"I'm fond of my own skin, and because of you I nearly lost it. So no, I'm not fond of you and I haven't missed you."

"He's in a bad mood today, don't pay any attention to him," said Misrak, the redheaded Tergnomus. Of all of them, he was the most extravagant looking.

"Well, I guess I'll have to give you work," Utrek said.

"I'll take her, she's proven she can survive down here," Sardesk, the strongest and hairiest of the four, offered.

"What's her punishment?" Utrek asked Tarcel.

"Undefined. You may use her as you see fit."

"Wonderful. You'll help Burgor for now," he told Nahia.

"Me? I was in charge of her last time. Let Sardesk have her."

"Yeah, I'll take her."

"You are the one who needs her the least," Utrek replied, shaking his index finger.

"Burgor is lame and needs help. You're going with him," he told Nahia.

"It's only a sprain. I'll be fine in no time."

"A pretty ugly sprain. She's coming with you, and that's that," Utrek ended the argument.

"But…" Burgor tried one last time.

"You're taking her, Burgor, and stop whining."

Nahia said nothing because she did not mind working with Burgor again. She already knew what he was like and preferred not to risk it with Sardesk, Misrak, or any of the others. Who knew how they would behave towards her. This place was extremely dangerous; the last thing she needed was more uncertainty. She preferred the bad she already knew, to the uncertain, possible good, which most likely would not be good at all. The Tergnomus were concerned with doing their work well and staying alive. Whatever happened to a punished human was none of their concern.

"Good, I'll go back up to the surface. I have a lot of work to do," Tarcel said.

"Like we all do, as it should be," Utrek replied.

Tarcel nodded and opened the door. Before leaving, he looked at Nahia.

"I wish you luck this time too."

"Thank you, Tarcel," Nahia replied. She saw something akin to compassion in the eyes of the grumpy Tergnomus of the dungeons. She was not altogether surprised. Tarcel was a bit cantankerous, but he did not have an evil heart. Or at least that was the impression he gave her.

"Very well. Your shift starts shortly, so go with Burgor and get ready," Utrek told Nahia.

"Okay." Nahia turned to Burgor, who snorted through his nose and then turned to open the door to the next room. Her punishment began. Nahia breathed in deeply three times. She hoped to survive it this time too.

Chapter 12

On the first underground level, Lily and Ivo were cleaning a long and shadowy corridor enclosed by two metal gates at the ends. Ivo was cleaning ahead and Lily was coming a few paces behind. The large Tauruk stopped and turned toward his partner.

"Are you doing well?" Ivo asked, a mixture of joy and concern in his beastly face.

"Yes, don't worry, I'm over it already," the Scarlatum replied, scrubbing the floor with energy.

"You're still a bit pale. Your skin is almost orange instead of its usual intense red," said Ivo, watching her closely by the light of a torch.

"Does it surprise you? I was terrified. And disgusted."

Ivo nodded.

"That thing appeared suddenly behind us, without a sound. I didn't even notice it. It's very stealthy."

"And treacherous."

"What are they called? I keep forgetting."

"Serpetuss. They're the most disgusting thing I've ever seen in my life. It made me sick to my stomach."

"It looked like it wanted to kiss you," Ivo smiled.

"Yeah, go on and laugh," Lily pointed the mop stick at him.

Ivo shrugged.

"It was funny, admit it. You looked so scared, your face…"

"Yeah, very funny," Lily rolled her eyes.

"You almost threw up on it. Good thing you didn't, I doubt it would've liked that," Ivo smiled.

"It was revolting!"

"It's just some kind of giant snake."

"Disgusting and loathsome!"

"I remember Nahia and Daphne telling us that they patrolled the corridors of the first underground level. According to them they're terrifying, but I didn't find them so."

"That's because you're an ox-head, and when you're as big and strong as you, nothing's terrifying."

Ivo was thoughtful.

"Maybe… indeed."

"And they're not only terrifying, they're revolting. I keep feeling like there's one lurking behind us," a shiver ran down her back and Lily shook it off. "Now I have to keep looking behind me all the time to see whether another one of those giant, nauseating snakes is lying in wait," she shivered again and shook her body exaggeratedly.

"I wonder if Taika and Aiden have encountered one of these Serpetuss. They've been sent to clean the north sector. We're in the south, do you think there'll be any over there?"

"Those things are everywhere. I bet they come across one or two."

"I don't think it would affect Taika, he's very composed. Besides, you know what they say about felines and snakes."

"I have no idea what they say about felines and snakes." Lily looked at Ivo blankly.

"Don't the Scarlatum have cats?"

Lily shook her head.

"Felines and Scarlatum don't get along well," she admitted.

"Huh… curious."

"You think it's curious?"

"They're adorable little fellows, especially when they're young. And very amusing, they do crazy things."

"Not for us. Don't you see that they're intractable and vicious?"

Ivo waved it aside as not so bad.

"They are a little vicious… but it's no big deal. They like their space and independence."

"They like to scratch and bite without reason. The Scarlatum can't accept such behavior. A mark on our skin is sacrilege."

"Oh, now I see the problem… your physical appearance."

"In order to be charming, one must look after all aspects of beauty. Having your body marked by scratches and bite marks is inadmissible."

"I see. What I meant is that cats and felines in general have a far superior reaction time to snakes and their ilk. Hence why it's very difficult for a snake to bite a cat."

"So, Taika won't be afraid of the Serpetuss."

"That's what I believe."

"But he's with Aiden, and that granite-head is capable of starting a fight with the beast to show that Drakonids are stronger than Serpetuss."

Well, that might also be the case," Ivo had to admit.

"I bet he ends up all crazy in the middle of one of his attacks, delivering cuts with his sword and lightning with his sphere at the Serpetuss."

"That would be worth watching," Ivo smiled.

"Could he be crazier?" Lily said with a frustrated look in her face.

"Taika won't let anything happen to him, don't worry."

"Yeah, I know that. He's the one with the most common sense out of all of us."

"I agree with that sentiment."

"Well, now that this corridor is cleared, we'd better focus on the mission at hand," Ivo said, looking down both sides of the corridor.

"You're right, that way I'll forget about that nauseating thing."

"From what Nahia and Daphne told us, the cell must be in this corridor, although we could be in the wrong one."

"Let me think…" Lily looked at both sides of the corridor. "Yes, I do believe it's this one, although this place is a labyrinth of corridors and cells without end."

"Yeah, I've got the same impression. It's going to take time to get used to this place. I find it very depressing."

"It's an underground dungeon, built out of black rock and poorly lit. It can't be very cheerful," Lily replied with a comical gesture.

"Thank goodness I have you to cheer me up with your optimism and charm," Ivo said with a smile.

"Of course. I'm not going to let this place affect me, I am the embodiment of joy and charm. Being here isn't going to rob me of my innate gifts."

"I was just thinking the same exact thing."

"You're very shrewd for someone as big and brutish as you."

"I am Ivo," the great Tauruk shrugged.

"Let's find the cell. I'll take the left side and you the right," Lily said, indicating with her mop.

They both started to slip open the cells' peepholes. They saw prisoners of different races. Lily found a Felidae, an ancient human, and a Tergnomus, which surprised her greatly, since they were a servant race.

"There's a Drakonid here… and I just saw an Exarbor," Ivo said, eyes wide with surprise.

"That's strange. Aren't both faithful servants to their masters?"

"I wonder what they've done to end up in here," Ivo said with a blank look.

"Yeah, a Tergnomus, an Exarbor, a Drakonid… I find it most strange. But let's keep going."

Ivo nodded.

Lily looked inside the next cell, sliding open the peephole. Although it was very dark, she made out what was unmistakably a human. And from their friends' descriptions, this could be him.

"Egil, is that you?"

The figure came to the door.

"Who's asking?"

"It's Lily, a friend of Nahia's and Daphne's."

"Lily, yes! I know. They tell me, Igneous Squad, Red Squadron."

"Exactly! That's me."

"It's a pleasure meet," Egil said, coming closer still, and Lily could see that he was still wearing the dragon mask.

"They're still keeping that horrid mask on? I can't believe it," she said angrily.

"I get used to. Not feel."

"Ivo is here, come," Lily motioned for the Tauruk to come over, and he turned and did.

"This is Ivo, another member of our squad," Lily introduced him and then moved aside so Egil could see Ivo through the peephole.

"Pleased to meet. You be Tauruk?"

"That's right. I am Ivo, the Tauruk. It's a pleasure to meet you, Egil. I've heard a lot about you."

"I know of you," Egil told him.

"I'm deeply sorry that they keep you this way… locked up here and with that mask on… for so long… it's horrible. No one should suffer this. I'm very sorry, honestly."

"Thank you Ivo. I endure. Life be tough sometimes. Good times and bad times. Now bad, tomorrow good."

"That's what I call being filled with optimism. I don't know how you do it. I wouldn't be capable if I was being held like you," Lily said, listening beside Ivo.

"And you have a great spirit," Ivo added. "An impressive one to endure all this punishment for so long and not lose hope."

"Be life. I fight today for tomorrow. Tomorrow good. Never lose hope. Hope be all I have."

"You're absolutely right. Tomorrow will be good. We'll achieve whatever we want," Lily said, cheered. "We also hold onto our hope of changing things, of getting rid of the dragons."

"We must do our best and fight for that better tomorrow, so that things like this never happen again. Not to you, or us, or anybody else," Ivo said, convinced.

"All together fight," Egil said firmly.

"The future that awaits us is most interesting," Lily commented, making a face that said it would be very hard,

"It's not the future of quiet, balance, and contemplation I dreamed of. But neither is the life I'm currently living, and it won't be the one that leads me along the Path of Dragons," Ivo said.

"That's for sure." Lily put her hands on his huge shoulder.

"What news?" Egil asked in a tone that showed great interest to know whatever information they had.

"Ufff… we have tons of things to tell you. We're going to need several days," Lily told him as she looked at both sides of the corridor in case Ufrem appeared.

"Have days?"

"Yes, we have a season-long punishment," Ivo said. "It will give us time to talk and particularly to get to know one another. I'm very interested in everything you can tell us about your world, Tremia."

"Yes, your world is most interesting," Lily agreed. "Dangerous, but interesting. The dragons are going to choke on it. I'm positive."

Egil nodded.

"Everyone well?"

"Yes, don't worry. Nahia and Daphne have been sent to the lower levels of the dungeons," Ivo told him.

"They send you greetings and a big hug," Lily told him.

"I happy they well. Nahia and Daphne friends. Good friends. Allies."

"You can count us among your friends and allies too," Ivo told him.

"Nahia's and Daphne's friends are our friends," Lily said. "And allies, of course. They trust you, and because of that we do too."

"That good. I grateful."

"Otherwise they wouldn't have sent us to talk to you," Lily said with a giggle.

"Must watch corridor, Serpetuss and Tergnomus come by," Egil warned them.

"Fine. I'll watch," Ivo offered. "Lily, you tell him everything, you're better at talking than I am."

"You mean that with my charm the conversation isn't just vivid but excellent?"

Ivo smiled.

"Exactly. I couldn't find the words," he humored her and began to scrub in front of the cell while he watched both ends of the corridor.

"I'd better tell you everything that happened in order. That way you can reach your own conclusions. Let me tell you everything and then you can ask me questions. Well, if you don't understand something I say, then you can ask or tell me to repeat it."

"Understand," Egil looked at Lily, giving her all his attention. Lily took a deep breath and began to tell him everything that had happened during the end-of-term test that had led to them fighting in Tremia.

On the second underground level, Daphne was following Portesus down a long, wide hall. They went along the middle, crossing it from west to east. The floor, walls, and ceiling were made of rectangular, black slabs with silver streaks. She found it curious. As a rule, everything that was silver-colored had to do with dragons, so she was distrustful. Several Tergnomus were getting ready to work on either side. They carried some sort of steel tridents, like long spears but with three tips. What would they need that for? To defend themselves? If that was the case, she would be in trouble. The Tergnomus watched her go by but did not say a word. They seemed very concentrated on their preparations.

"This level is a bit more complicated than the first one. I recommend you pay attention to what I have to tell you. It will save your life."

"Alright, thank you."

"Don't thank me. If you die it's more work for us, and we already have a lot to do. The lords insist on sending us 'help,' punishing pupils like you to serve here, but it's no help for us."

"It isn't? We clean, we feed…"

"Easy tasks that any Tergnomus could do a thousand times better than the other races. You don't help, you get in the way."

"I'll try to be useful and not bother you too much," Daphne replied, and it came out in a tone of resentment.

Portesus looked at her sullenly.

"Save your personality for the surface. Down here it won't do you any good, and it might bring about your demise."

She immediately caught onto the threatening tone in the Tergnomus' advice.

"I will," Daphne replied neutrally. It was not a good idea to antagonize the one who held her life in his hands.

They reached a door, reinforced with metal, at the end of the hall.

"Ready to go out to the cells?" Portesus asked her, indicating the door.

Daphne took a deep breath. "Ready."

Portesus opened the door with some heavy-looking keys hanging from his belt. They went out into the hall and Daphne saw a wide corridor opening in front of her. In the center of the corridor and all along it she saw braziers with fire burning in them to light the way. On both sides of the corridor there were bars, long rows of bars that went up from the black-stone, silver-streaked floor she had already seen to the ceiling, which was made of the same stone slabs. She had the impression that she was in the prison house of some great castle. There were no areas of natural rock or dirt. Everything was lined with those strange rectangular stone slabs.

"Follow me," Portesus said with a wave.

They went along the center of the corridor and the Tergnomus stopped after fifty paces. He indicated the bars on their left. Daphne looked and saw they led to a wall of rock. Then they started again and continued down the corridor.

"All that is just one cell?" Daphne asked.

"That's right. That's cell number one."

Daphne could not see the back of the cell since the only light came from the braziers in the corridor. They gave enough light but did not reach the bottom of the cell.

"It's also very deep."

"About a hundred paces, yes."

"Wow… then these cells are huge."

"There are larger ones in other sectors of this level."

"Why so big?"

"We have pretty sizeable prisoners, but the truth is that they were built to hold several prisoners at a time."

"Oh, I see. Groups of prisoners."

"That's right. Follow me and don't touch the bars, they're bewitched."

Daphne was left wondering. She followed Portesus, who went over to the bars of the first cell.

Suddenly, from the shadows in the cell appeared a winged creature that glided down. Before she could react, the creature attacked with its claws, like a great eagle's talons, and tried to reach them. Terribly startled, Daphne took a step back. The bars flashed silver and the creature's talons hit a barrier of silver energy. It took a good blow and bounced backward, feathers flying from the impact. Daphne did not know what kind of creature this was. She watched it as she got back to her feet. It was about her size, perhaps slightly bigger and humanoid looking. It had bird wings instead of arms, which it shook hard. Its legs and talons were also strong and birdlike. But its body and head looked like a human's, or a Fatum's. She froze. The creature gave off a shrill cry that sounded like a bird.

"Don't worry, as long as you don't touch the bars there's no danger."

"Are you sure?"

"Yes, quite sure. I've been working here for twenty years," he told her in a tone that was a mixture of sarcasm and irritation.

"I didn't mean to doubt your word. It's just something that surprised me, that's all…"

"If a Tergnomus tells you how something works, that's how it works. Never doubt what they tell you. We don't like to repeat things, it's a waste of time. We hate to waste time. And we detest even more those who make us waste time."

"Understood. I won't waste your time."

"Good, I have a lot to do, and time flies."

Suddenly, another creature came flying to the bars and opened its mouth. Daphne had no doubt what it intended. It was going to use some kind of magical attack, like their Elemental Breaths. She did not know how she knew, but she had no doubt.

"It's going to deliver a magical attack!" she warned Portesus.

"Easy," the Tergnomus replied calmly.

Daphne was expecting the creature to release fire from its mouth, but that was not the case. It released a green substance directly at Portesus and her. Daphne jumped back.

The bars flashed again and the green substance hit the barrier of energy, which could now be seen joining all the bars.

"Don't worry. They can't reach us on this side of the bars."

"Wow… good defense."

"All the cells have bewitched bars with energy barriers that respond not only to physical attacks but also magical ones."

"Quite impressive."

"It is, especially because the magical attacks can be of different kinds. This one, for instance, is a mixture of poison and magic."

"Poison with magic?"

"That's right. These creatures can launch a venom they mix with magic to increase its effect and reach."

"How nice… what are they?"

"They're known as Harpiyias. They're a species that's half-humanoid, half-bird. They have powerful talons, venom, and acid magic. They're very dangerous; they are raptors and see the rest of us as possible prey, no matter how big we are."

"Wow… never heard about them."

"It's because they are not of this world."

"They aren't? Then?" Daphne thought for a moment, since the Tergnomus did not answer. He just stared at her with a bushy eyebrow. "Oh, they're from another world."

"That's right. A far-away one."

"Fascinating. I only know the races of Kraido. Well, and now I'm beginning to know those of Drameia… because of the war."

"You should already know, but in case you don't, I'll confirm now to avoid a thousand unnecessary questions. There are many continent-worlds with all kinds of races and creatures. And yes, here on this level we have quite a few prisoners from those worlds."

Daphne opened her mouth since that statement, as Portesus had anticipated, had raised innumerable questions.

"And they…" she shut her mouth, because she guessed that the Tergnomus' reply would not be pleasant.

"They're very dangerous. Don't go near the bars and everything will be all right," he insisted, pointing at them.

Daphne looked at the two Harpiyias behind the bars as they watched her with half-closed eyes. The energy between the bars had turned transparent and was now barely noticeable.

"Then this place is very safe."

"Quite safe."

"Quite? Why only quite?"

"Because sometimes, as with everything in life, unexpected incidents occur."

"Someone puts their hand through the bars," Daphne ventured.

"That, and another, more serious, situation."

"More serious?"

Portesus nodded.

"It has happened occasionally that the magic gets consumed and then the defenses of some cell don't work."

Daphne's eyes opened wide.

"That's not good at all."

"No, it's not."

"Shall I make sure the magic is working properly?"

The Tergnomus laughed, a deep rumbling sound.

"No, absolutely not. That's too important. There are Tergnomus lives at risk. We can't leave that in the hands of a punished pupil."

"Aha… I see."

"You'll be in charge of going along all the sectors, which are numerous and long, and keeping all the braziers lit. They usually die out every now and then as the coal we use burns out."

"Oh, okay."

"It's a simple task but burdensome. You'll have to carry the coal in a cart throughout the level."

"I hope an animal draws the cart."

"Oh, yes, it does, of course."

"Thank goodness."

"A Fatum animal."

Daphne opened her eyes wide. He meant her.

"That's not funny."

"I wasn't trying to be funny. I'll show you where the cart is. Come with me."

Daphne shook her head with disbelief. Portesus was not joking. She looked down the long corridor, whose end she could not see, and sighed deeply. This was going to be torture.

Chapter 13

Nahia felt nervous. Underground level three was a very dangerous world, and she was about to step into it again. It eased her to think that Garran-Zilar-Denbo would be there and would protect her. It had done so the last time, and she hoped it would now too.

"Take your safety equipment and follow me," Burgor told her.

"The Repulsor?"

"And the hat. Don't tell me you've forgotten already," Burgor stared at her, eyes huge with disbelief.

"No… of course I haven't forgotten," Nahia said, pretending, and went to get her belt and hat and put them on. She had indeed forgotten, but she was not going to admit it to Burgor, who already had his belt on and was putting on his silver hat.

They went out, and Nahia immediately recognized the enormous cave lit by torches and the multitude of huge caves that opened inside that underground world made up of colossal caverns.

She shivered. Burgor closed the door and headed to the food carts.

"Follow me and remember to step on the silver path. If you've forgotten that, you deserve what you get."

"I haven't forgotten," Naha replied, and this time it was true. As they walked, the silver path became visible in front of them.

Burgor gave her an unfriendly look and went into the cave where the convoys of six carts pulled by Yakretils were. They had always seemed to her the most fascinating creatures, a mix between an ox and a large lizard. They were incredibly peaceful—the only peaceful thing down here—and Nahia liked them. She stroked them as she passed by the creatures.

"The convoy is already ready," Burgor informed her as he climbed onto the first cart.

"Loaded and ready, as it should be," Nahia said, using a common expression of Burgor's, and she climbed up beside him.

"A job well done ought to be acknowledged," Burgor said with a look that implied that he thought she was mocking him.

"That's what I was doing," she replied.

"Sure… today we have route three. Let's start, there's a lot to do and little time."

"Route three? Ours was route one."

Burgor looked at her, frowning.

"There is no 'ours.' You work the route assigned to you."

"The last time we always did route one." Nahia needed to do route one. Garran-Zilar-Denbo was on that route. If they did another, who knew what creatures and dangers she would meet.

"That was the one we had assigned. Now we have route three."

"But I want to do route one," Naha insisted. She needed to speak to Garran-Zilar-Denbo, and for that she had to do route one.

"That's the route I already know well. I'll be a lot more efficient doing that route. There will be fewer problems." Nahia was searching for reasons to persuade Burgor to change routes.

"We have been assigned route three, and that's the one we'll do. You're already delaying me with your odd requests."

"It's not an odd request, it's the best for the task," Nahia insisted.

"Then ask Utrek tomorrow, and stop pestering me!" Burgor exploded angrily.

Nahia bore the shouting and said nothing more. She knew she had reached the Tergnomus' limit and that it was not a good idea to push it.

Burgor urged the beasts and the convoy of carts started moving. As soon as they came out, instead of going straight they veered left. Nahia sighed deeply. They started route three. Anything might happen down there.

They entered a section of different caves as the silver path became visible in front of it. The large cave, which held another endless number of smaller caverns, was very similar to that of route one. Nevertheless, Nahia realized it was different. When doing the deliveries previously, she had memorized the caves along the way and which creatures and especially dragons there were in each one. Here, she had no idea what she might find, but they would certainly be dangerous.

They arrived at the first cavern where they had to unload, and Burgor stopped the carts. He got off without leaving the silver path.

"You know what you have to do."

Nahia looked inside the cave, but it was too dark. She could not make out what creature was inside. She focused on her work, glancing at the entrance out of the corner of her eye. They started unloading the meat. Nahia helped Burgor with the pulleys and they raised the trailer so the meat would fall. Three pieces went to the floor.

"Two pieces of meat here," Burgor said.

Nahia looked at him, and without protesting she hastened to retrieve the extra piece. At that moment, the creature held there appeared. It was like something out of a nightmare: half bear, half bird, and colossal. It started running on its four hairy legs with claws like a bear. Nahia pulled on the piece of meat, dragging it toward the cart with all her strength, propelled by the fright and fear of seeing the creature running toward her.

"It's coming for you. Hurry up," Burgor warned her but without much urgency.

Suddenly, the creature spread its large wings and pushed with its legs. It lifted off and came down on Nahia like a huge raptor, a strong and hairy one. The monster's face was that of a bird, but it also resembled that of a bear. It was coming at great speed to catch Nahia, who was retreating as best she could.

It was already falling on Nahia when her repulsor belt flashed and the monster was thrown back forcibly. It was as if an enormous force had hit it and it bounced, unbalanced in its flight, before crashing to the floor.

Nahia had fallen backward on the floor, but she saw that she was safe on the silver path, as well as the piece of meat.

"Phew… what a job," she snorted.

"Work is work. Load the piece on the cart, we must keep going."

Nahia stood up and looked at the creature, which seemed stunned. It was definitely unique. She could not say whether it was more bear or bird.

"What is that creature?" she asked Burgor as she loaded the piece.

"It's a Gryphon-Owl-Bear: a creature that's half bear, half owl. As you've seen, it's huge, and it likes to hunt small prey."

"You could've warned me," Nahia complained.

"A good worker is always alert on the job."

"I was alert, otherwise it would be eating me."

"As it should be. We keep going. Night is short."

Nahia climbed onto the cart with Burgor. She was annoyed at the Tergnomus, who should have warned her. She thought about it in more detail while the carts continued on their way and calmed down. It was no use getting angry with Burgor. She already knew him and knew he would not help her with anything. That was the way he was and he was not going to change, least of all for her, although they already knew each other. They had shared both ups and downs.

They continued with the delivery. No other creature appeared at the next caves, which Nahia was grateful for. She would rather not die from fright if she could help it, and that was a distinct possibility here. Her heart was beating fast.

"Are there dragons on this route?" she asked Burgor, just in case.

"No, there aren't any."

"Oh, good." Nahia was glad. Without Garran-Zilar-Denbo's protection, the last thing she wanted was to encounter a dragon.

"This route is called the route of birds."

"So… all the creatures prisoner here are birds?"

"Nearly all. Some type of bird, that is."

Nahia nodded.

"Yeah, like the bear-owl."

"That's it."

"Well, they won't be as dangerous as dragons, which makes me feel a little better."

Burgor turned and looked at her with amusement.

"Some of the dragons' worst enemies are held on this route, and they're as dangerous as them."

Nahia's eyes opened wide.

"Enemies of the dragons? Very dangerous? Who? What?" This was news to her. What dangerous enemies did the dragons have? This might be great news for the freedom cause. There might be a powerful ally down here.

"Why do you always ask so many questions? You're giving me a headache. We're here to work, not chat."

"I know, yes. But what creature are these that you're talking about?"

"It's not one creature, it's a species. There are several types of creatures in it. And don't ask me anything else. We're already entering their caves. You'll meet them presently."

They stopped in front of one of the caverns.

"Unload. A quarter of a cart here," Burgor told her.

Nahia got off the cart, following Burgor carefully. The word "danger" was engraved in her mind. She looked toward the cave attentively. Besides, a quarter of a cart was a lot of food. There had to be a very large or voracious creature here. Most likely, both.

"Get the pulleys moving," Burgor told her, seeing she was looking at the cave.

Nahia nodded and got to work. Although she tried to calculate well, a little more than a quart fell off the cart.

Burgor smiled.

"You know what to do."

"You could do it for once. We could do it in turns," Nahia suggested, although she knew what the Tergnomus's answer would be.

"I'm injured. That's why they put you with me," Burgor counted the pieces of meat. "Bring two back."

Nahia huffed in frustration.

"Okay..." she reached them quickly. She was right there, just a couple of paces from the silver path. She began to pull them toward the path. She looked toward the cave and did not see any suspicious movements. She kept pulling and heard a sound like a bird's, a loud shriek. Suddenly, a creature flew out of the cave at lightning speed straight toward Nahia. Somehow, she knew that although she was only a step away from the path, she needed to let go of the piece and take that step. She did so and fell on her bottom on the silver path. The creature flew low, flying in front of her at lightning speed, and grabbed the piece she was trying to retrieve.

Nahia looked down at her belt. It had not repelled the creature.

"The belt..." she said to Burgor.

"It happens sometimes," the Tergnomus shrugged.

"You don't say..." Nahia watched the creature, which passed flying low in front of them again with another shrill shriek. It was the size of a young dragon, but it flew and maneuvered at a speed at least five times that of a dragon. It was a mix between a hawk and a cheetah. The head and wings were those of a hawk, while the body and legs were those of a cheetah, tail included. That explained the amazing speeds it flew at for the size it was.

"It's... amazing..." Nahia muttered.

"It's the fastest powerful creature in the sky," Burgor told her.

"It has magic?" Nahia was taken aback.

"It does," the Tergnomus assured her, pointing at his hat.

"Mental and elemental magic. Don't you ever take off your hat, or before you blink, you'll be dead."

The impressive creature made another speedy pass in front of them.

"And don't you think you could've warned me?"

"That's not part of my job. Let's keep going. It likes to fly low and show off its splendor. It won't go back to the cave until we leave."

"I think it wants to eat me."

"That might be it too."

"It's huge. I don't know how it can even fly, especially not at that speed," Nahia got up on the cart, astonished.

"Huh, then wait for the next stop."

"Are there more like this one?"

"And bigger," Burgor told her, and although he did not smile, Nahia knew he was enjoying making her nervous.

They continued their food delivery. Nahia was paying even more attention now. She wanted no more unpleasant surprises. In the next two caves where they stopped, nothing happened. The creatures did not come out, and let them work in peace.

They went on along the silver path, which made a long curve they followed to enter a new colossal cave filled with prison caverns.

"This is the most interesting area," Burgor told her.

Nahia took it as a warning. She was grateful, although they said nothing. One look was enough.

"Eight pieces here," Burgor told her once they stopped the cart in front of a cavern.

With a leap, Nahia followed the Tergnomus, who was now limping more obviously than before. All the exertion must be affecting his injured leg. They unloaded quickly, which Nahia knew meant real danger. Luckily, the dump was eight pieces exactly. Nahia huffed; she would not have to retrieve any.

Suddenly, there was some kind of roar. Only it was not exactly a roar but a mix between a growl and a raptor's cry. From inside the cave, an enormous creature emerged, as large as a grown dragon and more unique, if possible. It had a powerful tiger's body, while its head and wings were those of a white eagle. It was magnificent. It radiated animalistic power. Its head and neck were covered in white feathers. The eagle beak was golden. This caught Nahia's attention. She thought back to the hawk-cheetah she had seen and remembered that it also had a golden beak. She found it curious.

The creature leaped forward, spreading its large wings. It truly looked as powerful as a dragon, except for the head. Nahia thought it looked more powerful than a dragon's. It approached slowly, and Nahia noticed it was watching her. Its eagle eyes stared at her in a way that made her nervous. She thought it was going to jump over her. She stepped back, driven by fear. The great winged beast landed a few paces from the path. The belt did not repel it. Nahia did not know whether it was because she was at the limit distance or because it did not work.

Burgor was already getting back on the cart to get out of there. Nahia wanted to get on, but this colossal creature was staring at her with intense interest. Burgor urged the draft beasts, and the convoy began to move away,

"Don't leave me…" she began to say, trapped by the fear the creature's attention filled her with. She knew Burgor would leave her there to her fate, without remorse.

The carts are leaving you, Human, she received the mental message of the eagle-tiger. Nahia froze; it was not only an intelligent creature, but it could send mental messages like the dragons.

"You're speaking to me…" Nahia could not move from the shock.

That's right, Human. My power allows me to send you mental messages.

Nahia received the message and realized that, although it was very similar to those the dragons sent, this one was different. She felt it differently. It came with a feeling of quietness that was different from the feelings dragons sent.

"Do you understand me?"

I understand you. I know the language of Kraido. It is always useful to speak the language of the enemy.

"Enemies? Are you our enemy?" Nahia had not known of the existence of these creatures, and least of all whether there was any conflict with them.

I am an enemy of your dragon lords, and hence you.

"Oh… I did not know."

You had better get on that cart, or you'll miss them. Your partner does not seem to be waiting for you.

"Yes…" Nahia made to go toward the cart but then hesitated.

Was it a trick? Would it attack her? The creature sounded sincere. Intelligent and sincere. Not at all monstrous or beastly like a dragon. But that was no assurance that it would not attack. It still might. She could not decide, and the cart was moving away. She looked at the creature; seeing how big and powerful it was, she hesitated even more.

Do not worry. You may go. I have no intention of harming you.

"Although we're enemies?"

Since you did not know, I will give you the benefit of this first encounter. Go, I will do nothing to you.

Nahia nodded and ran along the silver path. She did not look back, since she did not want to see the eagle-tiger fall upon her and kill her with its great golden beak. She went faster, careful not to leave the path, and reached the carts a moment later. Luckily, they always moved slowly.

"Thanks for not waiting," she told Burgor as she sat beside him in the first cart.

"Work doesn't wait for anyone, and least of all for blabbers."

"I'm no blabber."

"Aren't you? Weren't you just talking to the Gryphon-Tiger?"

"Well, only for a moment. It spoke to me."

"Don't talk to the prisoners. I told you that last time, and I'm telling you now. They're very dangerous; they'll kill you. Not that I care, but they will, and it'll mean more work for me," he said crossly.

"I appreciate all the love you have for me."

"I don't feel any love. You're here to work. Do it right."

Nahia shook her head. The Tergnomus did not get sarcasm. She was not surprised either. They only cared about doing their job well.

She was left wondering about the strange encounter. About how amazing that creature was, and the one before, and that they were enemies of the dragons. They were certainly not from Kraido, so they had to be from another continent-world. She wondered which one it might be.

"What world are those Gryphons from?"

Burgor looked at her.

I don't know, from some far-away one. They're cunning, be careful. They'll trick you and eat you."

"Wow, thanks for the warning."

"So that you don't get away from me."

Nahia sighed. You could not talk to Burgor, he was too much of a square head, or as Lily and Daphne would say, a stone-head.

He stopped the convoy at the end of the great cave, right before a bend that seemed to open onto another large cavern.

"Now, carefully and quickly," Burgor told her, and his tone was fearful.

"What is it? What's in that cave?"

Burgor snorted. he was nervous.

"A Gryphon-Lion. A king."

Nahia threw her head back.

"A king… among the Gryphons, you mean?"

"Yes, very dangerous."

Nahia looked at the cave and saw nothing.

"Understood. Whenever you say. I'm ready."

"We dump a whole cartload, and we get out of here like lightning," Burgor said.

"Fine."

"Let's go!" Burgor gave the order and got off the cart like lightning. His limp vanished, driven away by the fear he felt right then. Nahia followed him as fast as she could. They maneuvered the cart they wanted to empty, both concentrated on the levers and pulleys.

Nahia did not take her eyes off the cavern while she worked. They managed to get the cart in position and did the dumping. The whole load fell toward the cave. Immediately, they worked the levers and pulleys to lift back the trailer and then moved the beasts to place the cart in its position in the convoy.

And at that moment, the Gryphon-Lion king came out of the cave. Nahia froze. It was the most majestic creature she had ever seen, as great as a thousand-year-old dragon. It had the head of a white royal eagle, a lethal golden beak, and huge wings on the sides of a lion's body, including a long tail. It was tremendously powerful, both in body and presence. It oozed strength and power. The eagle eyes fixed on her. It spread its wings and showed all its power. Then it gave a cry.

"Let's get out of here!" Burgor shouted at her.

Nahia reacted and ran to the cart after the Tergnomus. They climbed into the cart and Burgor urged the beasts on. They left the place as fast as they could. Nahia took one last glance and saw that the great Gryphon had a silver chain tied around one of its legs. It had to be really dangerous if the dragons had taken extra safety measures. This intrigued her.

A cry from the Gryphon-Lion king filled the cave, and Nahia was grateful to have gotten out of there alive.

Chapter 14

The following morning, the torture that was going to last a whole season began. Only Aiden and Taika managed to get up to go to breakfast. The others kept sleeping, unable to open their eyes after the first night of their punishment. They had arrived shortly before dawn, and now they simply could not get up.

"Everyone, up!" Aiden tried to wake them.

"Don't know if they're going to be able…" Taika commented, watching Ivo sleeping soundly.

Nahia opened one eye and saw that Daphne and Lily were not getting up. She tried to open her other eye but could not. She closed the one she had opened, and without meaning to she went on sleeping.

"We have to go to the dining hall and then to line-up!" Aiden shouted, not giving up in his attempt to wake them all.

"Don't shout… we're not deaf, granite-head… it's been a very long night…" Daphne said reproachfully without opening her eyes.

"We'll get another punishment or something worse if you don't get up!"

"You go… bring us food…" Ivo muttered and pointed at the door with his finger.

"If Ivo isn't getting up to go to the dining hall, it's because they're really tired," Taika told Aiden. "Well, I don't intend to bring them food. It's their duty to get up and go to the dining hall."

"We'll let them sleep a little longer. Sleep is fundamental to recover from exhaustion, besides being necessary for the mind to function properly."

"When you can't sleep you have to rise to the occasion, no matter how complicated it might be."

"And we will. You and I will go to the dining hall and bring them food. We're a team. We won't let the squad fail."

Aiden stood, staring at Taika. The words of the white tiger seemed to have impressed him.

"All right then, for the squad. We can't let the squad fail and be dishonored," Aiden turned and went out the door.

Ivo shifted in his cot. "You're a shark," he told Taika with a half-smile on his face, without opening his eyes.

"Tiger. But I'll take the compliment," Taika smiled and then went out after the Drakonid.

A while later, they were all eating in their room.

"This isn't right. I want to protest against your behavior," Aiden said, crossing his arms.

"Protest noted, stone-head," said Lily, licking her fingers.

"And there's no rule that says we can't eat in our room," Daphne argued as she finished her chicken stew.

"Yes, there is. There's a place for everything. You eat in the dining hall. You sleep in your room." Aiden was not going to lose the argument.

"I could eat and sleep in the dining hall without a problem, in fact," Ivo said nonchalantly.

"That's definitely not allowed." Aiden shook his head.

"The funny thing is that the Tergnomus at the dining hall let us take food out," Taika commented. "They saw us and looked the other way."

"Well, that's odd, since those ugly little monsters are so bad tempered," Lily said.

"They're not so bad," Nahia defended them as she finished her serving as fast as she could.

"They are a bit on the monstrous side, no denying that," Daphne replied.

"As long as the two dragons didn't stop you, there's no problem," said Ivo.

"Those two are there to scare people, I doubt they're the least bit interested in whether we take food out of the dining hall or not," said Daphne.

"They're there to impose respect and obedience," Aiden specified.

"I'll give you respect and obedience," Lily snapped.

"With a hammer to the head," added Daphne.

Aiden made a face and turned his back on them.

"Our problem is that this is going to last a whole season. That's a very long time," Nahia said. "It's very likely we won't be allowed to bring food out of the dining hall that entire time."

"If we skip breakfast, do you think we can hold up?" Lily asked.

"I'm positive I won't," Ivo said. They had brought him two rations, like he usually ate.

"Yes, you will. We all will, including you, big guy," Taika said.

"Will we? And how will we?" Daphne wanted to know.

Taika told them.

"We can skip breakfast. Now we're having two meals a day. One to gather strength in the mornings and another to recover in the evening. If we do without the morning meal, we'll have less energy, yes, but our bodies will keep functioning and draw on our reserves until the evening comes and we can eat."

"It doesn't sound very promising, but if you think we can pull it off…" said Nahia.

"But we'll be hungry, and that unbalances the mind. I don't like it. I'd rather be at peace with my body and mind, both in equilibrium," Ivo protested, rubbing his large belly.

"Our bodies can go without eating for several days, as long as we drink enough water," Taika explained. "If it doesn't have food, the body feeds on everything it has accumulated, good or bad, in its system. Among my people, there is the ancestral practice of going without food for several days. It cleanses the body inside. It eliminates the old reserves and impurities we might have."

"Several days?" Nahia was interested.

"More than two?" Daphne raised an eyebrow.

"Among my people, the internal cleansing ritual requires ten days of fasting. Only drinking water," Taika told them.

"That's crazy. I'd die for sure. My body can't go without food for so long," Ivo said, shaking his head.

"I think I'd die too," Lily commented. "It sounds like an exaggeration."

"More than three days sounds impossible," said Daphne.

"I promise, you can all do it. Although it's not easy. And neither is this the right place to facilitate the correct way to do it. We do this using a state of relaxation, barely consuming energy."

"So, it would be impossible here, considering how demanding our schedule is," Nahia said.

"Even so, it doesn't sound possible or healthy. The body and mind must always be well fed," said Ivo.

"Taika is right. It can be done," said Aiden, who had turned around. They all watched him, interested in what he had to say.

"Explain yourself, little marble-head," Lily said. "The Drakonid also use fasting, but as a preparation technique for the rough times of war. The young ones spend twelve days without eating, only drinking water. This allows us to train our bodies to survive when there's no food available. It makes us stronger."

"Well, look at the little dragons," Lily said, shaking her hand.

"But you don't do it all at once, do you?" Nahia asked. Twelve days seemed too many.

"No, the first time we start with one day. Then three, later on five, then seven, ten, and finally twelve. We do it in several sessions, allowing for some time in between. Once we manage to reach twelve, we do this every three seasons."

"You do this every three seasons voluntarily? You're crazy," Daphne told him.

"You call us crazy, but I can go without food for twelve days and you can't even last for two."

Daphne was left with a blank look on her face, unable to retort to that.

"This crazy guy is kind of right," said Lily.

Taika looked out the window.

"We have to go to line-up."

"Fine. Let's see what the day has in store for us," Nahia said, not very cheered.

They all went out of the third-year barracks, sleepy but at least with their stomachs full. For that day—in the future, they would have to see.

Nahia arrived at the Sorcery Talent training with a conflicted heart. On the one hand, she wanted to learn new skills and maximize the use and power of the things she had already learned. On the other, she did not like attending that class because she had to go without her squadmates. They had been forced to go their separate ways because they all had a different talent class. She felt more vulnerable when they were not around her. She was so used to their continuous presence, especially in class, that when they were not there it was like her family was missing.

She sighed as she entered the room. Thinking about her family reminded her that it had been two years since she had last seen her grandmother, Aoma. She wondered how she was doing and whether things were going well for her. She hoped her health was improving. The village would look after her. She was an important member of the community. If Aoma was healthy, she would make sure the rest of the neighbors and villagers were too. It cheered her to think her grandmother was being well looked after.

She entered the classroom and saw a blue dragoness similar to the color of the sky. It seemed to have come out of the summer sky itself, as if it was a part of it and had taken on the form of a dragon. Its scales shone with the light glow dragon scales did. The streaks that ran down its back were white, as if it had passed through clouds at a great speed and shreds of white had stuck to its scales. For some reason, the fact that this dragoness was pretty did not put her entirely at ease. Surely it would be ruthless.

She stood before the dragoness and knelt with her forehead touching the floor. She watched her classmates out of the corner of her eye. They were the same ones from the previous year. The Sorcery Talent class had not lost any members, which cheered her up a little. She did not get her hopes up because she knew that at any moment one might die in that horrible, magical, martial Academy. They all knew this.

The Sorcery Talent is scarce. Only five chosen to train in the last course of the Academy. Pity. I was hoping to have more pupils this year, the dragoness sent them with a regretful feeling.

Nahia was surprised, because the feeling seemed sincere. But it might be lying to them, so it was better not to trust. One should never trust a dragon—that was a fundamental rule. And if it truly wanted to have more pupils, it might ask for fewer casualties in the Path of Dragons. Surely several of those who had not managed to reach this moment might have had the Sorcery Talent. But that was something they would never know. Rage began to catch fire in her stomach, and she breathed in deeply to quell it. She was bone tired from the punishment at the dungeons and the lack of sleep that went along with it, and she did not want any more trouble.

Stand up. What I must teach you this year requires your full attention. This is Sorginbor, my Exarbor Sorcery Talent assistant. Step closer.

The five stood up and kept their heads bowed. They looked first at the Exarbor, who looked younger and faster than the other Exarbors, if that was possible. Then they glanced at one another rapidly.

We begin with a big announcement. From this moment on, in this class you will not use any kind of Talent Sphere to help you with magic. A Sorcerer must be able to summon and conjure without any external help. Your inner power has to be strong enough to use your magic at all times and in any situation. That will save your lives, although right now you may not see it that way.

Nahia was not convinced by the announcement or the fact that it might save their lives. She would rather have the help of the magical object. It was true they might find themselves in situations without them on hand, and when they used a shield, many times it was impossible to use the sphere. Even so, she liked the help it provided. It was not great, but many times a small help was invaluable, since it helped manifest the skill one wanted to summon.

The first thing you will learn this year will provide you with a fighting advantage very few have. The rest of the Talents will not have it, so it puts you ahead of the curve. They are called Instant Skills. You will be able to use attacks whose response is so fast it is considered almost instantaneous. You will think the attack, and this will occur a moment later. A lot faster than any skill you have learned so far. Those other attacks cannot be instantaneous. They require a summoning time which can be reduced a lot, as you have been practicing. But no matter how much you improve and reduce the time required to launch an attack, it can never be instantaneous. On the other hand, the new attacks I am going to teach you will be indeed.

Nahia was intrigued by this new discipline. Whenever she had to use any of her elemental fire skills, whether breath, ball, claw, or maw, it always required time for her to summon them. In combat, that time seemed eternal. It felt like it took her an eternity to create and launch the attack. She knew she was not slow, but even so, it seemed slow to her. To be able to use an attack instantaneously sounded impressive. She wondered what type of attack it would be. She decided to listen and see what the dragoness taught them.

We will begin at once. You have a lot to learn and the year is short. I see we have a Flameborn with us. That pleases me. She will help me show you what you must learn in a faster and more efficient way. Step forward, Human.

Nahia did as was told, although she was not pleased that the masters knew what she was and made her their learning mascot. She inhaled through the nose until her lungs were full and exhaled all the air toward the floor, trying to calm down and not let frustration overwhelm her.

We will start with a very simple skill. It is not powerful, but it is very useful. It will serve as the base on which to build the rest of the skills. I want you to show me the palm of your dominant hand stretched forward, the one you usually use to create your Elemental Ball.

Nahia held up the palm of her right hand like the dragoness had asked. Unconsciously, she looked at her left hand where the Learning Orb should be and had to look back to the front, to the floor.

I want you to look at your palm for a moment. Memorize it. Then close your eyes and visualize it in your mind.

That posed no difficulty, and Nahia did so right away.

Now, create a flame, since your element is fire, like that of a candle in the middle of your hand. It must come out from your own palm; do not create it on top of it.

This was getting complicated. How was she going to make it emerge from her hand? How could a flame come out of her hand? It was going to burn.

Have the flame emerge from your hand outward. Concentrate and do it.

Nahia did not really understand the order, but there was nothing she could do but obey, so she tried. She visualized in her mind a small flame, coming out through the palm of her hand upward, like that of a candle. She could not create it; she had already guessed she would fail. She kept trying, but without luck.

Ban the fear of burning your hand from your mind. You are not going to get burned. Push the flame upward. It is your own elemental magic and it will not hurt you. You can do it.

It was easy to say but much harder to achieve. Was the dragoness tricking her, or was she really not going to get burned? She would not know until she did it, so she concentrated on making the flame come out of her palm. There was a golden flash around her hand and the flame formed.

Open your eyes and contemplate your creation.

When she opened them, Nahia froze. In the center of her upturned hand was a flame, burning straight. It was coming out of her hand, but she felt no pain. It did not burn her. It was as if it consumed air and burned only at the top. It amazed her.

And now send more energy to the flame.

Nahia did so and the flame grew in height and width. It gave off an intense heat and a strong light. With this skill she could not only create fire, but warm herself and light up dark places. She thought it was a most useful skill.

Now, put it out with your mind. You will not be able to do so any other way. Only the mind or elemental water magic can quench it, since it is not a natural flame but an elemental magic flame.

The explanation made all the sense in the world. Surely Lily would be able to put it out with her water magic, but Nahia did not have that elemental power, only fire. Adding more fire was not the way to put it out. She concentrated and put it out by imagining the flame being extinguished. She opened her eyes and it was no longer in her hand. She considered that a small victory.

Very well. Now you will all repeat the exercise. Each of you will create a flame of your own element. I want to see a fountain of water, a bolt of lightning for air, one of earth, and a flame of light. Get started.

They all stretched their upturned hands and closed their eyes. They started trying to create their elemental flames. It took them a moment, but they did it gradually. Nahia was very surprised at the shape each took. The water flame was indeed a small fountain, the water going up and down on the palm of her hand and falling to the floor. Would it be drinkable? If it was, that would be great. The lightning was awesome as it went up and down, sizzling and cracking. It made them all stand back, since it appeared ready to leap onto the first person to approach. It also gave off a bluish-white light. The light flame was very similar to her fire flame, only a lot brighter. It gave off a powerful white light that could light up a large room. When more energy was sent to it, it shone with great intensity and blinded them all.

What you must now achieve is creating that flame spontaneously, just by thinking it. That is the goal. Think it and it should appear at once in your hand, like an immediate reaction to the thought you had. It will take you some time to manage this, but I am sure you will all get there. Sorginbor will help answer any questions you might have. Get started.

The Exarbor reached for a large tome he carried on his back and opened it. He showed it to them.

"If you need… to consult the theory… come closer," he told them.

Nahia decided to try without the help of the large Sorcery tome. If she had already managed to create the flame, all she needed to do now was make it appear faster, a lot faster. She concentrated on doing this. One thing she did not think would happen started occurring as the class proceeded and she had more attempts under her belt: she created the flame faster every time. This surprised her, because it was precisely what she was supposed to do and what she wished would happen during classes but rarely did.

She kept trying, and by the time class was over she almost had it. She had reached a point where she was very close to summoning it instantaneously, but not quite. She watched her comrades, and although they were not doing badly, none were as fast as she was, at least for now. She left the class happy for once. Her magical skill was very good. Too good. Was her magic improving without her noticing? This little exercise pointed in that direction. She would have to pay close attention to her power in the classes of magic and Sorcery to see whether it was growing.

Chapter 15

A few days later, Nahia went to the Library and headed to the third floor where they were to study that year. As she was going upstairs, she looked all around her. Lately, she had the feeling that the librarian Exarbors were observing her. More than observing: they were watching her, and it was uncomfortable. It was probably nothing but her imagination, but this was how she felt. When she glanced at the Exarbor, they all seemed very busy. Some were taking books from the shelves, others were handing them to pupils, and still others were telling off whoever made the slightest noise. The usual, and they did it with their usual parsimony. Even so, she thought they were watching her somehow, and she could not explain it.

She reached the third floor and started to cross it with her head down and her eyes ahead. When she was halfway across, she saw what she had expected to find there this day and her heart skipped a beat with joy. Sitting at the last table at the far end were Ana and Logan. The joy she felt from seeing them compelled her body forward, and she headed toward them a little too fast and vigorously. She nearly crashed into an Exarbor.

"Watch out... pupil... you are not supposed to run..."

"I wasn't running, I was walking fast," Nahia stopped and turned to the third-year librarian in the hopes he would not tell her off.

"Running is... forbidden. Walking fast... is also forbidden," he said and pointed a twig finger with leaves at her.

Nahia had already been expecting this. These Exarbor were exasperating.

"I'm sorry. I'll walk slower."

"Yes, you will do that... or a punishment you will have..."

Nahia was surprised. Had the Exarbor made a sort of rhyme? If so, he must be a poet librarian. No, that was outrageous.

"There's so much to study and so little time," Nahia replied, pretending.

"The time to study is always scarce... therefore one must do one's best, or else they will fail the test."

This librarian Exarbor was definitely speaking in rhymes. Nahia did not know what to think.

"Thank you, I'll remember that."

"You had better make sure… if you want to endure."

Nahia blinked hard twice. This creature was so strange.

"Yeah, sure. Well, I'm going to study," she said and went to Ana and Logan's table at the far end of the hall.

"Trouble?" Logan asked her when she got to them and sat down.

"No, it's nothing I just came a bit fast and you know…"

"Yeah, they don't like the heels of our boots to leave the floor," Ana said, looking at the Exarbor, who was walking very slowly toward a shelf.

"I'm so happy to see you!" Nahia said, unable to hold back. She nearly hugged them both, but the poet Exarbor was already watching her. He had stopped and turned around. He watched her. They might not be fast, but they had excellent hearing. She smiled at the Exarbor, who put his twig finger to his bark lips. Nahia nodded and turned back to her friends.

"The joy is ours," said Ana, smiling as she put her hand on Nahia's fondly.

"A great joy," added Logan, who smiled and grabbed her arm for an instant, an unusual gesture from someone who always remained aloof and stern.

The small gesture went straight to Nahia's heart. Logan never showed his feelings. This small gesture was a treasure. It made her feel wonderful, and an indescribable joy traveled up from her stomach to her face.

"Together again," said Nahia, smiling happily, seeing them safe and sound. The few moments they spent together filled her with joy and hope.

"May that never change," said Ana, smiling shyly.

Nahia looked at them both and discovered they had both changed. They looked more mature, as if it had been a very long time since she had last seen them up close. It was not altogether untrue— time had passed, and this was the first time they were seeing one another since before the end-of-second-year test. But it was not that long. She wondered whether they were thinking the same thing about her. Ana no longer looked like the frightened little girl of their arrival but like a young woman. Logan looked more handsome and manly. Irresistible. She could not stop looking at him; it was stronger than her.

"You look good…" was all she could say, a little baffled by all the thoughts and feelings running through her mind.

"You look good too," Logan replied with his intense gaze.

"You're a terrible liar," Nahia smiled. "I have dark circles under my eyes from not sleeping and my face shows pure exhaustion."

"You look good, given the circumstances," Ana said sweetly. "We already know about the punishment your whole squadron received."

"If you do the right thing, you get punished," Nahia said with a shrug.

"Be careful that one of those punishments doesn't lead to your death," Logan warned her seriously.

Nahia sighed.

"I really try, honest."

"You must be more careful. You're too impulsive. We don't want to lose you. It would be… terrible…" Ana's eyes moistened as she held back tears.

"Ana is right. If you don't control that fire of yours, it'll end up killing you," Logan said, and his light eyes showed concern and something more that Nahia did not know how to interpret.

"You mean my fire because I'm a Flameborn?" she joked to make light of the moment.

"That too, but I meant your character." Logan jabbed his finger at her heart.

Nahia had to agree with them. They were right, she could not deny it.

"I'll be more careful, I promise."

Ana stroked her hand again and Logan looked at her with a spark of joy in his eyes, although a deep concern remained deep. He was really worried for her. Nahia could not help feel that those light eyes, his worry for her, and the spark of joy were irresistible. She looked at him and she could not keep her heart from being robbed by his gaze, loaded with deep feelings; his handsome face; and reserved and honest character. There was nothing she could do about it. She had to stop looking at him, feeling her stomach levitating. Apart from the fact that looking at his lips filled her with the urge to put her own to his and kiss him.

"Tell us, how did you fare in Norghana?" Ana asked her.

Nahia snapped out of her daydream and returned to reality.

"Oh yeah, Norghana. You're not going to believe what we lived through over there. And what we found out!" she said animatedly.

"That good?" Logan asked, raising an eyebrow.

"Better than good," Nahia said.

"Tell us all about it then," Ana said, her big eyes filled with interest.

Nahia looked around before she began. There were several third-year pupils with tomes of Mental Dragon Magic at the nearby tables, but they were immersed in their studies and were not paying attention. The poet Exarbor was already far enough away and would not hear her, but even so, Nahia lowered her voice so that only Ana and Logan would hear what she had to say. Calmly, she told them everything that had happened during their adventure in Tremia. She tried not to leave out any important details. She told them about Lasgol, Camu, the Rangers, of her relationship with Egil— who was still a prisoner in the dungeons—and everything else she could think of that might be relevant.

She took a pause to breathe, since she was speaking very fast. She had so many things to tell them and such little time. She looked around again before telling them about the most important subject. She did not see any danger and proceeded to tell them about Lasgol's golden bow and the promise he had made to her. And she revealed their great discovery: the huge dragon Lasgol had killed as proof of his statements and the promise he had made. Once she finished telling it all, she leaned back in her chair and waited for the reactions of her two friends.

"That's... amazing...." Both of Logan's eyebrows were raised high and his eyes were almost popping from their sockets.

"It can't be..." Ana could not quite believe it.

Nahia nodded repeatedly,

"It can be, and it is. I am a witness."

"Then... this confirms what Egil told you about the golden weapons his comrades had. It was all true," Logan said, remembering everything they had talked about before separating the last time.

"Yes, everything Egil told me is true."

"Then he is to be trusted and is true to his word. I wasn't sure it would be so..." Ana admitted.

"Absolutely worthy and honorable to the core. Not only that, he's an ally. His friends are fighting the dragons, and they're skilled

132

warriors we want on our side."

"They have to be good warriors if this Lasgol and his comrades killed a dragon. So, he has a bow capable of bringing down a dragon?" Logan asked as if he wanted to make sure he had understood right, some incredulity seeping into his voice.

"I know that for us in this world it seems impossible, but it is true. That bow has Golden Magic. And I can now confirm what Egil told me. Golden Magic can kill dragons," Nahia said.

"But with a bow… a weapon despised here…" Ana found it hard to believe.

"I can assure you that if you saw those Rangers fight with their bows against the dragons, you wouldn't despise them in the least."

"Perhaps the dragons don't despise them but fear them…" Logan ventured.

"After seeing what the Norghanian archers did to them, I can guarantee it."

"Then you're absolutely sure a dragon can be killed? It's not just a dream?" Ana asked.

"Absolutely sure. We have the proof. I wasn't the only one to see it, my whole squadron saw it. The evidence is irrefutable. Our squadron leader has forbidden us to speak about it under penalty of death." Nahia looked again all around. If the Exarbor heard her, she would be dead.

"Yeah, Irakas-Gorri-Gaizt doesn't want it to be known," Logan nodded. "If the dragon had died from other causes, it wouldn't hide it."

"It was riddled with arrows, through its eyes and mouth. Lasgol and his people killed it, and they used bows, among them the one with Golden Magic."

"Then there's hope," said Logan, making a tight fist.

"There's a chance." Ana put both her hands on the table.

"Now we have evidence that the golden weapons exist and can kill dragons. That the Golden Magic of those weapons can kill dragons. We have to spread this message of hope to all. We have to make them see that they can fight for the cause of freedom," Nahia said, full of passion.

"Yes, but we must be careful. We can't allow ourselves to be carried away and make any mistakes. We have to do it cautiously, without the dragons and those who don't share the cause realizing it," Ana warned, looking around to make sure no one was listening.

"Ana is right. This news is wonderful, but we can't be hasty. We must be extremely careful," Logan became serious and looked at Nahia with concern.

"I can persuade those of my squadron. They saw the dead dragon. I can explain who killed it and how. I think they'll listen to me, except for the Drakonid," Nahia said.

"No, you shouldn't openly risk yourself for the cause," Logan said, and his voice broke. Nahia wondered whether it was due to concern, or perhaps something else. She wished it was the latter.

"Logan is right. We must spread the message in secret. We must; you can't expose yourself."

"But if I don't spread it, I who know the truth, having witnessed it, it won't be equally strong. Don't misunderstand me, you've been doing an exceptional job talking to other pupils, but I have to tell this myself. They must hear it from me. That way there won't be any doubt. I'm the proof they need in order to believe."

Logan and Ana looked at one another and thought for a moment.

"We could do it here," Logan suggested.

"Meet them here, like now?" Nahia asked.

Logan nodded.

"It's not completely safe," he looked at an Exarbor, who was returning a tome to a shelf, "but it's safe enough. Ana and I have been speaking here to those who showed an interest for the cause and who we deemed trustworthy. We've been passing *the message* on. We've done pretty well, so far."

"We could invite those we trust to come here and you can pass on the message in person," Ana suggested.

"I like it," Nahia nodded.

"Then that's what we'll do," Logan said firmly.

Nahia took a deep breath.

"You know that ever since I've been here at the Academy, and even more so after Maika's death, I've wanted us to unite to fight the dragons and achieve freedom. Not only us, but all the races, including those from other worlds. My dream was that we would all unite with the goal of defeating the tyrants. That's the only way we can stop them from killing, here at the Academy and in Kraido, and also in other worlds like Tremia. You've been transmitting that message in the Academy, one of hope for all. Now we have evidence. It's not just a message of hope based on wishful thinking. It's not an unreachable dream. Now it's a message of hope based on true facts. The dream is reachable. The dragons can be defeated. Everyone has to know. Here, down on land, and in every subjugated world."

"That will be the new message to transmit," Logan said with determination.

"The dream is within reach. The dream will come true," said Ana.

"We'll achieve freedom, for us and everyone else," Nahia added, clenching her fists.

"The message will be transmitted," Logan said.

"You can count on us, we won't fail you," said Ana.

"I couldn't do it without you. You are the soul of the cause."

"No, you are the soul of the cause," Logan said, giving her a tender look that left Nahia defenseless. Her eyes moistened.

"We'll support you to the end," Ana promised.

"The dragons will fall," said Nahia.

"The dragons will fall," Logan repeated.

"The dragons will fall," Ana nodded.

Chapter 16

"Our first weapons training session of the year, yippee!" Lily cried in a tone filled with irony, a comical look on her face as they headed to the lesson.

"What do you think it will be on this year?" Daphne asked, wrinkling her nose, expecting something she was not going to like.

"Whatever it is, it will make us stronger and more loyal. The mastery of weapons is fundamental in order to graduate as a Dragon Warlock," Aiden said as he straightened, walking at the head of the group. It was where he liked to walk, hurrying them along and setting the pace.

"It will be tough, I bet," Taka said, glancing at his female comrades with eyes that could not hide his concern.

"Unfortunately, that's what I'm afraid of too," Nahia admitted. She had interpreted the white tiger's look.

"We'd better hurry up and get to class. Then we'll find out. Delaying it only makes us think even worse things," Daphne said with a sigh.

"True. The mind tends to think the worst when the reality isn't usually so bad," Ivo commented in a transcendental tone, looking peaceful.

"For you, surely not, since you're a beast and ooze strength out of every pore. But for us it'll be worse than we imagine, that's for sure," Lily retorted.

Ivo made a face that meant she was probably right.

"In any case, the best thing is to keep calm and seek serenity and balance."

"I don't give a hoot about that," Daphne grumbled, shaking her head.

"Don't worry, my beautiful, dear, grumbling comrade. I'll cheer you on. You'll see how it soothes your mind," Lily told her, throwing her arm over her friend's shoulder with a large smile on her face.

"Our Lily does know how to cheer a friend," Nahia admitted to Daphne.

"Of course, I'm charming!" Lily laughed and hugged Daphne,

and then she ran to hug Nahia too.

"This Scarlatum is a bit wrong up here," Aiden said, pointing at his head.

Nahia smiled like Taika and Ivo. It was these moments that relieved the tension of being in the Academy and united her to her comrades.

They arrived at the Weapons Building. It seemed to Nahia that they were entering a great fortress without walls. It was shaped like a perfect square, with an uncovered yard in the center. On the front wall of the main building were the knife, sword, spear, and shield drawn in silver. Those were the weapons they had to learn how to master. They had already mastered the dagger and sword, but they still had the spear left. She would rather learn to use the bow, especially after witnessing what the Rangers were capable of doing with them in Tremia. And of course, because of the existence of Lasgol's golden bow that could kill dragons.

They went in and headed to the third-year classrooms.

"What classroom did the Exarbor of studies at the square say?" Daphne asked.

"The Green Deep," Taika said.

"Yeah, now we're doing seas," Lily said, indicating the name of the classroom in front of them. "Black Ocean."

"They have a peculiar way of naming classrooms," Nahia commented, "don't you think?"

"What might seem strange to us makes perfect sense to our masters, we're simply not capable of seeing it," Aiden told them.

"What we can see with perfect clarity is your granite-head," Daphne told him.

"The fact that you can't understand our lords' logic isn't my problem," Aiden replied.

"The fact that you don't see that 'our lords' are abominable tyrants is everyone's problem," Daphne told him.

"You forgot to add granite-head," Lily said, making a face.

Aiden snorted and shook his head.

"You think whatever you want and I'll think what I think."

"Unfortunately…" Daphne commented.

It took them a while to find the classroom. They went in. Nahia had the feeling that they were going to have a very hard time. As they entered, they saw two other squads and the instructor. It was a colossal red male dragon. It was so big it had to be over nine hundred years of age and tremendously strong, with muscles that looked ready to burst out from under its scales. Its chest and legs looked uncommonly strong, like those of Irakas-Gorri-Gaizt. Its head was intimidating, with several horns that curved backward and the crest that ran down its back. Even more frightening were the eyes, red as live coals that shone with inner fierceness. Without a doubt, with that awesome size it could not be far off from a thousand years.

This year, your last one in the Academy, I will be your weapons master. I am Beldur-Gorri-Handi. I teach with discipline, and I expect the maximum respect from my pupils. You have had the chance to fight with the dagger, sword, and shield. You have already mastered those disciplines. The third year begins with the study of fighting with the sword and shield. This is the preferred combination of many Dragon Warlocks. The sword provides the skill to kill, and it's a lethal weapon with a good reach. The shield is the protection you all wish for in combat. Together, they form a combination difficult to surpass. In battle it will give you an advantage against practically every other combination of weapons. There is almost nothing more fearsome than a warrior skilled with a sword and shield.

Nahia knew that the dragon was right, but she preferred magic to a sword and shield. She was better at it and it did not exhaust her. The dragon had forgotten to mention—no doubt on purpose—the strength and energy necessary to fight with the sword and shield. They both weighed quite a bit. In order to fight with both of them, you had to be very strong. She now had some muscle but was not that strong. Already the dagger and shield were a horror to fight with. With only the sword, it was slightly less tough. And this was after working on her physical strength for almost the whole second year. She did not even want to think about how hard it was going to be for her to fight with the sword *and* shield.

She noticed Daphne and Lily were looking at her, and their looks were of worry. They were thinking the same thing. The combined weight of the sword and shield was going to crush them. They would not be able to fight with both. It would be too much, even after all the efforts they had made to improve their physical strength. On that note, the truth was that Nahia barely recognized herself now. Compared with how weak and scrawny she had been when she had first arrived at the Academy, she now looked like a totally different person. After two years of suffering, her body had improved a lot. Her arms and legs were nearly twice as big as they had been. And there was no fat to them—she was all muscle. Well-worked muscle she had developed at the gym and in class. But, unfortunately, it was not enough. She was going to need more muscle in order to be able to wield those two weapons. As she well knew, developing muscle and endurance required a lot of hard work and sacrifice. It was not pleasant, but it did not scare her. She would make it; she had to, there was no other way.

So that the learning is faster and more efficient, we will use instructors from each of your races once again. Pay absolute attention to what your weapons masters teach you. Let me remind you that we are at war with Drameia and whatever you learn here will be of great use in battle. It will save your life and, at the same time, it will help the dragons conquer that world.

The idea felt like an aberration to Nahia. She did not want to help the dragons conquer Tremia; quite the opposite. If there was anything she did not want to do, it was fight for the dragons and least of all, help them conquer that world. Yet she would not be able to stop them if she was dead, so she had no option but to learn this combat discipline and avoid dying here because she had failed the class.

From a side of the room, the instructors came forward. They consisted of a Felidae, a Drakonid, and a Tauruk. They were carrying swords and shields for the class. The three bowed before the great dragon respectfully. Then they glanced at the three squads. The Tauruk stood in front of them.

This kind of weapons instruction will be harder this year than it was the previous years. It is imperative that you all give your best effort during training, because otherwise I will have to leave you behind. And you know the consequences of not passing this class, so you had better do as I say.

The threat, and knowing that this class was going to be even harder, made Nahia shiver. She was no longer so confident she would pass. The dragons never warned them in vain. She gave her comrades a troubled look and they returned it. The three women knew they were going to really suffer and also that they simply could not fail.

In order to incentivize you a little more, this year we will change the location of the training. It will not be in this room, or even this building. You will train in The Arena.

The announcement left them not only perplexed but even more worried than they had been, especially Nahia, Lily, and Daphne, who could already see problems piling up. They had not been expecting this at all. The Arena was a place of competition, one that brought up horrible memories. The class was already becoming too complicated.

Of course, as you will be training in The Arena, you will practice in the combat-elimination format, or duels, as we call them. It will be a full experience that will help you progress quickly. In order to become a master of weapons, we require blood, sweat, and effort. I know all of you are ready for this sacrifice. Nothing less is expected of you. Follow your weapons masters to The Arena to begin the training.

The Tauruk addressed them with a deep and powerful voice.

"I am Urus. Take your equipment, Igneous Squad."

Nahia looked him up and down. The powerful Tauruk had muscles more carved than Ivo. He carried a shield on his back and a sword at his waist. He was the living image of a beastly warrior. With those powerful arms and wide, muscular shoulders, he could split a person in two easily.

They did as they were told. One by one, they fetched their gear, and when they were all ready, they waited for their weapons master.

"Follow me to The Arena in silence," he told them, and without another word they left.

On the way there, they exchanged uneasy glances. They arrived at the round building that invoked such bad memories. When they went in, Nahia had a sick feeling that made her stomach turn and which increased once they came out of the passage into The Arena. Entering the site of the spectacle and stepping onto the sand made her feel awful. Bad memories of her experience here assaulted her. She did not want them repeated, but being here, it was more than likely that some kind of horror or suffering would come to them.

Urus stood in the north area of the round, sandy plaza. The squad followed him.

"Line up and wait."

They did so as the enormous Tauruk watched them in silence. Nahia realized that he was waiting for the other squads to arrive. Once they did and stood to the south and east of the plaza, Urus addressed them.

"It is up to you to pass this training. Willpower and courage are necessary. Find them within you."

Nahia was having worse and worse feelings about what was going to happen here.

"You already know how to use the sword and shield separately. Therefore, the combination of both will come naturally. Gather around me, forming a circle," he told them, indicating around him with his finger.

They did so quickly.

"Now I will show you the basic movements of offense and defense. You will repeat them in series of forty. You must learn to do them as if you had been born with a sword in one hand and a shield in the other."

Nahia found the comment a little funny. But the thought evaporated as soon as she heard "series of forty." She was horrified. She had her shield in her left hand and the sword in the right, and she was already feeling the weight of both on her arms. This was already a bad beginning.

"Watch my offensive and defensive movements. Then repeat them like I do. You must be like my shadows. I start right now."

Nahia watched how the enormous Tauruk did the series. For him, moving the sword and shield was easy. He had tremendous strength. He could surely spend several days doing series of forty without resting. It was their turn, and already with the first series Nahia knew this was going to be torture and agony. The moment she finished, she felt the effort in both arms. Not much, but enough to be able to calculate it was going to be really tough. She wrinkled her nose. Sometimes she hated being right. On this occasion she would have loved to be wrong.

Urus went on with the movements and they all followed suit. Luckily, he taught them a dozen different attacks and defenses. When he switched from one movement to a new one, they were able to rest while the weapons master explained the next movement, and the explanations were long and detailed. The Tauruk spoke as if every word that came out of his mouth was a great truth in the art of fighting with the sword and shield. At least, so it felt to Nahia, who was listening carefully. It had to be due to how deep his voice was and his intimidating presence; this combination was capable of turning a simple "hello" into a death greeting. It also made him capable of persuading anyone that what he said was the absolute truth.

Nahia managed to finish the first day of training. Tired, but she had finished, and she was very pleased. Lily did too. Daphne almost did not make it, but in the end, she finished thanks to her inner strength. The boys had no trouble, something she had expected. The three were strong and resilient. They finished the first day with the feeling that things would get tougher in the next classes.

Unfortunately, they were not mistaken. The next sessions got tougher and tougher. Urus would tell them what they were doing wrong and teach them how they should do it, which gave them a respite they needed like the air they breathed. But the day came when the technique was good enough and there were no corrections or breaks. And that day, filled with repetitions of offensive and defensive movements, was the first in which Nahia, Daphne, and Lily were unable to finish. When the class ended, Urus came over to them with a look of disgust he did not even bother to hide.

"I advise you to go to the gym and work those muscles. Otherwise, you won't be able to pass this class."

The three were well aware of this fact. They would have to ask for Logan's help once again. Luckily, Nahia knew he would help them due to his good nature. And she would be delighted to spend time with him. Yes, she was going to enjoy that a lot, even if she had to suffer. She might even suffer gladly as long as she was with Logan. No, she was going to suffer, but with a smile on her face. You had to look at the bright side of the problem.

Chapter 17

A few days later, at sundown, the Igneous Squad was eating in the dining hall like a pack of hungry wolves. They had to get their strength back before heading to fulfill their nightly punishment.

"How are you all?" Taika asked with his soft, silky voice, concern in his tone. He looked at each one with his cat-like gaze.

"Much better now," said Ivo, who had just finished eating two whole rations. "Although I think I still need a little more to reach my balance."

"Balance? What balance is that?" Lily looked at him, amused.

"That between mind and body. My mind is anxious because my body doesn't have all the energy it needs to work in fullness. So, I'll go for another ration. I think with that, my body and mind will balance out and I'll achieve peace and harmony."

"Only you could come up with such a theory," Lily told him, making a face that meant it did not fit him at all.

"You'd be surprised. There are tomes by great thinkers who elaborate on this in depth. You should read them. It would do you good," Ivo advised her.

"Eating too much doesn't become my waist or graceful, curvy figure, that's for sure." Lily shook her head and her finger.

"The fast we're doing in the mornings must be helping to keep you splendid," Daphne told her.

"Oh, yes, but I don't like to go hungry. Although I'd rather fast than put on weight, don't you have a single doubt about that."

"In that case, by the time we finish our punishment you'll look spectacular," Nahia told her, smiling.

"Don't bet on it. If I get too thin, I'll lose part of my irresistible attractiveness. Some curves always add a special charm to a feminine figure," Lily explained coquettishly.

"Who cares about curves or no curves. What we need is muscle. The more the better," Aiden said in a tone that showed his annoyance with the conversation as he flexed his right arm.

"There goes granite-head with his reactionary Drakonid ideology," Lily moaned.

"But this time he's right," Taika defended him.

"And how's that?" Daphne asked, raising an eyebrow.

"Because if we want to survive and live many more years, muscles are the most important. I'm not saying curves aren't attractive, but muscles are fundamental. Without muscle, the body can't survive in the long run. Or at least that's what my people believe," Taika told them.

"And they believe correctly. My people also believe that the body needs muscles, the more the better," Aiden added.

"We don't have a problem with that. We are born with a mountain of muscle in our bodies. That's why we have to eat so much," said Ivo.

"You eat so much because you love it. Don't involve your body and muscles in this," Lily said accusingly.

Ivo smiled.

"You aren't wrong."

"Are all of you coping well with the fast?" Taika asked them, seeming to want to make sure they were all well.

"No problem," said Aiden.

"I, like Lily, don't like to go hungry, but I can hold up pretty well until nighttime," Daphne told him.

"I'm okay. I was already guessing we would be told that we couldn't take so much food out of the dining hall every day, so since we have no other option, we just have to endure," said Nahia.

"Yeah, it was to be expected. The third day, the kitchen Tergnomus stopped us," Taika said.

"The dragon lords don't allow it," added Aiden.

"Because they're cret...." Daphne began to say, but she shut up when Taika made a sign not to continue. The tiger glanced to his right. Daphne followed his gaze. One of the guardian dragons in the dining hall was looking at them.

For a long moment, they all shut up until the dragon's gaze went to another table.

"How are you handling the punishment?" Nahia asked the others.

"Quite well, if it weren't for those disgusting Serpetuss," Lily protested. "I can't bear them; they disgust me so."

"Apart from that, fine," Ivo said. "We've already updated Egil, he's very happy with what's going on in Tremia. Well, not with what's happening, but with how his people are holding their own against the dragons. He's proud of the fierce resistance the Rangers, Ice Magi, and all of Norghana are posing to the invasion."

"It is reason to be proud indeed," Nahia nodded. "We should be fighting like them. More fiercely still," she said and began to light up. The flame started in her stomach, and she felt its heat come up to her face.

"Take it easy… I can see your eyes lighting up," Taika told her, and he looked back unobtrusively at the guardian dragon.

"Do my eyes show it?"

"Yup, they get ember-colored when you start to get excited," Lily told her.

"And when you have one of your seizures, even more so. They glow as if they burned outwards," Daphne added.

"Wow, I didn't know that…"

"Logical, you can't see yourself," Lily said with a giggle.

"Is it only the eyes, or something else too? Do I get all red?"

"On the contrary, you go pale, like snow. As for that, it doesn't show," Daphne told her.

"That's funny…" Nahia did not know what to think of that.

"I know. It's good to know when it happens," Taika said. "We can help you."

"Yeah, that's true…"

"On the other hand, with granite-head, we can't tell when he's going to have one of his seizures. Which doesn't surprise me, because he has to make everything more difficult for the rest of us," said Daphne.

"That's him…" Lily added.

"Don't be so mean. Leave Aiden in peace," Ivo told them.

"I don't need anyone to defend me. I can do it myself," Aiden retorted, annoyed.

Ivo shrugged.

"As you wish."

Nahia decided to change the subject to cut off the argument.

"Ask Egil if he has any idea where his friend Ingrid might have hidden the golden weapons. Lasgol and his friends haven't found them, and it's very important they do so. Perhaps we might get lucky and Egil can think of where they might be," she told Lily and Ivo.

"Fine, we'll ask him." Lily nodded.

"Daphne, try to get all the information you can from the

prisoners in your area."

"I'll try, although there are some with murderous intentions."

"I can imagine, but do what you can. Don't take any risks, but if you find something out it might be useful. If there're any other prisoners like Egil, it might be good for us," Nahia said, thinking about possible opportunities they could take advantage of.

"My enemy's enemy is undoubtedly my friend," Taika commented.

"That's what I'm thinking. We might have to forge odd friendships to help us in the fight for freedom." She said the last part in a low voice.

Taika nodded.

"It's a good idea."

"If you don't mind, don't talk about the cause, or about going against our lords in my presence. I'd rather not know any of this. I don't want to be involved. Keep me out of this entirely," Aiden told them.

"Unfortunately, we don't have a choice but to bear with your company all the time, so suck it up and bear with us. Stay absolutely quiet," Daphne told him.

"You know what'll happen to you if you breathe a word," Lily told him, passing her thumb along her neck.

"I'm not afraid of you. You two or anyone else," Aiden said, lifting his chin.

"Maybe, but I bet you don't want to stand up to the five of us," Daphne threatened him. Aiden waved his hands, not wanting to continue the conversation.

"Aiden isn't going to betray us," Nahia said, looking at the Drakonid, more in hope than in certainty that this was true.

"Let's finish eating, the dungeons await us," Aiden said. He did not want to hear anything else.

Nahia was thoughtful. Unfortunately, they had not been able to keep Aiden out of it. It was impossible. He was always with them, day and night. They had tried, but he had found out gradually. They had tried to keep the secret and only talk about the important matters when the Drakonid was not with them, but it had not worked. Things slipped out or Aiden suddenly came back in the middle of a conversation and heard things. Other times the comments slipped out from sheer frustration and hatred toward the dragons. The

Drakonid now knew, not only what they thought but also of their efforts and goal of achieving freedom. The Drakonid presented a risk they had to live with; there was no other solution. Nahia hoped he would not betray them, but neither she nor anyone else in the group would risk their neck for the Drakonid's loyalty. They could only wait and see.

A while later, Lily and Ivo were scrubbing the floors of dark rock at the beginning of the corridor where Egil's cell was. They were waiting for a couple of Tergnomus who were making the food delivery to finish their task there and go to another sector. So far they had not had many problems with the Tergnomus. As long as they did a good job cleaning, everything seemed to go well. They strove to do it well to avoid any trouble. The plan was that the two of them would do the sector where Egil was held and speak to him while Taika and Aiden cleaned other sectors and were alert in case they needed to provide support.

The two Tergnomus finished delivering the food to the last of the prisoners in the corridor and left. Lily and Ivo exchanged glances and headed to Egil's cell. Everything looked to be in order, they should not run into any problems. At that moment, a Serpetuss appeared behind them. Lily saw it by sheer chance and she grabbed her mop, ready to hit the creature if it came too close.

"Stop… don't hit it with the mop… or we'll be in deep trouble…" Ivo whispered in a quieting tone while he stayed absolutely still.

Lily was shaking off the nasty shiver and grasping the mop with both hands, her knuckles white. She knew she must not move in the presence of one of those guards, but she found it very hard to maintain her poise.

"If it comes any closer, I'll hit it."

Ivo's eyes opened wide. The thing was, the Serpetuss came to sniff at everyone in the corridor. This one was no different. It came to Ivo, and rising up to the Tauruk's face, it smelled him with its forked tongue. Ivo did not move; he let the creature examine him and remained calm. They both had their bracelets on, so if they did not do anything weird the creature would let them be. The Serpetuss seemed satisfied and turned to Lily.

"Don't come…" she muttered under her breath, making a tremendous effort not to step back and remain still in her place.

The creature snaked its way forward until it was in front of the Scarlatum who had the mop stick in front of her, parallel to her body as if she were hiding behind it. The creature guard rose on its body until its head was level with Lily's and sniffed at her with its tongue.

"Stay still… and calm…" Ivo told her, seeing that his partner was about to lose her cool and do something they were going to regret.

Lily was clenching the mop so hard it looked like she was going to shatter it into splinters. The muscles in her face were so clenched that the little horns on her head looked like they were going to launch themselves into the air. Ivo thought the Scarlatum was not going to be able to control herself. She was about to burst, so he prepared to fight.

The Serpetuss sniffed at her one last time and, turning half its body, looked at Ivo. Then it left, snaking its way along the center of the corridor.

Lily's whole body began to shake uncontrollably, as if she were having one of Nahia's seizures.

"I hate those things!"

The Serpetuss stopped and turned around. It stared at Lily with its snake eyes.

Lily closed her mouth and stayed very still. Ivo feared it would attack them.

The creature made a sound like a grating hiss. Lily and Ivo understood at once that it was a warning. A deadly one. They did not move a muscle. The Serpetuss looked at both, poked its tongue out in their direction, and then turned to continue down the corridor.

Ivo snorted under his breath, very relieved. Lily remained silent for a moment longer, afraid that the creature might come back. Once it had vanished down the end of the corridor, Lily cursed under her breath.

"Nauseating thing! To the abyss with you!"

"You must learn to be calmer, more balanced, with these creatures," Ivo tried to soothe her with his peaceful, relaxed tone.

"The next time I see it, I'll freeze it on the spot!"

"I don't think that's a good idea. I'm positive the creature has magical defenses, otherwise it wouldn't be in the dungeons."

"Well, I'm going to skewer it from side to side with my sword."

"Hmmmm… I don't think you'd be able to do that either, it has scales similar to the dragons. Besides, the Tergnomus won't let you come down here with a sword," he shook his large horned head from side to side.

"So, we bring it hidden!"

"I think it'd do you good to do some breathing exercises. You're redder than usual, and you are a very intense red…"

"Of course, I'm red and intense! That filthy monster nearly licked my face and then almost attacked me!"

"Breathe, or else your horns are going to fly off your head," Ivo told her, spreading his arms and then closing them, doing breathing exercises so that Lily would imitate him.

"Stop doing that!"

"Do as I tell you. Inhale through the nose to your lungs," he told her and did it, "and exhale long and steady," he finished, looking at Lily.

The Scarlatum was furious and disgusted. As a rule, Lily was charming, but when she got angry, she turned as red as her skin, or even more. It took her a long moment to calm down. Ivo kept showing her the breathing exercises of breathing and relaxation, but Lily ignored it and breathed at her own pace. Once she was calmer, she spoke.

"You're right. I must learn to control myself around those things. Our punishment is long, and we're going to encounter them almost every night."

"That's the attitude," Ivo smiled at her.

"I simply can't cope with them, it's beyond me."

"You'll manage, don't worry. It will go better every night. You'll get used to it as we encounter more of them."

"You really believe that, or is it one of your philosophical theories about how to overcome things we don't like?"

Ivo laughed.

"Both."

"You're impossible, you over-thinking, philosophizing ox-head."

Ivo smiled and shrugged.

"I'm Ivo."

"Yeah… yeah… let's go and see Egil, see if I can get rid of this bad feeling, brrrr!"

"Okay. Open the peephole, I'll watch."

Lily went over to the cell and slid the peephole open.

"Egil, we're here," Lily said.

"Hello both of you. I happy to see you," Egil greeted them. "Serpetuss?"

"Yeah, that disgusting thing approached us."

"That seem to me. Careful. Be dangerous."

"Yeah, that's perfectly clear to us."

"How do you not go blind in there all the time in the dark?" Lily asked him.

"Tergnomus open peephole three times a day. Torch light come in. Then close again. Four if count food, like just now."

"Well, how nice of those grumpy little dragon servants," Lily commented sarcastically.

"Little, but enough."

"Give me a moment and I'll make you a ball of ice. It doesn't glow as much as Daphne's, but it will give you some light since it's so white. In the total darkness of your cell, it will allow you to see something."

"Thank you very much, Lily."

"It's a pleasure to be able to ease the suffering of your captivity a little," Lily said, and then she concentrated on creating a very condensed ball of ice so it would last without melting as long as possible. Then she passed it through the peephole.

Egil took it to the far end of his cell, which was sunk in darkness.

"Yes, light up a little. Fantastic."

Lily smiled.

"You're a champion. You have an incredible spirit."

"Not so much, you good person."

Lily smiled and studied him from head to toe.

"What I wonder is how come you're not all wasted away from being cooped in here for so long without ever coming out. You ought to be unable to move a single muscle and feel all cramped, but you don't look it," Ivo said in a fascinated, surprised tone.

"I do exercises."

"Exercises? In there? But this cell isn't over four paces long and four wide!"

"Don't need more. I run without moving," Egil said, and he started to run in place. "Also jump in place," he said, and he began to jump, lifting his knees high. Then he switched to jumping, moving his arms and legs. "Also do squats and pushups. Many a day. Not have more to do here inside, so exercise a lot. Using weight of my body can do exercises. Be important not to get weak and sick, like Ivo say."

"The fact that you do all that in there is fascinating." Ivo was scratching his ample chin. "It's as if you had your own mini-gym."

"And are they feeding you properly?" Lily worried.

"Yes, food is no problem. Lots of meat and cheese. Good for body."

"Thank goodness they feed you well in this nightmarish dump," Ivo snorted in relief.

"It seems to me that even if you were left in the middle of the sea, you'd find a way to survive. You'd drink salt water or something like that," Lily said.

"Salt water can be desalinized and drunk. I know how," Egil replied.

Lily put her hand to her forehead.

See? What I just said! You're capable of finding ways to survive anywhere."

"Adapt or die," Egil told her.

"Yeah, well, that's an extremist philosophy, not one of my favorites. I prefer to find balance, but very true," Ivo agreed.

"Your dominion of our language is improving a lot," Lily congratulated him. "Do you need us to bring you any more books? We could smuggle them in, they don't search us."

"Yes, please, language books if you can. I have dictionary, but conjugate verbs I am no good."

Lily laughed.

"That's not important, we understand you perfectly. But we'll try to bring you some books that explain how to conjugate."

"I want learn," Egil insisted.

Lily nodded.

"Consider it done."

"I appreciate it."

Lily looked both ways to make sure the corridor was deserted.

"I have a question from Nahia. It's about the golden weapons."

"Go ahead, ask."

"Ingrid is imprisoned, like I told you, and Lasgol and the others don't know where she hid the golden weapons. You wouldn't happen to know where she might have hidden them?"

Egil was thoughtful.

"Ingrid be great Ranger. Get to be First Ranger, be the first woman to do it."

"See, I already like this friend of yours," Lily said, smiling.

"Very good friend, great leader."

"Can you think of where she might have hidden them?" Ivo asked from his watch post a little further back.

"Hmmmm... I would say the Abyss, but Camu and Lasgol will have already looked there."

"From what Nahia told us, your friends have looked everywhere with no luck."

"Given the situation, with the dragons' invasion, they surely left no stone unturned in order to find those weapons," Ivo commented.

"Yes. They look everywhere. Leader of Rangers not have them? Sigrid or Dolbarar?"

Lily shook her head.

"No Rangers have them, including the leaders. That's what Lasgol said."

Egil thought for a while longer, then he shook his head.

"I no idea where Ingrid can hide them. Sorry. Perhaps only she knows," Egil said ruefully.

"That puts us in a tight spot, because she's a prisoner in a city-state off the eastern coast of Tremia."

"Yes, be important problem."

"Well, I'll tell Nahia we don't have any news."

"Someone's coming," Ivo warned them suddenly.

Lily closed the peephole, and in the blink of an eye she was scrubbing in front of the cell. It was a Tergnomus. They pretended to be working and let him pass by.

The Tergnomus turned to them.

"This corridor is more than clean, go on to the next one."

Lily and Ivo looked at one another. They did as they were told and went on to the next sector. For that night, talking to Egil was over.

Chapter 18

One level below, Daphne was pulling her cart loaded with charcoal down the endless corridor. She was tired. She had been walking along the labyrinth that was the second underground level for hours. She crossed by two Tergnomus, who carried their tridents on their shoulders. She still did not know how they used them, since the curmudgeons practically did not talk to her. They passed her by, and since Daphne knew they would not greet her if she did not do it first, she did.

"Good evening," she said in a dry tone.

"May it be so," the one with the darkest hair and an annoyed face replied.

Daphne smiled inwardly. She did not understand why the Tergnomus were always angry or in such a bad mood. They seemed to her a strange race. She seized any chance she had to make them talk. She did so because she knew it bothered them, and this amused her. It was the only entertainment she had during the nightly working hours that felt eternal.

She saw a brazier that had gone out and went to fill and rekindle it. She always made sure she walked along the center with her cart, close to the braziers. She did not go near the cells because she did not trust that the protection barrier would work. She assumed it did because there were no loose creatures wandering the corridors, but she preferred not to check. The few times she had taken a look from a prudent distance she had gotten a good scare. A creature always came out, trying to kill her, so she now went down the center without straying too much.

She got to the brazier and stopped pulling the cart, which was nothing but a large wheelbarrow. They loaded it with coal and she had to go around this sector making sure all the fires were burning and pouring more coal on those running low. Since they were underground and there were no torches or oil lamps, those braziers were the only source of light in that dungeon underworld.

She saw a figure move in the cell to her right. It did not reveal itself and she did not try to see it. Better to keep her distance.

Although they might be dangerous, she found it cruel that the prisoners only had those fires as a source of light. They were kept going day and night, yes, but they could not compare with the light of the sun. From what she knew of healing from her Healer Talent and her elemental light magic, nothing compared to sunlight. Its properties were beneficial for the health. Keeping the prisoners down here without seeing the light of the sun for so long was going to weaken them and make them sick. Of that she was positive, unless nocturnal creatures dwelled there. An idea came to her mind: no doubt that was what the dragons intended with these underground dungeons. Not only did they keep them locked up safe, but they also made their enemies sick. That explained why they kept the prisoners from natural light, with barely circulating air, and in a damp, lugubrious atmosphere. All factors that contributed to weakening the body and causing illnesses. Indeed, that was why they did this. She thought it most evil. Dragons were abominable beings.

She got to work and filled the brazier with coal with a small spade she carried in her cart. Then she lit it. She could not do like Nahia and use her power to create fire, so she carried an oil lamp and a small ceramic container with fuel in the cart. She poured the fuel, which was nothing more than a special oil that burnt easily and for a longer time than regular oil. She did not know how the Tergnomus made it, but it was one of their creations and they were very proud of it. They had made that clear to her more than once. The little curmudgeons were as proud of their work and everything that had to do with it, as they were grumpy, perhaps the former more than the latter. She soaked the coal well and then started the fire with her oil lamp.

"Thank you," a voice said behind her.

Daphne started, putting her hand to her chest and almost knocking down the oil lamp. She recovered and, turning around, she looked toward the origin of the voice. She was alone in that section of the corridor, so it had to come from one of the cells.

"You thanked me?" she asked, not going near the cell. She could only see half inside, and not very well. The far end was all shadows.

"Yes, I did," a voice said, and a figure came out of the darkness and approached the bars.

Daphne stiffened. She remembered that as long as she did not go near the bars, she had nothing to fear. If the cell's magic worked, of course; if not, she would be in deep trouble. Just in case, she stood in a defensive stance and called on her inner dragon. She gathered elemental light energy and prepared to use it.

"You don't need your magic. I'm not going to harm you."

Daphne narrowed her eyes to better see the figure that was speaking and froze when she saw it. It was a humanoid-like creature, a little taller than her, and thin. Its features looked feminine, like those of a young woman, yet there was something extremely odd about her. She was covered in plants and their leaves. Not only covered—it was as if the plants were a part of her. They came out of her feet, ankles, elbows, and wrists, even her head. She had no hair, but long green leaves fell down to her shoulders. Her skin was unlike regular skin; it looked as if her legs, arms, torso, and face were enveloped in plant leaves of different intense shades of green. Daphne had the impression they were all jungle plants.

"Who are you? And what are you?" Daphne was staring at the creature with wide eyes.

"I am Oihane, of the Selvaris," she told her and bowed slightly.

"You're… half human, half plant…" Daphne stammered, unable to believe what she was seeing.

The young Selvaris smiled.

"To you I am a mixture between a human and plants, yes. But I am much more than that, in ways too complicated for you to understand. For now, we'll leave it at that. Your mind would not understand the complexity of my physiognomy, least of all that of my whole being."

Daphne managed to snap out of her astonishment after a moment.

"I'm quite smart," she replied.

"Then you will understand me when I tell you that for me you are a mixture between a human and a hummingbird."

"I'm a lot more than… oh, now I get what you mean."

Oihane smiled.

"You and I are complex beings. Let me tell you that I'm very sorry you can't fly. Those wings of yours are beautiful."

"Thank you… you are really amazing. Like something out of a jungle."

"That's because I come from one. My species, I mean," she indicated behind her and a dozen others like her revealed themselves.

There were men and women of different ages, all grown-ups.

"Wow! I didn't know there were so many inside one cell."

Oihane nodded.

"You've never come close to look. You always pass by along the center, without coming close. We see you."

"I never saw you. If I don't get close, it's out of precaution."

"Understandable. It's better to be too wary than to end up dead for not being wary enough."

"Exactly."

"You have nothing to fear from us," Oihane assured her and indicated her people with a wave of her arm and hand. Daphne noticed that the leaves of her wrist and elbow moved as if they had a life of their own.

"I hope that's true," Daphne replied, not trusting her entirely. If there was something life had taught her, it was that there was plenty of evil in the world, and although it mostly came from the dragons and their servants, she was distrustful.

"It is. And you will see. Then you will believe me."

Daphne watched her and had to admit that she did not look dangerous, her or her people. They looked like… plant beings. They were not frightening, at least in appearance.

"How do you speak the Kraido language?"

Oihane smiled.

"I learned it on my world, before I was captured. Some of us studied the dragons, our enemies. If you want to defeat your enemy, it's better to know all you can about them. Lack of knowledge kills you."

"What world are you from?"

"A very distant one. A green world where plants cover the whole surface. A world of jungles and tropical forests. It's called Biziohian, but the dragons call it Jumeglia. They have conquered it, destroying a quarter of the great continent, the most populated areas."

"That's horrible. I'm so sorry those monsters have done that to you and your people," Daphne said, and it came straight from her heart.

Oihane looked at her, surprised.

"You're not like the other dragon servants."

Daphne wrinkled her nose. "I'm a slave to the dragons, just like you."

"But you're not a prisoner like me."

"I am, but in a different way. They have me at the Academy, learning to fight for them or die. And death follows after every step I take."

Oihane nodded.

"And you don't see it as an honor? There are those who work here and serve the dragons, and those who are in the Academy, who see it as a real honor."

Daphne shook her head.

"Not in my case. I see it as a terrible punishment. One I don't wish for myself or anyone else. We're slaves, inferior beings without any value to the dragons. They enslave us, make us fight for them, and kill us."

The Selvaris was thoughtful, watching Daphne with a glow of curiosity in her light-green eyes.

"Perhaps you and I have more in common than I thought."

"Very likely."

"If you could put an extra load of coal in that brazier, I would appreciate it. We have a couple of sick people and they need it," Oihane made a sign to two members of the group, who nodded. They were two elders and they came to the bars, seeking the light of the braziers. They looked unwell. The plants of their bodies were wilting and those that were not had a dull, lifeless, gray-greenish sheen. It was clear they were sick. When she realized this, Daphne observed Oihane and the others more closely. She took a couple of steps toward the bars to see them better. She squinted and noticed that the others also had parts of their body where their colors were turning gray and the plants were wilting. Even Oihane. The young Selvaris's leafy hair was dried and wilted at the ends, and a couple of plants on her elbows were a grayish hue. They were all sick.

"Of course," Daphne turned and poured a double load of coal not only in that brazier but in all of those that lit up the cell. Then she went back to Oihane. The others watched her with interest. The two elders, helped by a couple of the younger ones, were basking in the firelight.

"We appreciate it from the bottom of our hearts. Our people depend on light; without light we can't exist."

Daphne was not surprised by this. This race was half plant, and plants could not survive without light. She realized that the ruthless dragons were going to let them die there. They would slowly wilt away, drying up until they died. It was horrible.

"Why do they have you here if they've already conquered your world?" It seemed odd to Daphne.

Oihane sighed and looked at her people.

"They have conquered our world, but our people refuse to give up. They're still in the fight. We are hostages. We belong to the great houses of our nation. They have us here to keep our families from fighting against them."

"That's despicable. They're abominable," Daphne shook her head, angered.

"They are. But our people will never give in. They will fight for freedom to the last drop of sap."

"Then they are brave."

"That they are. All my people are."

Daphne wondered how they would fight the dragons. They did not look very strong. Perhaps they had magic. She decided to ask.

"Do you have powerful magic to fight the dragons?"

"We have magic, but it's not powerful enough to defeat that of the dragons. Their magical defenses prevent us from using our magic against them."

Daphne nodded. She understood what Oihane meant.

"What kind of magic do you have?" Daphne wanted to know.

"Nature magic. Based on plants, mainly. We have great healers."

"That's what I guessed. But if you can't do anything against the magical defenses of the dragons, and I'm assuming you can't pierce their scales either, then how do you fight them?" This had her wondering. She could not imagine how they could fight.

"We can't get through their scales," Oihane shook her head. "But we don't need to."

"You don't? But then what? I don't understand. How do you fight them?"

Oihane nodded and then smiled.

"We have great knowledge of the world of plants, and that gives us an advantage we have learned to exploit: poisons."

Daphne was shocked. She had not been expecting that.

"You have poisons that affect the dragons?"

Oihane nodded.

"We have several. They're not strong enough to kill them yet, but we keep experimenting, and the day will come when we succeed. For now, we have managed to make them sick with a very powerful mix of different poisonous plants from our world."

"Sick to the point that they can't fight?" Daphne wanted to know. This was fascinating. She thought about Nahia; she was going to be very interested. They might be able to use it or develop it in their fight against the dragons.

"Sick to the point that they can't fly and can barely walk," Oihane explained.

"That's wonderful!" Daphne nearly applauded.

Oihane lowered her gaze, and her face showed sadness.

"The problem is that they manage to recover. They return and continue committing atrocities. We can't poison them for long. Their defenses are almost as strong as their own bodies. They're too strong in every aspect."

"Even so, what you're telling me is a great advancement. One we haven't achieved in this world. Don't stop searching. If you develop a poison that manages to knock them out, it would be something awesome. We could use it. It could be used in Drameia, and in other worlds."

"My people continue resisting and are still searching for the poison that will finish off the dragons. One day we'll find it. I am sure," Oihane nodded with hope in her eyes.

"You've made me immensely happy. We, the enslaved peoples of Kraido, didn't know this was even possible."

Oihane nodded.

"It is possible to poison them. Dragons aren't immune to poison. It affects them."

"I'll spread the word among my people. They must know this."

"Indeed, but it requires the creation of a very special poison, with plants I don't even know grow in this world or not." Oihane pointed upward with her finger. Daphne noticed that her nails were also green but crystalline.

"I see. We might not have them here."

"Another important thing is how to poison them, which isn't easy either. The dragons are as clever as they are wicked. We have to use all kind of stratagems in order to succeed."

"I can imagine that." Daphne was thoughtful about how they would go about doing it. Weapons, like daggers, swords, and spears, could not be used to inflict wounds and poison the blood, since they did not penetrate their scales. She thought of the head and mouth. That was the only way she could think of, when they opened their mouth. Only, as a rule, they only opened their mouths to use their elemental breath or tear a head off someone with a bite. They would definitely not be easy to poison.

"Thank you again for tending our braziers," Oihane said gratefully.

"You don't need to thank me. I can't bear to see what they're doing to you. It makes me furious, and I'll try to help you in any way I can. My people hate the dragons, for taking away our freedom and what they do to us," Daphne fluttered her wings and snorted in frustration. "It's despicable, hateful, and having you here, without light and getting sick, is too."

"It's our fated disgrace for not being able to defeat the dragons. Unfortunately, the strong races subject the weak."

Daphne wrinkled her nose and frowned, enraged. Blasted dragons. She wanted to go against them, do something to fight them. She had an idea. One that was no great feat, but it might help the Selvaris.

"Your magic can't get past the bars. But do you know if ours can?" she asked Oihane.

"Yes, yours can, as long as it's dragon magic."

"Mine is dragon magic."

"Then you can get past the barrier."

"Great! I have something for you." Daphne looked right and left to see if anyone was near or coming. She saw no one. The corridor was deserted. She closed her eyes and gathered elemental energy from her inner dragon. She stretched out her right hand, palm up, and concentrated on creating a ball of elemental light energy. She did it without problems. The ball lit up the whole cell and part of the corridor.

"Light, how wonderful!" Oihane cried.

Daphne stretched out her left hand. She took elemental light energy and transformed it into healing energy like she had learned to do with her Healer Talent. With the healing energy, she created another ball and loaded it as full as she was able. She opened her eyes and looked at both balls. One created light and the other emitted a healing energy.

"I'll try to pass them on to you," she told Oihane.

"Go ahead," the Selvaris motioned for her to hand them to her. Daphne did not want to touch the barrier with her hands, not only because it might cause her some harm, but because it might alert the Tergnomus that something was up. She decided to use her mind. She concentrated on the ball of light and sent it as if she were launching it at an enemy, only very slowly and making sure it passed between two bars. It took her a while, but the ball of light went through. The barrier let it in, recognizing the dragon magic. Daphne heaved a sigh of relief.

"Take it," she told Oihane.

The Selvaris held the ball in her hands. She closed her eyes and let it bathe her completely. At once, her color improved a little. She opened her eyes and smiled.

"You have no idea how good this feels," she told Daphne and handed the ball of light to the two elders, who took it amid smiles.

Daphne nodded and did the same with the ball of healing. Oihane took it in her hands, and her face showed great joy.

"It's healing magic. This radiates it. I can feel how it penetrates my body."

"Healing is my Talent. I can't cure you, it's not among the things I've been taught, but I can create non-specific healing energy. It must do some good, even if it's small. Or at least I hope so,"

"I am sure it will help us."

"I hope so. The ball of light will last a couple of days. The healing one I'm not sure about. You'll have to tell me."

"Of course. We'll let you know how long it lasts and its beneficial effects," Oihane assured her as she handed the ball to her people.

"I'd better get on with my work. I don't want them to notice this," Daphne said, looking once again in both directions. "If anyone comes, you'd better hide those spheres."

"Don't worry, we'll hide them at the bottom of our cell. Covering them with blankets and our own bodies will be enough to hide their light."

"Perfect. I'm happy to have made you acquaintance."

"We are even happier," Oihane told her with an honest smile. "There aren't many good people left in the world."

"I'm grumpier than I am good, but I'll accept the compliment. And there are good people left, they're just scared. They don't want to die, and in the world of dragons, dying is very easy."

Oihane nodded.

"You're very right."

"I'll be back tomorrow. I'll make two more balls if they've been good for you. If you need more just let me know, although it's a little risky. You can see them from the corridor."

"I think two will be enough. We'll know tomorrow. A thousand thanks for what you've done."

"You are welcome. Today I help you, tomorrow you help me," Daphne smiled at them.

Oihane nodded.

"You can count on that."

Chapter 19

On the third underground level, Nahia was doing the food delivery with Burgor atop the first cart of the convoy. It was the same route every night. They traveled in silence. She was disappointed. The weeks went by, and she had not persuaded Utrek to change her route no matter how much she had insisted and despite the reasons she had given him. She had spent all her ideas to argue for route one.

"You didn't like Utrek's umpteenth refusal, huh?" Burgor said with a Tergnomus smile which always looked evil on their peculiar faces. In Burgor's case, Nahia had already realized that, indeed, he always had a hint of evil or resentment.

"You grow more perceptive."

"Don't think so. I'm always the same."

Nahia shook her head. Irony and sarcasm were not the Tergnomus' forte. They were an odd race. Even the Exarbor picked up on double meaning, but the Tergnomus barely. Thinking about it, the Exarbor were slow of movement but quick of mind. The Tergnomus were small, ugly with those long noses and ears, and not very mentally astute.

"How's your leg? Is it already healed?"

"It's almost better," Burgor massaged it a little.

"Great, then we'll take turns picking up the extra pieces that fall off the cart during delivery."

"I said almost, not completely. You'll keep picking them up."

"But…"

Burgor urged the beasts and looked ahead, ignoring her. Very typical of him when he did not want to talk about something.

Now that Nahia knew what kind of creatures were in the caves, there was not much danger most of the route. Granted, she did not know them all, because some did not come out when they delivered the food. She did not mind; she preferred it that way, less risk. But there was an area that made them both very nervous—the section with the Gryphons—and they were approaching it.

"Watch out now."

"I will. The Gryphons… have they ever killed anyone that you know of?" The idea crossed her mind and she asked as it did.

"All the prisoners have killed at some point, and so have these. They're powerful creatures; they will kill, not for food or the pleasure of killing, but to demonstrate their power and dominion."

"Oh, I see. They mark their territory."

"Yes, and they do it with blood. That's why working down here is so dangerous. That's why they punish some of you by sending you to this level."

"Yeah, so we don't return to the surface."

"Exactly. You keep testing your luck and you'll see. Sooner or later, it will desert you and I'll have to take whatever remains of you above."

"Thanks, you're a dear."

"Of course I am," Burgor looked at her bad humoredly.

Nahia smiled. There was no way he had picked up on her sarcasm.

They came to the cave of the Gryphon-Hawk-Cheetah. The creature saw them and flew out of the cave like lightning, passing low over them.

"Can't it escape? I mean from its cave?"

Burgor shook his head.

"It has a silver necklace around its neck. If it flies away from its cave, it receives a discharge of energy that hurts its head. Dragon magic, advanced."

"Wow, very interesting."

"Don't they teach you Mental Dragon Magic at the Academy?"

"Well, yes, we're just starting with it."

"Well, that's the kind. Very powerful magic. It attacks the mind and brings down the Gryphons."

"I see. Don't they have magical defenses like the dragons?"

"They do. That's why they're forced to wear the necklace. It neutralizes them."

"Ahhh, I see."

Come, human, let's play, it will be fun, she received the message from the Gryphon-Hawk-Cheetah, which flew by in front of them.

Nahia huffed. *Not fun at all. Highly dangerous,* she thought. The creature was set on playing with her. If an extra piece of meat dropped off the cart and Nahia had to retrieve it, the creature played a game to see who was faster—it or Nahia. Of course, it was the creature, so Nahia had to find ways to trick it if she lost. And losing meant it would eat her instead of the piece of meat.

"It wants to play…" she told Burgor, who did not receive the creature's mental messages.

The Tergnomus shook his head.

"These things only happen to you."

Nahia sighed deeply. He was not wrong about that.

"Let's unload carefully."

Burgor nodded.

They got to work, Nahia with one eye on the creature's fast, low flying. They unloaded carefully. One extra piece fell off. Nahia looked at Burgor.

"We could leave it…"

Burgor shook his head.

"Each creature has its established food and is given what it's due. The job is done well, always. There are no shortcuts or excuses."

Nahia had already guessed the Tergnomus would say something like that. He would not let her do a sloppy job, and he would not go for the extra piece either on account of his limp.

Come, human, one extra piece. You have to retrieve it. Let's play.

Nahia took a deep breath. The closest piece was not far. She could do it. The problem was that the blasted Gryphon flew tremendously fast. She watched its flight.

Ready? I am.

Nahia saw it was now circling over the fallen pieces about fifteen paces above. She could only do one thing. Trick it. She thought about it and decided. She made as if to go for the piece and took one step off the silver path. The Gryphon-Hawk-Cheetah came down for her at top speed. Nahia was already expecting this, so she lunged back to the path. The creature almost got to her, and when it saw Nahia stepping back it swerved right at great speed. It could not go for Nahia because the repulsor would reject it.

With a leap, Nahia got to her feet and sprinted toward the piece, grabbed it, and pulled it toward the silver path. The creature swerved swiftly and attacked again. Nahia calculated the distance. This time she might have time; the creature would not catch her, or so she hoped. She pulled hard on the piece while the huge flying creature flew toward her. She stepped on the silver path. The Gryphon-Hawk-Cheetah brushed past her without reaching the path.

Well played, human. I like you.

Nahia, who was breathing hard from the effort, raised her gaze toward the creature.

"Thank…. thank you…" she said brokenly.

"Let's keep going, there's no time for games." Burgor was already sitting in the first cart.

"Oh, you…" Nahia had to bit her tongue and ran to climb on the cart.

They arrived at the cave of the Gryphon-Eagle-Tiger and Nahia got off to unload. This delivery was safer. For some reason, the Gryphon-Eagle-Tiger did not threaten her or give her the feeling it wanted to harm her. Not like the Gryphon-Owl-Bear or Gryphon-Hawk-Cheetah, who had very bad ideas.

How are you today, human? It greeted her, coming out of its cave to receive them.

Nahia watched it. It was imposing, Enormous, strong, and feline, apart from its powerful eagle traits. A lethal combination.

"I could be better. Your comrades want to eat me."

The owl and the hawk?

"Yeah, them. Couldn't you tell them I have very little flesh, and also that I don't taste nice?"

I could tell them, indeed. But I doubt they would heed me. I have no influence over them. They are a different species.

Nahia stared at it. She was halfway between the cave and the carts.

"Aren't you all from the same species? Aren't you all Gryphons?"

We are, yes, but each sub-species has its own hierarchy. Because they are not from mine, they have no reason to obey me.

"Oh, I see," Nahia started unloading. Burgor was glaring at her. He wanted to get out of there as soon as possible.

But you can always appeal to the king.

"The Gryphon-Lion?"

Yes. He is a high Gryphon, and because of that all the Gryphon sub-species must obey him. But besides, he is not just any high Gryphon, he is a king. All of us here owe him obeisance.

"That's fascinating. Yeah, I might try. The thing is, he doesn't seem to want any contact whatsoever. Whenever we pass by, he screams and threatens us."

He's marking his territory. He doesn't want you to get close.

"Yeah, I figured, so I don't think he'll want to speak to me."

"Try. You might be surprised."

"I might, because if I don't, one of these will end up eating me."

That is quite likely, yes.

"Thank you anyway."

You are welcome. I like talking to you. There is very little distraction down here, as you well know.

"Yeah, easier to say none."

The Tergnomus don't provide much as far as conversation or sympathy go, to tell the truth.

"I perfectly understand you." Nahia looked at Burgor, who was fuming, he was so angry. "I'm going to get back to my job."

Very well, Human. Good luck and see you tomorrow.

"Yeah… I'm going to need it."

With a leap, Nahia climbed onto the cart, ignoring Burgor's glare of hatred. He had forbidden her from speaking to the Gryphon-Tiger. She ignored this ban because the creature, apart from being fascinating, was kind.

They arrived at the cave of the Gryphon-Lion king. Burgor threw a look at Nahia, which she understood without needing words: *Quick, there's danger.* They got off the cart and began the unloading maneuver. As they were turning over the whole load in the cart, the gigantic creature came out of the cave. Nahia was awed by its magnificent and regal presence, and the power it radiated. The white royal eagle head swerved the way the raptors did. It opened its lethal golden beak and shook its huge wings on the sides of its powerful lion body. It gave a cry, a mix between a shrill bird shriek and a deep lion roar. It was a blood-curdling sound.

Nahia was sure it was saying, *This is my domain, leave.* But, after the conversation with the Gryphon-Tiger, she decided to try her luck. She still had many nights down here, and she did not like her odds of getting out of here alive. They were too slim.

"Good evening, Your Majesty," Nahia greeted him as she bowed deep.

Burgor made a face of absolute shock.

Nahia remained doubled at the end of the bow as a show of respect. She was hoping it would please the magnificent creature, although she had no idea whether it would work. Perhaps it would be better to kneel with her forehead touching the floor as the dragons demanded.

What do you want, human? Why do you greet me respectfully? she received the Gryphon king's message. She once again thought that although the mental message was similar to that of the dragons, it was also different. She had no doubt that if her eyes were closed, she would be able to tell the difference.

"I'm Nahia, Your Majesty," she replied, still doubled down with her head low and without looking at it.

Why do you address me?

"I need the help of the king of the Gryphons, Your Majesty,"

I would assume it is because your life is in danger in this area of the dungeons, in the Gryphons' domain.

"That's right. The delivery route is dangerous in this area…"

My Gryphons make it difficult for you.

"Yes, they want to eat me…"

And why should I bother helping a Human who brings me food in a prison, and who is my enemy on top of it?

"Forgive my boldness, Your Majesty," Nahia apologized. As she spoke, she saw out of the corner of her eye how Burgor straightened the cart, already unloaded, and was heading unobtrusively to the first one of the convoy. She already guessed what the Tergnomus was going to do shortly. She wanted to say something else to the powerful king, but the response had been so cutting she did not know what argument to use. "I'm sorry to have bothered you…" was all she could say.

I can sense your power. More than your average Human; in fact, a lot more. That interests me. The slave races of Kraido have power inherited from the dragons, but it's not usually much. You are an exception. The eagle eyes were fixed on Nahia, who remained doubled down with her head low.

Nahia saw a chance and decided to take it.

"I'm a Flameborn."

I do not know the concept, but I want to know more about you. It might be interesting. The days are long in this prison and the nights even more so, although without the sun it is hard to tell the difference. You may rise.

Nahia straightened up, although she did not look directly at the great creature. She did not want to risk angering it. She guessed it might have the same airs of grandeur as the dragons and their bad habits.

"I'm a Human slave, who has… I think… greater power than

normal. The dragons call those who are born like me Flameborn."

The great Gryphon shook its eagle head in a movement that Nahia interpreted as of assent.

I guess the flame means you have the elemental power of fire.

"Yes, that is correct. Although the dragons say it happens very seldom, I am not the only one at the Academy. Another comrade, also human, is a Stormson."

Of the air element, interesting. Yes, it seldom happens and I understand it to be true because we Gryphons have not seen anyone like you either. This is, therefore, a special situation.

Nahia did not know whether it was or not, but the Gryphon was right in that it was not very common, least of all that it was her and Logan, two humans who were also friends.

"It might be… I don't know."

Very strange coincidences are seldom such. The fact that two Humans with great power exist at the same time, when it is rare to have even one, is significant. There is something behind it.

"Something? How… what could it be?" Nahia asked in a worried tone. This might be bad for her and Logan.

The great Gryphon king shook its wings hard. Burgor, who could not stand it any longer, urged the draft beasts on and started to leave. Nahia thought about running to the carts but then dismissed it. She was talking to a Gryphon king. Perhaps it would help her stay alive down here. That was the important thing.

Something like a transcendental destiny.

"I don't know whether I understand…"

The Tergnomus is leaving. Are you not going with him?

Nahia looked at the convoy, which was already moving. It would soon reach the bend and vanish after it. Then the route was nothing more than a long tour that led back to the beginning of the route where the carts were.

"Yeah, well, I'll follow shortly."

Those who are like that Tergnomus live a common life, not significant at all. Then there are beings, singular ones, like you, like me, who do live transcendental lives. Their actions have transcendence, not only on their own lives, but on the lives of those around them. It might even be life-changing.

"I'd like it to be that way… the purpose, I mean. And to reach it."

I hope that, if that purpose is honorable and good, you may reach it.

"May I ask…? Why are you a prisoner?" Nahia could see the thick chain tied to the right foreleg of the creature and the silver necklace on its neck.

The dragons defeated me in battle and I was captured. They brought me here and keep me prisoner, along with several of my loyal ones who were captured with me.

"In what world was this?" Nahia wanted to know, since they were not from Kraido.

My world is called Gryphoros. It is very far from here. Our oldest and most hated enemies are the dragons.

"Have the dragons conquered Gryphoros?"

The creature rose high and showed its golden beak

They've tried many times but have not been able to. They attack us every now and then, trying to invade us, but we reject them. We have been fighting against the dragons for thousands of years. We are irreconcilable enemies. We hate each other to the death. So it has always been, and so it will always be.

"Several thousand years… that means a long war. Then you fight against the dragons and are capable of defeating them?"

Of course. There is nothing a dragon fears more than a Gryphon flying at great speed to attack it.

Nahia thought the king was slightly exaggerating but said nothing. Perhaps the Gryphons were more powerful than she thought.

"Can you… kill them?"

We can, and we do. Otherwise, we would already be a conquered people.

"I wish we could too," Nahia said and looked out of the corner of her eye to see whether the cart was out of sight. It was. Burgor would be on the final section of the route. He would not hear what she was going to say.

Do you wish to fight against the dragons? Kill them?

"With all my being," Nahia said. She said it without thinking, giving voice to her feelings.

The Gryphon king moved its head and its eagle eyes widened.

You are a complete surprise. A slave of the dragons who dares pronounce herself against them.

"I want freedom for my people, for all the peoples of Kraido. More than that, I want freedom for all the worlds conquered by the dragons," she said, full of passion.

That is wanting a great deal, but it does you credit. You are different from the others, not only because of your power, but because of your spirit. I like that.

"I say what I feel. The dragons are also our enemies. We serve them because we have no way of fighting against them. But we are searching for one, and when we find it, we'll rise against the dragons."

An honorable goal, but a tragic one, I fear. The races of Kraido do not have the power to fight the dragons.

"We have the spirit, courage, and daring. We will find a way."

The Gryphon king made some noises that sounded to Nahia like laughter.

I definitely like you, Flameborn. What is your name?

"My name's Nahia."

Mine is Arran-Lehoizuri.

"It's an honor, Your Majesty."

I grant you free access to this area. The Gryphons will not bother you again.

"Thank you very much, that's a big relief."

Now, go with the Tergnomus before they believe I have killed you and eaten you.

"Yes, of course." Nahia turned and started walking, following the silver path. One sentence from her conversation kept cycling through her mind over and over as she left Arran-Lehoizuri.

There is nothing a dragon fears more than a Gryphon flying at great speed to attack it.

Chapter 20

The class of Magic had become the most hated by all. The punishments for not being up to the dragon Buru-Beira-Gogoa's standards were terrible. They did not only suffer headaches at the end of the class, but they lasted several days. Daphne blamed it on the cumulative effect of weeks of punishment. Unfortunately, she did not know how to alleviate it. Healing the mind was beyond her skills.

"If I don't make it today, my head's going to explode. That would be horrendous, it's so big. Be careful with my horns in case they pierce you," said Ivo on their way to magic class. He was clearly joking, but there was a touch of despair in his voice too.

"Cheer up. If Aiden and I have survived, you will too," Taika said encouragingly.

"It's been a dishonor that we were only able to do it during the last class. We deserve all the punishment we've received," Aiden said.

"You really have to be a granite-head to say something like that," Daphne chided him.

"No one deserves to be punished," Nahia corrected him. "It's cruel and unnecessary."

"Our dragon lords know what's best to help us learn. It's taken me weeks, despite the punishments. Imagine how much longer it would've taken me without them," Aiden said, defending the dragons' brutal way of teaching with sheer conviction.

"Exactly the same. Weeks," Lily told him.

Aiden shook his head.

"It would've taken me months. Our lords know how to make us improve faster."

"It took me two weeks, and it would've taken me the same amount of time without the punishments and suffering. It's totally unnecessary," Daphne argued.

"That's what you think. We'll have to see." Aiden would not be convinced.

"It took me three weeks, and I did not like any of the migraines I had. I almost got wrinkles from frowning so hard. And that would be a tragedy!" Lily touched her forehead with the tips of her fingers, very worried.

"Some wrinkles or, even better, scars are the least you can expect from good training," Aiden said.

"Can he be more of a marble-head!" Daphne raised her arms to the sky.

"Regardless, today Ivo's going to make it. I'm positive," Taika told them and patted his back in encouragement.

"It won't be for lack of studying and trying…" Ivo shrugged.

"You'll do it. Today you'll be capable of seeing the aura with total clarity," Nahia said with assurance.

He was the only one who still had not achieved it. The rest of the squad had done it already, with great effort and suffering. They were all able to make out the aura of the others, some more easily and clearly than others, but they all could. For Nahia, it was now easy. If she looked at any of her comrades and called on her Mental Aura Seeing skill, she could see them at once. She did not even have to consume much inner energy. Not only that, she was now capable of making out the mental aura of everyone in the class with one use of the skill. Daphne and Lily also could, but it took them two or three summons. Aiden and Taika could only see one, for now. Ivo, poor thing, could see none. He had been punished in each and every class. He said his head was now twice its usual size, from how swollen it was and from so much pain. The size was actually the same, it had not changed, but it felt that way to him.

They went into the room and prepared to receive another lesson on Mental Dragon Magic, filled with the fear this class always brought on. The mental punishments were so devastating they not only left their minds sore and stunned, but their whole body seemed unable to respond. They were rendered useless. Any movement they tried to make sharpened the pain that assaulted their minds. They could only lie there on the floor and suffer the torture until it passed. And in the beginning, it had lasted a long time. The thing was, no one was stronger or better at resisting the mental punishment than anyone else. Taika, Ivo, Aiden, Lily, Daphne, and Nahia suffered the same and took equally as long to recover. Race and physical strength had nothing to do with the mind, which was what the dragon punished.

Today we will begin with Mental Attacks. It is something I am sure you will all want to master and stand out on. Those who still have not managed to see the

173

mental aura will train separately. We cannot allow them to slow down the rest, Buru-Beira-Gogoa sent them, along with a feeling of urgency.

"Those behind… with me…" Membor indicated.

Ivo heaved a deep sigh and with a bowed head, went to the Exarbor. With him came the Kapro of the Hurricane Squad, who also had not been able to pick up the mental aura of his comrades. Nahia felt awful for Ivo. She, Daphne, and Lily had done everything they could to help him, but it was as if his mind and magic were not capable of such a feat. From what Buru-Beira-Gogoa had said, everyone was capable, so Ivo had to do it.

Very well. Now is when we will see who among you has superior dragon magic and who has only been blessed with basic power. Those who can attack another's mind have superior power. Those who can only see it but not attack it have basic power. There is no halfway here. You either have superior power or basic power.

This revelation left Nahia confused. What would happen to those with basic power? Was it going to punish them too? She hoped not, for the good of everyone. Besides, basic her foot. If they had gotten to this third-year class, they all had moderate power. This was how she understood it at least. She watched the dragon. Its eyes shone with excitement. Not a good sign. Too much exultation—nothing good would come from this.

In order to attack another's mind, you first have to sense their aura. Once detected, you must focus on it. The next step is to attack it. For that, you will use the elemental energy each of you has. You will do this as if you sent a powerful elemental ball, only the impact and explosion will happen in the rival's mind, not against their physical body.

Nahia froze. She was going to have to send a ball of fire to the mind of another person. No doubt the burst would kill them. A ball of fire incinerated a person; it could kill several if the range and power were increased. How was she going to send one at someone's mind? It would definitely kill them.

By the anxious looks, so typical, that I am seeing, I understand that you are all thinking you will undoubtedly kill someone by doing this. Be at ease, it is not so simple. A ball of fire, for instance, Buru-Beira-Gogoa looked at Nahia, *bursts into flame and consumes everything around it with fire. But when it is a Mental Attack, the ball itself does not exist. It is not anything physical that is created and thrown. It is only mental. Its destructive power is much less. Let us say that a regular ball of fire can only pain slightly greater than a migraine. A very powerful ball of fire would be close to the pain and suffering my punishments inflict. Therefore, do not be afraid of killing anyone. You will not be capable of such, for now. But let me tell you that it is possible. Not for the inferior races, of course. That is a privilege of the dragons, of the most powerful beings.*

Nahia sighed in relief. She did not want to kill anyone, least of all accidentally in magic training. The end of the message disturbed her though. *They* could not, but a powerful dragon could. She imagined a dragon like her leader killing her with its mind. It definitely seemed possible. That troubled her. That the powerful dragons might kill them using their minds was something they had not counted on, and it was absolutely terrifying. She cursed their bad luck under her breath. It was not enough that the dragons were so tremendously strong, and had devastating claws, and had elemental breath attacks that destroyed anything in their way. They could also kill with their minds, with a simple thought. She imagined the colonel of the Academy killing whoever it wanted with its mind. She shivered. Worst of all, she was sure Irakas-Gorri-Gaizt could do it. It was one of the most powerful dragons at the Academy.

The first one of each squad who managed to identify the mental aura, take a step forward.

Lily and Daphne looked at Nahia with encouragement. Nahia was not in the least encouraged—she was rather uneasy—but she could only do as she was told. She stepped forward, trying to stay calm and breathe deeply. That magic was very powerful. If she managed to master it, she would have a new power she could use in the fight against the dragons. It would help her on the long and painful path to freedom. Yes, that was what must happen. It was a new weapon that would help her. The dragons did not realize they were arming her to fight not *for* them, as they were expecting, but against them. They would pay for that mistake dearly.

The dragon looked at her, and Nahia immediately dismissed those thoughts of revolt from her mind. If she had feared they could read minds before, now that she knew the dragons could access them, she was even more afraid. Buru-Beira-Gogoa was teaching them to use their mind to attack the minds of others. They already knew it could be used to kill, and it had been hinted that such power could be used for other things as well. One of them might be mind reading. She pondered on it and was almost sure it was so. The dragons had the ability to know what they were thinking. Perhaps not all of them, but surely some powerful ones could do it. It would not surprise her in the least. She hoped and wished she was wrong. But she had a bad feeling about this.

Nahia looked out of the corner of her eye and saw that Lorena, the Fatum of the Hurricane Squad, who was to her right, had also stepped forward. She did not know her well, only by sight. But she understood she was very good at magic. Probably better than her. The Fatum race was better aligned to magic than Humans. The Fatum also looked at her out of the corner of her eye. She did not seem to be very calm. Nahia would have preferred Markus, the Human of the Hurricane Squad, so that the competition would be equal, Human against Human, but she had not been that lucky.

The exercise will consist of a mental duel. Each of you must attack the mind of your rival. You must do so as I have explained. Whoever manages to do so first will win the duel and the exercise. The one who loses will suffer the consequences of the attack, as it cannot be otherwise. Go ahead.

There was no time to dwell on it further. Nahia looked at her rival and closed her eyes. She concentrated and summoned her Mental Aura Seeing skill, which they had been practicing for weeks. She instantly sensed Lorena's mind. Nahia could see it without trouble. It was a round aura, a mixture of infinite hues of blue and white. It shone bright. Nahia now knew this was because her mind was very powerful. Buru-Beira-Gogoa had told them that the brighter the aura of a mind, the stronger it was and the more difficult it would be to attack it. It seemed to Nahia that the Fatum's mind was very bright, which was not good for this mental duel.

Focus on your rival's mind and attack it as if you were attacking the body with an elemental ball, only with your mind. The ball's level of power must be the same you would normally use.

A ball of fire was something Nahia could create already without thinking after two years at the Academy. But she had never created one in her mind. She looked at her right hand automatically, which is where she usually produced them. No, she could not create it there. She focused on her rival's mind aura and gathered energy from her inner dragon. She took the regular amount, although she did not understand why she could not carry out the attack with a smaller dose. If the attack was successful, a regular amount would do enough harm. It would be better to use a smaller dose of magic. But that was not the teaching method of the dragons. For them if there was no pain, there was no gain.

She did not have time for all these thoughts. She had to attack, or she was going to suffer a terrible headache. Lorena already had the ball created in her mind and was ready to launch. Nahia created hers in her mind. She could see it, spherical, burning, charged with energy, only that instead of on her hand, it was in the middle of her mind. It was a very weird feeling, and she was surprised.

Suddenly, she felt something strange, as if a force wanted to enter her mind. She frowned and tried to understand what was happening, but it was too late. She received Lorena's Mental Attack in full. A tremendous storm ball burst in Nahia's mind and she felt a very sharp pain. Her ball of fire vanished. She put her hands to her head unwillingly, from the suffering. She could not think. She only saw the pain that enveloped everything. She was defenseless. Somehow she knew she had to react, that if this was real combat she would be at her enemy's mercy. But she was unable to clear her head or move a muscle. She only felt a strong ache in the middle of her forehead that did not let her see, think, or act.

Winner of the duel: the Fatum. As you see, the Mental Attack has not killed the Human. Neither has it left her incapacitated on the ground. Yet it has left her defenseless by means of the pain that affects the mind. There is no need to tell you that in this state, even an Exarbor can defeat you and kill you. You will do well to not be caught off guard like this.

Nahia heard what the dragon was saying and wanted to recover to prove she was all right, but it was impossible. The pain was so sharp that her mind was annulled, and with it, her whole body. There was nothing she could do, not even escape her current state. She bore the pain by clenching her jaw, and after a moment the intensity of the suffering began to decrease. She waited and the pain decreased even more. Now she could think. She opened her eyes and lowered her hands, breathing deeply several times. Gradually, the pain subsided until it was gone. Nahia straightened up and huffed in relief.

Although it might seem that you cannot defend yourself from a Mental Attack, that is false. There is a way to do so which your own mind provides. A moment before the attack, the Human felt that her mind was being attacked. For a brief instant, the mind feels the invasion of an external magical force. At that moment, you have a chance to defend yourselves. I will teach you how to do it. But first you must learn to attack, which is more important. If you attack first and manage to penetrate the enemy's mind, you will not need to defend yourselves.

That crushing logic of the dragons did not convince Nahia at all. Attack first and kill. That way there was no room for a response. A mentality that favored death and destruction.

Very well, try again. Let us see whether the Human has learned the lesson and reacts, or is once again defeated.

Nahia held back a moan. She did not want to confront Lorena again. This exercise was dreadful.

Attack. Now!

The order reached them, unappealable. Nahia had no choice: she either reacted or was going to suffer again. As fast as she could, she located the mental aura of her rival, focused on it, and created the ball of fire. She did not think twice, and with her mind she lunged it at the Fatum's mental aura. The ball went from mind to mind like lightning. It seemed to vanish from Nahia's mind and appear in Lorena's. An instant before it exploded Nahia felt a resistance, as if the ball had bumped against an invisible barrier that did not let her into the mind of her adversary. She guessed it was the mind of her rival rejecting the attack. She could not let that happen. She did not know what to do, but the ball of fire had to penetrate. She decided to push it with her mind. She sent more energy to help her ball cross the barrier. She could not manage. She kept sending more energy, determined to not fail. Her rival was tough, but so was she. On the third attempt, she succeeded. The ball of fire burst in the midst of Lorena's bright blue-white aura. An instant later, the aura lost its brightness and the colors faded.

With a dull moan, Lorena doubled down in pain. She put her hands to her head and remained bent with a look of intense pain. Nahia did not see it because she still had her eyes shut, but she felt that her attack had been successful. She opened her eyes and saw her opponent. Nahia immediately felt sorry. Poor Lorena, she did not deserve such suffering. Nahia wondered whether she had really defeated her or whether the Fatum had let herself be beaten so that Nahia would not have to bear the punishment twice. Had she done that? Was she such a good person? In the merciless and brutal world of the dragons they lived in, this seemed highly unlikely. But Nahia wanted to believe so, that Lorena was a good person, compassionate, and had let her win. She would ask her as soon as she could. But for that day, Nahia decided to believe there were good people and that they had not all been dehumanized in that soulless academy of suffering.

I see the Human has reacted. Very interesting. That was a very swift and powerful attack. Well done, Human. As for the Fatum, during duels you always fight to win and never trust your opponent. Otherwise, pain arrives, and then death.

They were all watching Lorena suffering, half bent, unable to react and recover. Nahia knew there was nothing the Fatum could do other than wait for the pain to subside. She was completely beaten, defenseless. Nahia realized then how powerful attacking the mind of a rival was. If they were left like that, it was an extraordinary weapon. It served to incapacitate enemies and kill them if necessary, something Nahia would rather not do. In that state, you could deliver a blow to the nape and head and that was it. It was not necessary to kill them.

Watch out. Now, all of you get into pairs and start dueling. Pairs of different squads. I advise you to fight with everything you have. You know what happens to the loser.

The class was long and very tough. The duels went pretty well for some and quite badly for others. Nahia did not lose again, but she allowed herself to be defeated out of sympathy. Daphne only lost twice, once against Lorena and once against Markus. Lily, three times. Aidan and Taika were not capable of attacking the mind of their opponents, so they lost all the fights and suffered true torture. When at last the duels ended, they were all very sore, all except the great Tauruk and the Kapro, who had not participated.

The only good thing to come out of that day was that Ivo was finally capable of seeing mental auras, and for the first time he did not suffer any punishment in class. He was delighted, not so much about his success, as for not having suffered. They all left the class with their heads bowed, except Ivo, who was smiling. Nahia could not stop thinking that this skill, Mental Attack, was truly powerful and incredibly dangerous.

Chapter 21

Nahia walked quietly into the library and went up to the third floor with her shoulders hunched and a look of being overwhelmed. She did not want to draw any attention. She was just another third-year pupil having a hard time in her classes. That was what she wanted the librarian Exarbor to think. She did not need spying eyes on her.

She crossed the whole third floor with her head down, huffing every now and then. She was very bad at pretending, but she was following Lily's directions. According to her friend, girls like them, charming and intelligent, could fool all the Tergnomus and Exarbor of the Academy without a problem. Nahia did not agree with her, but she decided it was better not to argue with Lily, mostly because she would never persuade her to the contrary. It was very clear that Lily's self-esteem was always sky high. From what she had heard Taika say, that was the case with all Scarlatum. And they believed their very own Scarlatum had even more self-esteem than was usual for her race.

She raised her gaze as she reached the last tables at the far end of the floor. Her eyes saw Logan at once. She felt something move in her stomach and began to feel her inner flame stirring. She realized it was not that, which surprised her. As a rule, the flame lit up when she became angry, and she was able to identify it without any trouble. When she was with Logan, something similar to her flame lit up, but this was different. It gave her a very pleasant feeling and a special nervousness she never felt at any other time. She had the imperious need to not only see him, but to be with him. She wanted them to be together, that somehow, they would put Logan on her squad and they could share the whole day and night in each other's company. These feelings, which had begun in the first year, had been growing with the passing of time. They were already in their third year, and now the feelings were very strong. Nahia found it hard to control them. She suspected what it was, but she did not even want to consider it. Her existence was already complicated enough without getting involved in a sentimental relationship on top of it all. No, better to dismiss the idea. Besides, it was more than likely that Logan did not have the same feelings for her, beyond those of the friendship they shared, a great bond between them.

She dismissed those thoughts and saw that Ana was beside him. She looked at Nahia and then turned her gaze back to Logan. Nahia realized then that the look Ana had given her and the one she was giving Logan were very different. She also noticed that Ana always appeared with Logan, almost never on her own. It was as if she sought him out before the three met. She probably sought him out more often. Did Ana want to have him for herself? These thoughts awoke a new feeling in Nahia, one she was not familiar with. She felt a discomfort that led her to think badly of Ana. She realized that this feeling was not a good one. It was one she had already spoken to Lily about, the expert on these subjects, and which she recognized as jealousy. Nahia shook her head. She did not want anything to do with that evil feeling. She dismissed it and felt terrible for thinking badly of Ana, who had not done anything wrong and was a very good friend of hers.

She walked up to them and greeted them unobtrusively while she located the position of the nearest Exarbor. One of them was looking at her. She did not like that. She still felt as though she were being watched, and if that was so, it could only be for the dragons. That made her nervous. She was on the point of turning and leaving the way she had come and not meeting her friends, but she calmed down and sat with them at the long table that had ample space for four people.

Logan turned toward her.

"We have those you wanted to see, they'll be here shortly."

Nahia nodded.

"Thank you, good job," she replied, also in a whisper.

"It wasn't hard to persuade them. They were eager to speak with you," Ana said.

"Great. Before they get here, tell me how your missions went in Tremia. We haven't had time to talk about it, and I'm very interested to know the situation of every kingdom."

"Fine, we still have time before they arrive. Ana, why don't you begin?" Logan gave the floor to her.

Ana nodded and her face darkened.

"It was a horrible experience, terrible, but I'll tell you about it." Ana sighed deeply, seeming very affected. "The goal of the Dragon

King Itx-Urd-Arr, the blue king, is to conquer the west of Tremia. That includes, from what we were told, the Kingdom of Rogdon and the Massig Tribes of the Steppes, as well as the savage tribes of the Usik of the great forests," she started to explain. "I don't know much about Tremia, but I believe it encompasses the whole upper west coast of the continent."

"Yeah, that's a little below and west of Norghana, where I was," Nahia said, who had memorized the maps Egil had made for them.

"We got there from a Pearl that's in the west." Ana looked at Nahia in case she knew which one it was.

"I know where it is. To the west, right in the middle of the continent, south of the Pearl where the deserts begin," she explained.

Ana seemed to be memorizing the location in her mind.

"We went to the north and entered Rogdon, crossing what had been a beautiful walled city. Now it's destroyed. It was called Silanda."

"I can imagine, yeah. It was a border city, the armies of the blue dragon will have laid siege to it and taken it," Nahia guessed.

"That's right. The city fell, and from the damage I witnessed when we went through it, they defended it to the death," said Ana, bowing her head. "I also saw the funeral pyres."

"They burn the dead," said Logan.

"Yeah, it's horrible. There were several burning when we arrived. The smell… it was horrible." A couple of tears ran down Ana's cheeks.

"They do it to prevent sickness," Logan told her.

"I guessed as much. Even so, it's a horrendous smell and it was a terrible experience. I'm still having nightmares…"

"The war is cruel and terrible," Nahia nodded, feeling sympathy for her friend.

"From Silanda we went north, to the capital, Rilentor. It's under siege, but they're resisting. The Rogdonians are good warriors. They call them the blue and silver lancers, because of their colors and their wonderful riders with spears."

"Could you see them?" Nahia asked her.

Ana shook her head.

"They're all inside the city, defending it."

"Do they have magi?" Logan wanted to know.

"Yes, powerful. Several magi they call Magi of the Four Elements.

They're resisting the attacks of the dragons."

"Four elements? We have six," Nahia commented thoughtfully.

Ana shrugged.

"It's what our soldiers there told me. They mentioned fire, water, earth, and air magic."

"They don't have the elements of light and darkness," Nahia nodded.

"And they're resisting?" Logan asked.

"It seems their magi can use any of the four elements at any given time, so if a dragon with a particular element attacks, say for instance a red fire dragon, they defend themselves with water magic. And so it goes with every other, except the two they don't have."

"Well, that's very interesting," Nahia commented.

"It is?" it did not seem so to Ana.

"Magi of the Four Elements. Very curious. We only master one element each. Between the three of us, we're short on one type of magic to face one of those magi."

"I see what you mean..." Logan understood.

"Being able to switch elements according to their needs gives them a fantastic advantage, especially if they're powerful magi."

"And it seems like they are, because the dragons of the blue king can't seem to be able to kill them."

"I wonder what they'll do if they're attacked with light or darkness magic."

"Against light you can use any of the other elements except darkness, which they don't seem to have," said Logan.

"True. But against darkness?" Nahia wanted to know.

"Mmmm... I'd use air to dispel it, with strong winds and lightning," said Logan.

"Good thinking, that might work. You have a good head," Nahia smiled at him, looking into his eyes.

Logan smiled lightly.

"Thanks, so do you," he replied, looking back at her.

Their eyes were suddenly locked. For an instant they stared into one another's, unable to look away. Nahia realized that all those feelings were emerging again.

"The siege was a horrendous experience," Ana continued, ending the moment Nahia and Logan were sharing.

"Huh... did you participate?" Nahia asked, returning to the

conversation,

"Yeah, we had to attack one of the gates of the city. It was horrible. Lots of people died, both from our army and theirs. More from ours, from what I was able to see…"

"Then your mission was similar to mine," Nahia told her.

"Mine also involved participating in the siege and taking one of the gates," Logan commented.

"It appears we all had the same mission. It makes sense. The dragons are quite stubborn when it comes to these things. They gave all the squadrons the same missions, only in different places around Tremia."

"Yeah, each squadron supported one of the dragon kings," Logan reasoned.

"All I know is it was a terrible experience. We had to fight for our lives and kill Rogdonians. I feel awful for what I was forced to do. I did not want to kill them, but it was their life or mine." Ana covered her eyes with her hands and wept.

"Don't beat yourself up. You did what you had to. It's a war. Kill or die. There's no choice," Logan told her, putting a hand on her back to comfort her.

"It's not your fault, Ana. It the dragons' fault; they sent you there to fight and kill for them. Don't blame yourself, blame the dragons," Nahia said.

Ana tried to calm down and seemed to manage after a moment.

"Thank you, I know. It's what I keep telling myself. But it's hard to swallow."

"What do you know of the Massig and the Usik?" Nahia asked her.

Ana wiped away her tears and went on.

"The soldiers told me the Massig are a race of Humans with red skin that roam the great steppes on horseback. A part of the army of the Blue Dragon King, with a group of dragons, was sent to defeat them."

"Did they succeed?" Logan was interested.

Ana shook her head.

"From what it appears, the steppes are immense and the Massig are spread out in numerous nomadic tribes. They don't have a capital; they just move constantly throughout the steppes. They don't even have an army as such, but they have fierce warriors. The soldiers consider them savage tribes who ride horses. They fight with bows and arrows. They haven't managed to defeat them because when they see a dragon, they scatter. They don't go into battle. Since there is no city to lay siege to, there's nothing to conquer."

"Well, they seem smart these Massig, and the fact that they're nomadic tribes helps them avoid an invasion," Nahia commented in wonder.

"It's a good tactic indeed. If you don't have to defend a city, and were unable to defeat the dragons, I'd do the same thing. Run away from any direct confrontation," said Logan.

"I was also told that when the dragons aren't with the army, the Massig do attack, swift raids, and then they disperse again into the great steppes."

"That's a very good strategy," Logan nodded.

"So, then they haven't been defeated yet." Nahia wanted to be sure.

"No, because the dragons can't catch them."

"And the Usik?"

"Those are even worse," Ana made a horrified face.

"What do you mean?" Nahia did not understand.

"If the Massig are savage and tough, the Usik are even worse. They live in an endless forest; it must be gigantic. From what I was told, it's said they live in the tops of the trees. The regiments that went into the unfathomable forests of the Usik never returned."

"They haven't come back? None of them?" Nahia's eyes opened wide.

"That's what I was told. The dragons can't protect the soldiers inside the forest because it's so thick and dense. They can't see what goes on inside. The Usik are savages with green skin, primitive and ugly. They don't allow anyone into their forests, killing anyone who enters."

"And the dragons haven't found a way to defeat them?" Logan asked.

"They hide in the trees or among the thicket. They can't see them because of their green skin, they camouflage very well. The dragons razed parts of the forest, but the common consensus is they haven't reached many natives. The forests are so immense and the weather so humid, that burning them doesn't seem to work either. The fires go out."

"Or the Usik put them out," said Logan.

"Yeah, maybe. The campaign against the Usik is going very badly. A lot of soldiers belonging to the blue dragon king have died, and they've achieved nothing."

"That's good news—not the deaths of our soldiers, that's awful—but that the dragons can't crush those savages."

"It's the habitat they live in, it protects them," Logan reasoned.

Ana nodded.

"Yeah, and that's all I know."

"Great, Ana. The more information we have of what is going on in Tremia, the better," Nahia told her.

"It seems the dragons are having difficulties in the west. That is indeed good news," Logan stated.

"And what about you, Logan? How did your mission go?" Nahia said, looking into his eyes with a sort of shyness in case her feelings returned.

Logan returned her gaze, and once again there was that instant when their gazes locked. It happened almost magnetically, as if their eyes sought each other's at a subconscious level and once they met did not want to move away.

"I hope it was better than my experience," Ana said wishfully.

Logan looked at Ana and the magic of the moment with Nahia vanished.

"In my case, I had to support the White Dragon King, Aiz-Zur-Tor. The goal was to conquer the middle of the continent. It's a wide area that includes the Kingdom of Zangria, a little to the north, the Kingdom of Erenal, more to the south, and the Central Sea. All on the upper half of the continent."

"That's just below Norghana, a little more to the east," Nahia told them, closing her eyes to go over the memorized maps in her head.

Logan nodded.

"We came out of a Pearl in the east and had to travel a long way, heading southeast to reach the Kingdom of Erenal. Then they made us march along an even longer road to reach the Kingdom of Zangria. Most of the mission was spent traveling from the capital of one kingdom, to the capital of the other. Both are under siege by the armies of the white dragon king. The king has his armies divided in two groups, one attacking Zangria and the other Erenal. Our squadron's lot was to attack the capital of Zangria."

"What are the Zangrians like? Will they hold out?" Naha asked, interested.

"The Zangrians are an interesting race. They're Humans but short and heavy-set. Ugly, with lots of hair, and good warriors. They're not tall, but they are wide and strong."

"Then they'll hold?" Ana asked.

"I'm afraid not. Their magi aren't very powerful or many in number."

"Then they won't. Without magi, they won't be able to hold back the dragons' attack," Nahia said in a grim tone.

"That's what I fear. We participated in the siege on the capital. We took one of the three main gates that access the city. The Zangrians defended themselves like lions, but against the dragons there was little they could do."

"Then Zangria will fall," Nahia guessed.

Logan nodded.

"Very soon, unfortunately."

"The dragons will kill thousands," Ana said ruefully.

Nahia and Logan said nothing, but they both knew it was true.

"What can you say about the Kingdom of Erenal?" Nahia asked him.

Logan made a gesture of annoyance.

"I think something similar is happening there. Their magi aren't able to defend themselves from the dragons. I believe it will also fall."

"At the same time as Zangria?"

"I think it might hold a little longer, from what I could see there, although we did not take part in the siege, so I can't be sure. We were told that the Kingdom of Erenal has a powerful army that uses advanced military tactics. But I know nothing of their magi. They might be able to withstand."

"Maybe not…" Ana bowed her head. She seemed relieved.

"And the Central Sea?" Nahia asked him.

"It seems to be controlled by a race of pirates. They did not stand up to battle. They escaped from the dragons in their ships. I don't think they'll help the cause."

"Well, that's bad news. I was somewhat cheered by what was happening in the west," Nahia said.

"It's more than likely that both kingdoms will fall rather than stand up to the dragons," Logan said in a sorrowful tone. "We must have that premise in mind when we make decisions."

"Yeah… they will all fall in the end…" Ana was losing hope.

"Don't say that, Ana. Tremia will manage to expel the dragons. We'll help them do it," Nahia said.

"It just seems so difficult…"

"It is, but we'll do it," Logan assured her as he shared in Nahia's feeling.

There was a moment of silence. The three were thinking about how complicated the situation in Tremia was and how difficult it was going to be to go against the dragons.

"They're here," Ana said with a nod.

Chapter 22

Nahia and Logan looked up and saw two figures coming toward them. Nahia recognized them at once: they were Brendan, of the Ardent Squad, and Logar, of the Searing Squad. She was glad they had decided to come. Unobtrusively, she rose from Ana and Logan's table and went to sit down at the end table. She waited for the guests to reach her.

Brendan and Logar stayed in character and did not greet Ana and Logan as they passed them by.

"Sit down," Nahia told her two squadron comrades with a wave of her hand. The two nodded and sat in front of her. Her back was to the wall.

Ana, beside Logan, turned unobtrusively.

"Give us the signal when you're ready," she said to Nahia in a low voice.

"Fine." Nahia opened the tome on the table and acted like she was studying.

Logan and Ana looked at the Exarbor.

"Welcome," Nahia greeted her two squadron comrades and looked over their heads to see whether their group raised suspicion. There were some other third-years at different tables in groups of two, three, and some alone, all studying. Among them were her squad comrades, Lily, Daphne, and Ivo at one table and Taika alone at another. Aiden, of course, had not wanted to have anything to do with all this and was practicing alone in one of the halls of magical training. The Exarbor librarians were now busy with their tomes and helping the pupils. Everything looked normal.

"We're pleased to be here," Brendan told her.

"We've heard some rumors… and we wanted to speak with you," Logar admitted.

"Rumors? What do they say about me?" Nahia raised an eyebrow and stared at Logar.

"The Felidae-Lion looked over his shoulder, making sure no Exarbors could hear him before he said, "Many things are rumored… all dangerous… that you speak against the dragons… that you want to free the slave races… that you want to start a new insurrection…"

Nahia took a deep breath.

"They're saying all that about me?"

"That and more," Logar assured her.

"No one dares to even imagine going against the dragons, least of all being bold enough to express it. The fact that you have, and risked your life on more than one occasion, draws attention. A lot of it," Brendan told her.

"Is that why you're here? To find out whether it's true or not?"

They both exchanged looks and then looked at Nahia.

"We're not here for rumors or gossip. We respect you, for the way you've always treated us and our squads," Brendan told her.

"And also because your squad and your friends, here beside you, greatly respect you," Logar said.

"We want to know whether the 'message' that's being spread is true," Brendan told her.

"If you really believe it with all your heart," Logar added.

Naha nodded.

"I understand your position. You risk a lot simply by talking to me about 'the message.' So, and because I respect you, I'll be straightforward and absolutely honest. The message is real. I give you my word, and I'm asking you to join the cause."

Brendan and Logar looked at one another, and then their eyes turned to Nahia.

"We're listening," Logar said.

Nahia raised her right hand and Brendan and Logar waited.

"Now," she signaled Ana and Logan.

They both rose and went straight to where the two nearest Exarbor were. They started asking questions to distract them and allow Nahia to have some time to persuade her two guests.

"Listen to me carefully, because what I'm going to tell you is of great importance and absolutely true."

"Go ahead," Brendan said.

Logar motioned for her to continue.

Nahia explained the message to them, what the dream was, and how they could achieve it with weapons of Golden Magic capable of killing dragons. She explained who had killed the dragon they had seen dead in Norghana, and how. She told them everything in the hopes that by being honest she would persuade them. Once she finished, she was silent for a moment, letting them digest all the information she had given them.

After a long moment of reflection, they spoke.

"Your dream is one many of us have and share," Logar said.

"It's not my dream, it's our dream—everyone's dream. The same way that this isn't my cause, it's our cause, because we won't be able to reach freedom if we don't all fight for it," Nahia said.

Logar nodded.

"Wise words."

"If the Golden Magic exists, and those weapons are capable of doing what you say they can do, then there's hope," Brendan said.

"I promise you, it's true."

"We believe you, we know you're an honest person," Logar said.

Brendan nodded.

"I believe you. And your words fill my heart with hope. Thank you."

"Thank you both for trusting me."

They both nodded.

"You can count on me. I want to fight for freedom—for us, not for the dragons. If there is a chance, if there is hope, I want to fight," Logar said, convinced.

"Thank you for joining us. I swear, there is a chance. We can kill them. That's our chance and our hope," Nahia said with conviction.

Logar nodded.

"I'm with you."

"Count on me too," Brendan told her. "Living like this isn't really living. If I have to die, I'll die fighting, not as a slave defeated by my own fears. I don't want to miss the chance to rise because of fear."

"That's how I feel too," Nahia said. "Thank you for joining the cause."

"What do you need us to do?" Logar asked.

"I need you to speak to your squads and tell them what I've told you today. Only to those you trust. Leave out the Drakonids, they're a risk, and anyone who is too subjected to the dragons, or convinced there is no other destiny than being slaves until death."

"Understood," Logar said.

"Only our squads?" asked Brendan.

"First your squads. Then pass the message to the squads of the second- and first-years. Each squad can deal with their own in the three years."

"It's a good strategy," Brendan nodded. "But we need to persuade each third-year squad so that the message goes down."

Nahia nodded.

"We won't be able to persuade all of them, I'm sure of that. But this is the plan we have now. It's not perfect, but it's a start. Once we do that, we can see which squads still need to be persuaded. Then we'll think of a new strategy."

"If they find out, the dragons will make us tell them who leads us before they kill us," Logar warned her.

"I know. I'll die… but the message and the cause will not. They will continue, because there will be others to take the baton from the fallen. If I die—if we die—I'm sure others will take our place, so we have to make sure the message reaches them and sinks into their hearts."

"We'll make sure it does," Logar told her.

"I hope you survive, Nahia," Brendan told her.

"Better to hope that the cause succeeds. Whether we survive or not is secondary. The only important thing is achieving freedom for all," Nahia emphasized the message.

"I already had great respect for you, Flameborn. But now I have even more," Logar said.

"I feel the same way," Brendan joined him.

"Go, and be very careful. We need the message to reach as many people as possible."

"We'll do that," Brendan promised.

They both rose and left.

Nahia was left thinking. She had found a lot of time to meditate about freedom and the sacrifice it required. She had known she was going to die here at the Academy since the day of the ceremony at her village. Dying here for freedom did not seem so bad to her. It was a price she was willing to pay for everyone else's freedom.

Ana and Logan had already stopped their distracting maneuvers to avoid suspicion. They turned toward her at her table.

"How did it go?" Ana asked her with great interest.

"Wonderful. They believed me. They saw the dead dragon. They couldn't explain how it had happened, but now they know, and they're both joining the cause of freedom," Nahia told them, motivated and happy.

"Good news," Logan nodded, and for once his serious face lit up with a small smile.

"Wonderful." Ana clenched her fists hard and smiled.

"They're going to tell their squads everything I've told them, those they trust. I've already told them not to risk it with the Drakonids or with anyone else they don't fully trust, to not tell them for now. We need the message to spread, but we must do it cautiously."

"That's the way," Logan said, nodding.

"You do the same. Then see about the second- and third-year squads, whether you can give them the message too."

"Alright, it's time to act," Logan said determinedly.

"I hope everything goes well…" said Ana, fear nagging at her throat.

"Take it easy and everything will be all right. If you don't see it clearly, don't trust anyone," Nahia advised her.

"Don't take any risks until you're completely sure," Logan told her with the same concern.

Ana nodded repeatedly.

"I don't understand why you're not afraid. I'm overwhelmed…"

Nahia smiled.

"Who says we're not afraid? I am, I'm terrified. I bet Logan is too."

Their friend nodded.

"I am. Only fools do not fear death."

"Or stupid people," Nahia added.

Ana looked at them both with moist eyes.

"I hope we escape death."

Logan and Nahia looked at one another. They both knew their chances were small, almost nonexistent. But even so, they would go on.

"We'll make it," Nahia promised.

Chapter 23

A few days later, Nahia was in Talent class. Zeru-Urdin-On, the powerful blue dragoness, had chosen her again to demonstrate how they ought to cast a spell. She was in the middle of the class while the rest of her comrades watched her. There were many days when Nahia regretted being a Flameborn. It drew too much attention, which she hated.

Stretch out your hands, Human, the dragoness ordered, and the order came along with a feeling of quiet, as if trying to soothe her. This surprised her; it was not what she was used to. The mental messages always came as relentless and urgent commands. Was the dragoness being kind? She doubted it. She would have to see what followed.

She did as was told and Sorginbor, the assistant Exarbor of Sorcery moved back quite swiftly for someone of his race. That did not make Nahia very confident. She had no idea what the new exercise intended, but the fact that the Exarbor moved away was not a good sign.

Now I want you to look at your hands for a long moment, until you memorize their appearance. Then close your eyes and concentrate on that memory. See them in your mind, and once you do, nod.

This was very weird. The dragoness had asked her to nod. But their all-powerful leaders never sought communication, they only sent orders. It took her a moment to overcome her surprise. She stared at her hands, turning them. Then she concentrated and visualized them in her mind. She nodded once she could see them.

I want you to use your elemental fire power in a direct manner. The fire must come out of your hands as if they were burning and projecting the flames. You must not do it like when you use Elemental Claws. It must be like an explosion of fire coming out of your hands. An instantaneous one. That is the most important aspect. Go ahead. Concentrate and try it. Remember, envision fire coming out of your hands.

Nahia took a deep breath and concentrated on successfully doing what the dragoness teacher had asked of her. She thought of an explosion emerging from her extended hands. She gathered elemental energy from her inner dragon, and instead of creating a sphere, or a claw, or maw, she threw it out. She opened her eyes and saw how energy flew from her hands, but it was not fire. She had released elemental energy in its pure state.

That was not bad, but you must turn your elemental energy into fire as you throw it. Try again.

The failure made Nahia hesitate. She realized she had done it wrong and did not want to err again. She repeated the exercise, and this time when she sent the energy to launch from her hands, she first turned it into fire. She opened her eyes and saw intense flames coming out of both of her hands. They only reached a couple of handspans and created a fan of fire around her hands, but it was most impressive.

Very well. Now move your hands and direct the flames. You must send energy to feed the flames, or else they will die out.

Nahia moved her hands right and left, and then up and down. She continued sending energy so the spell would not die out. She was very surprised; this skill was powerful. The flames, thought short, were intense, as powerful as Dragon Breath. They would incinerate anyone trying to approach her. Besides, she noticed it was much easier to conjure and maintain it.

Very well. You have learned the Fire Hands skill. I want the rest of you to learn to develop your Elemental Hands: ice, storm, light, and earth. This is the Sorcery spell most used once it is mastered. The reason? How simple it is to conjure, and how efficient it is. But for this, you must learn to conjure it instantaneously. You must think and instruct your hands to expel the elemental attack at the same time. Start practicing.

The five stood at a prudent distance, like Sorginbor had done, so that no accidents happened. And they started practicing. It took them the whole class, but by the end of it, they had all succeeded. They performed even better than Nahia had expected. She could not summon her Fire Hands instantaneously, yet—there was a second of delay between her mental command and the fire emerging from her hands—but for the first day she thought it a tremendous achievement. Besides, she was the only one to do it so fast. It took the rest practically the whole class to make the spell work at all.

But no matter how much she tried to make the spell happen faster, she could not. She had the impression that succeeding in making it instantaneous was going to be harder than she had imagined. For her it was good enough, it was still fast, but she knew

Zeru-Urdin-On would not accept anything less than instantaneous.

She watched her comrades to see what their Elemental Hands were like. They all had the same reach and shape, but they surprised her quite a bit. The Ice Hands were like her fiery ones, only they froze everything in front of them. No doubt they would cancel her Fire Hands if they had to fight one another. The Earth Hands were the most interesting. Rocks and stones with stinging, lacerating edges and shapes shot forward, destroying themselves when they reached the range limit. The Light Hands gave off a light so bright they blinded whoever was in front of them. They would be perfect against any kind of darkness spell, or when fighting in the shadows. But the really impressive ones, and which raised some envy, were the Air Hands. White-blue bolts loaded with energy zigzagged out of the fingers and discharged on anything they met. The effect was amazing, the ten bolts of lightning discharging over and over again giving out blue sparks. If they hit a person, the discharges of energy would kill them in the blink of an eye.

At the end of the class, they each left happy with the new skill they had developed. Nahia could not wait to tell her squad.

That evening, at the dining hall while they were eating, Nahia told her comrades about it in full detail.

"The Air Hands sound incredible," Aiden commented, looking at his own stretched-out hands.

"Careful with those little paws, I'm right in front of you," Lily told him. "Magic might shoot out and burn my face with a lightning bolt."

"I'm not a Sorcerer, I don't have that skill," Aiden told her. "And a burn on your face would give you character."

"It would disfigure me, which is completely different." Lily felt her soft, firm red cheeks, as if making sure they were perfect. "What a disgrace. If I had a mark, it would be my ruin."

Aiden shook his head and made a face of disbelief.

"The fact that it's instantaneous is amazing," Taika commented. "I didn't think that was possible. There's always some time between invoking a skill and it occurring."

"Yeah, and the more difficult or the harder the skill is to create, the longer it takes," Daphne said.

"The instantaneous factor I believe is only for those with the Sorcery Talent." Nahia stared at the Talent Mark on the back of her right hand.

"I'd love to have instantaneous Air Hands," Aiden said.

"But you're not a Sorcerer, so there you go, suck it up," Lily said with a comical face.

"The dragon lords have granted me the Barbarian Talent, and I couldn't be happier."

"Oh sure, because how could your lords possibly make a mistake… and heaven forbid you go against their judgment," Daphne retorted.

"Tell me, how you are doing in your Talent classes?" Nahia asked, wanting to know all about her comrades and their Talents.

"I'm doing great," Aiden said at once.

"How strange that you're so good at everything…" Daphne commented with irony.

"I'm not lying. I'm very good at it. We've learned the skill Unstoppable Frenzy. It's spectacular. It allows us to attack with greater aggressiveness, strength, and speed. We use our magical energy to summon the skill. We're more aggressive, stronger, and faster than a Fighter, Warrior, or Defender. It makes us into impressive fighters. We get to be unstoppable."

"Out of curiosity… this skill only affects attacking, right? Not defense," Ivo asked him.

"Yes, of course it's an attack skill. It makes us formidable attackers."

"Yeah, I find it a little unbalanced. All offense and no defense," the Tauruk told him. "It doesn't seem right."

"Use it with caution," Taika warned him. "Being exposed while attacking too aggressively is dangerous."

"It's one of the most important skills a Barbarian has. I must use it," Aiden told them, ignoring their warnings.

"Yeah, as if you weren't crazy enough to begin with, they had to go and give you a skill to make you even more insane," Lily said with sarcasm.

"I'm not crazy."

"You do become somewhat of a loon every now and then," Daphne told him. "With this new skill, you'll be even worse."

"Say what you want. It's an honor to be a Barbarian, and I'll use

Unstoppable Frenzy as often as I can."

"This lunatic will kill us all one day, you'll see," Lily told the others.

"How are you doing, Ivo?" Nahia asked him.

"I can't complain," he said. "I'm still having trouble with the magical part, but the knowledge I'm acquiring is amazing. I like the Druid Talent very much, more than I initially thought. The study of nature I find fascinating. Lately I've been spending more time in the library studying nature tomes than practicing magic."

"Shouldn't you be doing both?" Nahia asked him.

"Yes, I should, you're right, just to be more balanced," he smiled, "but sometimes I get so lost in the tomes of natural knowledge that it's as if I were captured."

"Really, letting yourself be captured by a book. You're the oddest Tauruk I've ever met," Aiden told him.

"I'm Ivo," the great Tauruk shrugged.

"What skill are you learning?" Taika asked him.

"Now that we know how to cure poison, we're learning to poison others. I still don't fully understand it, but I'll be able to shoot poison similar to the way Nahia uses her Fire Hands."

"Oh, that's very interesting." Nahia liked the sound of that.

"Well, carry the antidote to the poison always, just in case," Daphne recommended.

"Don't worry, you know I like balance. If I'm going to poison, I'll also know how to counter that poison."

"That's because apart from being beastly, you're great," Lily told him, laughing.

Ivo let out a deep guffaw, which was joined by his comrades. Even Aiden smiled, something rare from him.

"How about you, Taika? Are you doing well?" Nahia asked.

"I think I'm doing well. I have an advantage over the rest of my comrades because of the combination of my race and elemental magic. Being a Felidae with elemental darkness magic is a favorable combination for the Shadow Talent."

"I'd say it's the best combination," Daphne said.

Taika nodded.

"It's possible, yes."

"What skill are you developing?" Aiden asked with interest.

"Great Silent Leap. We already mastered Creating Darkness,

which in my case is quite powerful, and Stealthy Movement. That way you can't see us or hear us. Now we're learning to take a big leap to fall on our enemies from the darkness."

"I like that, a surprise attack," Aiden nodded.

"Yup, when we finish the leap, we knock down the opponent, leaving them at our mercy," Taika explained.

"A very good skill." Nahia approved.

"Once I master it, I'll let you know."

"I don't think it will take you very long, you're quite the physical specimen," Daphne told him.

Taika smiled lightly.

"Thanks, I doubt I'm all that."

"Don't be modest, you know you are," Lily told him and blew him a kiss.

Taika smiled and went a little red in the face.

"And you, Lily? How are you doing?" Ivo asked her.

"Well, I'm the best in my class by far," Lily said confidently and spread her hands and made a face that it could be no other way.

"Come off it!" Aiden replied.

"I'm the most charming one in every way, physical and magical," Lily assured him with a coquettish smile.

"Of course you are. There's no one more charming and ravishing than you in the whole Academy," Daphne told her.

"Thank you, partner. You, as pretty as you are, could also be charming and compete with me for queen of the charmers."

"Not with my surly character," Daphne replied, wrinkling her nose.

"Yeah, I won't disagree with you on that. That character of yours… charming, what you call charming… is really not…"

"And very proud of it," Daphne said, happy to be cantankerous and quarrelsome.

"What are you learning now?" Taika asked, interested.

"We're working on an impressive enchantment skill called Hallucination. Once you manage to affect another person's mind with it, you make them see things. And not just anything—no, you can get them to see their most horrendous nightmare. It's really impressive. People almost literally die of fear. I still haven't mastered it, but when I do, I'm going to make this rock-head suffer through his worst nightmares in front of everyone, and in full daylight. You'll see, it will be very funny."

Daphne laughed out loud.

"I don't see the fun in that," Aiden complained. "Don't you dare use your spells on me," he warned her.

"I'd only use it to know what your worst nightmare is. What you're afraid of," Lily told him. "I have an interest in learning…"

"I fear nothing. I am a Drakonid, born to fight. I don't fear anything. And don't you dare even look at me with a spell."

"Now I'm really curious," Daphne said.

"Leave me alone, or I'll be forced to use my Unstoppable Frenzy skill."

Lily and Daphne smiled. They did not say anything else; they did not want Aiden to get upset in case he had one of his seizures.

"You're left, Daphne, what can you tell us? How's it going?" Ivo asked her.

Daphne huffed. "I'm doing good, and bad, as usual."

"It can't be that bad," Lily said.

"Oh yeah, it's worse," Daphne replied. "The Talent classes require that I be at the library studying physiognomy of the 'fighting slave races,' as the dragons call us. It's necessary so that my healing magic is more effective. Otherwise, it's too generic and doesn't do so much good. As you know, with the punishment we all have to bear every night, plus weapons classes, I'm dead on my feet. My head can barely cope with studying. So, on that hand, bad."

"Yeah, we're all a bit like that," Nahia told her.

"We are more, because these three don't suffer in weapons class like we do," Daphne pointed out.

"Maybe not, but we suffer more in magic class," Ivo replied, nodding with his big horned head.

"On the side of healing, it's getting better. I'm happy because I can now heal different kinds of wounds and injuries. The Healing skill is easier every time. If I manage to study a bit more, I'll be even better. But I'm happy. I'd never have imagined that I could heal a wound or an illness with magic. It's unbelievable. I can even create a Ball of Healing, which radiates healing magic. It's not very powerful yet, but it does heal everything that's not very specific or serious."

"We certainly appreciate it very much," Taika told her. "I'm sure we'll need your care."

"Especially the crazy barbarian granite-head," Lily said with a comical face.

"I doubt it, I won't be needing it much." Aiden crossed his arms over his chest.

"So, I'm happy with my progress, but the way will be long and arduous," Daphne said and smiled, and her face showed the exhaustion she was feeling.

"I'm glad to see you happy, and even smiling, which is rare for you," Nahia told her and also smiled at her friend.

"Don't get used to it, it's an exception," Daphne said and frowned, wrinkling her nose.

The group smiled at the Fatum's grimace.

"We have to get to our punishment, it's time," Aiden announced, getting up.

"Oh… dear…" Lily protested.

"Yeah, we'd better go," Nahia said.

They left the dining hall and headed to the dungeons. As soon as they stepped outside, they all felt the mounting exhaustion wearing them down. Unfortunately, they had no choice but to endure and complete their punishment.

Chapter 24

Daphne pulled the cart along the middle of the corridor by the braziers, on the second underground level of the dungeons. She was already used to pulling the load, although it was heavy and burdensome, but since she was always so tired, she took it with resignation and without really thinking about it. She arrived at one of the braziers running low and got to work. She looked toward the long-barred cell in front of her. Inside was a race of aggressive creatures. From what Oihane of the Selvaris had told her, they were the Growr.

She finished loading the brazier and walked over to see them. At first, she had not dared to get close—she was not in favor of approaching the cells—out of mere precaution. But since nothing had happened during all the time she had been down here and the season was about to end and with it, her punishment, she risked it. The truth was, she was intrigued by the beings and creatures the dragons had locked up down here. A powerful Growr came up to the bars when it saw her. They were humanoid creatures with a physique similar to that of a great ape, but they looked more dangerous. They had large fangs that protruded from their mouths, and the nails of their large feet and hands were claw-like.

"Growr!" it growled, banging its powerful chest with its fists to show how strong it was. It wore primitive leather breeches with a belt made of leather too. On its torso it wore a shirt lined with feathers and on its head a crown, also of feathers. It had to be some tribal chief. Others behind it were similarly clad and wore necklaces instead of the crown.

"I see why they call you what they do. You don't need to get all cocky every time I come by. I have no intention of fighting you. You're a beastly gorilla with brutal, murderous tendencies."

The Growr paid attention to what she was saying, so Daphne guessed that although they looked like savage creatures without reason, they really were not. They might be primitive, but they were intelligent. Their clothing indicated this. Besides, if they were mere animals, the dragons would not bother putting them in prison: they would just kill them. Those creatures came from one of the conquered worlds, and they were sentient, organized beings.

The chief studied her from head to toe and said something that sounded like unintelligible, halting growls.

"Sorry, but I don't understand you," Daphne replied with a shrug, opening her arms for emphasis. She was surprised that the chief would address her. As a rule, it growled at the top of its voice and threatened her, jumping and thumping its chest so she would leave.

The chief pointed at her and then motioned for her to come closer.

"You want me to get close? I don't know if that's such a good idea." Daphne wrinkled her nose and tilted her head to one side.

The chief insisted again. Daphne could see all its powerful muscles, which intimidated her. She knew the barrier of energy between the bars would not let the Growr do anything to her, but even so… that creature was primitive and wild, awe-inspiring, and she even felt a little fear.

"Fine, I'll get closer."

Daphne almost touched the bars. The chief Growr stared at her carefully. The rest of the small tribe also had all their attention on her as they crouched, staring at her.

"What is it you…"

She could not finish the sentence. The chief leaped for her with its huge, powerful arms in front of him. It hit the barrier of energy between the bars and fell backward with a hard thump, shoved back from the strength it had used to leap forward and the rejection from the barrier of energy.

"I'm thick-headed, but it seems to me that you're even more so."

The chief got up, sore, and began to growl. It shook its arms and screamed at the top of its voice. Its growl-screams were joined by the others. They all started screaming, shaking their arms and showing their fangs aggressively. Daphne had no doubt that if they managed to grab her, they would rip her apart.

"What a bad attitude you all have, really. I'm leaving," she said and went back to her cart to continue her route. She stopped in front of the brazier, looked at the Growr, and with her spade mimicked putting out the fire. The shouts multiplied, enraged.

"You deserve to have no light, but you're in luck. I don't want any problems with the Tergnomus. I'll leave it on. Savages, worse than savages," she called to them as she traveled down the corridor.

She went on with her task while she got over the fright the Growr had given her, replenishing the low braziers and loading those that were already out. Although there were intractable creatures like the Harpiyias and the Growr down here, she stopped to watch those who most surprised her while she did her route every night. It made her job more entertaining and her exhaustion more bearable, which had multiplied enormously. It was the accumulation of days without proper rest.

Among the locked-up creatures were different types, and some caught her attention greatly. One of those was the Centaurus, a race of creatures that were half Human and half equine. She stopped in front of their cell and greeted their leader, Gizozaldi, or at least that was the name she thought she had understood. They had introduced one another and exchanged greetings and words in their respective languages for several weeks now.

"Good evening." Daphne raised her hand in greeting.

The Centaurus came to the bars and greeted her with a wave of his hand too. He said something in his language, but Daphne did not understand beyond it being some kind of greeting. Daphne could not believe such creatures existed. The lower part of the body was that of a horse and the upper part was that of a man, only it had horns, like Ivo's but somewhat shorter. They were an intelligent species, and she had tried to verbally communicate with them, although unsuccessfully so far.

"Do you need a Ball of Healing?" Daphne asked him and mimicked one with her hands. It was frustrating not to be able to communicate, although they had made progress. Not like with Egil, unfortunately, but of course Egil was a prodigy when it came to understanding and learning things. The Centaurus had explained and shown her that he had several wounded among his people in the cell. They must have arrived shortly before. She had no idea where they had come from, but she had decided to help them as she had done with the Selvaris.

The Centaurus nodded and bent over, bowing his head in a show of respect and surely gratitude. Since he was so tall, almost twice her size, even when he bent down to greet her, he still seemed very tall.

"Very well, I'll prepare one for you right away."

Gizozaldi said something in his language which Daphne guessed meant "thank you." She proceeded to create the Ball of Healing. What she did now was charge them with as much healing energy as she could without them destabilizing and exploding. She had to tread very carefully, because if she charged them too much, she might injure someone instead of healing them. An explosion of energy, even a healing one, was still explosive energy that would harm whoever it caught.

The Centaurus who were with Gizozaldi came over to see how she created the ball. They always did. It seemed to interest them a lot. Daphne wondered whether they had some kind of magic, but guessed they probably did. Even the Growr must have some, or the dragons would not be interested in them. Indeed, the more she thought, the surer she was that she was right in her assumption. The races the dragons had locked up here must all have some type of magic.

She finished creating her healing ball, and using her mind she passed it through the bars. Gizozaldi took it in his hands and then handed it to his people to use on the wounded.

"I'll get back to my route, I don't want to delay," Daphne took her leave.

The Centaurus said goodbye to her with strange sounds, a mix of a pleasant language and neighing.

The next stop she made lately was with the two races of creatures Daphne called "the Levitators." They were disconcerting. She had no doubt they both came from the same world because they had many similarities, even though they were different races.

She left the cart in front of the cell of the creatures she had named the Dark-Levitators. She had no idea what they called themselves. Oihane did not know them; they were not from her world, and she had not seen them other than when they were brought down, and then for only a brief moment.

She stood in front of the cell and watched them. They were most singular. They all formed a line and levitated about four handspans off the ground, upside down. This had her mystified: they levitated upside down. It was crazy. Their bodies were humanoid but they did not move, they simply levitated. They were tall and slim and had no hair, their heads more oval-shaped than hers. Their eyes were also oval, perpendicular to the oval of the head. It was very funny. Their skin was anthracite-black, as were their eyes, although those were somewhat lighter. They had no irises. All of this gave them a ghostly appearance. Their long arms ended in hands with seven fingers. The long legs also ended in feet with seven long toes. They wore dark robes with elegant anthracite embroidery. And if all of this was strange, there was something even stranger: their wings.

Daphne always looked at them with extreme curiosity, because they were something she had never seen before. Instead of having bird wings, or even wings like hers, they had wings shaped like seven-pointed stars. And that was not the only weird thing about them: the wings whirred. It had to be a very light vibration. And this must be how they levitated. It was very strange; they were all strange.

She walked up to the bars. She did not fear being attacked since they always remained immobile, levitating upside down with their eyes open. They seemed to be lost in the great beyond. She guessed they were either meditating, like Ivo liked to do, or asleep, or perhaps in some kind of trance that helped them cope with their incarceration. Somehow, they seemed to her like large bats, which hung upside down but also levitated upside down. It was weird, very weird.

She watched them for a long moment, as she always did.

"Hello there, how are you today?" she asked them. There was no reaction. She was sure they would not react, even to fire. They did not even seem to breathe, although they did have a nose, long and sunken.

"You are most fascinating," she said as a goodbye and left. She knew they were not going to react to her presence.

She went on with her route and, a little further on, on the opposite side of the corridor, she stopped to see the other race of creatures that had piqued her interest. She walked up to the bars. The beings inside were the absolute reverse of the Dark-Levitators. She thought of them as twins, because they were practically the same when it came to their anatomy: same oval head and eyes, same slim body, same hands and feet with seven digits each. Contrary to the Dark-Levitators, these had a pale skin, practically albino, which shone with a light so intense and clear, it hurt to look at them. They wore robes, also white, with embroidery done in a darker white to stand out. They were all white, even their eyes without irises. They also levitated, but they did not do it upside down, instead floating right side up. Hence, for her they were the reverse of their "cousins."

She stepped up to the bars with her eyes half closed because it hurt to look at them, even though she was used to the intense and powerful light of her own elemental light magic. The wings were also identical and whirred. It was barely noticeable because the light they gave off. The whole cell was lit up brightly. There were ten of them. She could not tell whether they were young or old, but she had the feeling they were not very old. Their face and hands were smooth, without any wrinkles or marks. They were also in a trance or some similar state, probably to survive this place. Perhaps to regenerate wounds? She had no idea. She would have to ask Ivo, who knew the most about meditation and keeping the body and mind in balance.

"Well, I'll go on, I just wanted to greet you," she told them, but none reacted.

She left the Luminous-Levitators and went on with her work. She had always thought the races of Kraido were unique, but now after meeting those two, they did not seem as peculiar. There were disconcerting creatures locked up down here. She felt bad for them. They had been taken out of their worlds and dragged to these dungeons of darkness and suffering. Prisoners until the dragons freed them, if they ever did, which she highly doubted. She had always thought the races of Kraido had been very unlucky with the dragons. Now she knew that the same thing happened to races from other worlds.

She kept working, lost in her own thoughts, and arrived at the Selvaris' cell. When she realized, she stopped.

"Hello, Oihane, how are you?"

The young Selvaris, who always waited for her with a smile, waved at her.

"We are much better, thanks to your kindness and magic. You are a blessing of light and healing in the midst of this world of shadow and suffering," she said in a grateful tone.

"It's nothing, I enjoy being able to help you. The Healer Talent at first seemed like a total waste to me, that it was a mistake, but little by little I find I enjoy it more and more."

"A waste? Why would you say that?"

Daphne sighed.

"I'm better at hitting than healing," she said, making a fist.

Oihane smiled.

"Oh, I see. Well, now you can do both, that's good."

"Yes, true. At least something good has come from suffering through the Academy and the dragons."

"That's a positive attitude."

Daphne looked at them and heaved a deep sigh.

"I don't know how you endure down here…" she said sadly. "I couldn't, not in these conditions…"

"Of course you could. You must survive. You can't lose hope but have faith that one day things will change and keep fighting for that day to come. We will."

"You're very brave, and you're absolutely right. We must fight and get out of here, of course we must. Blasted dragons!" she cried, enraged.

"That's the spirit."

"I have plenty of spirit. Sorry to have lost it briefly, you'll never see me like that again. We must get over our own fears and fight against those soulless monsters."

"You can count on us for that."

"Rest assured that if there's anything I can do for you, I will," Daphne promised, furious not just because of the situation the Selvaris were in, but for having lost faith because of the struggles they all faced.

Oihane nodded.

"I know. But don't take risks. The dragons will kill you. They don't lock Kraido people up here, they kill them."

"Even so, I'll find a way to help you."

"You have a brave heart, Daphne."

"Rather grumpy and quarrelsome, but thank you for the compliment."

"How much longer is your punishment?" Oihane asked Daphne with interest in her rather sad eyes.

"There's not that much left. The season is about to finish. Once it does, the punishment will end."

Oihane nodded.

"I will miss your nightly visits. All of us will," she said and indicated the rest of the group with a wave of her hand. They all smiled at Daphne.

"I'll also miss these visits."

"You will? Now you'll be able to sleep at last, something you sorely need. You have such dark circles under your eyes that not even your own light makes them vanish."

Daphne laughed out loud.

"That's true. The other day I looked at myself in the mirror and saw a nightmarish monster."

Oihane laughed.

"Not that bad."

"Yes, it is, but it's all right. I'll recover. I've become used to eating once a day, sometimes not even that, and barely sleeping. I did not believe I'd make it, but here I am. Looking like a monster, but I'm all right. My friend Lily, who is on the level above us, is taking it a lot worse. Her physical deterioration has her desperate. I really don't care whether I'm pretty or ugly, or that exhaustion makes me a little more irascible. I already am. Lily doesn't though, she lives for her beauty and charming personality."

"I'd like to meet her."

"Who knows, maybe you will one day. When you're free."

"I think it will be easier to see her down here like you, but I agree with you that it would better to meet in freedom."

"May it be so," Daphne said wistfully. "Before I leave, I'll give you a ball of light and another of healing, fully loaded."

"Thank you so much, you are wonderful."

"I'm cheeky and have little patience, but I think my heart's in the right place after all," Daphne admitted, almost as a confession, and then proceeded to create the two spheres.

A while later, Daphne was going back, all her chores done. As she went along the last stretch, pulling the now-empty cart, she was thinking about her conversation with Oihane. She wanted to find a way to help them. Not only them, but all the creatures and beings who were locked up in there. She could see no way of freeing them, just like she did not know how to free the races of Kraido. But Oihane was right. They could not lose hope. They had to keep fighting with that goal in mind. She thought about Nahia and her inner flame, which burned for freedom. She seemed never to get exhausted, despite the problems they faced and the difficulty of what they intended. A difficulty that was practically an impossibility. Even so, Daphne left the dungeons that night with the conviction that they had to fight for the freedom of everyone, to the end.

Chapter 25

Their nights of punishment were passing by, and Nahia no longer had any trouble with the Gryphons. They let her work in peace, even the Gryphon-Hawk-Cheetah. But she was always alert to potential danger; she saw that the Gryphon-Owl-Bear and the others looked at her as if she were a delicious piece of meat they wanted to eat.

That night, when she went down to the third underground level to work, she was met with a surprise. Utrek was waiting for her.

"Tonight, there's going to be a change of route," he told her.

"Really? What route?" she asked, interested.

"Route one for Burgor and you."

"Oh, good." Nahia hid a smile. At last, she would be able to speak with Garran-Zilar-Denbo, something she had been wanting to do for a long time.

"And just so you know, I'm not doing this because you've been boring me with your requests for a change of route, but for logistical reasons. The job always comes first and foremost."

"Yes, of course," Nahia replied, very serious.

"Now, get to work. I'll let you know when there's a new change of route."

"I'm not staying on route one?"

"Didn't I just tell you that it will be according to the requirements of the job?" he snapped angrily.

"Yes, of course, sorry."

"Now get to work, come on." Utrek waved her off so she would leave.

A while later, she and Burgor were on route one, sitting on the first cart of the delivery convoy.

"Happy?" Burgor asked her in an acidic tone.

"As far as can be expected, yes, I'm happy."

Burgor snorted.

"Let's hope you don't stop to chat on this route, because we have a lot to do."

"If I stop to chat, it's so they don't eat me alive."

"In my opinion, it's because you can't keep quiet."

·You Tergnomus don't get eaten as much as we humans do, so I have to take precautions."

"That's because we don't stop to chat with the prisoners."

"It's because you're lucky enough to taste bad."

"We don't taste bad!"

"That's what I've been told," Nahia shrugged.

The Tergnomus did not say another word until they reached the dragons' sector, he was so offended.

"You know what happens here. If you leave the path or get into any kind of trouble, I don't intend to help you. I'll leave you to your fate," Burgor warned her.

"Yeah, you've done it before," Nahia replied, and she could not help it sounding angry.

"I won't risk my life for you, blabbermouth."

"Yeah, you don't need to swear it, I know that already."

"Good. Start working, and fast."

The first dragons did not pose much trouble. She and Burgor worked quickly, unloading the food as fast as possible. They made sure not to leave the silver path so the repulsor belt and hat would work. It was the only way they were protected from the dragons' physical and magical attacks. But only on the silver path.

They stopped at the next cave and started unloading quickly. They maneuvered and tilted a full cart. Burgor was nervous. It was obvious from how fast he went and the sweat that moistened his forehead. The Tergnomus did not usually sweat, which was significant. Neither did they hurry. They liked to do all their jobs with precision, taking all the time necessary.

Human flesh. Fresh, the mental message reached Nahia. It was a powerful message, accompanied by a feeling of amusement. Nahia knew at once who had sent it.

A colossal red dragon came out of the cave. Spreading its wings, it took a powerful leap and landed in front of them, maintaining the safety distance.

The jump caught Burgor off guard, and he received a tremendous scare. He fell on his backside on the floor. The dragon opened its mouth and showed its fearful maw. It seemed to be going to eat them or use its fiery breath. Nahia looked at it, surprised. What was it going to do? Was it going to kill them? She had no time to wonder.

The dragon delivered a roar that left Burgor lying on his back, unconscious.

Nahia noticed and went over to the Tergnomus. He had fainted from the dreadful fright.

"What have you done to him, Lehen-Gorri-On?"

Nothing irreversible. I only frightened the Tergnomus a little. Did you know that if you scare these creatures enough, they faint? Can you believe it? It's most amusing.

Well, no, I didn't know… but yes, now that I've seen it, I believe it. You shouldn't do that, you might kill them."

I don't think so. I do not know why you worry so much for one of them. They are pretty annoying creatures, and they taste awful.

"You still want to eat me?" Nahia asked, more at ease, seeing that nothing bad had happened to Burgor.

Of course, I still want to eat you, Human flesh is exquisite.

"I'm glad to see you too. How are you?"

I am as well as I can be, locked up in these dungeons underground, condemned to die here.

"Well then."

You are fiery. I like you, Human.

"Then you won't eat me."

Did I not just say I like you? Lehen-Gorri-On said, passing its tongue along its sharp teeth,

Nahia sighed. "Are we going to quarrel again?"

No, Flameborn. Garran-Zilar-Denbo wants to speak to you. He is waiting. I only came out to greet you.

"It's always a pleasure to see you, Lehen-Gorri-On."

Same here, Flameborn.

"Don't eat Burgor, you'll get me into trouble," she told the dragon as she headed to the great silver dragon's cave.

Do not worry, the last time I ate a Tergnomus I had heartburn for a month.

Nahia shook her head and walked fast to the cave. She had to be back before Burgor woke up, before he knew she had left. She reached the entrance of the cave and Garran-Zilar-Denbo came out to meet her.

My heart rejoices to see you again, Nahia, it sent her with one of its powerful messages.

Nahia was also deeply glad to see the powerful, silver Primeval Dragon again. She ought to feel fear before such a colossal presence, but for whatever reason this was not the case. She watched it for a moment, as if she wanted to make sure her memory of it was correct. Its massive body—over two hundred and ten feet long—had impressed her the first time she had seen it and did so again. The enormous head of a horned male and that thousand-year-old gaze of the silver eyes imposed respect and fear. The dragon's entire powerful body, an intense silver color, gave off silver flashes Nahia knew were due to the powerful magic it possessed. It was a being of great power, and the magic it radiated made Nahia's skin crawl. Simply being in its presence, one had the impression of being before a semi-god. But despite being in front of the most powerful dragon she had ever met, she did not feel any danger. She trusted it. Not for its appearance, both majestic and awesome, or for its undeniable power, but for something else she could not quite explain. She trusted the great silver dragon implicitly.

"My soul rejoices to see you too, Garran-Zilar-Denbo."

I have been waiting for you.

"It's been very difficult to get to you. I'm sorry. I tried, but things didn't go very well above."

No need to apologize. I know that meetings like this are very difficult to arrange.

"I don't know if I'll be assigned this route tomorrow… maybe not."

I understand. Then we should focus on what is important, in case we cannot meet again.

"Yes, that's best."

Come inside my abode. It will be quieter. Although it may not seem so, even down here there are eyes and ears we must protect ourselves from.

"All right." Nahia went into the cave, but before she did, she looked back toward the route, trying to see those ears and eyes. She did not see any spies.

How are you doing at the Academy? Tell me, I am very interested, Garran-Zilar-Denbo said, decreasing the power of its messages when it saw Nahia frown as she received them.

"Are you interested because our destinies are linked?"

Our destinies are entwined, not exactly linked. They might be later on, but for now they only entwine.

"Hmmm, they join and separate and join and separate? Is that it? They cross?"

213

You will understand better as the events that mark your destiny take place.

"And those that mark yours?"

That is correct. See? You are already beginning to understand. The decisions and actions we both make will have consequences on our own destinies. As both destinies are entwined, they will also influence each other.

"That's why you're so interested in how I'm doing at the Academy. Because it will affect your destiny."

That is correct. It might be small or great, but it will affect me. I have the feeling it will be great, although for now it is only a feeling.

Nahia nodded. More or less, she understood and also realized why the great silver dragon was worried about her.

"Well, I couldn't say how I'm doing at the Academy. I'm suffering in Magic class, but in Sorcery I'm doing pretty well. In Weapons I'm doing terrible. Worse than that, really."

Garran-Zilar-Denbo moved its head up and down, nodding.

It is only natural. You have great magical power, but your body is not that of a warrior.

"Yeah… sometimes I'd like to be a dragon… to have both magical and physical power."

You might one day.

Nahia looked at Garran-Zilar-Denbo with utter confusion.

"Become a dragon? That's impossible."

Who told you it is?

"Well… no one… but it's impossible for a Human to transform into a dragon. Not even in my dreams does it seem possible."

And what if I told you there is one way to do so?

"A way for someone like me to become a dragon?" Nahia shook her head. The idea overwhelmed her. But Garran-Zilar-Denbo's message carried a feeling of veracity. It was not lying; what it was saying was true.

There is indeed. But I do not think this is the time to talk about it. It would take time, which is something we do not have.

"Fine. Let's focus on what's important. Only one more question… about it…"

Go ahead, Nahia, ask.

"The opposite can also happen, right? I mean… dragons can transform into Humans?"

They can, indeed, into Humans and other creatures and beings. But not all dragons. Only the most powerful. Primeval Dragons like me that are thousands of years old.

"Oh... wow... you flabbergast me..."

There are many things regarding Dragon Magic and its power that you do not know. You will learn more with time.

"Yeah, I don't know a lot about that, I realize that more and more every passing day. Can you become a Human?"

Garran-Zilar-Denbo raised its head and Nahia thought she could see a smile on its face, although being a fearsome dragon, she could not really tell.

I can indeed. I am one of those who do have the power to do so among my people.

"That's amazing! Why don't you? We could plan an escape with you in Human form!" Nahia was very excited.

Take it easy, little Flameborn, it is not that simple. For a dragon to take on the form of another being, it requires a complex magical process. It also needs to consume a great source of external power, since the inner power of a dragon is not enough to complete the transformation. And even if I had that external source of power, this collar around my neck would not allow me to perform such an act.

"Oh... wow... for a moment I got all excited about the possibilities."

It is understandable. Besides, I cannot abandon my faithful to their fate.

"You mean the Faction of the New Tomorrow, right? The one formed by dissident dragons of the five clans that seek to change the Path."

Yes, them. I am their leader. They are my responsibility. Together, we have fought to stop the bloodshed and the obsession for absolute power and dominion that have ruled our race for thousands of years. I cannot leave them to their death here.

"But there must be others that escaped, aren't there? Perhaps if you could get to them..."

There are. And they are awaiting my return above, on the surface. But I will not return without my faithful.

"I see. This loyalty to your people does you credit." Nahia understood the great silver dragon, and she found it a being with lofty principles.

Do not worry about that now. What is important at this time is that you follow your destiny.

"You put a lot of weight on this supposed destiny of mine. What if it's not so important? What if it's nothing but a regular destiny? Or worse, what if I die in the Academy?"

That could happen, yes, but I believe you will find a way to survive. I believe it because we are linked and entwined in the threads of a destiny of great importance. One that might change not only this world, but others as well.

"That's a lot of destiny." Nahia made a grimace. It was too much for her.

It is, what little I have been able to see, but I believe in its great impact on this and other worlds.

"I'm not so sure, but what I can promise is that I will try to survive, and I will fight to achieve the freedom of the slave races of Kraido, and that of other worlds. I'll fight to free them from the dragons."

That goal, that destiny you pursue, is perfectly aligned with what I have been able to glimpse.

"Let's hope I live to accomplish it," Nahia said without too much hope that it might be so.

If you do not mind, I would like to have a vision. It will help me interpret the movements in the threads of destiny according to your latest decisions and actions.

"Yes, of course, no problem," Nahia offered.

Garran-Zilar-Denbo concentrated and Nahia felt a powerful magic radiate from its body. This magical radiation reached her, bathing her entirely. The powerful dragon began to flash bright silver at intervals. It happened like the slow heartbeat of a huge heart. Nahia was calm because she had already had an experience like this with the great Primeval Dragon and knew nothing would happen to her.

The rhythm of the flashes increased, just like the power they came with. Nahia closed her eyes to protect them from the powerful light. Even with her eyes shut, she could feel the brightness increasing in power and frequency. She was about to move away just in case.

Stay, I need you beside me to be able to glimpse beyond, Garran-Zilar-Denbo said, and it felt like a plea.

Nahia stopped and stayed beside the great dragon while the flashes came faster every time. Finally, a last flash, huge, lit up the whole cavern. She felt a charge of powerful magic filling everything.

"What did you see?" Nahia said, opening her eyes, barely containing herself.

I have examined the threads of destiny... in the middle of a vision... using all my power… it is the only way I can see something, it sent her, and Nahia felt Garran-Zilar-Denbo's utter exhaustion.

Nahia nodded.

"Do you have good or bad news?"

Our entwined destinies are consolidating… also the third one we identified the last time we did this.

"That of Lasgol and Camu?"

Indeed, I have seen the Human again… blond… with the young Higher Drakonian… your destinies are joining… but are not all linked yet… you must join them…

"I thought I had. We're already allies. I met them in Tremia, and we're now collaborating in the fight against the dragons."

There might be something else missing… for the destinies to entwine.

"Do you know what it might be?"

I am afraid I could not see it… I do not know what it might be…

"I'll try to find them again and see what it is."

Do that. It is very important… they are the key to your destiny and you for theirs…

"All right."

One more thing… I have glimpsed, very far and very faint, a fourth thread, an additional destiny entwining with ours…

"Wow, that's new. Could you see who it is?"

Unfortunately, no. It still has not begun to entwine… but it is… I felt that it also comes from Tremia… and not only one person… it is more than one…

"Do you know how many?"

It is not clear yet, but I saw five points of light…

Nahia huffed.

"That's not very much information to locate them."

I am sorry… it is all I was able to glimpse.

"Don't worry, I'm sure I'll cross paths with them. I'll be alert. Five points of light, I'll remember."

Very well… remember the scale… it has power that will help you with your destiny… with your choices… it will guide you.

Nahia touched the silver scale at her nape under her hair.

"I'll keep that in mind."

Very well… now go… be very careful… the threads of destiny… show great danger.

"I can imagine. Thank you, Garran-Zilar-Denbo. Until we meet again." Nahia said goodbye and left.

She reached Lehen-Gorri-On.

"Have you been good?"

The Tergnomus is alive. Take him, and good luck.

"Thank you, I'm going to need it."

Nahia put Burgor in the cart. She climbed up and urged the beasts on. She headed back, thinking about everything she had talked about with Garran-Zilar-Denbo and the repercussions it would have.

Chapter 26

It was the last night of punishment, and Nahia was feeling a bit strange. On the one hand, she wanted to be free of that torture and be able to sleep and rest properly. She was worn out. And not only her, all her comrades were the same: the Igneous Squad, the Ardent Squad, and the Searing Squad. Exhaustion was affecting everyone. Some bore it better than others, but in general they were all equally exhausted.

"Ready for work?" she told Utrek as a greeting when she saw him in the prep room of the Tergnomus.

"That's the spirit, I see Burgor inspires you."

Nahia looked at Utrek and then at Burgor, who was getting ready beside a closet.

"He inspires me in a way that's hard to explain," Nahia replied with sarcasm.

"The Tergnomus have that innate ability. We inspire others with our work and hard effort."

Nahia could not help grinning. The inability to pick up on irony seemed generalized among the Tergnomus.

"Oh, indeed."

"Today you have a change of route," Utrek informed them suddenly.

"Change? Why?" Nahia did not like that, least of all this being the last night.

"Functional needs," Utrek replied, using one of his favorite answers.

"What route?" Burgor asked.

"Route four. Maintrek is sick and can't cover it."

Burgor frowned.

"All right, I'll deal with it."

"Very well, off you go." Utrek sent them on their way.

They started their shift and Burgor led the carts to the left, along a cave they had not visited before. Nahia began to worry. She was safe on route one because of Garran-Zilar-Denbo's protection, not on route four. She began to have bad feelings about what awaited them.

"What's route four like?"

"Like any other route. It's work."

"Yeah, I guessed as much. But what kind of prisoners are there on route four?"

"Lesser prisoners."

"Oh, lesser… then they're less dangerous, right?"

Burgor shrugged.

"All the prisoners are dangerous," he said and urged the beasts to go faster.

"Then why are they lesser?"

"They aren't as important to the dragons. And stop asking a thousand questions, you're giving me a headache."

"I'm asking because you never give me any warning."

"That's not my job…"

"Yeah, yeah," Nahia cut him short. She knew all the answers of the cantankerous Tergnomus.

The way along the new route was not so different from the others they had done. The caves they went by were similar. What she did find odd was that no one came out to fetch the food when they unloaded it.

"There are prisoners in these caves, aren't there?"

Burgor glared at her with a look of disbelief.

"Of course there are prisoners. Otherwise, why unload food?"

"That's what I was wondering."

"Less questions and more work."

They arrived at an area that surprised Nahia. There were fires at the entrances of the caves. It was the first time she had seen this. She thought perhaps it was because of the temperature of the place. But no, the temperature was normal, neither warm nor cool. The atmosphere was damp and grim and there was very little light, only some torches along the silver path.

"Are those fires allowed?" she asked Burgor.

"They are."

"What creature…" Nahia was about to ask. It did not seem to fit that there were creatures that built fires, but she stopped when she saw the first one. It was a Human.

"Unload!" Burgor said.

Naha climbed onto the second cart from the back of the line and grabbed a piece. It did not make sense to tilt the cart for a single piece. The Human, a middle-aged man, came up to the piece and slowly picked it up, slinging it on his back. Without a word, he headed back to the cave.

"Who is it?" Nahia asked Burgor blankly.

"A Human prisoner."

"When you don't want to collaborate, you nail it," Nahia said.

"Who cares? He's a prisoner, keep working."

"I've already unloaded."

"Who told you it's a single piece?"

"There's only one Human…" she started to say before realizing there were ten more around the fire.

"Some people are too smart for their own good…" Burgor said grumpily. "Unload four more."

Nahia did as Burgor ordered.

"Who are they?" she asked again.

Burgor ignored her. Seeing that the stubborn Tergnomus was not going to tell her anything, she did not ask again. They went on with the route. Things got even stranger at the next stop. The prisoner was a Fatum, also middle-aged. With him were half a dozen Fatum, male and female. Nahia could not explain why the dragons would have Humans and Fatum down here.

They continued on the route, and at the next cave they stopped. Around the low-burning fire, another half dozen prisoners waited, this time Scarlatum. They unloaded three pieces and Nahia stared at them. She could not hold back her question.

"Who are you?"

The Scarlatum prisoners looked at her for a moment. They did not answer. They fetched the pieces and took them inside the cave.

"No chatting, we have to finish our deliveries," Burgor said in an angry tone.

Nahia waited a moment longer to see whether any of the Scarlatum would speak to her. They took one of the pieces and started roasting it over the fire. That was most strange.

At the next stop, something similar happened. This time they were Felidae who, like the Scarlatum, fetched the piece without replying to any of Nahia's questions. There were a dozen of them:

tigers, panthers, and lions.

"Can you talk to me? What happened to you?" Nahia insisted. She wanted to know what was going on here and why they were locked up.

"They won't answer, move on," Burgor said.

Nahia huffed in frustration and continued with their deliveries. At the next cave, beside the fire, a dozen Tauruk-Kapro were waiting. They unloaded the pieces. Without waiting a moment, they started roasting two of them.

"This is most strange…" muttered Nahia, who could not understand why the dragons would keep these prisoners locked up. They belonged to the slave races. The dragons did not bother sending them to the dungeons. They killed them, like they did with them at the Academy.

They got to the last cave with fires before leaving that sector of the caverns. Waiting for the delivery were several people: Drakonids. If having prisoners from the other slave races down here made no sense, having Drakonids in prison made even less.

"Five pieces," Burgor told her.

Nahia sighed and helped the Tergnomus with the unloading maneuver. Six pieces fell off.

"Retrieve the extra piece," Burgor told her, pointing his finger at it.

Nahia sighed. She did not think the Drakonid would attack her, but in this underground world anything might happen. One of the Drakonids stepped forward. He signaled to Nahia to come for the piece.

Nahia did not know whether to trust it. Her senses told her not to. She watched the Drakonid for a moment. Although it was difficult to know his age because of their race, she thought he was older. She thought of asking him who he was, but thinking back to her lack of success with the others and since he was a Drakonid, she dismissed the idea.

She had no choice, so she stepped forward to retrieve the piece carefully, looking at the Drakonid in case he tried anything. She reached one of the pieces and grabbed it to drag it. She was about to step back when she heard a question.

"Who are you? You look familiar."

Nahia looked up toward the voice. It was the Drakonid. She

could not help looking surprised.

"I'm… Nahia."

"Nahia. Pretty name. Nahia who?" the Drakonid asked in a deep, calm voice.

"Nahia Aske."

The Drakonid was thoughtful. Then he smiled.

"I thought you were familiar."

Nahia was very surprised by this.

"Do you know me?"

The Drakonid shook his head.

"No, I don't know you. I haven't had the pleasure. Not until today."

"Then who are you? What are you doing here? How come you're all here?"

"Those are too many questions. I see you have an inquisitive mind. That is good," the Drakonid said and smiled again.

"I don't understand what's going on here."

"What's going on here is no longer important. All of us are doomed to die here. It's only a matter of time."

"I'm sorry…"

"You have nothing to regret. It's not your fault. Those of us who are down here accept our fate. We did so a long time ago."

"Don't speak to him, let's go!" Burgor scolded Nahia in a temper.

"Just a moment, I'm coming."

"No moments! Get on the cart!" Burgor ordered her.

"But I need to know…"

"Do as the Tergnomus says. You shouldn't speak to me. It's for your own good."

"But who are you? Why am I familiar?"

The Drakonid smiled.

"I'm a shadow of the past that will soon fade away. Don't take an interest in me. Go on your way. Live a long life. Try to make it happy and prosperous."

Nahia did not know what to do. The Drakonid did not answer her questions, and Burgor seemed more annoyed than usual.

"Get on the cart, now!" he shouted at her.

Nahia looked at the Drakonid one last time in case he said anything else, but he said goodbye with a nod and turned back to the fire. Nahia had to resign herself and pulled the extra piece toward the cart. Then she loaded it, ran, and climbed onto the cart beside Burgor, who urged the beasts to get away from there.

For a while, they did not speak and continued their route. At last, Nahia decided to ask.

"Why are you so insistent that I not speak to the Drakonid?"

"I've told you that you talk too much. We're here to work. Stop talking to the prisoners or it'll cost us both our lives. I don't care if you die, that's your choice, but I don't want to die because of you," he told her and glared at her with hatred.

Nahia was silent for a moment, thinking. Something did not quite fit.

"Other times, you've left me where I was without caring what happened to me. Why not here?"

Burgor snorted, annoyed

"Do. Not. Speak. To. The. Prisoners. That's it."

She did not like the answer, but Nahia knew that Burgor was not going to tell her anything. When he shut up and refused to talk, there was nothing to do.

They continued on their route, and the final stretch had no incidents. Nahia finished her shift with a strange feeling inside her. She did not know what it was, but she felt that she was missing something important. She had to resign herself though and went up to the surface to go to sleep. In no time they would return to their training, and she was already beginning to feel the accumulated exertion. It was like a huge slab that pressed on her back and head as she went back up. She also realized that every time she found it harder to get back up to the surface. The endless stairs were an additional punishment at the end of every shift.

She came out of the dungeons and breathed in the night air. At least she was alive. She would fight to stay alive and try to help the prisoners she had just seen. Perhaps they no longer had hope, but Nahia did—both for her and all of the slave peoples of Kraido. One day, they would reach freedom. One day she would free those poor, unhappy wretches at the bottom of the dungeons.

Chapter 27

Several weeks had gone by since the end of the punishment, and even though it was over and she could now enjoy her well-earned additional rest, Nahia did not seem to be able to fully recover. She was not the only one. Lily and Daphne also seemed to struggle. The accumulated exhaustion did not seem to want to leave them entirely. The consequences remained. The sustained effort they had to make at weapons training, plus the supplement of physical exercise at the gym so they did not lag behind, did not aid their full recovery.

That evening they were all in the bedroom, getting ready to go to sleep, giving their bodies a chance to rest before the next day of tough training.

Sitting on her bed, Nahia was lost in her own thoughts.

"Everything all right?" Lily asked her.

"Yeah… I'm just tired… and a little worried."

"Exhausted is the normal mood in this place," Lily joked, poking her tongue out as if she could not bear even her soul.

"What's bothering you?" Daphne asked Nahia as she lay on her own bed and watched her.

"What could possibly bother her here? Not dying tomorrow?" said Lily, raising her arms in an obvious gesture.

Nahia looked at the Scarlatum and nodded.

"Yeah, that too, but I was thinking about what happened in Tremia… Drameia."

"We survived the mission, but I'm worried about the ones fighting there…"

"On our side or the other?" Daphne asked, raising an eyebrow.

"The other," Nahia admitted, lowering her voice and looking at the screen that separated them from the boys.

"You're worried about Lasgol, Camu, and the Norghanians you met? The ones we helped to free their friend Gerd from the war camp?" Daphne asked in a tone of interest.

Lily poked her head out of one end of the screen to see whether the boys were paying attention to their conversation, especially Aiden.

"Can we talk?" Nahia asked in a low voice.

"Yes, don't worry, granite-head's sleeping," Lily nodded.

"I can't get them out of my head. Them and Egil. We have to find a way to help them."

"From what we saw at the battle of the capital, they're pretty well off with those Norghanian Rangers," Lily commented.

"And Lasgol was able to kill a dragon with his golden bow. I don't know how he did it, I can't even imagine it, but he did. We all saw the corpse of the great winged monster."

Nahia nodded.

"But they won't be able to hold out for long. The casualties they're suffering are high. The capital will be taken and their forces will fall. The dragons don't allow defeats. The red dragon king is the most savage and deceitful of all of them. He'll go himself to destroy the city rather than suffer a defeat."

"The casualties in our army are even greater," Lily reminded her, looking sad. "And they're innocent people, sent to die on the battlefield because they are slaves to the dragons."

"Because of the dragon lords' excessive greed and desire for conquest," Daphne added.

"Yeah, and we are among them, let's not forget that," Lily said.

"I think we need to help each other," said Nahia. "I'm sure that if we collaborate with Egil, Lasgol, Camu, and their friends, we'll not only help them but also our people."

"I don't see it as clearly. If we help those Rangers, we'll only be letting more of our own get killed…" Daphne scratched her temple and was thoughtful.

Nahia thought it through as well. The situation was complicated, since they were on the side of the bloodthirsty invaders, the side of evil, and this was unquestionable. The Norghanians, all of Tremia, were defending themselves from the dragon invasion. Unfortunately, part of the invading army were the slaves the dragons sacrificed in their war without any consideration, poor souls who were not to blame for what was going on and who did not deserve to die. But neither did the Norghanians or the other inhabitants of Tremia.

"We're on the wrong side. We fight on the side of evil. We and the other slave races that form the dragon army," Nahia said, summing up her thoughts and those of her two friends.

"That's true, no one's arguing against that," Lily told her. "But do you want us and the soldiers of our army to die instead of our rivals?"

"Of course she doesn't want that," Daphne intervened. "The question is how to stop innocents from dying on both sides."

Nahia nodded repeatedly.

"That's what we need to try and accomplish: that no innocents die. Whichever side they're on."

"That sounds impossible, because they're going to fight to the death one way or another," Lily said.

"It won't be easy, I know. But we can try to help both sides, the innocents on both sides," said Daphne.

"That's what we have to do, you're right. What I don't know is how." Nahia let out a loud, long sigh of frustration.

"What we're hoping to do is very complicated. There's no easy way of doing it," said Daphne.

"And it'll be very dangerous," Lily added.

"Danger is our middle name," a small smile appeared on Daphne's face.

"That'll be yours, mine is 'Irresistible'," Lily joked, tossing her long hair to one side with a sensual shake.

"Mine is 'grumpy'," joked Daphne.

Nahia smiled. Her friends were trying to diffuse the situation, and she was grateful for it from the bottom of her heart. She had too many worries she did not know how to solve in her head. Being able to talk with them, even if they could not find a solution, was good for her. Keeping them inside was bad for her emotional health, she could feel as much.

"So, you fully trust Egil's friends," Lily said after a moment. "You're determined to help them, so it must be because you trust them. Or are you taking a risk?"

"That's a good question." Daphne joined her as she sat on the bed with her legs crossed and shifted her wings to adjust them. "In Norghana, at the war camp, we risked our lives to help them. Yes, I know it was because we were looking for the golden weapons capable of killing dragons and they have them, but even so, we risked our lives. We'd better be able to trust them. I trust Egil. There's no malice in him. He won't betray us despite everything he's going through. He should be enraged, furious, frustrated and wanting to kill everyone, but he isn't. That's surprising and shows strong character. He has the noble soul of a good person. The others... I don't know them. I can't tell. What do you say, Nahia?"

Nahia sighed deeply and pondered her answer. It was a good question, an important one.

"Yes, I trust them. Don't ask me why, but I trust them completely. We've agreed on an alliance, to help each other."

"So, you trust them," Daphne said.

"Yeah, at least those I've met so far."

"And those are Egil himself; Lasgol; the Higher Drakonian, Camu; and what's the name of the other two Rangers who were with them?" Lily asked.

"Molak and Luca. Yes, I trust them. They gave me the impression of being trustworthy."

"What do you know about the two new ones?" Daphne asked her. "They weren't on Egil's list. They aren't any the Snow Panthers he told us about."

Nahia closed her eyes, remembering what she had talked about with Lasgol and his two comrades.

"They're not Snow Panthers. They're from a similar group. I don't remember the name they mentioned…"

"So, it seems the Rangers, instead of having squadrons, have groups with different names," said Lily.

"I'm not sure about it all, but I do know that these two groups exist and are comrades of Egil," Nahia said.

"What else do you know about them?" Daphne leaned over, interested.

"Molak is a Sniper. Apparently, he's very good at releasing from great distances with a large bow. From what I understood, he can shoot double the range of a dragon."

"Wow, that *is* impressive!" Lily cried.

"Shhhh, you're going to wake up the rock-head," Daphne said, putting her finger to her lips.

"Okay, I'll lower my voice, but I still find it awesome. That means this Molak can attack a dragon from outside its reach. That's wonderful." Lily was imagining in her mind what that might be like.

"Remember that a dragon can close distances very fast," Daphne replied so she would not get too excited.

"Yeah, and then destroy you, I know."

"Luca is a Man Hunter which, from what I gathered, is a Ranger who specializes in pursuing and capturing criminals, outlaws, and the like."

"What are outlaws?" Lily asked.

"That's what I asked," Nahia nodded. "They're people who do evil: rob, kill, things like that."

"To other humans?" Daphne was surprised, and her face showed it.

Nahia nodded.

"Their society is very different than ours. If one of us commits a crime, steals or kills—which almost never happens, since we live under the yoke of the dragons and have enough problems without creating more—the Drakonid soldiers deal with our punishment."

"Which by the law of the dragons is death," said Lily.

"That's right. In their world they have Rangers and soldiers who pursue those who do evil deeds to their neighbors. They don't have dragons that dominate and subjugate everyone," Nahia waved her hands in frustration.

"They don't for now," Daphne rectified.

"We must help them so that such a thing never happens, so Tremia doesn't become Kraido," Nahia said, convinced.

"Yeah, we have to stop it, although it seems too dangerous and unlikely in my opinion," Lily said, bowing her head.

"Let's not lose our hope so quickly. Nothing is truly impossible," Nahia said in a hopeful tone.

"And Lasgol? What kind of Ranger is he?" Daphne asked.

"Lasgol is something special. For starters, he's like us. He has magic, which the other Rangers don't have," Nahia explained. "Magic he's trying to recover, just like his memory."

"The Immortal Dragon robbed him of both," Daphne said, who knew the story.

"Yeah," said Lily, "I remember you telling us, Nahia."

"Apart from having magic, he's like five different types of Rangers. He's a prodigy."

"Look at this Lasgol!" Lily smiled.

"Besides, Lasgol and Camu seem to be part of my destiny, a very important part from what Garran-Zilar-Denbo glimpsed in his visions."

"I'm not sure I trust this dragon…" Daphne said doubtfully.

"I definitely don't trust it. After all, it's a dragon," Lily said, shaking her head.

"Garran-Zilar-Denbo is a dragon, but not like the others. That's why it's being held a prisoner in the depth of the dungeons. The dragons have sent it there as punishment until its death," Nahia told them. "For wanting to change the Path of the Dragons. It's supposed to be the leader of the dissenters: the Faction of the New Tomorrow. But we have no record of its existence. Where are the dragons that form it? Why haven't they tried to rescue their leader? It doesn't sound too credible to me…" Daphne was doubtful, and the more she reasoned through it, the more doubts she had. Her face said it all.

"Dragons are dragons. They're evil beings without souls. I also find it hard to believe that any of them would want to be civilized, knowing what they're like," said Lily, who did not have doubts and was absolutely sure they could not trust dragons.

"I know, but I believe Garran-Zilar-Denbo. I want to think that this destiny that links us is the one that will lead us to freedom. I don't know how or when, but I want to think that if we join Lasgol and his people and Garran-Zilar-Denbo and its followers, we'll be able to make this dream come true."

"It seems to me like too much wishing and too much trusting," Daphne warned her.

"Yeah, I'm thinking the same thing," Lily said. "Hasn't it occurred to you that all of this might be a stratagem this dragon is using to buy its own freedom?"

"Garran-Zilar-Denbo? No, I don't believe so…"

"Think about it. It tells you of a joint destiny, one of freedom, a dragon and a prisoner. I think it's using you," said Lily.

"She's not wrong, you know. It gains your trust, tricks you, you help, and then it betrays you. It's a dragon, after all," Daphne warned her.

Nahia sighed deeply.

"I know you want to protect me, and I am really grateful. I also understand that you don't trust a dragon you haven't even met. But I've been with this dragon, and there's something that inspires me to trust that it's telling the truth. I don't think this is a trick."

"You wouldn't be the first or last to be deceived," said Lily.

"I know… I know…"

"Take it as a warning," Daphne told her. "Don't be too confident. There's nothing bad about being a little suspicious, least of all when you're gambling with your life."

"You're right. I need to be careful and not trust blindly. It's a dragon, after all."

"Exactly," Lily nodded hard.

"In any case, whether Garran-Zilar-Denbo is an ally or will ultimately betray me, we must find a way to free Egil."

"And Oihane and her people!" Daphne added.

"Rescuing Egil and the other creatures from the dungeons is madness," Lily warned them.

"Madness we must somehow achieve," Nahia said.

"We need to think carefully," said Daphne. "But we must do something. We can't let them die in the dungeons. None of them will ever get out alive. Even if its madness, we have to do something, knowing the situation they're in."

"That's true. Otherwise, we'll lose our own humanity…" Nahia shook her head.

"It's madness that will mean our death. The dragons will discover us and eat us alive," Lily said with perfect certainty.

"I'm not saying you're not right, Lily, but letting them die… down there, in that world of darkness, without hope…" Nahia was shaking her head.

"I feel the same way. Those creatures don't deserve an end like that," Daphne said.

"No one does," said Lily. "But we can't rescue them. We'd need an army for it. Besides, one that can kill dragons, because otherwise we'd still fail."

Nahia and Daphne looked at one another.

"You might not be wrong."

"Of course I'm not," Lily said, sure of it.

"There are armies fighting the dragons right now. And some, like Lasgol, can kill them…" said Nahia.

"And they'll want to save Egil," added Daphne.

"You're both crazy," Lily told them. "This is monumental madness."

"Well. We don't have to be hasty. Let's keep the idea in our minds. We may find a way. It doesn't have to be right away. It can be in the near future," Nahia said.

"That's right. We'll think of a way, calmly, but let's not dismiss the idea. We have to manage to get those people out of the dungeons," said Daphne.

"Like I said, you're both crazy." Lily made a face of disbelief.

Chapter 28

Autumn was becoming more evident at the Academy. The summer temperatures had vanished and now it was cool all day. A breeze that pushed gray clouds threatened to bring more than cold winds. The trees and gardens were painted ochre, and the spirits of the Igneous Squad were the same color.

That morning, they were at The Arena. They had weapons training. They had been practicing offensive and defensive moves for weeks. Urus was making them repeat to the breaking point, without any mercy. They were all capable of doing the movements without mistakes and decent skill. But Nahia, Daphne, and Lily could not finish the classes. They were improving and getting closer to the end, but they never finished. Exhaustion overwhelmed them in the end.

"Today we'll begin exercising in pairs," Urus announced as soon as they lined up in front of him.

This was new, and Nahia cheered. If they did not have to do a thousand repetitions, they might be able to finish the class. Practicing in pairs was less tough, they all knew this, and she saw the same sign of relief on Daphne and Lily's faces.

"You'll do the whole class in pairs. One will attack and the other defend. Then you'll switch. You'll do all the movements."

Nahia liked this a lot more. Without a doubt, she would get less tired practicing with a partner. She had to hold back a small smile of joy.

"At the end of the class, you'll fight me so I can check your improvement."

They did not like this at all. She thought she had heard him wrong. How were they going to fight a duel with a weapons master who was also a beastly Tauruk? It could not be, she must have heard wrong. She looked at Taika, and judging by his look of concern she realized she had indeed heard right.

"Get into pairs," he ordered them.

Nahia paired with Daphne, Lily with Ivo, and Taika with Aiden.

"One in a defensive position and the other in an offensive one. Start with the first attack and defense movement. Now."

They began the movements, and Urus counted the repetitions out loud so they would not lose a beat. They all strove to do the moves well, since they already had them memorized, and they did them almost without thinking. Once they finished the first round of exercises, Urus ordered them to change partners. And so they did throughout the class, until the dreaded moment arrived.

Urus ended the exercises for the day. Just as Nahia had calculated, she, Daphne, and Lily had been able to finish thanks to the exercise and partner switches. The three were exhausted and could barely stand, but they had managed to finish the class, an important milestone for them.

"Very well. Now you'll fight me so I can see how much you have progressed in class," Urus told them.

Nahia swallowed. She could barely stand; she was in no shape to fight against anyone, least of all a Tauruk weapons master. It was crazy. She would not withstand even the first blow. As she thought about it, she realized that if this happened, Urus would not let her pass his class. This demoralized her. She was making great efforts in class and out of it at the gym, and the little reward she received seemed unfair. She sighed. Life was unfair, of this there was no doubt. She would have to overcome it somehow. At that moment, she did not know how she would do it, but she had to find a way.

"The strongest ones first. I'll start with you, Tauruk," he told Ivo and signaled him to step up. "Everyone else, form a circle around us. Watch and learn. Don't intervene in any way, don't even speak. Concentration is imperative in a duel."

Ivo snorted through his large nostrils and stepped forward until he was standing in front of the weapons master.

"It's free combat, but you can only use your sword and shield in the way we have practiced," Urus told him.

Ivo nodded.

"Understood."

"Stand in position," Urus said, and they both took a defensive stance. Urus greeted him with a nod and Ivo did the same. "The combat begins."

Ivo did not attack. He stayed in the defensive stance awaiting the attack of the master, which was not long in coming. With a fast movement on The Arena, as if he were sliding on ice with both feet, he came at Ivo and delivered a combined attack of steps one and two. Ivo was surprised, first by the speed of the attack and then by its power. He blocked the first move with his sword instinctively, and then he felt a smack on his back that went from his arm to his shoulder. The second blow he blocked with his shield, and when Urus's sword hit him, it struck him so hard Ivo nearly lost his protection.

They all watched the fight, stunned. And they were not the only ones watching their weapons master fighting one of his pupils.

The other two squads were also doing the same exercise. Nahia watched the combat, and now it was Ivo who was attacking at an order from Urus. His movements looked clumsy and slow compared to the master's, but he hit hard. They could hear the blow of metal on metal. The swords were dull, without edge, to avoid accidental deaths, even the masters', which Nahia was grateful for. But even a blow with the flat of the sword hurt a lot; it could break bones just like the shield, since they were both solid steel.

Ivo tried his best. He hit and defended himself from Urus's terrible blows, trying to equal the master's power. He could not. Urus's blows were much stronger. In the end, the master disarmed Ivo with a feint of his sword. Ivo's dropped on the arena. Urus followed up the attack with a strong blow to the ribs that made Ivo double down to one side. Urus finished him off with a slash to the stomach that sounded hollow and painful. Nahia's eyes opened wide, unable to believe the master could deliver such blows at Ivo.

"You have been defeated. Your movements are slow and clumsy. Your technique is poor. You must improve. You may go."

Ivo left, holding his rubs and bent over with pain His face showed acute suffering. The blows had been hard.

"Your turn, Drakonid," Urus told Aiden and pointed the sword at him.

Aiden straightened up and went to face the master with the confidence that always guided him. Aiden was not afraid. His eyes shown with pride, for being there and for facing his instructor. Nahia had to admit he had courage, seeing what Urus had done to Ivo. Common sense, however, was a different story; Aiden did not have much of that.

The combat began, and soon they saw it was going down the same path. Aiden was slightly faster and more agile than Ivo, but he hit with less power. Urus attacked and defended himself with greater speed and power than the Drakonid. Aiden tried everything. At least everything he knew and had learned so far. But he could not put pressure on Urus, who ended up defeating him with a slash to the stomach and a thrust to the heart. Both blows were executed with tremendous strength that left Aiden breathless and bent over with pain.

Urus spoke.

"You have been defeated. Your movements are also slow, although not clumsy. Your technique is regular. You must improve. You may go."

Taika was next. Here, things changed. The Felidae-Tiger was much more agile and a lot swifter than Ivo or Aiden. More so than everyone in their squad really, and although he hit with less strength than his previous comrades, he was far more accurate. They fought for a while, and the instructor had a hard time defeating him, it was not as simple as it had been with Ivo and Aiden. He had to work harder. He finally managed to hit Taika in his right leg, which left him limping, and finished him off with a reverse shield blow which left him lying on the ground.

"You have been defeated. Your movements are fast and your blows accurate. Your technique is acceptable. Your power should be greater, you must improve. You may go."

And then the fateful moment came for the girls. Nahia did not start shaking because she did not even have the strength to do so.

"Let the Human step forward," Urus said.

Nahia tried to maintain her composure and walk with her back straight, although inside she was nervous and scared. The blows she was about to receive would be painful, and there was no escaping them. Well, there was—defeating Urus—but that was nothing more than a fantasy, given the circumstances. She stood in front of the instructor and breathed in deeply, seeking to calm her nerves. She was not going to win and she was not going to get off free from the beating, but she would try to do her best, because she had to pass this class if she wanted to stay alive.

The combat began and Nahia stood in a defensive stance. Instead of waiting for the instructor's first attack, which would surely wreak havoc on her arms, she decided to attack first. She had nothing to lose, since she was going to be defeated anyway. She moved forward and delivered a direct thrust at the face of the enormous Tauruk.

Urus did not seem surprised by the sudden attack. He covered his face with his shield and her sword hit the metal and was thrown upward. Nahia knew she had a moment to follow with a second attack before the instructor's counterattack, so she delivered a cut to his right thigh as he had done with Taika. In fact, it was a very similar attack combination to the one the instructor had used on Taika. Unfortunately, the result was not the same. Urus saw it coming, and with a swift downward movement of his shield he blocked the attack again. Nahia had already expected to fail, but she had tried, so she was pleased. And then pain came. Urus's counterattack was brutal. A tremendous blow on Nahia's shield rendered her left arm useless and made her shield fall to The Arena. He followed with a thrust to the stomach, which Nahia tried to deflect with her sword but could not. When both swords clashed, her arm cramped and she had to drop her weapon, which fell on the ground. Urus's sword stroke hit her in the stomach hard and she doubled down in pain, an intense pain that hurt so much she dropped down to her knees.

"You have been defeated. Your movements are pretty fast and your blows quite accurate, but not enough. Your technique is acceptable. Your strength and endurance are unacceptable. You have to improve a lot. You may go."

A moment later and not before, because she was unable to, Nahia straightened up, her body and pride both sore. She had fallen like a weak combatant. That hurt more than the blows she had received. She went back to her place in the circle. She was not sure whether she would be able to stand much longer, she did not have the strength for even that. She felt like a pitiful warrior when, beaten by exhaustion, she had to sit down on The Arena floor.

After Nahia's disastrous duel it was Daphne's turn, and she stepped forward with a grim look. She already knew what awaited her, and she was muttering something under her breath, surely nothing nice. The combat began and Daphne also launched an attack with the little strength she had left. Her enraged face was a clear sign that she was not going to leave anything in reserve. She delivered a cut to Urus's neck, which he blocked with his sword, and she followed with a stroke to his chest. The weapons master blocked it with his shield, and there Daphne's strength ended. Her face was livid and her arms could not hold her shield and sword, so she let them drop at her sides.

Urus looked at her blankly, as if it was a ruse. Daphne had attacked with all the strength she had left. All of it. Now she could barely hold herself up. The weapons master had no mercy. With a swift slide forward, he hit her first on the sword and then the shield. Both blows were delivered with tremendous force. Daphne's arms could not bear the punishment, and her sword and shield fell to The Arena floor. A moment later, Urus swept Daphne off her feet with a blow of his sword on her calves. Daphne's legs swung upward and the rest of her body went backward as she fell on her back. As she lay on the ground, exhausted and sore, Urus put the tip of his sword to her throat.

"Attacking the way you did is not intelligent. If you are defeated in combat because the rival is better than you, so be it. All-or-nothing assaults are for losers. You must always maintain a cool head, even if there's only a small chance of victory. Let me assure you, there always is one in a fight, no matter how uneven it might look at the beginning. You must maintain faith in the technique you've learned, in your ability to use your weapons. Being exhausted is no excuse for launching one single, desperate attack."

"Fine…" Daphne mumbled from the ground with a look of pain.

"You have been defeated. Your attack was not fast or accurate enough. Your technique is not acceptable. Your strength and endurance are unacceptable. You must improve a lot. You may go."

Daphne had trouble getting up from the ground; she did not seem able to do so. They all watched her, not knowing whether to help her or not. Ivo made as if to go and help her, but Urus immediately stopped him, pointing his sword at him.

"The pupil must get up by herself. No one can help her," he sentenced.

Ivo seemed to disagree but said nothing. He knew he could not go against an instructor's order. The punishment was the same as opposing a dragon: death without excuse.

At last, Daphne managed to get up, pick up her sword and shield, and return to the circle.

Now it was Lily's turn. She was the last, and she went to stand in front of the instructor. Seeing what had happened to Daphne, Lily decided to use a defensive strategy and not waste the last of her strength in a desperate attack. She was going to lose anyway, and she did not want to get chastised like Daphne on top of it. The combat began and Lily waited in a defensive stance for the instructor's attack. She had her shield in front of her and her sword at mid-height, ready to defend herself. She was expecting a combination of strong blows with the sword and prepared to bear with it. She was wrong. Urus did something no one was expecting. He made a great leap and fell upon Lily, striking her shield with his own. The combined attack—the power of the leap, Urus's weight, and the hard blow of the shield—threw Lily backward as if a bull had charged her. She ended up on the ground several paces backward, on her back, unable to continue.

Urus watched her, defeated on the ground, and shook his head.

"Don't expect to be able to fend off every attack with a mere defensive stance. As you have just seen, the rival might surprise you with an attack of force. It might be one like I just performed, or it might be a similar one, hitting with the sword. It might even be an attack without a leap. Or a run, which is also very effective. Expect the unexpected, not always the same movements you have studied and practiced. In most of the cases they will serve you, but not always. If someone charges at you, whether at a run or leaping, what you must do is simple: move away with a swift sideways slide. Then you turn and face the enemy; you will have them if you are fast enough, because they will be exposed." Urus executed the movements so they could all see. When he finished explaining, he turned to Lily, who was still lying on her back on The Arena without the energy to get up.

"You have been defeated. Your defense was not fast enough, your technique is not acceptable, your strength and endurance are unacceptable. You must improve a lot. You may go."

Lily rolled on The Arena floor, and with great difficulty she managed to crawl on all fours to her place in the circle.

"We will repeat this exercise at the end of every class. For your own good, I hope you improve. What I have witnessed today is not at the level of what is expected of you. I know you see it as suffering, but one day it will save your lives on the battlefield. Do not doubt it."

Nahia had no doubt that what Urus was saying was true. The problem was how to overcome his class. It was too much for them. At that moment, she could not imagine herself fighting against the instructor and surviving the duel. It seemed impossible to her, to hold up even for two seconds of combat against him. And that meant she would not pass weapons class.

Chapter 29

The first days of autumn training went by. They were all making great efforts at the three disciplines: Weapons, Magic, and Talent. The mid-term test was getting closer, and no one wanted to be left out for not being up to the standard required by the instructors. Aiden, Ivo, and Taika were working hard in the Magic classes and afterward studying and practicing at the library. Nahia, Daphne, and Lily were giving their all in Weapons class and then at the gym, trying to strengthen their bodies. Luckily, they were all doing fairly well in their Talent classes, something they found hard to believe.

Just like the leaves fell from the trees, every member of the Igneous Squad fell before the formidable Urus in the middle of The Arena in the compulsory duel at the end of the class. If anything marked the weapons class, that was sweat, pain, sand, and more pain.

"Class finished," Urus said once the last duel had ended.

Daphne, who had been the last one, dragged herself to her place in the circle.

"Courage," Taika whispered to her.

"The progress I see is satisfactory. You are not all as good as you should be," said Urus, looking at Nahia, Daphne, and Lily, "but it's acceptable progress."

That surprised them because he had given them a royal beating. They had tried, but it was like hitting a rock wall.

"You may go. Class dismissed," he finished and left with a serene demeanor.

Nahia looked at Daphne and Lily with astonishment. It was the first time in two seasons that Urus had said anything positive.

"Did I hear him right?" Lily whispered as they turned to leave.

"He can't have said something good about us." Daphne shook her head with a look of feigned incredulity.

"You heard properly. Our formidable weapons master told us we are progressing satisfactorily." Aiden puffed himself up and lifted his chin as he faced the exit passage out of the south side of the round building.

"We must've done something well," Ivo shrugged. By the look on his face, he was pleased with what they had achieved.

"The duels went well," Taika said in an optimistic tone.

Daphne looked at him with wide eyes.

"What do you mean, well? Speak for yourself, because it wasn't like that for us."

"Taika held up the most. At least ten attacks from the instructor. A true feat," said Ivo.

"Rather than holding up, let's say I managed to avoid his blows," Taika smiled.

"You have enviable agility," Nahia admitted.

The squad left The Arena. They were worn out and exhausted from the blows they had received, but each of them felt a little more cheerful after the weapons master's comment.

"I held up better than ever, so I'm very proud," Aiden announced, lifting his chin.

"Yeah, you did really well today," Daphne admitted. "You managed to endure eight offensive and defensive moves, a real achievement."

"That's what I think. I did my best. Without losing my head, I must say," Aiden admitted.

"Well, if you lose your head with Urus, there's not much of a problem. He'll leave you unconscious with a blow of his shield to your face, so don't worry," Lily said, laughing.

"Most likely, yes," Aiden nodded.

"I'm improving. My defenses held up pretty well, but I'm still struggling to attack," Ivo commented.

"Well, with your strength, wherever you hit him should be enough," Daphne told him.

"Yeah, that's what I try to do, but the master won't let me."

"You just keep striking that hard and everything will be all right," Lily smiled at him.

They crossed the Square of the Path and Nahia inwardly felt like she was doing awful, but that at least she was trying with all her heart.

"I'd be happy getting to the end of the class with enough strength for three attacks. That's all I ask for," said Nahia with a long sigh of exhaustion.

"That makes two of us," Daphne said. Her eyes were so sunken in it looked like exhaustion wanted to swallow them into her skull.

"I was able to launch four today. I can't feel my arms or legs and

I think I'm going to faint at any moment, but I did it," Lily said, stumbling. Aiden, who was beside her, grabbed her by the waist so she would stay upright.

"Well, so gallant for a granite-head," she said with a wink, but her head fell backward and she tripped.

Aiden kept her on her feet and helped her walk.

"We're almost to the barracks. Don't worry, we'll get there," he said, although they were still quite a way off.

"I'll hold up… don't worry," Lily replied.

Aiden held her better so she would not fall to the ground and lifted her by the waist.

"Wow… I feel like I'm flying… I'm like a Fatum from the old days," Lily said, her mind drifting.

"The poor thing overexerted herself today," Ivo said.

"The thing is, we either overexert ourselves in every class or we're done," said Daphne, whose natural ill temper kept her going. But she was on the verge of falling over just like Lily.

"It's true, but we are making significant progress," Taika said.

"You think so?" Aiden asked, looking at the tiger to see what he meant.

"I don't see it as clearly either…" Ivo joined in as they went around the castle and faced the bailey.

"Today Urus praised us, and none of us are failing catastrophically in class."

"Well, *we* are, a little," Nahia retorted.

"Don't think that way. You're finishing the class, which is a real feat. Particularly, seeing the way you started the year. In two seasons, you have improved a lot. The fact that you can't take on Urus doesn't mean you're failing the training," Taika reasoned.

"You think that we'll… pass?" Daphne asked him, doubt in her tone.

"I do. You're holding up until the duels and doing better every time," the Felidae said.

"I'm not that optimistic. About you three I mean," Aiden said.

"Granite… head…" Lily said as her eyes were closing.

"You're an enviable comrade," Daphne said, full of sarcasm and with a disgusted look on her face.

"I say what I think. And you know I'm right. I always tell the truth."

"You do? And what about Magic class, rock-head?" Daphne rebuked him. "You're not doing well there."

Aiden heaved a deep sigh, still carrying Lily in a firm grip.

"True. I'm not doing well at all. I might not even pass," he admitted with a dull voice, dropping his chin onto his chest.

Daphne and Nahia looked at one another in shock. Such an admission was not usual for the Drakonid.

"Are you feeling well, Aiden?" Nahia asked him.

"Yeah…of course…it's just that I'm not as optimistic as Taika. Especially when it comes to magic," he said as they headed to the barracks.

"If you think about it, we're not doing that bad in magic either," Taika argued.

"What do you mean? Ivo, you, and Aiden are doing terribly," Daphne rebuked him, the argument keeping her on her feet. Ivo had come to her side in case she fainted. It would not be the first time, and it would not be the last.

"That's not entirely correct. Ivo and I aren't capable of performing mental attacks, that's true, but we aren't all expected to. We're expected to pick up the mental auras, and we've achieved that."

"Oh, well… if you look at it that way… I guess so," Nahia cheered up. She felt some optimism for her comrades.

"And Aiden, who's only capable of attacking with his mind half the time, has improved a lot since the beginning, when he only managed one out of ten attempts."

"That's true…" Nahia admitted.

"Do you believe we'll pass the two classes? Really?" Daphne asked him.

"I'm maintaining my optimism. Maybe not, because you never know with dragons and their impossible expectations, but I believe we'll be allowed to pass to the second part of the year," Taika said.

"I think you're more than optimistic," said Ivo, who was not at all convinced.

"We'll have to see and be surprised," Taika told them with a smile as they reached the barracks. Lily had been asleep for a while, and Daphne fainted at the door. Ivo held her and carried her to the dorm on his shoulder.

Nahia went into their room, thinking that Taika was somewhat right. They had done their best and improved a lot. At least when it came to the expectations they had for themselves, considering the difficulties they faced. But the dragons might tell them they did not measure up. In fact, that is what Nahia thought would happen. Although she tried, she could not be as optimistic as Taika. The only hope she had left was that the Felidae was smart and astute, and if he said so, he must be right, at least in part. There was nothing for it but to wait and see.

She looked out the window before getting in bed and realized that autumn was already letting winter in, and this meant that in no time the mid-year test would take place. Just thinking about it gave her a shiver that ran down her back. She decided to sleep because she could not even think, she was so tired. She dropped down on her face in her cot and fell asleep before her body even finished falling.

The last week of autumn training became crucial and required one last effort from everyone in each of the three disciplines. In magic training, things went slightly better in the mental duels. They had all suffered, but they had all improved, Aiden and Taika quite impressively. Even Ivo could now see the auras of all his comrades, although he could not attack them. Nahia would never admit it, because it was a cruel and ruthless method, but Buru-Beira-Gogoa had gotten results from making them suffer. Just thinking about it gave her a headache. The good news was that they had its approval to take part in the mid-year test. The sighs and snorts of relief the three squad boys had let out had been loud and noisy, especially Ivo's.

And then the final day of autumn came. They had weapons training. It was one last practice session, very much in line with the latest ones. They all crashed against the impenetrable wall that was Urus and ended up sore, lying on The Arena floor. But something positive came from their sweat and pain.

"That wasn't bad. Better than the last classes. That's enough for now. You have my permission to take part in the mid-year test. Go and rest," the weapons master dismissed them.

Nahia, Daphne, and Lily jumped up and down with joy and shouted so loud that the noise bounced off the round walls of The Arena.

"I knew we would make it," Taika told them.

"You are a very intelligent tiger," Ivo said, laughing.

"I'm glad we did it," said Aiden.

"If *you're* glad, little marble-head, imagine us," Lily said.

"Look, I'm smiling from ear to ear," Daphne said, beaming.

"That is a major achievement," Aiden said.

"We did it!" Nahia cried and the three girls dropped down on the floor. They stayed there, sitting on The Arena. Taika, Ivo, and Aiden looked at them and a moment later sat down beside them. They were all so tired they just stayed there for a long while. They had managed to overcome the Weapons class, and the best way to celebrate was resting. Right there. And there they remained until dinner time. Hunger was stronger than exhaustion, and they all went to eat something. They did not talk much, although there was a joyous glow in their eyes for having managed to reach the mid-year test. They went to sleep early and fell, laid out on their beds. Before they could count to three, they were all fast asleep.

The next morning, a tremendous roar woke them all up. Aiden had not even finished getting ready, which meant it was very early.

"What's… going on?" Nahia muttered with one eye closed and the other just a quarter open.

"I don't know, but something's up," Aiden replied as he looked out the window.

A second dragon roar made it clear that something was indeed up.

"We'd better get going, and fast," Taika suggested.

"I can't even raise my head," Daphne complained.

"Well, I can't even move my perfect hips to turn over…" Lily was trying to turn over in her bed, unsuccessfully.

Nahia sat up in her bed, and that one small movement made her whole body ache like a nightmare. She felt as if Urus had beaten her ten times, one after the other.

Ivo had stood up and was stretching his arms.

"This is no way to start the day. We ought to begin quietly, without urgency or shouting. This isn't good for our souls."

"You're not wrong, but I don't think that's what the dragons want," Daphne said as she massaged her head.

Several more roars, one of which was Irakas-Gorri-Gaizt's, made it very clear they needed to report immediately.

"Our leader is calling!" Aiden cried as he opened the door to leave.

They went down to line up with uncertainty in their hearts. Nahia wondered what awaited them now.

Chapter 30

Red Squadron, line up in a row! Without delay! Irakas-Gorri-Gaizt ordered as they arrived at a run from the barracks to line up. They were not the only ones; all the third-years were running to line up in front of their leaders.

The Igneous Squad stood in line before their leader on the left, the Ardent in the middle and the Searing on the right. Nahia looked at Brendan and Logar out of the corner of her eye. They were also looking at the other squads, and when they noticed her, they nodded at her unobtrusively.

Then she looked at the other squadrons. Ana's Blue Squadron was nearby and Nahia was able to see the look on her friend's face, which, as always, was anguished. She wished there was some way to calm her, but apart from not having one, Nahia was not calm herself. Anyway, she had to admit that being surrounded by her squad comrades gave her a sense of security that was quite soothing. She sought Logan and found him at once. It was as if her eyes could find him in the midst of the most intense darkness. She noticed his handsome profile and her heart began to race. She had to quiet it: now was not the time to get excited about anything.

The six leader dragons roared in unison.

All firm! Irakas-Gorri-Gaizt ordered them.

A huge red dragon appeared, flying over the castle. It was Colonel Lehen-Gorri-Gogor, leader of the Academy. It came down and landed in front of the castle, looking toward the square where they were lined up. A moment later another huge dragon, this one white, appeared the same way. It was Commander Bigaen-Zuri-Indar. It landed on the Colonel's right. They roared to announce their arrival to everyone, demanding the attention of all present at the bailey.

After a moment, the Colonel let out another roar. It was going to address them.

It seemed odd to Nahia that they had not been told when the mid-year test would begin. As a rule, they announced it at least a couple of days before; this was a very unpleasant surprise. She looked at Daphne and Lily and made a face that meant this was not good.

Who knew what kind of creatures they would have to face in order to pass the test. Surely the most difficult to defeat and bloodthirsty. That they were going to suffer, she had no doubt. After all, they had been through a nightmare in the first and second year, so the third year would not be different. In fact, she expected it to be worse.

Very well. As time is of the essence, my speech will be brief. You have been training for two and a half years in Drakoros. In this test which is about to begin, you will show your worth. Do so and you will be on the Path to become Dragon Warlocks. Do not disappoint me. Do it well. This year's test will not be held here. This year, given the situation, it will be a mission of war in Drameia, it sent, along with a strong feeling of importance.

Nahia opened her eyes wide. They were being sent to Drameia. She had hoped they would be going back, but for the end-of-the-year test, not this one. Things were more serious than she had anticipated. They were being sent back to war. She heard a couple of sighs and looked at Daphne and Lily. They both looked like they expected problems.

Squadron Leaders, the Commander sent them.

The six leaders roared at once.

You have each been given a mission to carry out.

The six roared again.

Very well then, go on your missions and fulfill them.

They did not even have time to assimilate it.

We leave immediately. We will now be brought the field gear.

A group of Tergnomus appeared from administration in a single-file line. They were carrying backpacks and weapons. Nahia thought that Hiputz the supply manager must have known this was going to happen, since they had to prepare the gear for all the squadrons. She wondered how many other things the bad-tempered supply manager knew about. They were given a long sword, a dagger, a shield, a Battle Sphere, and the backpack. Nahia was already used to the weight of the weapons, but the backpack added an additional load she would have to get used to. They had already done it the previous year, so she did not foresee any trouble.

Once they all had their equipment, the line of Tergnomus vanished into the long administration building.

Red Squadron, we march! Irakas-Gorri-Gaizt ordered.

They started out, and with them, all the other squadrons. They marched in perfect formation as they had been taught. First went the

White Squadron, then the Blue, Brown, Crystal, and Black, and finally theirs, the Red Squadron. They left the Academy and headed to the Arrival Gate, where they would take the portal to leave the realm of Cael-Utrum, where they currently were, and enter the sixth realm of the dragons. It came to Nahia's mind that this was the only neutral realm not ruled by any of the five clans. Now they were heading to one that was, that of the Red Dragon King. In its realm, everything belonged to it, including the Humans on the surface that were its servants.

They reached the Arrival Gate, and Nahia felt a shiver when she saw the Pearl. That was the only way to enter or leave that realm. At least for the slave races. Not for the dragons: they could always fly down to the surface of Kraido. In front of the Pearl, surrounded by the six lookouts, the Guardian of the Gate was waiting for them: Sarre-Urdin-Olto, the great blue dragon. The leaders conversed with it, and shortly after the great silver sphere that was the portal, took shape above the Pearl. They got ready to cross, and they all entered the portal at an order from their leaders.

They appeared at a Pearl Nahia recognized. They were in the realm of the Red Dragon King. Several dragons appeared, flying over the portal. They were watching them. This was nothing strange: it was due to the great rivalry between the five dragon clans. From there they made another journey, which was already familiar, to the Great Pearl of the Red Dragon King, which allowed travel to distant continent-worlds. There, the great portal that would take them to Tremia would open. Nahia was nervous about returning to Egil's world. She wondered if she would have the chance to meet with Lasgol, Camu, and the Rangers. She would have to wait and see, since they did not know what their mission would be yet. Only that it was in Tremia.

The Red King's dragons escorted them, flying above them until they arrived at the Great Pearl. They found it surrounded by a multitude of human soldiers and their carts with supplies. There were dragons flying over and around it, as if watching over it. They had not yet opened the great portal.

Stop. Maintain your formation, Irakas-Gorri-Gaizt ordered them once they reached the south side of the Pearl.

Suddenly, the colossal portal began to take shape. Above the lookouts that surrounded the Pearl, a dozen silver dragons flashed in

249

their efforts to open the great portal. It took them some time. When the great silver sphere finally formed, they all marveled at its colossal size and power.

We have permission to cross. In formation. To the portal! Irakas-Gorri-Gaizt ordered.

They headed to the ramp that went up from the ground to the top of the Pearl, not without trepidation. They all ascended to the portal, and a moment later they were jumping in.

They woke up in camp tents which already looked familiar.

"We're in Tremia," Taika announced.

Aiden was already outside the tent.

"I wish they'd improve these bracelets once and for all. I hate this headache," Lily protested.

"Don't worry, I can alleviate the headache," Daphne offered.

"That's wonderful, thanks," Nahia said as she rubbed her temples without much luck.

"Well, I'd ask them to make these tent ceilings a little higher," Ivo commented as he got up and bumped the canvas, tearing it with his horns.

Attention, everyone. Line up, they received Irakas-Gorri-Gaizt's order.

"Ugh, our leader's already calling," Lily moaned.

"Everyone, out, let's line up," Aiden said urgently.

They went outside and lined up in front of their leader, waiting along with the other five in front of the great glacier shaped like a semi-ruined castle. They were on the Reborn Continent, and within the gigantic ice structure by the Pearl they had arrived through. Nahia looked around. The invasion camp was half-deserted. There were fewer than five hundred soldiers there and a similar number of carts with supplies. It did not surprise her. The rest were already attacking the Tremian kingdoms. Three dragons were flying above the glacier in circles, watching.

The mission begins. This will be an easy mission, an escort one. Each squadron will escort a convoy of a hundred carts with supplies. The carts must reach their destination. Our mission will be for Erre-Gor-Mau, the Red Dragon King, inside the territories under his rule: the Reborn Continent, the kingdom of Norghana, and the Frozen Continent. This mission will be in Norghana. The other squadrons will perform similar duties for the other kings, Irakas-Gorri-Gaizt announced.

Nahia looked toward Ana and then Logan. They would be receiving the same orders and would go their separate ways once they left the war camp. She hoped everything would go well for them and that they would make it back alive. Irakas-Gorri-Gaizt considered the mission easy, but Nahia had the feeling it would not be that way.

Off you go. Our convoy to protect is the one with red runes on the carts.

Outside the war camp, they saw the five convoys waiting for them. Each convoy had the colors of the dragon king it belonged to. Nahia and her squadron comrades went to the head of the red convoy. Ana, Logan, and the others did the same, and the leaders flew off.

I will wait for you at the Reborn Continent Pearl. March on, Irakas-Gorri-Gaizt sent them.

They started out, and the convoy of carts followed at once. They had no problems reaching the Pearl, which was a little to the south. When they arrived, it was already open and there was a ramp for the carts to go up. The black leader manipulated the runes of the portal and set their destination. Then its squadron and convoy went in, and after them the black dragon. One by one, each squad, convoy, and leader entered the Pearl once the leader had set the destination. Nahia saw Ana and Logan leave and felt uneasy for what might happen. A while later, she was going in with her comrades.

They came out of the Pearl and fell to the ground. Nahia looked at the place: she already knew it pretty well. It was the northern Pearl, the one in Norghana. It was situated in what the Rangers called the Lair, and the valley surrounding it was the Shelter. Both Lasgol and Egil had told her about it. Lasgol had left them his parting gift inside the Lair the last time Nahia had set foot in that place.

She looked up at the sky and saw two dragons patrolling. They flew in circles above the Pearl in opposite directions at about six hundred paces above them. One was red and the other blue. Judging by their size, they were young. If those dragons were here, there would not be a gift inside the Lair this time. They were watching the Pearl, and based on the height they were flying at, they were being cautious.

The rest of the squadron stood up and watched the place. They all recognized it. Brendan and Logar looked at Nahia and gave her a little nod.

Spread out and surround the Pearl. Cover the carts from this position, Irakas-Gorri-Gaizt ordered.

"Yeah, let's spread out, fast," Taika urged them.

They all moved quickly.

Suddenly, the carts began to appear. The first one came through and the driver, well taught, urged the beasts to get on their way. Four soldiers were sitting at the end of the cart. Nahia realized they had to clear the arrival area. A moment later, another cart appeared and the driver did the same thing. The carts came out one after another and the convoy took form down the hill to the west. All the carts carried four soldiers who escorted it. The great convoy had a hundred carts and four hundred soldiers protecting them.

They all carried supplies of some kind. Food, weapons, clothes, and the like, except for one that traveled in the center and was not like the others. Nahia could not take her eyes off it. The back of this cart featured a large silver box that had dragon runes engraved on either side. It shone even in the overcast sky. Nahia did not know what it held, but it was definitely something for the dragons. She had the impression that it was something important, and if it was, the dragons had not bothered to hide it. This did not surprise her, because the dragons did not understand the concepts of subterfuge and dissimulation.

"That's a monumental number of supplies," Lily said with a whistle once the whole convoy was formed.

"You'd be surprised how quickly they run out," Ivo told her.

"If you laid your hands on it, I bet they would," Lily laughed and covered her mouth so no one else would hear her.

"Ivo is right. They have to feed and equip thousands of soldiers," Taika commented.

"And a few dragons," Daphne added.

Nahia nodded, "True."

"An invasion, especially if there are cities to lay siege on, requires countless supplies," Taika explained.

"Well, here they come," Lily said.

"Don't be too confident. The Norghanians won't want these supplies to reach the troops," Taika warned them.

"You think they'll attack the convoy?" Daphne asked him.

"They very well could. I would if I were with them," Taika

replied.

"They're right. Hungry, weakened soldiers don't fight well. Besides, they lose morale," Ivo said.

"Will they steal the supplies?" Aiden asked.

"They'll destroy them if they can't steal them," Taika guessed.

"That's something only cowards without honor would do," Aiden stated.

"We're at war. There is no honor in war, only survival," Ivo told him.

"Well, whatever it is, this isn't going to be an easy escort mission, is it?" Daphne asked.

"I doubt it. This has high odds of becoming complicated," Ivo replied.

"Well, that's nice…" Daphne protested, wrinkling her nose.

Nahia looked at the wide valley surrounded by tall mountains. Everything looked quiet. A hawk flew out from the trees, flying at top speed and soaring up to the covered sky before disappearing into the clouds. She did not know exactly why, but Nahia remembered what the Gryphon king had told her: *there's nothing a dragon fears more than….* That hawk was flying so fast and maneuvering with such ease that it would be impossible for a dragon to catch.

She felt better. The dragons were formidable, but they could never beat a hawk.

We follow the convoy, Irakas-Gorri-Gaizt ordered.

They started marching behind the long line of carts and headed west toward the entrance to the valley. Nahia felt confused. The way in and out of the valley was high up, through a cave at the top of one of the peaks. How were the carts going to go that way?

Chapter 31

They traveled the valley, which was already covered in snow in several areas. They were at the end of autumn, and in that region of Tremia it was already snowing heavily. The whole mountain range surrounding the valley was painted white. Not just the highest peaks, but the whole mountain almost to its base. The temperature was also cool, but without getting very cold. Their clothes would protect them in any case.

They reached the end of the valley, and Nahia still had the same question in her mind. How were the carts going to get out of the valley? What she saw left her with even more questions. All the drivers and soldiers got off the carts when they reached the end, at the foot of the high range. They started climbing to the cave Nahia was already familiar with, which had an exit on the other side. The carts, though, were staying there. It made no sense. Were they going to leave all those supplies there? And what about the strange silver cart?

"This is very weird," Lily commented.

"They can't just leave the carts with food here," Ivo said, who did not like the scene at all.

"I doubt they'll do that; the soldiers need these supplies to continue the invasion," said Taika.

"The dragon lords will have a clever strategy," said Aiden.

"There goes little rock-head about his beloved dragon lords," Lily snapped at him.

"They must have thought of something," commented Ivo. "They're not going to leave the carts grouped here. Maybe they've dug a tunnel for them to go through."

"I don't see any tunnel. And the drivers left them behind..." said Nahia.

"Well, if it's not by land, it'll have to be by... air..." Taika reasoned.

As the Felidae-Tiger was finishing his sentence, four young dragons came down from the sky. With their front and back claws, they each grabbed a cart and lifted it. The draft animals were left hanging, held by their strong harnesses. The dragons rose until they cleared the range and vanished on the other side.

"Yup, it's by air," Daphne nodded.

"How smart is our tiger," Lily smiled.

Taika shrugged.

"It's only logical."

Cross to the other side of the range and protect the carts. The Igneous Squad will protect the west, the Ardent the east, and the Searing the north until the carts start moving on, they received Irakas-Gorri-Gaizt's message as it flew above them.

Nahia thought that if the Norghanians wanted to attack the convoy, this was a good moment. All the carts were at a standstill and disorganized. It would take them a while to organize and form the long line once more. She thought again and realized that despite the slight chaos, there were four dragons working and one watching over the carts. They would need many archers to attack with any chance of success. There was a thick forest to the north and another one to the east. They could be hiding there, but if they were Rangers out there, she would never see them, that was for sure.

The three squads watched the surroundings with alert eyes. But nothing happened. The convoy reorganized and began its journey anew. Nahia felt disappointed and relieved at the same time. The former because she did not want the supplies to arrive; no supplies meant the dragon army would not be able to fight and would lose morale. The latter because she did not want the soldiers accompanying the carts, Humans mostly, to die in an ambush. Then she realized *they* could also die in the ambush and the idea seemed even less appealing.

A few hours later, the convoy was moving along the road heading north. Irakas-Gorri-Gaizt had ordered them to split up. The Ardent Squad was in the lead, the Searing Squad in the rear, and the Igneous in the middle. Their leader was flying over the column of carts, making sure the way was clear.

Nahia could see the silver cart right in front of them and, of course, she could not stop wondering what might be inside.

"What do you think is inside?" she asked Daphne.

"No idea, but the engravings are dragon runes, so something bad for sure."

"Now we know why they don't teach us to interpret dragon runes at the Academy. It's so we won't know what's inside their secret boxes," Lily said.

"You're not wrong," said Aiden.

"I'm not?" Lily looked at him with interest.

"No, indeed you're not. Among my people it is believed that the dragon runes have a meaning of their own, as if it were a small tome, and its language is secret. Only the dragons know it. Those runes likely indicate the nature of what's in the silver box."

"Besides being irresistible and charming, I'm smart. I have everything," Lily said, beaming.

"It must be something important," Nahia commented. Whatever was inside of it called to her. She felt the scale at the back of her neck to check whether it was burning, but it was not. It was not indicating that it had anything to do with her destiny. Perhaps it was not calling to her and it was only a feeling brought on by the intrigue she felt. "It might only contain gold and precious stones to bribe rulers and buy mercenaries."

Aiden looked at her with astonishment.

"Our dragon lords don't need to bribe rulers, and least of all buy mercenaries without honor."

"Of course not, granite-head. Wars are won by themselves. Your beloved dragons arrive at a continent-world, everyone surrenders at their feet, and the world is conquered. It's that easy," Daphne said.

"Exactly what's happening here," Lily added.

"I didn't say... well..." Aiden did not know what to say and looked ahead with his chin up.

"Don't worry about that box. What's important is doing our duty and getting out of this mission alive," Taika said. "Everything else is secondary."

"That's a great truth," Ivo agreed. "Let's focus on surviving."

"Eyes open, everyone, and stay alert," Daphne said, and they concentrated on the Felidae-Tiger's advice.

They went on in a northern direction. Nahia guessed they were going to the capital, since they were following the same road they had traveled on the last time they were here. But when they arrived at a crossroads, the capital already in sight, they veered west.

"We're not going to the capital?" Daphne was surprised.

"It seems the new course is northwest," Taika guessed, looking at the sun the clouds were covering.

"Does anyone know where we're going?" Lily asked.

Nahia had one of Egil's maps in her boot, but she did not want to take it out in case the soldiers saw her.

"We'll find out further on," she told her comrades.

"It doesn't seem like the capital has fallen yet," Taika commented as he stretched his neck to better see the great city in the distance.

"I only see smoke columns," said Daphne.

They came to a hill, and through the trees they were able to see what was going on in the capital. Part of the city was ruined. Another part seemed to be on fire, columns of smoke rising into the sky. But the walls seemed to hold and the doors were walled up with metal and rock.

"Is it just me, or is the city still standing?" Lily asked.

"It hasn't fallen. They're withstanding the dragons," said Nahia, shocked and thrilled by such an accomplishment.

"Check the war camp of the Red Dragon King," Ivo pointed out. "I can also see smoke columns."

"True, it looks like they've been attacked," Taika said.

"I count fewer troops than when we were here," Daphne said, who could now see better.

"There are also fewer dragons, look," said Nahia.

About half a dozen dragons were flying over the city, making attacking passes to rise again to the sky. Above the war camp, another half dozen dragons flew in circles and seemed to be watching the area.

"The attack on the camp is recent. They still haven't managed to put out all the fires," Aiden said, shocked.

"What's burning are the supply carts and the store tents," Ivo noticed.

"So odd that you should know where those particular tents are," Lily told him.

"Each one notices what they notice," he shrugged with a smile on his face.

"Yeah, it looks like an attack on the supplies," Taika corroborated.

"Well, that's not good news for us," said Daphne.

"Why do you say that?" Aiden asked, not understanding what the Fatum meant.

"What are we transporting, granite-head?" she asked back.

"Oh, yeah, I see." Aiden stared at the carts.

"We're starting down the hill, we'll lose sight of the city soon," Taika warned them.

The convoy of carts followed the road at a slow but steady pace. They had to keep up, but they had lagged a little while they studied the capital.

"Does anyone see anything of interest?" Nahia asked, standing on her tiptoes.

"You can see lots of small flashes around the dragons when they come down to attack. The Norghanians continue defending themselves with their explosive arrows," Taika told them.

"It also looks as if the Ice Magi are doing their best, because now it's raining over the spots where the fire dragons have attacked," said Ivo.

"They're putting out the flames with water magic," said Nahia.

"That's right."

"Well, it looks like the Red Dragon King hasn't been able to take the capital yet," Daphne commented.

"It's only a matter of time. It won't hold much longer," Aiden stated.

"You, little granite-head, had better not say anything while we're here," Lily warned him.

"Why wouldn't I say what I think?"

"Because your opinion isn't shared by the rest of us?" Lily retorted, looking at him sternly.

Aiden shrugged.

"I'll save my opinions if they're not to everyone's liking."

"Yeah, you do that," Daphne snapped.

Nahia felt bad for Aiden, but Lily was right. No one in the squad wanted to hear that the dragons were going to conquer the city, or win this war, as the Drakonid was certain was going to happen.

The way down became steeper, and they lost sight of the capital. Nahia was comforted by the fact that the Norghanians were still resisting. It was really amazing. She had to admit that Egil and his friends were tough and difficult to submit.

They continued the march along a wide road toward the north and slightly east. They kept traveling until night came. Irakas-Gorri-Gaizt ordered them to light torches and go on a while longer. Finally, they stopped at midnight so the draft beasts could rest and eat and drink.

We will rest where we are until first light and then we will continue, Irakas-Gorri-Gaizt sent them as it flew around them a couple of times and then came down to land at the head of the convoy.

"It looks like we won't get proper rest," Ivo protested as he sat on the ground behind the silver cart.

"It looks that way. We must suffer the rigors of the campaign. This will make us stronger," said Aiden.

"This small wingless dragon is completely insufferable," Lily raised her arms to the clouded sky.

"They haven't given us tents for this mission," Daphne said, shaking her head.

"Let's eat something and hope the weather doesn't get worse," said Taika.

"Shouldn't we keep watch?" Lily asked, looking around.

"The soldiers on the carts have watch shifts," said Aiden.

"Yeah, there are two on either side of the carts, twenty paces off," Nahia counted, having already noticed.

"In that case, let's eat. So much walking has given me an appetite," said Ivo, already looking for the ration in his backpack.

"You've never been without one," Lily laughed.

Ivo shrugged and started eating his smoked meat.

They ate, alert but at ease. As they were finishing, it started to snow. Large flakes fell from a black sky that did not let them see either the stars or moon.

"And now what do we do?" Lily asked. "This weather is not good for my skin," she said, putting on her hood.

"This is nothing." Aiden shook off a few snowflakes from his shoulders.

"We could sleep under the carts, that would be the best idea," Taika suggested

"Yeah, I think we have no choice. It's starting to snow heavily." Ivo had his hands open, and the rhythm the flakes were falling at now announced a good snowfall.

They followed Taika's suggestion and slept under the carts, the boys under the one behind them and the girls under the silver one. When she got under it, Nahia felt a shiver. She was not sure whether it was because of the snow or the large box they had above them. The cart was just like the others, except that instead of supplies, it had this strange silver box. It intrigued her. She found it hard to sleep, not so much from the uncomfortable situation but because her mind was trying to figure out what might be inside.

It did not stop snowing all through the night, and at dawn the snow was still falling.

"It's morning, everyone, up," Aiden, who was up already, woke them.

Nahia opened her eyes and saw that everything was covered by snow. She came out from under the cart and put on her cloak and hood.

"Does it always snow in this kingdom?" Lily asked as she came out from under the cart.

"They call it the white kingdom, so I guess the snow is here to say," Nahia said with a face that implied they had to bear it.

Attention, everyone. We start marching! Irakas-Gorri-Gaizt sent them.

"Time to move on," Lily said with a big sigh.

"As long as it's only snow, it's not that bad," Daphne commented.

Nahia was hoping the same, and thus went the next day of traveling. It snowed all day and all night without stopping, so they slept under the carts again. At dawn, they awoke to a beautiful landscape. Wherever they looked, everything was white. It was snowing still, but only a little, as if the storm had decided to give them a break.

"I have to admit, it's very pretty," Ivo said, contemplating the landscape with delight.

"The trees especially. They're completely white," said Daphne.

"I still say this weather is bad for my skin. It's going to age us, you'll see," said Lily, who was not enjoying the white landscape or the incessant snow.

The third day of traveling, they turned due north. The mountains in the distance were tall and completely white. The storm above them, and which seemed to be following them, discharged snow and sleet every now and then. It did not bother them so much when they walked, since the rhythm of the carts they followed was slow. As long as they did not get soaked, they would not have any problems, and so far, their clothes were holding up well under the weather.

At dawn of the fourth day, things went south.

The soldiers sounded the alarm at first light.

"Alarm!" cried one soldier.

"Alarm!" cried another, and the cries were followed by others and more shouting.

Chapter 32

They came out from under the carts like lightning. They formed in groups of two with their shields raised and swords in hand. They looked around but could not see the enemy. The cries of alarm went on, but they could not see anyone attacking them.

"Did any of you see who's attacking us?" Nahia asked nervously.

"I can't see anyone." Ivo, the tallest, was looking in every direction.

"There are no signs of struggle," Aiden realized in a blank tone.

"So?" Daphne said, wrinkling her nose.

Alert! Sentinels have vanished during the night! Irakas-Gorri-Gaizt sent them, along with a feeling that was a mix of rage and frustration. It flew over the column of carts. Its enormous shadow looked like a giant specter out of a nightmare.

Nahia looked at the carts in front and behind. There were no soldiers missing on them, each one had four. Then she looked left and right and saw that several soldiers a little ways ahead and also further behind were looking in what seemed to be the spots where the sentinels had vanished.

"Let's go and see what's going on," she told her comrades.

"It's not prudent," Taika stopped her. "We have protection between the carts. Beside the road we'll be out in the open."

"Taika is right," Ivo nodded hard. "Out there is nothing but snow and more snow on flat land. There's nowhere to hide."

"Besides, our leader hasn't ordered it," Aiden added.

"All right, let's be sensible," Nahia nodded. She wanted to find out what had happened, but she knew her comrades were right, more so in this land where there were plenty of archers.

For a long while, the soldiers searched for their missing comrades without success. The snow that had kept falling during the whole night had erased any prints. There was no way to follow a trail. Not far off, on both sides of the road they could see forests. Nahia guessed the sentinels had been taken there.

"Why have they taken the sentinels, and why haven't they attacked us?" Lily asked.

"That's a very good question, and I can only think of one answer," Daphne replied.

"It might be some kind of mental game," Ivo suggested.

"Mental game?" Aiden asked blankly.

"They want to scare us," Taika explained.

"No one scares me, I'm a Drakonid," Aiden said stiffly.

"Yeah, but those poor soldiers might have been frightened, rock-head," Lily told him.

"Oh… I hadn't thought of that."

"Yeah, thinking isn't exactly your thing," Daphne replied.

"I think it's an intimidating tactic. Besides, this way they take no risks," Ivo reasoned.

"Well, since you're the expert on all things mental, why don't you start telling us what you think the enemy is doing with us," Lily said.

"I'll try, but interpreting the enemy's actions isn't simple," Ivo smiled at her.

Make a move on! We keep going! Irakas-Gorri-Gaizt sent them after checking the whole area and finding nothing,

"Keep going? And what about the poor wretches who have been captured?" Nahia could not believe it.

"They must've been taken away. I doubt they're still around," Taika told her.

"They'll have killed them. It's the most efficient solution," Aiden said, convinced.

"Could you be more of a granite-head!" Lily cried, unable to believe he had made such a comment.

"Have a little compassion, you heartless Drakonid," Daphne said reproachfully.

Aiden looked at them, as calm as could be.

"We're at war in enemy territory. It's the most likely thing, and you all know it. If you want to tell each other children's stories to feel better, go ahead."

Nahia knew Aiden was right, but she did not want to admit it. She wanted to think they were still alive.

"In any case, we should try and find them."

"That's not the mission," Aiden corrected her.

"Even so, it's the right thing to do," she replied.

"In war, the right thing is rarely done," said Ivo.

And on that occasion, it was not done. They continued on their route north. They had no idea where they were headed or how long it would take them to get there. Irakas-Gorri-Gaizt had not told them. This did not surprise them, since it only informed them of what needed to be done, nothing else. Not knowing only increased everyone's uncertainty.

Nothing strange happened during the next three nights. Nahia and most of her comrades barely slept, expecting a new attack that never came. But on the fourth night, more sentinels vanished.

With the first light of day, the soldiers sounded the alarm again.

Everyone, be alert! The enemy is near! Irakas-Gorri-Gaizt sent them as it started reconnoitering all the land around the convoy.

"They're definitely playing with us," Taika said, making a face that said he did not like this at all.

"It's what I thought," Ivo said. "They're making us afraid and uneasy. They want us not to sleep, to tire and to demoralize us."

"Well, it's not going to work on us. Not sleeping and being exhausted is part of our routine," Lily laughed.

"You're so right. If anyone can play this game, it's us," Daphne agreed.

"It's a game for cowards. They should show their faces. Come out and fight," Aiden said, fiercely annoyed.

"See here, you crazy little thing, here everyone fights how they want and can," Lily told them.

"It's dishonorable, and I'm no crazy little thing,"

"Yes, you are, and you know it," Lily grinned.

"I just hope they're not killing them…" Nahia said sadly.

"There's no trace of blood or bodies. Whoever is doing this, they're an expert on this type of attacks," said Taika,

"Do you think it's the Rangers?" Ivo asked Nahia.

"Maybe, yes. They have specialists who can hide in the mountains and forests and survive for days without anyone finding them," Nahia explained.

"Yeah, Egil told us they're experts at camouflaging themselves in the forests and mountains. Even more so in the winter," Daphne added.

"If it's them, I don't think they'd kill the sentinels," said Nahia.

"Didn't they also have Assassins?" Lily asked.

Nahia nodded.

"They do, but I hope they haven't sent them."

"Whether it's them or not, Irakas-Gorri-Gaizt hasn't found them," said Ivo, pointing at the great red dragon as it zigzagged in low passes along the column of carts and the surroundings.

"What I said. They camouflage themselves in the snow-covered environment and the dragon can't find them," Daphne commented.

Move on! Keep marching! it ordered after a while, seeing it could not locate the attackers or the missing sentinels.

"I hope they don't kill them…" Nahia felt awful for not being able to do anything about the missing soldiers.

They went on and arrived at a deserted village. If anyone had ever lived there, they had left a long time ago. It was the consequences of war and having a main road nearby. They had gone by two other villages, and in one of them they had seen people. The other one was deserted. They seemed to have left the villages near the routes the troops went by, like the one they were on.

The following day, Irakas-Gorri-Gaizt stopped them.

They have blocked the road! Everyone, be alert to a possible attack! it sent them with a feeling of rage and alarm.

Six huge trees had been felled and lay across the road, preventing the carts from going on.

"This is indeed a textbook ambush," said Taika, looking everywhere.

"Let's not get nervous. Shields up and alert," Daphne called.

For a moment, they all waited to be attacked. The soldiers were frightened and surrounded the carts, betraying the fear they felt. A while went by, but there was no attack. Irakas-Gorri-Gaizt came down upon the trees and with its claws picked them up, freeing the road of obstacles.

"If they're playing with us," Aiden said angrily, "our leader shouldn't be doing this."

"Let it work a little. It will be good for our leader, it might bring it down a peg or two," said Lily.

"It's the first time I've seen a dragon do something useful," Daphne commented.

Aiden cursed in his language and ended with a "lack of respect." The others ignored him.

The days of traveling passed by, and the strange game the

Norghanians were playing with the convoy continued. Every two or three nights, sentinels vanished, or their road was blocked, and Irakas-Gorri-Gaizt had to work hard to clear the path more than once.

Suddenly, at the head of the column they heard several explosions. The soldiers sounded the alarm and everyone looked at the origin of the sound.

They are attacking the head! Irakas-Gorri-Gaizt sent them as it flew low over them to get to the front of the line.

"Have they caught the Ardent Squad?" Nahia asked, very upset.

"I think so… and the first cart," Aiden said, standing on the side of the road and looking ahead.

"Oh no!" Lily put her hands to her head.

"I can help them," Daphne offered as she looked toward the site of the explosions.

"Perhaps I can too," Ivo joined her.

"Let's go see what happened and help!" Nahia was unable to hold back and started running.

"We haven't been ordered…!" Aiden's protest was left behind.

They had all run off except for Aiden, who remained at his post. But when he saw the others run off, he cursed under his breath and followed them.

They arrived at the head of the convoy and encountered a troubling scene. Three of the squad lay wounded on the ground. Nahia recognized Cordelius, the Kapro; Evelyn, the Fatum; and Elsa, the Scarlatum. Around them were Brendan, Lara, and Draider: the human, panther, and Drakonid were looking everywhere, hiding behind their shields. Behind them, the draft beasts of the first cart were lying, badly wounded, on the ground.

"Cover the wounded!" Nahia said as they arrived.

"Let's form a circle!" Taika told them.

They stood around the three fallen who were hurting on the ground, closing the half-circle formed by their standing comrades.

"What happened?" Nahia asked.

"We stepped on some kind of traps on the ground," Brendan told her as he looked at both sides of the road.

"There were elemental explosions of fire and earth," Draider explained.

"I managed to jump to one side when I felt the trigger go off, but they couldn't," said Lara, looking at their wounded comrades on the ground.

"I'll see how they're doing," said Daphne, and setting her shield aside, she sheathed her sword and knelt to see to the wounded.

"Did you see anyone?" Taika asked.

"No one," Brendan shook his head.

"The traps had been set beforehand and were well hidden. There was no sign of them," Lara said.

"There's nothing to be seen on the ground, it's covered with snow," Draider said.

"They have burns and lacerations on their feet and legs from the explosions. I'll cure them as best as I can," Daphne said.

"Tend to my comrades first," Cordelius asked her.

"All right," Daphne nodded and started working on Evelyn first, who was writhing with pain.

The soldiers behind her checked on the two draft animals. They could do nothing; they had already died. The first cart could not go on.

There is no one nearby, I will search again, Irakas-Gorri-Gaizt informed them, flying low over them.

"I doubt it'll find anyone," said Taika.

"I doubt it too," Brendan joined him.

"They're going to keep attacking without showing themselves," said Lara.

In the defensive circle, they were tense and looking in every direction, but they were aware that they would most likely not be attacked.

Daphne worked without pause and healed their wounds. It took her a long time, and the whole column had to wait. Once she finished, she stood up, drained from the extensive use of her healing magic.

"I've cured them as best as I could. They won't be able to walk for days. Their boots and breeches have protected them some, but not enough. The charges on those traps were important. It's elemental damage, similar to ours."

"Won't they be able to go on?" Brendan asked with a look of concern.

"I'm afraid not. The wounds need time to heal and scar over properly. They won't be able to walk for a couple of weeks," Daphne explained.

"Yes, we will," Cordelius said, trying to stand up. He fell to the ground at once amid shows of pain.

"The soles of my feet are ruined," Elsa said, moaning.

"And my ankles," said Evelyn.

"Take it easy. Don't overexert yourself, that'll make your wounds worse," Lara recommended.

"This complicates the mission," Draider commented.

"We'll take care of our comrades," Brendan assured them.

Nahia looked at the three wounded and knew the Ardent Squad had been neutralized. Three wounded required their three comrades to protect them, maybe even carry them.

Take away the wounded from the first cart. We keep moving, Irakas-Gorri-Gaizt sent them.

Nahia could not believe that their leader would not even ask about the state of the wounded on the Ardent Squad. Well, she could believe it; it was a dragon, and by definition it was ruthless.

They got Cordelius, Elsa, and Evelyn on the fifth cart where they carried clothes, making them comfortable. The soldiers moved the first cart off the road and shared the contents among the next three. It seemed to Nahia that this was overloading them, but Irakas-Gorri-Gaizt's orders were never contested.

Igneous Squad, you take the lead now. Make way. Move on, it sent them and flew low over their heads to emphasize the message.

"How nice, now we have to go first and step on explosive tramps." Lily commented, filled with irony.

"No, look," Taika pointed at a group of soldiers with spears who got in front of them, about a hundred paces ahead.

"What are they going to do?" Ivo asked, surprised.

The soldiers started walking in a line. Before each step, they tapped the ground in front of them with the butts of their spears to check whether there were any traps hidden under the snow.

"That's very dangerous," Daphne commented.

"I don't think Irakas-Gorri-Gaizt cares," Nahia said.

"Our leader does what's necessary to ensure the mission succeeds," Aiden commented.

"Well then, your beloved leader could walk ahead of us," Lily suggested.

"That would be an outrage. Our leader flies through the sky, he doesn't walk in the mud and snow," sad Aiden.

"Yeah… yeah…" Daphne made a face that clearly said she did not want to hear any more.

Chapter 33

The convoy went on toward the north. They passed forests and lakes, all covered with snow. The storm stopped for a couple of days, so they enjoyed some good weather. The soldiers who went ahead of them found a dozen spots where traps had been placed. Unfortunately, every time a trap was found, several soldiers were badly hurt. Daphne helped them as best as she could with her healing magic, but their wounds were serious and required extensive care. They put them on the carts at the rear and kept going. Irakas-Gorri-Gaizt did not allow them more time than the bare minimum to look after them before ordering them to continue on their way.

Two days later, they had to cross an enormous forest completely buried in snow. A great snowfall had occurred not long before. The road went through the forest, and the snow made it feel like they were entering a different world, a perfectly white one. Everything was a beautiful shade of white. Night came and they had not finished crossing it. They had to sleep right there. Nahia and her comrades slept under the first two carts. Luckily it was not snowing and the storm seemed to have stopped. The temperature was not too low, allowing them to rest.

In the wee hours of the morning, a dozen explosions woke them all suddenly.

"What on earth was that?" Daphne asked in a bad temper.

Ivo half rose from the scare and hit his head on the underside of the cart, one horn getting stuck.

"I can't believe it!" he cried, upset.

"We're under attack!" Taika warned, rolling out from under the cart.

Aiden did so too and stood on the road.

We're under attack! Weapons, everyone! Irakas-Gorri-Gaizt sent them from where it was standing ahead of them in the middle of the road. It spread its huge wings and took off.

Another set of explosions was heard further behind, followed by another one.

Nahia came out from under the cart and saw that carts were

burning in different sectors of the column.

"They're using explosive fire arrows!" she warned,

"Who is? There's no one to be seen!" Lily cried.

"Cowards! They attack us at night and from the shelter of the forest trees!" Aiden cried.

At that moment, Nahia saw more explosions. The middle of the column of carts was on fire.

"I can't see the archers!" Ivo said, craning his neck to see.

"We can't see them at night. The sky's covered. We only see the arrows they release as they burst," Taika said as he looked at either side of the burning carts.

"What do we do?" Lily asked.

"Let's protect the front of the convoy," Nahia said. She could see Brendan, Lara, and Draider further behind, protecting the carts where their injured comrades were.

They heard new explosions, now at the back of the column. Another section of the carts began to burn.

Irakas-Gorri-Gaizt flew parallel to the burning carts and threw its breath of fire toward the forest.

"Our leader will roast those cowardly archers," Aiden said confidently.

The great red dragon turned at the end of the column and flew low, throwing its fiery breath at the forest on the other side where the carts were burning.

"It's going to try… but whether it'll succeed, I'm not so sure…" Daphne commented.

"What do you mean?" Aiden found the comment outrageous.

Irakas-Gorri-Gaizt flew over them and turned along the left side of the column of carts, spraying fire at a low flight a hundred paces from the carts.

"It's attacking without having located them," Taika realized.

"It's trying to burn two areas parallel to the column, one on each side," said Ivo.

"But the archers might be a lot deeper into the forest," said Nahia.

"How deep?" Taika asked her.

"From what I know about the Rangers, they could be releasing from three hundred paces quite easily. The targets are huge," she said, pointing at the cart beside them.

"So, our leader is somewhat awry with its fiery breath," Lily chuckled.

"Besides, with the forest blanketed in snow, I doubt the fire will be effective at all," Nahia argued.

"That's true," Taika agreed.

Igneous Squad! Protect the silver box! Irakas-Gorri-Gaizt sent them as it now flew in circles around the middle of the column where the cart that carried the box was.

"Move on, quickly!" Aiden was already running to do his master's bidding.

The others followed.

"Be careful!" Brendan shouted as they passed him.

"Don't worry, we will!" Nahia shouted back.

They reached the middle of the column. Over thirty carts were burning, and the soldiers were trying to put out the flames.

The squad's surprise was great when they found the cart carrying the silver box empty.

"What happened?" Nahia asked one of the soldiers.

"We don't know… we were putting out the fires from the carts, and when we looked the box wasn't there anymore."

"They took it?" Daphne asked in disbelief.

"We didn't see… we don't know…" the solders looked confused.

"What a coincidence that this cart wasn't attacked," Lily said.

"Definitely not. This was a ruse. The goal wasn't to burn carts, it was to steal the box," Taika guessed, looking around at the carts being consumed by the flames and the soldiers trying to put the fires out.

Igneous Squad, recover the box! Searing Squad, to the head of the column! Irakas-Gorri-Gaizt's message reached them.

Several more explosions followed the message. They fell right and left of where they were and made them crouch. The animals brayed, frightened, while the soldiers tried to free them so they would not burn to death.

"Recover the box?" Lily could not believe it.

"They have to have taken it into the forest," Nahia said.

"There are fresh tracks here," Taika indicated the ground. "They go into the forest, east."

"Do we follow them?" Lily asked.

"Of course we follow them. We've received an order from our

leader. We must carry it out," Aiden said without hesitation. He raised his shield and headed into the forest.

"We'd better go after him or he'll get killed," Ivo said.

"Fine, let's go," said Nahia, knowing that they had no choice. They had received an order, and they had to obey.

They went into the forest, following the trail. There were at least six pairs of footprints. Nahia thought it was impressive the way they had managed to steal the box away. Suddenly, ahead of them, flames fell through the frozen trees. They looked up and saw Irakas-Gorri-Gaizt clearing the way for them.

"Two-by-two formation, and stay alert," Taika said.

"Magic wielders in the middle," Aiden said.

Ivo and Aiden went first, Nahia and Daphne in the middle, and Taika and Lily brought up the rear. They were all carrying their shields and had their swords ready.

"Prepare elemental balls," said Taika.

Nahia, Daphne, and Lily did so. In one hand they gripped their shield and in the other the magical spheres, ready to be used. The problem was that in the middle of that snow-covered forest and at night, they could not see anything.

Irakas-Gorri-Gaizt's breath came now from the left, lighting up that side. But they could not see any Norghanians or the box.

"Stop," Taika ordered.

"What is it?" Lily asked.

"I've lost the trail… I don't see any more prints," said Taika.

"That's impossible. The ground is covered in snow, there have to be footprints," said Ivo.

"Well, there aren't any," Aiden said in a frustrated tone, looking down at the snow-covered ground.

Irakas-Gorri-Gaizt flew past them on their right, throwing its fiery breath over that area as it passed. Nahia looked at the area and saw that it barely had any effect on that tundra of snow and ice. As they had traveled north the temperature had dropped, and there, in the middle of the frozen forest, Nahia felt the cold more than on the road, protected by the carts. The fiery breath of the powerful red dragon was achieving little other than illuminating the areas. But they had not seen anyone in the trees either.

"They've erased them," said Nahia.

"Is that possible?" Lily asked.

"It's the only possible explanation," Taika agreed.

"If that's the case, they must be Rangers…" Daphne guessed.

"Yeah, and we're in the middle of a snow-covered forest…" Nahia looked around.

"Our odds aren't good," Daphne shook her head.

"We have to follow orders. Forget about the danger. It's our duty," Aiden reminded them.

"And where are we going then, granite-head with a death wish?" Lily asked him.

Aiden looked around.

"I don't know…"

Go east, I've found the box, they received Irakas-Gorri-Gaizt's message.

"Let's go, in formation," Taika set the pace.

They moved through the snow-covered trees and thicket. Nahia looked up, but now the white trees did not let them see more than small patches of darkness that came through. They seemed to be in a dreamscape, surrounded by white everywhere, with hints of nightmare breaking through.

They trod firmly and carefully with every step they took, because under the layer of snow that covered the ground there might be branches, roots, rocks, and other things that might make them miss a step or stumble. Luckily, the space between the trees let them pass and they did not have to maneuver too much.

Irakas-Gorri-Gaizt threw its breath on an area and maintained it there. It was where it wanted them to go, so that is where they headed, taking extreme care in case there were enemies nearby. They reached the spot, and indeed the box was there, half buried in the snow.

"Here it is," said Lily.

"I don't see anyone around, but be careful," Taika warned them.

"How did it see the box from above, buried in the snow?" Ivo wondered.

"It didn't see it," Nahia told him.

"Didn't see it? Then how…?"

"It's the runes: they give out power. I can feel it," Nahia said, noticing her skin crawling.

Daphne walked up to the box and laid her hand on it.

"I can feel it too. It radiates dragon magic."

"Your hair is standing up," Lily said.

Daphne stepped back and her hair dropped.

"Bad news. It's open, and there's nothing inside," Taika said as he looked inside the box through one of the opened sides.

"It can't be," Aiden hastened to check. "Empty," he confirmed and looked around.

Irakas-Gorri-Gaizt flew over them. It seemed to be about to land but flew past, seeing there was no room to land between all the trees everywhere. It was too large a creature to be able to land in the middle of the forest.

Aidan and Taika took the box and lifted it to show that it was empty.

The contents have been stolen! We must find it!

Taika and Aiden lowered the box.

"Do you see any tracks to follow?" Aiden asked Taika.

The Felidae-Tiger bent down and checked the surroundings. He shook his head.

"They buried the box and erased their footprints."

Keep to the north. I can feel the power of the stolen object, they received the dragon's message.

They moved on in formation, slowly but steadily, alert to every tree and bush covered with snow. In that mix of darkness and white it seemed that at any moment an enemy would appear from behind a tree. They proceeded nervously.

They arrived at a ravine that went north. Irakas-Gorri-Gaizt flew over, also north. Suddenly, the ravine became deeper and stretches began to appear that were filled with earth and brush. They reached a point where the ravine was completely covered with earth. There were even trees on top.

"Do we continue this way?" Lily asked in a tone that indicated danger.

"The trail says they went through there," said Taika.

"It makes sense, they went under the surface so the dragon couldn't find them," said Ivo.

"If we go in there, it'll be very dangerous." Daphne also recognized how risky the situation was.

"There's no choice. We must recover what they've stolen," Aiden said.

As if enforcing what the Drakonid was saying, they received the

275

message of their leader from the air.

Do not stop. Keep going. Recover what has been stolen. It is of great value.

"We go on," Aiden said.

"Very carefully," Nahia warned them.

They entered the covered area of the ravine. A moment later, they realized they were now traveling along an underground passage. Over their heads were earth and tree roots.

"We need light, I can't see a thing," Taika said.

"Aiden, take my place," Daphne said as she stepped beside Taika. The ball of light she had ready in her hand began to give off light and lit up their surroundings.

"Great," Taika said gratefully. "Shields up."

"Keep quiet now. Sound can travel quite far through enclosed spaces," Taika told them.

The others nodded.

They went on along the ravine, which was now a wide tunnel of earth. They saw footprints on the damp floor. They were not hard to follow. Nahia thought they had not hidden them in their haste, or perhaps because they did not think they would follow them this far. They came to a wider area that opened up in three directions: one north, another east, and the third one west. One tunnel followed each direction.

Taika studied the tracks on the floor and saw that they went on to the north. He motioned for the group to take that passage and the others nodded. They went into the tunnel that led north. Nahia thought they could not be too far—at the other end of the tunnel, wherever it went. It had to be a way back to the surface.

Under Taika's and Daphne's feet there was a *click*.

"Oh no…" muttered Taika.

Two earth traps exploded with great thunder and strength. They filled the tunnel with earth and dust, stunning and blinding substances shooting out. Being inside the tunnel the explosion was intensified, since it bounced off the walls of the passage. They received impacts from every direction, as if they had been hit with a tremendous ball of earth that had burst into a thousand pieces. They were half deaf, completely stunned, and blinded. Daphne fell. Taika felt the Fatum fall and tried to help her but lost his balance. His ears were ringing and his head was reeling. Nahia tried to keep her balance, but she bumped into Aiden.

"Retreat!" cried Taika as he fought to get back on his feet and grab Daphne's hand.

Ivo and Lily retreated, stumbling, to the fork, unable to see anything. They were the ones who had suffered less from the impact of the traps. Nahia and Aiden, half deaf and blind, tried to retreat. But they were dizzy and fell. They began to crawl. Taika managed to grab Daphne and drag her back.

Ivo managed to see something out of one eye.

"Enemies!" he cried. An instant later, an air arrow hit him in the chest. It burst and Ivo received a discharge like a lightning bolt that knocked him down and left him shaking on the floor.

Lily was able to clear her head a little.

"Ivo!" she cried when she saw him on the floor, and then she was hit by another arrow in the chest, this one of earth. When the tip burst, it stunned and deafened her, incapacitating her.

Nahia could not see anything between the smoke and the earth that surrounded them and the little vision left in her eyes. She tried to gather energy to use her magic, but she found it impossible. Her head and ears were hammering with such force that she could not concentrate enough to use her magic.

Taika and Aiden managed to stand and sought to confront their enemies, but they could see nothing in the midst of the cloud of stunning substances that surrounded them. Aiden got hit in the stomach, and a tremendous discharge made him double down in pain and fall on his knees. Taika received another earth arrow in the chest and the explosions finished him off, blinding and stunning him. He was defenseless.

Unable to use magic, they were lost. They could not defend themselves with their weapons, and magic was their only escape in that situation. Unfortunately, the trap they had fallen into was formidable. If they could not use magic, they would not be able to get away. They were lost.

Chapter 34

Nahia glimpsed a figure down the east tunnel. She barely saw it, but she recognized the clothes—they were the kind the Rangers wore. She had already guessed they were the ones behind the attack, so she was not surprised. They had set a trap for them down there and they were going to die, unless they were able to persuade them not to kill them somehow.

"Rangers!" she shouted in the Norghanian language like Egil had taught her.

Daphne realized what Nahia was attempting, and she joined her.

"Friends!" she shouted from the floor, also in Norghanian. Egil had taught them a few words and expressions to use in Norghana, precisely in case something like this happened. The fact that Egil had foreseen this possibility was even more proof of his great intellect.

There was a silence. Then a voice asked in Norghanian, "Rangers friends?"

"Yes, yes! Lasgol, Egil," Daphne said in a loud voice so they would hear her well.

"Molak and Luca," Nahia added, also loud.

There was again a tense silence. Then they heard some whispering and someone ran off.

Aiden got up suddenly and tried to clear his vision, using his shield to dissipate the blinding cloud that enveloped them. This time the arrow burst in the middle of his forehead, and the lightning bolt it discharged went into his head and down his body, rendering him unconscious on the floor.

"Aiden!" Lily cried and felt around until she found him. He had a pulse, and Lily huffed in relief. Then she searched for Ivo on the floor and made sure he also had a pulse.

Taika remained at a crouch. He was trying to recover in order to attack.

The cloud of blinding and stunning dust, earth, and other substances faded gradually. They began to be able to see. Nahia could glimpse out of one eye. The other one was useless for now. Her head was beginning to clear as the hammering subsided. She looked right and left. Three archers, dressed entirely in white, with hooded cloaks and scarves covering their faces, were aiming their bows at them. There were two women and one man. She could only make out their eyes; everything else was the color of snow. They looked like beings out of the forest itself, as if they were its defendants, and her and her friends, mere intruders to be hunted. Nahia realized she was quite right in her thought.

After a moment, a fourth archer appeared, the one who had run off. He arrived, whispered something to his partner, and aimed his bow at them.

"Everyone, stay put," the other archer said.

This she understood. Nahia translated, and no one moved. They did not know what they were waiting for, but it was good for them. Once the dizziness and stunning passed, they would be able to use their magic. The problem was, if the Rangers realized they were using it, they would release at them. Nahia thought about using Fire Hands. It was almost instantaneous, but that would not help them with the archers entering the other tunnels, at over five paces each. Her Fire Hands would not reach them. Besides, there were two archers in each tunnel. If they attacked one way, the others would shoot at them. They were in a very unfavorable position. The traps and archers had left them hurt.

"No magic," one of the women said.

Nahia and Daphne understood. They told Lily and Taika not to use it for the time being, until they saw where it all led to. They did not know what was going on or why they kept them like that, but they simply had to wait. They did so for a long while. So long that Ivo and Aiden recovered. They stayed on the floor, following the indications of the archers with their bows. They motioned for the others to mimic them, and they all sat on the floor and waited.

Finally, they heard running footsteps and two more Rangers, also in white, appeared from the southern tunnel, the one they had come in through. These two greeted the others with a brief nod and came to where the Igneous Squad was sitting. They carried bows on their backs, but they did not reach for them. The two Rangers took off their hoods and scarves.

"Molak! Luca!" Nahia recognized them.

"Hello there, Nahia," Molak greeted her.

Luca smiled at her and gave her a nod.

Molak motioned her to get up.

"Friends," Nahia told Molak and then pointed at the four archers still aiming at them.

Molak looked to where Nahia indicated and nodded. He told the archers something and they lowered their weapons but remained with their bows armed and staring at them.

"Friends," Molak told Nahia, indicating the squad.

"Yes, friends," Nahia nodded.

Molak made a gesture of understanding.

Nahia turned to the others.

"They're friends. Don't attack. I know them."

"They're the enemy..." Aiden told her in a low voice.

"They're friends. Accept it. Don't do anything stupid," Daphne told Aiden in a serious tone.

"I'll watch him," said Ivo.

Molak indicated for them to stand up, and they did so.

"Lasgol, Camu, Gerd?" Nahia asked.

Molak pointed at the floor and shook his head. Then he pointed north and nodded.

"I see, they're in the north," Nahia pointed in that direction.

Molak nodded.

Luca pointed at the group.

"Squad?"

"Yes, Igneous Squad," Nahia remembered she had told them about her comrades. "Daphne, Fatum. Lily, Scarlatum. Taika, Felidae. Ivo, Kapro. Aiden, Drakonid," she introduced them with a wave of her hand, and as she named them, each one gave a nod. Aiden merely made a face.

Luca introduced his people.

"White Foxes: Frida, Elina, Sugesen, Gonars," the four uncovered their heads and took off their scarves at a gesture from Molak so they could see their faces.

Nahia nodded.

White Foxes," she repeated, doing her best to mimic what Luca had said.

"Yes, White Foxes."

"Like Snow Panthers."

"Yes," Luca nodded. "Snow Panthers: Ingrid, Nilsa, Astrid, Lasgol, Egil, Gerd, Viggo."

"Yes," Nahia nodded. She understood.

"Ingrid, Astrid, Viggo?" she asked

Molak and Luca shook their heads and then shrugged.

They suddenly heard roars. It was Irakas-Gorri-Gaizt. Somehow, its roars reached them down there.

Nahia pointed at her squad and then upward, indicating that the dragon was looking for them. One thing she realized was that here, underground, Irakas-Gorri-Gaizt's messages could not reach them, and it was definitely sending them.

Luca nodded.

"You're looking for this," Molak told them and reached into his backpack, taking out an object. As soon as he uncovered it, Nahia felt its power. They all stared at the object with great interest. It was a silver sphere. It looked like a large pearl, and it emanated immense power.

"What is it?" Nahia asked, and she made a question movement with her head.

"Dragon magic," Luca said.

"Dragon power," Molak added.

"The dragons already have magic and power. Why would they need this pearl?" Daphne asked.

Luca and Molak looked at her blankly.

Daphne pointed at the pearl and then shrugged.

Luca nodded. He took his knife from his Ranger belt. Aiden tensed at once, and Ivo noticed and put his large claw on his shoulder.

"Easy now…" he whispered in his ear.

Luca showed them the knife and then the palm of his hand. He pointed at himself with the knife and shook his head, then pointed at Nahia. He motioned for her to get closer, and Nahia complied. She wanted to know what the Ranger was trying to explain to them. Luca indicated for her to show him the palm of her hand. Nahia understood what he wanted to do. She did not like it much, but she trusted them, so she offered him her hand. Luca made a cut so swift Nahia did not even feel it. Blood began to come out of the cut on her palm. Luca put the knife away and held Nahia's wrist. He put her hand over the sphere Molak had in his own hand, without touching it but close.

They were all staring, amazed. What was Luca doing? What did he want to show them?

A drop of blood fell on the silver pearl. The pearl reacted, emitting a silver flash. A moment later, it radiated a silver energy over Nahia's hand, who felt a singular tingling. The sphere flashed again and stopped glowing.

Luca let go of Nahia's hand and she looked at her palm. The cut had vanished. Completely. It had not even left a scar.

"Look!" she showed her hand to the others.

"That sphere has healing power," Daphne said.

"A lot of power, even I can feel it," Ivo commented.

"Yeah, it's a powerful object," Taika nodded.

"The dragons use it to heal themselves? Is that what they're telling us?" Lily asked.

Nahia turned to Luca. She pointed upward, then at her hand, and then at the sphere.

"Yes, healing for dragons," Luca confirmed.

"That's why we stole it, so they can't heal," Molak said, nodding.

They could not understand it, but they got the basics. The silver pearls had power that allowed the dragons to heal. Perhaps more things. Surely others things as well, Nahia thought.

There was an explosion along the south tunnel. The Rangers were restless.

"Another squad is coming. We just set more traps," Luca said, indicating Nahia and her comrades, the south entrance, and then the floor.

"We must leave," Molak said and indicated his friends and then east.

Nahia pointed at the silver pearl.

"Are you taking this? The dragon will chase you. It can feel it," Nahia warned Molak and then pointed upward. Then with her hands she mimicked the pearl flashing upward, toward the dragon.

They heard another one of Irakas-Gorri-Gaizt's roars.

Molak understood.

"We know, but we're taking it anyway. We can't let them heal the wounded dragons. It's terribly hard to hurt them. We'll take the risk."

Nahia did not understand it.

"Thank you, Nahia," Molak told her and put the pearl in his backpack.

Nahia guessed they would take the risk.

"Say hello to Egil from us, from all of us," Luca said and included everyone with a wave.

Nahia nodded.

"Greet, yes."

Suddenly, Frida, Elina, Sugesen, and Gonars raised their bows. Before they could react, they released. There were four earth explosions and the whole place was filled with a stunning, blinding cloud.

"Get down on the floor, they shot at the ceiling," Taika told them.

They threw themselves on the floor while above them the cloud enveloped everything.

"Blast them! We must pursue them and recover the silver pearl," said Aiden, standing. At once, he was stunned and blinded.

"I don't think you're going anywhere, little granite-head," Lily told him, "so stay very still."

A few moments later, the Searing Squad arrived with Logar leading them. He found them on the floor, the stunning cloud still above their heads.

"Are you all right?" he asked without getting too close.

"Yes, but with a few injured from the traps," Daphne told him.

Nahia looked at Daphne and saw that she and Taika had cuts on their legs. She had not seen it before. "So are we," Logar said, indicating those behind him.

"The human, Balk, was carrying a comrade and the Tauruk, Valka, another. The Fatum, Beck, brought up the rear.

"The attackers?" Logar asked.

"They fled east," Aiden said before anyone could stop him, and he indicated the tunnel.

Logar looked at the passage and then at his injured comrades.

"I think we'd better go back south. If we follow this tunnel, more surprises could be waiting."

"My thoughts exactly," said Nahia.

"Give me a moment and I'll try to help you," said Daphne as she began to apply her healing energy on herself.

"Don't worry, we're not going anywhere," Logar told her.

Nahia and her comrades waited until the cloud dispersed before getting up. When they finally did, Daphne was already well enough to help the others. The first one she tended to was Taika, who was right beside her.

"Did the leader send you?" Aiden asked.

"Yes. Since you weren't coming out, he sent us to help you," Beck replied,

"Our leader isn't going to be happy with this…" Logar told Nahia under his breath while Daphne helped the rest of his squad.

"I know. It's going to have a mighty fit," Nahia nodded.

"Three squads with wounded and whatever was in the box gone."

"I'll tell you when we're alone," Nahia whispered to him and looked him in the eye.

The Felidae-Lion understood there was something interesting to share.

"All right. Without risks."

Nahia nodded.

Once Daphne had helped all the wounded, the two squads withdrew, careful not to step on more traps. The wounded ones could not walk, so they were carried between two. At the ravine, already in the open, Irakas-Gorri-Gaizt located them and flew over them several times.

Aiden was pointing east with his sword. Irakas-Gorri-Gaizt flew off in that direction.

Go back to the carts. And don't have any more accidents!

They did as ordered and got back to the carts. The attack had finished and the soldiers had managed to put out practically all the fires. They chose several carts and put the wounded in them. Daphne assured them their wounds would heal, they only needed some time.

Irakas-Gorri-Gaizt did not return until dawn, which surprised Nahia and her friends.

"Do you think it will have managed to recover the silver pearl?" Lily asked.

"I hope not, for the sake of the White Foxes," Nahia said wishfully.

"You should hope so," Aiden said, annoyed.

"And you should wish that you and your people were free instead of the dragons' smiling slaves. Then you'd see things a different way," Daphne snapped at him.

Aiden was about to reply, but when he saw the looks of the others he shut up. He was in the minority, and he knew it.

"We'll find out depending on the lecture," Nahia said.

"Yeah, we're going to be seriously punished if the silver pearl isn't recovered," Daphne shook her hand hard for emphasis.

"We'll just have to wait and see," Ivo shrugged.

"At least we've learned a very valuable lesson," Taika commented, and they all turned to look at him.

"Explain that," Lily said.

"We Dragon Warlocks are powerful with our magic and the knowledge we have of fighting in hand-to-hand combat. But here, in the forests, we're no match for the Rangers."

"The forests are full of treacherous traps, and they shoot from covered areas, like cowards, without revealing themselves," Aiden said, upset.

"Well, there are some who don't learn their lesson, even if it hits them in the center of the forehead," Lily laughed.

"Yeah, it's a lesson the dragons are also learning the hard way," Nahia commented.

"Yeah, but even though they're like this rock-head, in the end they'll wake up," said Daphne.

"Yeah, I'm afraid of that," Nahia nodded.

We leave at once! they received the order.

Several days went by without attacks or mishaps, and Nahia, who had checked her map, thought she knew where they were headed. She told her comrades.

"We're going to the walled city of Olstran."

"Where is that?" Daphne asked from the cart.

"It's a point of resistance north of the capital. Egil told me that part of the Norghanian royal army is likely taking shelter there. It's a very difficult city to lay siege to. It's withstood several in the past."

"Then the dragon army will need supplies," said Taika.

"And silver pearls for the dragons," Daphne added.

"We'll soon find out," Taika said and pointed to the horizon.

The road was beginning to slope down, and they clearly saw a walled city on a high plain. It was large—not as grand as the capital, but still a great metropolis. As Egil had foreseen, it was being besieged, and it was withstanding the assault. They could see several dragons flying over the city and columns of smoke coming from inside it. A part of the red dragon's army was camped to the north of the city. They headed there.

For a week, they rested in the war camp at Olstran. During this time, they heard nothing of Irakas-Gorri-Gaizt, which they were all grateful for. They did not know what was going on, but this siege was going worse than the one at the capital. On the one hand, there were fewer soldiers and dragons attacking the city, and on the other, the defenders seemed to have reinforcements. The soldiers at the camp told them that Shamans from the Frozen Continent had come down with enormous warriors with skin of ice. They were helping the Norghanian soldiers. Hence the war camp was north of the city. They could not allow more reinforcements to enter it.

"They must be the Wild People of the Ice we encountered before," Daphne commented.

"They were tremendously strong and ugly," said Lily.

"I didn't like the gangly ones with the javelins, they looked like they were covered with frost," said Ivo.

"Our armies will defeat them," Aiden said confidently.

"The Shamans must have a powerful magic, from what I heard. They make you see and do things, the soldiers say," Nahia explained.

"That's enchanter magic," Lily recognized. "I'd like to see them in action."

Unfortunately, they could not see anything else. The next morning, Irakas-Gorri-Gaizt ordered them to form into three squads and march on. They were going back to the Academy. The mission was over.

The return journey was a long one, but luckily quiet. They returned with the empty carts, those that had survived the attacks, led by the drivers. The soldiers who had not disappeared, stayed for the siege. They had no other encounters with Rangers or any other Norghanians. Since they had all recovered from their injuries, they traveled relatively fast. The only setback was the constant presence of Irakas-Gorri-Gaizt, since it did not leave them at any moment. They arrived at the Academy and realized they were exhausted. They had traveled an enormous distance, and on foot. Luckily, they did not have to deal with any serious injuries or casualties. What none of them understood was why they had not received any scolding from Irakas-Gorri-Gaizt, neither on the way, nor when they returned. Nahia concluded that it had to be because it had recovered the silver pearl. This made her fear for Molak, Luca, and the White Foxes' fate.

Chapter 35

They still had not recovered from the mid-year test when they had to return to one of the hardest classes, one none of them liked. Not only that, but winter had already arrived, and with it the cold and stormy skies. Nahia liked winter less and less. She found it icy, and up here in this floating realm among the clouds, even more so. She found it hard, both physically and emotionally, and her body turned off, just like her spirit. For some reason, the snow and the frozen landscapes of Norghana seemed much nicer to her than those of the Academy. She blamed the Academy itself. It had to be that.

She looked up, saw the black clouds that threatened them with storm, and the freezing wind blew in her face. It smelled and felt like damp cold, the kind that got into a person's bones. She definitely did not like winter up here.

"Ugh…. Mental Magic training again," Daphne moaned with a snort, disgusted.

"Not one of my favorites," Lily shut her eyes tight and shook her head, as if foreseeing what was about to come.

"And you complain…" Ivo sighed deep and made a resigned face. "I'd rather be in Tremia making Rangers' elemental traps explode than go to training now."

Lily burst out laughing, and the others joined her.

"I could say the same thing," Nahia said, patting the Tauruk for courage.

Although they were all capable now of seeing mental auras and identifying when they were being attacked with a mental attack, not all of them could attack with their minds. Ivo could not manage it, and that was why he walked to class with his shoulders down, dragging his feet.

"It's a very tough, frustrating class, but we have to pass it. We must make the effort," Taika said, not walking as nimbly or lightly as he was used to. It was not because of the wounds from the mid-year mission, which had healed well. His feet also felt heavy on the way to the training, as if they did not want to go and he was forcing them forward.

Nahia looked at him fondly. The Felidae could not throw mental attacks either. At least he took it more in stride than Ivo, who considered it a lost cause. Taika did not give up. He had a fighter's heart; he was a tiger, first and foremost, in body and soul.

"That magic is hard to learn and master. We've known that since day one at the Academy. We're in our third year. Now we must prove that we are worthy and pass these classes," Aiden said.

To the girls' surprise, who were all able to use Mental Magic, there were times when Aiden was able to perform Mental Attacks, although they were few. But he was not demoralized by his failures and did not give up. Quite much the opposite—he spent day and night trying to achieve it. For him, it was a matter of honor. There were several Drakonids who had already succeeded, and he could not be less than them. Nahia thought that, even if all the third-year Drakonids failed in mental attacks, Aiden would keep trying until he succeeded. That was just how he was. No one could be more stubborn and hardworking than him. Hence, in part, the reasons for the nicknames Daphne and Lily so fondly used for him. The other part though was because of his blind love for his dragon lords, which the rest of the squad neither understood nor shared.

Nahia looked up at the sky and remembered an old saying her grandmother had explained to her when she was little. "There is no one blinder than the one who doesn't wish to see the truth." Aiden was the clearest example of that saying. It did not matter how evil, bloodthirsty, or destructive the dragons were. In Aiden's mind, they could do no wrong. They always had a reason to behave the way they did. On more than one occasion Nahia had been on the verge of hitting him on the head with her shield, but it would not be of any use. The saying played through her head again with the voice of her dear grandmother.

"Today I'm going to manage to do all the mental attacks," the Drakonid told them confidently as they arrived at the magic building.

"I bet you will, with your head filled with sand," Lily told him with a mischievous smile.

"I've given up, it's impossible," Ivo admitted, scratching his large head. "It's simply not for me."

Taika nodded with a long face.

"I don't want to give up, but it's true. I don't believe I'll succeed. Even so, I'll keep doing my best."

"You two ought to keep trying. It's marble–head who should give up. He causes enough trouble with everything else," Daphne said with a look that said she meant it.

"Don't be mean, Daphne, Aiden has the right to succeed just like us," Nahia replied. She understood what Daphne meant and why she said it, but it was not fair.

"Oh, he has a right, I'm not denying that, but it would be better if he stayed the same. Another uncontrolled weapon in his arsenal is bad news for us," she retorted.

"I'll manage to master the mental attacks. I am a Drakonid, and therefore I must succeed. And I won't lose control."

"Sure, until you have your next seizure," Daphne snapped.

"Let's be optimistic. He might not have one for some time," Ivo said cheerfully.

"Better see what today has in store for us in there," Lily said, raising an eyebrow as she looked at the building,

"Whatever it is, we'll overcome it," Taika said in a great show of strength.

"Together we can," Nahia joined him.

What was in store for them was Buru-Beira-Gogoa, the fearsome dragoness who enjoyed torturing them. Without wasting an instant, the class began.

You have two ways of defeating your enemy with a Mental Attack. One is with a direct attack of great intensity, which is what we have been using until now. The ball of elemental energy is the most efficient way to attack, since its explosion produces an important harmful effect and is easy to execute. But you may also perform the other elemental attacks you know in the same way: Elemental Claws, Maw, or Breath. They are all usable but not as easy to execute or maximize their power. That is why we focus on the elemental balls.

It was a lot easier for Nahia to create the elemental ball of fire than the other three skills, so she understood what the dragoness was saying.

I encourage you to experiment. Perhaps some of you will be better with one attack or another. It is not common, but it can happen. In the world of magic, there are always exceptions for everything.

Nahia was left thinking that she would like to try it. Perhaps she would be faster with Elemental Claw. Surely not with Elemental Maw or Elemental Breath. She wondered whether any of her comrades would be more lethal with those attacks. Perhaps Lily. Yes, she bet that with Elemental Claws or Elemental Maw she would do better than the others.

The second way to defeat an enemy is what is known as a Sustained Mental Attack. It is something we dragons favor, and one of the attacks we use and enjoy the most. What you have to do is attack with your elemental energy, but instead of making the elemental ball burst, you must envelope the enemy's mental aura with it without it exploding. It must swallow the rival's mind so they suffer the elemental effects for an extended period of time. If it is fire, you will make the mind of your rival burn. If it is water, you can freeze it, and so on and so forth. You will send more and more energy without destabilizing and bursting the ball. That will make the mind of the enemy suffer exponentially until it yields completely. It is similar to strangling someone until they are rendered unconscious or die. With this attack, that is what you are after. Rendering someone unconscious or killing them.

Nahia was already nervous just from listening that she could kill someone with this attack. An accident might happen. This dragoness did not care if anyone died in class. In fact, it would celebrate if that happened. It would surely interpret it as an achievement of the difficulty of her classes and her method of teaching. It was crazy that they had to go through all this dangerous training.

We are going to begin practicing. For this exercise you will work on Membor, my assistant Exarbor. You will attack his mind and bend him in the two ways I have just explained.

Nahia's head was thrown back from the unpleasant surprise. The dragoness could not be serious. How were they going to attack the poor Membor? That was the most inhumane thing she had ever heard of. That Exarbor looked about two hundred years old, and his wooden body seemed to decompose a little with every move he made.

I see your looks of concern about harming Membor. The inferior races are nothing more than that. One of the main reasons for that is your pathetic sense of empathy. You must not worry about the Exarbor. Membor is prepared for this function. He is not just any Exarbor, he is an Exarbor with power, like any of you. Dragon blood also runs through his veins.

This revelation left Nahia dumbstruck. And not only her; Daphne and Lily were looking at one another in shock. An Exarbor with magic. That meant that among the two non-combatant races there were others with magic. Nahia had sometimes wondered, but since she had never seen an Exarbor or Tergnomus using magic, she had assumed they did not have it. Assuming things was a bad trait and empathy was a very good one, whatever the dragons had to say about the matter.

Flameborn, step forward. I want to see how you do it.

Nahia took a deep breath, and although she hated to be singled out for what she was, she hid it. She did not want any more trouble, least of all with this dragoness. She stepped forward. Membor moved with his usual parsimony until he was in front of her.

First, attack. Go ahead, punish the mind of the Exarbor with a direct attack.

Nahia did not want to do that. She felt awful for poor Membor. It was like hurting an old man.

Before you say or do anything you might regret, you should know that the Exarbor is capable of defending himself. Not only that, he can also counterattack, so do not take pity on him, because he might defeat you.

Once again, Nahia was shocked. That did not make her feel any better, but at least she would not be attacking a defenseless being. If the dragoness was telling the truth that is, because, knowing dragons, it might be lying.

Bend your rival. Now, the dragoness ordered, together with a feeling of victory.

Nahia did not want to do it, but if she refused, she was as good as dead. The dragoness would kill her right there and then. It would not allow such a lack of respect to its honor. She sought Membor's mental aura and found it at once. It did not surprise her that it was a combination of intertwined greens and browns. She called on her inner dragon, gathered a good amount of energy, and created a ball of fire in her mind. She did not maximize it in any way, neither in power or range. She did not want an accident to happen.

She threw the ball with her mind. She saw it heading for the Exarbor's mind. It would impact and the exercise would be over. But that was not the case. The Exarbor's mind flashed and a barrier of energy surrounded it, forming a ring. The ball reached it and was unable to pass through. Nahia was surprised; that ring-shaped barrier that enveloped his mental aura and protected his mind was definitely magical. She was watching the Exarbor use his dragon blood to create magic and defend himself. She was able to detect how he sent more energy to defend his aura.

Keep attacking, the order came and startled her.

Nahia knew what she had to do and sent her own energy to the fireball to help it get through the defensive mental ring. At once, the Exarbor sent more of his own energy to defend it. Things were getting interesting; Nahia had to be careful that her ball did not explode since it could not get through the defensive ring, or she would lose control of it. Suddenly, something odd happened. There was a green-brown flash in the Exarbor's aura and Nahia felt that her own was being attacked. Almost without time to think, she instinctively sent energy to protect her own mental aura. She created a ring of energy, an intense red, and defended herself from the Exarbor's mental attack.

Well done. Defend yourself from the counterattack.

What had begun as a simple command was becoming more and more complicated by the moment. She had to attack, maintain the ball of fire, and at the same time defend herself. She focused on the latter and discovered that Membor was attacking her with an Elemental Earth Claw. If the claw got through her defensive ring, it would seriously harm her. She detected the claw as if it were a real, physical one. It was frightening. It had three rocky fingers with sharp edges and ended in a tip that was stuck in her defensive ring. Nahia sent more energy to strengthen it. The Elemental Earth Claw tried to penetrate her mind and break through her defensive barrier.

Nahia realized she had to push back, so she pushed her fireball against the Exarbor's barrier. The flames that came out of her ball seemed to burn the defensive ring's energy and penetrate it. Whoever managed to break the other's defensive ring would win.

There was a moment of intense struggle, and suddenly, at the same time, both attacks managed to defeat the defenses. Nahia's fireball exploded in Membor's mind as the Exarbor's claw struck Nahia's mind. Nahia doubled down with pain and fell to her knees. Membor swayed back and forth with a look of pain on his tree-like face.

Excellent demonstration of magical mental attack and defense. As you can see, ties might occur. It is not common, but here is an example. Let it be a lesson to attack with all the intensity and speed you can, because you may end up like the Flameborn, defeated.

Nahia felt a tremendous pain in her head that did not even let her think. She was defeated, half useless.

Very well. We will continue with the fights as soon as my Exarbor assistant recovers. Get ready: whoever loses will suffer.

After class, Nahia went to the library. She waited at the end table of the third floor while her headache ran its course. She was nervous. She still felt like someone was watching her the moment she set foot in the library, and she could not get rid of that feeling. She checked the floor; everything looked normal. Third-year pupils were studying, alone or in groups, all in silence. Several Exarbor came and went, carrying tomes from the shelves to the tables with their slow, weary pace. No one was looking at her. Everything seemed the way it ought to be, and yet she was restless.

Ana and Logan appeared on the floor, and at once Nahia felt happy, her aches vanishing. The two new arrivals checked the scene briefly and then crossed the floor. Ana was looking at Logan out of the corner of her eye while he looked straight ahead. They reached her but did not sit at her table. They chose one beside it to pretend. They sat together and pretended to study the tome they had brought.

"We have to talk about what happened during the mid-year test," Nahia whispered.

"Yeah… but you have a meeting. Afterward," Logan said.

Ana gave her a nod. Two third-year pupils were approaching them.

"Alright," Nahia whispered back.

The two figures crossed the floor and came to stand in front of Nahia. Before they could say anything, she spoke.

"Go and ask for a tome of third-year magic and come back with it to study here."

The two nodded and turned to where the nearest Exarbor stood. They spoke to him, and once they had the tome they came back to Nahia's table. They sat in front of her and opened the tome as if they were studying.

Nahia waited a moment to make sure no Exarbors were watching them.

"I think it's now safe to talk."

"Thank you for seeing us, Nahia," said Nielse, the Fatum from the Rock Squad. He had been a comrade of poor Maika, and Nahia had seen him at the dungeons serving punishment.

"Hi, Nielse, I'm glad to see you again. How's your Serpetuss' repulsion going?"

Nielse made a face of horror.

"Badly, but lately I haven't been sent to the dungeons, so I'm doing better."

Nahia smiled and nodded.

"It's better that way."

"Is the prisoner still doing well?" Nielse asked with interest, referring to Egil but without naming him, just in case.

"Still is, yeah. He's a great collaborator to the cause. We must make sure nothing happens to him."

"I understand," Nielse nodded.

"And you don't need to thank me. It's me who should thank you for coming to see me."

"It's an honor that you're taking the time to see us," said Mark, the human from the Stone Squad who had shown interest in the cause.

Nahia was very surprised they felt so honored to talk to her. After all, they were the ones taking risks just by listening. She saw that Ana and Logan were getting up to distract the Exarbor and decided to be straightforward.

"Listen to me, both of you. I'm going to tell you what I know, what I've seen, and what I've lived. I want you to pay close attention, because it's very important and I can't afford to repeat it. The risk is great, as you can imagine."

They both nodded.

"Go ahead, that's what we've come for," Nielse told her.

Nahia lowered her voice as much as she could and told them everything about the golden weapons, the possibility of finishing off the dragons, the need to join the fight for freedom, and, most of all, the importance of transmitting the message of hope to all the slaves of Kraido. She was honest and straightforward; it was the only way. When she finished, they both looked at her with bright eyes. Nahia wanted to think she saw the glow of hope in them.

"I had heard something, but what you're telling us is much more than I expected," Nielse said, nodding.

"It's a revelation. Something we never thought could happen," Mark added.

"I swear it can. They can be killed, and therefore we can defeat them."

Mark nodded repeatedly too.

"It's a lot to digest."

"I know. Think about it carefully. Joining me and the cause comes with enormous risks, and you don't need me to tell you what the punishment will be if we're found out."

"It won't be the dungeons, we'll be killed on the spot," said Nielse.

"That's right," Nahia said honestly.

"The risk is great and the punishment terrible," Mark said thoughtfully.

"Yeah, but the reward is greater if we achieve freedom for everyone," Nahia said.

"You're absolutely right, Nahia. Count me in. I saw what happened to Maika, and the same will happen to me, I have no doubt about that. It's only a matter of time. I'd rather die trying to reach freedom than serving *them* without hope," Nielse said.

"Well said," Mark joined him. "We're going to die on some far-away battlefield or at the whim of some dragon any day, so I'd rather die trying to reach freedom. At least I'll die for something worthy."

"You fill my heart with joy. I wish everyone was like you," Nahia said gratefully.

"I believe that when the message reaches more ears, there'll be more like us," said Nielse.

"A lot more," Mark nodded.

"I hope so. For now, this is what I need you to do. The message has to keep spreading. The more people it reaches, the better," Nahia told them.

"Absolutely, we'll do that," Nielse said.

"Between Nielse and me, the Brown Squadron is covered," Mark said.

"Great. I also need you to carry the message to the second- and first-years of the Brown Squadron."

"We'll do it, don't worry," Nielse promised.

"Don't take any risks. If you don't see a clear way, don't pass on the message," Nahia warned them, not wanting to take any more risks than necessary. The danger was too high.

They both nodded.

"Thank you for trusting us," Mark said.

Nahia felt happy to have comrades like them. They thanked her when she was asking them to risk their lives. It was impressive, and it filled her with pride. With them, the cause for freedom would move forward. Sooner or later, but in the end they would triumph. She was going to fight for people like them.

The two boys said goodbye and left. Nahia remained thoughtful. They needed to find someone in the Light and Dark Squadrons. They had both suffered terrible casualties, perhaps that would help. Yeah, it would, most likely. Something good to hold onto after seeing so much death. She thought about telling Ana and Logan. She raised her gaze, looking for them, and realized that an Exarbor was heading directly to her table. She froze. Had she been found out? What did that Exarbor want? Why was he coming toward her?

She looked for her friends and saw them entertaining two other Exarbors. The one coming toward her did so at a slow, deliberate pace. Nahia thought she would have a heart attack while she watched the Exarbor approach her so slowly. With every step he took, her heart beat faster.

Chapter 36

The librarian Exarbor walked up to Nahia and looked at her. He took a moment to speak. Nahia could not contain her nerves.

"The… Chief Librarian… wants to see you."

"I haven't done anything," Nahia frowned.

"I didn't say… you had… done…"

"Oh yeah."

"Go up… to see… the Chief Librarian."

"To the fifth floor?"

"Yes… to his… office."

Nahia thought for a moment. She had no idea what was up or what the Chief Librarian wanted, but she could not refuse or she would end up in the claws of the dragons.

"Fine, I'll go."

The Exarbor nodded, and then turning very slowly, he pointed at the stairs with his arm.

"Right away?"

"It's… very bad manners… to make someone wait."

That was weird. The Exarbor was making sure she went at once.

"True. Okay, I'm coming." Nahia got up and headed to the stairs. The Exarbor followed her. As she walked, she looked at Ana and Logan out of the corner of her eye. The two were looking at her unobtrusively. The looks on both of their faces were troubled.

Nahia went up the stairs to the fourth floor. She noticed that the Exarbor was following behind her. She had thought of slipping into one of the magical training halls to think about what to do beforehand, but she was not going to be able to with the Exarbor following her. She had to resign herself and continue to the fifth floor. When she arrived, she found it empty, although she knew there were several Exarbors around. She had been caught before when she tried to steal a dictionary for Egil.

She headed to one of the three doors in front of her, the one to the north, and went down a corridor that had about twenty more doors on the sides. The Chief Librarian's office was at the end of the corridor. She looked back and saw that the Exarbor was watching her from the top of the stairs. He had apparently been told to make sure she did as requested. She looked at the door of the office, made her decision, and knocked.

"Come in," she heard the leathery voice of the Chief Librarian.

Nahia opened the door and went in. The room was well-lit. Sitting in an armchair, behind a large carved oak desk, was Liburex.

"I haven't committed any crimes," Nahia said. She knew that Liburex had a tome where he had two serious crimes of hers written down, crimes that would cost her life if he told Irakas-Gorri-Gaizt.

The Exarbor smiled and the bark-like skin over his mouth curved.

"No one… has said… otherwise."

"Then why am I here?"

"I wanted to… say hello…. It's been … a long time… since we've seen each other."

She certainly had not been expecting that answer.

"Say hello? Why?"

"We are acquainted… I was wondering how… you're doing."

"I'm doing well, thank you," Nahia replied. The situation had her on edge.

"Indeed, that is… the rumor…"

"The rumor? What rumor?"

"That you're doing well… you are very popular… among your people."

Now the situation was beginning to make sense. Liburex knew something, or suspected something. Nahia wished it was the latter, because if it was the former, she was as good as dead.

"Not so much. I get along well with my squad, that's all."

"And other… squads… too."

"Yeah, well, with the whole squadron."

Liburex smiled again.

"We can … play this game… as long as you like… but it's a waste of time… for both of us."

"What game?"

"Deceit… won't work…. I know the truth… about the 'cause'."

Nahia felt an enormous void opening in her stomach. She was doomed. She had been found out.

"I don't know…" she tried to feign ignorance.

"Have you ever… noticed… the lamps… that light the library?"

Liburex cut her short.

"The lamps?" Nahia tried to remember what they were like. Yes, they were there, they provided light, but she could not fully remember them.

"I haven't noticed..."

"Sure... neither you nor anyone else.... It's curious... since light is necessary to see, read, study... and no one pays attention."

"I don't follow," Nahia made a gesture of annoyance.

Liburex smiled with his mouth and lips of bark.

"The library lamps... like those in many other places in this Academy... have a wooden base," he pointed his wooden finger, a leaf on the knuckle, at the dark lamp that stood on one end of his desk.

"I still don't understand..."

"Do you know anything of the magic of the Exarbor?"

Nahia could not be more confused. She had no idea what Liburex was talking about or where he was going with all this.

"Err... no. No idea." She shook her head.

"It's not something they teach you at the Academy... since the dragons consider us useless for war... so they don't see fit to teach you our magic... which they also consider useless... although it isn't, in the least."

"Not all the Exarbor have magic, do they?" Nahia was trying to understand this.

"Indeed, only a small part... same as the other races... like yours... the Human race."

"What kind of magic do you have? Nature?" Nahia asked. Although she knew of Membor's magic, she was trying to gain time to understand what was going on here and how to get out of it alive.

Liburex nodded with a rustle. When the Exarbor leaned over, they seemed to be ready to snap.

"Indeed... nature... with a special connection to trees and woods.... Let me show you... that way you'll understand better."

Liburex pointed at the lamp again, and this time he shut his eyes. Suddenly, his body gave off a green glow. Nahia could sense his magic. An intense green aura surrounded the Exarbor's whole body. A moment later, a thread of green energy came out of his finger and headed to the lamp.

Nahia watched with great interest. She was intrigued. For some reason, she did not have the feeling that the Chief Librarian's magic was dangerous. The thread of energy coming out of Liburex's finger reached the lamp. It went to the wooden base and enveloped it. Suddenly, and to Nahia's great surprise, the lamp turned on. Somehow, Liburex's magic interacted with the wooden base, which turned on the lamp. A moment later, the lamp went out. The thread of green energy unraveled from the base and returned to Liburex's finger and aura.

The chief librarian opened his eyes and the magic faded, as well as his aura.

"Did you like… the demonstration?"

"Yeah, it's amazing. The magic interacts with the wood."

"That's right. The same way I turned the light on… I can interact with the lamp… for other interesting things…"

When she heard that, Nahia finally understood what had happened.

"Other interesting things like listening," she said.

Liburex nodded, smiling.

"I knew you'd understand… with a simple… practical demonstration. You are… intelligent."

Nahia swallowed.

"You've been listening to our conversations."

"That's right…. They are most interesting…"

"That's terrible. They're private conversations," Nahia felt a mixture of rage and frustration.

"About very… serious matters…. About which… I have permission from our dragon lords… to listen to and report on."

"You're an informant for the dragons!" Nahia accused him, feeling the flame light up in her stomach.

"I am… otherwise I couldn't be the… Chief Librarian. The dragons want loyal servants… especially in posts of responsibility."

"And you're a loyal servant," the sentence left Nahia's mouth as if she spit out an insult.

"I am," Liburex nodded.

"Then turn me in and have me killed! I don't regret it, and I never will!" Nahia shouted at him, and she stood up.

Liburex raised his wooden hand.

"Sit down and… keep your cool… please," he asked her in a quiet voice.

"Maybe I should incinerate you on the spot for being an informant. I'm sure you'd burn easily," Nahia threatened furiously.

Liburex smiled.

"Indeed, I would burn fast and fierce. But that would sentence you to death… and as far as I know, I haven't yet said … that I'm going to turn you in."

That left Nahia's mind completely blank.

"What's going on here? Are you tricking me so I don't turn you into ashes?"

"Absolutely not… If I wanted to turn you in, I would have done so already… I wouldn't risk you setting me on fire."

"Then what?" Nahia stared at him with a frown.

"Sit down and I'll explain… and extinguish your fury…Flameborn… I don't want an accident to happen, and… flames to consume me."

Nahia thought of running away. But if he had heard their conversations, he knew their plans and everyone involved in them. Logan and Ana. She could not risk their lives. She would listen to what the Chief Librarian had to say. But if it did not convince her, she would incinerate him. She would fall, but not her friends. This is what she would do. She sat down but kept her flame burning in her stomach. If she needed it, she would use it with all her power and there would be nothing left of that Exarbor informant, not even embers.

"Explain yourself," she said, glaring at him.

"As a Chief Librarian… I must inform the dragons of any word or action against them… like, for instance, starting and organizing a rebellion… which is what you've been doing…"

"But you haven't."

"No, I haven't."

"Why not?"

"You see… young Flameborn… you are not the only one who believes in the cause of freedom… as you see when you recruit others…. There are those who wish for freedom… in all the slave races."

"Not in the Exarbor and Tergnomus."

"And that is… where you are wrong… young Human. Of course, there are many among… the Exarbor and the Tergnomus who wish for freedom…. There are even some among the Drakonids…"

Nahia shook her head.

"I don't believe it. They've never shown any interest. They are faithful servants of their dragon lords. They didn't support rebellion before and never will. They didn't join the Great Insurrection."

"There is some truth in that… but you're wrong…. There are many among the most servile races who wish for freedom."

"Are you one of them?" Nahia said as if daring him to answer.

Liburex smiled.

"Let's say that I'm interested… in the best future for my people…"

"That's not a direct answer."

"I'm not… a direct Exarbor…"

"I can see that. Are you going to turn me in to the dragons? Me and my friends?" Nahia felt the flame growing inside her. If he answered wrong, she was going to burn him and half the office.

"That is not my intention… I'm not going to end the rebellion…"

Nahia looked him in the eyes to guess whether he was telling the truth. She could not decide whether he was being honest or not. His deep eyes did not show any feeling.

"In that case, what do you want from me?"

"Although it will surprise you… I want to help you."

"You do? Why?"

"Because of what I just told you… I want the best for my people…. Your rebellion, if successful… might bring about exactly that. Although I have to admit… that the odds of your being successful… are practically nil…. That's why I'll lend you my assistance… but from a distance."

Nahia's mouth twisted.

"I see. You want to see whether we succeed, because that would be very good for your people. But since you don't believe we will succeed, you don't want to take the risk and have the dragons kill you."

"That's a simple way of putting it… but yes… you are not wrong."

"And you're not very brave."

"The brave usually live short lives… I help my people… and they need me alive… dead, I can do little for them."

"But I can die."

"I like your spirit… you are achieving something very few might…. Organizing a rebellion against the dragons is an impressive feat… and I'd rather you did not die…. That's why we're having this conversation…"

Nahia was thoughtful.

"How can you help me with the cause?"

"In the first place… by telling you that not all the Exarbor, Tergnomus… not even all Drakonids are faithful to the dragons. You can… find allies among them… allies who might be of great use…"

"Hmmmm… maybe. How do I know you're not going to betray me, me and my friends?"

"That's a good question… you can't know… you can only hope."

"And if I don't want to take the risk? If I incinerate you right here?"

"Then you'll die… and with you the rebellion you're trying to raise…"

"I'll save my friends."

"From a danger that might not exist… because I haven't betrayed you yet… and I've known your intentions for a long time."

"I don't like risks, least of all when there are innocent people involved."

"Innocent or not, they have all joined the cause of their own free will…. They all know the risk they are taking… you yourself told them all, each and every one of them…. If they're with you, it's because they have made their choice… despite the risks. As for betraying you… any of them might do that before I did…"

"They would never do that," Nahia replied, offended.

"You're wrong… people are not as strong and brave… as you believe…"

"Those who join me are."

"You are making a mistake by thinking that… there's weakness in everyone… in some more than in others… even if you don't see it."

Nahia was left thinking. If she killed Liburex, it would be her end and perhaps the end of the rebellion. The cause was not secure enough yet. They needed a little more time for the message to reach everyone; and not only at the Academy, but below, on land. She also needed some more time to organize the structure of the rebels. Right now it was only her, helped by Ana and Logan. Many things to do that needed time, since they had to be done carefully.

"You put me in a difficult situation."

"Whoever plays very dangerous games... must accept the risks they bring."

The thing was, he was not that wrong. From the first moment, Nahia had understood the risks implied in attempting a rebellion to win freedom. But she had always focused the risk on herself and her own life. If she had to die, she accepted it. But now she realized that Ana's and Logan's and all the others' lives were also at stake. She had not given enough thought to this fact, and now, before the decision she had to make, they weighed as much as a mountain. Trusting Liburex was risky, she knew that. She remembered Garran-Zilar-Denbo's words in the past. Not to trust anyone, and least of all the Exarbor and the Tergnomus. She had to make a decision, a risky one. It might be the end of everything if she was wrong. She hoped not.

"All right, I won't kill you. I expect the same courtesy on your part."

Liburex smiled.

"As I said, I want to help you... killing you doesn't interest me... it would bring nothing to me... or my people."

"All right, I accept your help. I understand that you don't want to take an active part in my plans." Liburex shook his head, which rustled.

"I'll be a... passive observer."

"I understand. One question. Do you listen throughout the Academy?"

"We do indeed."

"And if I don't want you to listen to me?"

"Look for a place... without wood near."

Nahia nodded.

"I'll do that."

"Good luck.... You're going to need it... leader of the rebellion."

"I'm not..." Nahia was quiet. She did not feel or consider herself the leader of anything, least of all a rebellion.

"Yes, you are... you just haven't... internalized it yet."

Nahia left Liburex's office and crossed with two Exarbor waiting for him. She passed by them without a word. She had a lot to think about. This meeting had been very strange, and she was left with a feeling of great uncertainty that devoured her stomach.

Chapter 37

Contrary to what happened in their Weapons and Magic training, Nahia enjoyed the Talent training more and more with every class. She had to admit that she liked Sorcery; not only that, she was very good at it. Perhaps she liked it because of that. Besides, the Sorcery instructor, Zeru-Urdin-On, the powerful blue dragoness, was no despot and torturer, but the very opposite. To her surprise, she had found a dragoness who was not evil and with a rotten heart, like nearly all other dragons. Like, for instance, the Magic instructor, who took great joy in making them suffer. This exception to the rule allowed her to study and learn in a much more pleasant, easy, and fruitful way. At least, Nahia saw it like that. She had to do her best, that never changed, but the instructor treated her well, which was unthinkable and very motivating.

Flameborn, step forward and stand in the middle. Today you will volunteer again. It is not that I have it in for you. You are quite skilled, and the class is more efficient if time and magic are not wasted, she received Zeru-Urdin-On's message. As always, it was accompanied by a feeling of quiet, something Nahia was grateful for. It was shocking, the difference between these mental messages and those of Buru-Beira-Gogoa. If she could, she would tell the tyrannical crystalline dragoness a few home truths.

She stepped forward and saw that Sorginbor, the assistant Exarbor of Sorcery, had appeared with a wooden dummy. The goal was to destroy it, but from a distance. He placed it thirty paces away from Nahia, a distance he carefully measured. That was different. Nahia did not have any Sorcery skill she could launch from thirty paces; not even her fireball could go that far with her mind. She did not wonder but waited to see what the instructor dragoness told her.

As you see, today we are going to practice with a dummy. The goal is to destroy it from afar. I can see by the looks on your faces that you are all thinking that you do not have a Sorcery spell that reaches that far. That changes today. You are going to learn a very powerful spell: Elemental Thunderbolt. You can throw it far distances. You will begin with a distance of thirty paces, but with this spell, once you master it completely, you may reach enemies at two hundred paces.

That is for those of you who are more powerful. Those of you with less power should still reach a hundred or a hundred and fifty paces.

Those distances seemed enormous to Nahia. The Dragon Warlocks did not have such long-ranged magic. But it seemed the Sorcerers did. She found that having a spell like that was a big advantage. She could attack enemies from a distance and defend herself from them before they reached her. Of course it seemed advantageous, but now she only needed to learn how to cast it. It could not be that easy.

Very well, Flameborn. I want you to focus on the dummy. You must create an Elemental Thunderbolt, in your case of fire, and launch it at the dummy. The more energy charge you use, the more damage you will cause. It will also be more complicated to get the spell right. Therefore, start with a small charge of energy.

Nahia took a deep breath and then let out the air slowly. She focused on the dummy and closed her eyes. She gathered energy from her inner dragon and turned it into fire. She followed the teacher's recommendations and did not charge it much. In her mind, she shaped it like a burning thunderbolt. It started to fall apart, so she focused even harder. She had to contain the thunderbolt and not let it destabilize, or she would not succeed. It took her a long moment to get it. Once she finally had it stable, she launched it at the dummy. As she did so, she opened her eyes, and with great surprise she saw a thunderbolt of fire hitting the dummy. There was a great flame and the dummy was completely destroyed.

The Flameborn has not only done it well, but on her first attempt. You are improving a lot, not only in your Sorcery magic, but also with your power as Flameborn.

Nahia was so surprised that it had gone well on the first attempt that she could not believe it. Besides, she had incinerated the wooden target. There was nothing but a pile of black residue on the floor. If she had done that to a wooden dummy, she did not want to even think what could happen to a human.

As you have seen, this spell is very powerful. It is not instantaneous, but if you manage to cast it in combat, you will finish off your enemy. It is a mortal spell. Enemies without magical defenses will die, one out of ten times. Those who do have them will suffer serious damage and will have to defend themselves by strengthening those defenses. This will give you an advantage for your next attack. Now, I want the rest to try, each with your own element.

Sorginbor brought out five more dummies and placed them thirty paces away from them so they could practice. Nahia watched the others to see how they did before attempting another attack on her new target. For a long while, her comrades tried without success, so she conjured a Fire Thunderbolt again. This time, she charged it more. The bolt struck the dummy, enveloping it in huge flames. There was only a little pile of black dust left on the floor.

Do not charge it more, Flameborn, or we will have a mishap. Practice on the distance, not the power of the bolt.

Nahia withdrew twenty paces more. Since the classrooms were enormous, dragon-sized, there was lots of space to practice. She tried from fifty paces away and noticed that it was a little harder, but she succeeded anyway. The poor Sorginbor brought her another dummy.

They kept practicing, and soon her companions started to succeed. By the end of the class, everyone had succeeded, and Nahia was now capable of hitting the dummy from a hundred paces without problem. She found the Ice Thunderbolt very interesting because it completely froze the enemy on the spot. If it was charged, it froze the victim to death. The Earth Thunderbolt was destructive: it looked like a stalactite had crushed the dummy with a tremendous blow. The Light Thunderbolt was interesting because it was the first time Nahia saw that Light could kill. The bolt's discharge was so intense that the Light power would kill the being, even if it did not destroy the dummy, which appeared to be left intact. Although the one she found most terrible was without a doubt the Air Thunderbolt. Aiden would love to have access to it. A powerful bolt, like something out of a frightful storm, discharged on the enemy and fulminated them. It was impressive.

At the end of the class, Nahia felt good. This was definitely her favorite class. Unfortunately, she would have Weapons training the following day and would suffer again. But at least she was happy today. She was leaving class with a tremendously powerful, useful spell.

That evening in the dorm, they were getting ready to sleep. Nahia was so pleased with the new skill she had learned that she decided to tell her comrades about it.

"I have to tell you about Sorcery practice today. It left me dumbstruck, and I think you'd be interested to hear about it."

Daphne, who was lying down, already in her bed, half-rose and looked at her with interest.

"If it impressed you so much, you'd better tell us all about it."

"Yeah, and besides, stone-head might stop doing pushups and crunches for a while, he's making me nervous," said Lily.

"You can't see me from behind the screen," Aiden replied, who was exercising in front of his bed by the door like he did every evening.

"But I hear you, and you're making me anxious" the Scarlatum said.

"That's because you know you should be doing physical exercises yourself instead of lying in bed."

"Of course I know! And I've already done them at the gym!"

"Don't argue with granite-head, it's in vain," Daphne advised her.

"And I'm not lying in bed, I'm taking care of my skin before going to sleep."

"I don't know how someone can waste so much time on completely unnecessary things," Aiden replied, and he went on with his series of pushups.

"What did I say?" Daphne said to Lily.

"Come over, all of you, and I'll tell you," Nahia said

Taika, Aiden, and Ivo came over to listen. They stayed standing and alert beside the screen.

"We've started learning the Elemental Thunderbolt skill—well, a Fire Thunderbolt in my case because of my element. The others each cast with their own element, and it's really awesome," Nahia commented.

"Do tell," Taika encouraged her.

Nahia explained what it consisted of and what had happened in class. When she finished telling them, Lily whistled.

"Well, isn't this Elemental Thunderbolt powerful!"

"Apart from being powerful, it has a very important aspect which is almost more important than its destructive power," Taika commented.

Ivo turned to him.

"What do you mean?"

"Yeah, I don't know what you mean either," said Daphne.

Taika nodded and explained.

"What makes this skill so powerful is its reach. All our magical skills, the elemental ones, are very short-ranged. This one is the first to reach a range of two hundred paces."

"Ohhh… yeah, that's true," Daphne agreed. "My elemental magic is all about proximity. Healing, now that I think about it, requires physical touch too. I have to be touching or almost touching the person in order to heal them."

"All my elemental magic is short ranged and my Druid skills are, at the most, able to reach fifty paces," said Ivo. "Although it could also be that I'm limited because of my poor mastery of magic."

"I don't think it's that," Aiden told him. "All magic skills have an intrinsic maximum reach. My Barbarian skills are all limited to the distance of one-on-one combat. Of the elemental ones, only the Elemental Ball has some reach, but it doesn't get to fifty paces, and I always throw it with my hand."

"Elemental Ball doesn't reach beyond twenty paces if you throw it with your mind, that's for sure," Lily told them. "But the skills I'm learning now as a Charmer do have a range of over a hundred paces, although not as far as the two hundred Nahia's skill can reach."

"I hadn't thought about that, Taika, but you're right, the range of this skill makes it even more powerful," said Nahia.

"Since we're on the subject, how are we all doing in Talent class?" Lily asked with interest.

"I'm improving a lot," Ivo commented, and a smile appeared on his beastly face. "I'm still finding magic difficult, but I have made great progress, at least for how clumsy I am with magic. I like my nature studies even more than I did before. It's a world filled with so many wonderful things to learn that I'll need three lifetimes to learn it all."

"And we hope you to live at least five," Lily told him, smiling.

"What skill are you learning now?" Taika asked, curious.

"My new skill involves creating a circular area, strong creepers that emerge, not only trap the victim, but also poison them. It can be deadly, depending on the poison applied," Ivo explained. "It's a combination of several skills I already have, but enhanced."

"That's what I was thinking," Taika commented, "because you can already trap with creepers and throw poison."

"That's right," Ivo nodded.

"It sounds like a great skill which will help us," Nahia commented. "Try to make it big enough to trap a dragon," she joked, although it was not entirely a joke.

"Hah! I'll try," Ivo smiled.

"You shouldn't…" Aiden began to say.

"Don't even start, stone-head," Daphne told him.

"You'll regret it…" Aiden went on.

"Shhhh, rock-head, shut up," Lily told him.

"In any case, it'll take me a long time to master this skill. It's very difficult and it requires being good at magic which, as you all know, I'm not."

"You'll get there, I'm sure," Nahia said cheerfully.

"Without a doubt," Lily cheered too. The others nodded in support of the great Tauruk.

"We're improving our Barbarian skills in order to be even more ferocious and unstoppable in combat. We'll each become an attack force so beastly and overwhelming, that the enemy will run away," Aiden announced.

"That's because you're so ugly, not because of the skills you're developing," Lily laughed.

"Go on and mock me, but you'll see."

"What skills are you developing? Immediate attack, I'm guessing," Taika said.

"That's right. The Barbarian skill is all about attack, not defense. We've learned Rage, which is even more powerful than Unstoppable Frenzy. It gives us more strength, velocity, and envelopes us in a state of fury. The combination of both is unstoppable."

"So, in battle you're going to be like a furious, rabid bear," Lily commented.

"Blinded with rage and fury," Aiden specified.

"You'd better develop your healing skill with this one nearby," Lily said to Daphne, shaking her head.

"Yeah, I was thinking the same thing," Daphne said, nodding.

Aiden ignored them.

"Now we're working on Mental Rage…"

"Oh, you already…" Daphne began to say, but Aiden continued without letting her finish.

"… which is a mental state where the mind can't be affected by skills such as those of a Charmer," he looked at Lily with narrowed eyes.

"Don't be annoying! You'll take away the main incentive I had to improve," Lily huffed, upset.

"I still haven't succeeded, but I hope to do so soon. Then I'll be

311

safe from external mental manipulation." He again glared at Lily.

"We might get lucky and you won't succeed," Lily smiled.

Aiden glared at her again.

"I will. I always do what I set off to do. But in this case, I'll also do it to prove it to you, and because I don't want you to be able to affect me."

"I'll always affect you. I'm irresistible and you know it," Lily winked at him and posed coquettishly for him.

Aiden made a horrified face.

"Taika, tell us about your Talent, please," Nahia intervened to end the spat between Lily and Aiden, who were getting increasingly riled. She feared that if they went on like that they would end up in a real fight, and this had to be avoided at all costs. Luckily, Daphne was no longer messing with Aiden as much. Sometimes however, she could not help herself, but she had reduced her arguments with him a great deal. This was because Nahia had asked Daphne to do so several times, and she was finally heeding her. She had also asked Lily, but so far Nahia was not having any luck with the Scarlatum.

"Yes, of course," Taika nodded, also realizing the conflict with Aiden. "We're learning an interesting skill that gives us a bit of distance in combat, something we lack, since our skill is for one-on-one combat."

"The best kind," Aiden assured.

"We have strengthened our fighting technique with Dark Daggers. It's a skill that allows us to throw two dark daggers the enemy can't see from a distance of ten paces."

"They don't see them at all?" Daphne asked blankly.

"Not until the last moment."

"No one can see them?" Ivo asked.

"No one who doesn't have some kind of light or divination magic."

"Ahh, then I could see them," Daphne said.

"If you use your light magic, yes, you could see them."

"That sounds like a very good skill," said Aiden.

"That's what I think too. It gives us some range, and it will help us at the beginning and end of fights," said Taika.

"How are you doing at the skill?" Nahia asked him.

"Pretty well, this one doesn't worry me. But the one that does is Form of Shadow."

"Nice name. What does it consist of?"

"It's a very powerful skill, and the last one we'll learn. It allows the body to take the form of a shadow so it can't be seen, harmed by any weapon, or hit by any enchantment or spell. Of course, in the absence of light magic, which would prevent the skill," Taika looked at Daphne.

"That's phenomenal!" Nahia cried.

"But in that state, we can't attack or use our magic. If we do, we come out of the state."

"Hah… I thought it was too good to be true, with such a powerful skill…" said Lily.

"Everything has its balance. Not everything can be good: there has to be a counterpart for balance…" Ivo mused.

"If that's true, I'm not fully convinced with this skill of yours," Aiden told him.

"Another thing is that it only lasts for a short period of time, only a few moments. It can't be used for long periods of time," Taika explained.

"Even so, I think it has a lot of potential," Nahia said.

"Yeah, I can also see its uses," said Daphne. "Well, I'm learning the opposite of these harmful and deadly skills."

"Healing?" asked Taika.

"Yeah, and the good kind. After spending endless hours in the library studying, my magic and knowledge have become one. Don't ask me how it happened, because I don't understand it very well myself, but they have. This has allowed me to take a big step forward. I've managed to make my one-on-one healing quite powerful. What that means is, if anything should happen to any of you that isn't excessively serious, I'll be able to deal with it a lot better than before."

Lily clapped her hands in delight.

"That's wonderful!"

"Congratulations!" Taika said.

"An admirable achievement," said Ivo. "My healing skills go no further than shallow cuts, minor blows, and poisoning from natural poisons."

"Which is also an achievement," Daphne said to Ivo.

"Isn't it? I think it is," Ivo nodded, quite pleased with his achievements.

"We're learning Multiple Healing now," said Daphne. "It's very complicated, but I see amazing potential. If I succeed, I'll be able to heal you all at the same time simultaneously, even in the middle of a battle. It's an amazing skill."

"You'll be able to heal the whole squad at the same time?" Aiden asked with wide eyes.

"If I manage to master the skill. Not everyone can, as I've been told. Only those who have the greatest magical talent."

"Then you'll nail it," Nahia told her.

"Don't be so sure. So far, I'm doing very badly. I haven't been able to."

"I'm with Nahia. If there's anyone who can make it from your Talent class, it's you," Lily told her, nodding reassuringly.

"How far away can you be and still heal the whole squad?" Taika asked her.

"You'd have to be close, not over three paces away. Otherwise, I wouldn't be able to reach you with the skill."

"So, the closer the better," Lily laughed

"Yeah, formation distance would be ideal, but I should also be able to do it with slightly more distance. Well, if I get there at all."

"You will, you have very powerful magic," Taika told her,

"I'll let you know when I'm better at it."

"Yes, please," Nahia told her. She found this very interesting. Having a healer who could heal a whole squad in battle would be an incredible advantage.

"And what about you, Lily? What are you learning about your Talent?" Taika asked her.

"As you know, I'm the best in my Talent class thanks to my natural charm, obviously," she said, turning around while smiling and tossing her long brown hair.

"Also, the most vain and cocky," Aiden replied.

"You wish you could walk with this charming beauty at your side," she told him coquettishly.

"In your dreams. No thank you," Aiden refused, shaking his head.

"What are you learning now, Enchantress?" Daphne asked, interested.

"I already mastered the Hallucination skill. It took me longer than I expected, but that's done at last. With it I can affect the mind of another person, and make them have hallucinations. They find themselves trapped in their worst nightmare. We're taking it to the limit: death."

"Wow, does it produce so much terror?" Nahia asked her.

"Yeah, to the point that you could die of fear. If Aiden wants to, we can try it now," she smiled at him.

"Yeah, very funny. Don't you dare."

Lily winked at the Drakonid.

"And if that skill's impressive, the last one we're learning is even more so. It's the pentacle of Talent," she went on explaining.

"And what would that be?" Ivo asked.

"It's called Enchant-Being, and it allows you to enchant a person or being so they lose their own will and are left under the absolute control of whoever has enchanted them."

"You remove their will?" Nahia was very impressed.

"Yup. For that you have to be a very powerful Enchanter. Not everyone in my class is going to make it. I will, since I'm the most powerful one in class."

"It must be a very complicated skill to master," Ivo guessed.

"It is. I didn't say I'll be able to do it easily, only that I will. It will take me a lot of work and effort, but I'll get there. I'll put my work and power into it, and my natural charm will do the rest."

"Without a doubt," Daphne nodded, confident that her friend would succeed.

"How far can this enchantment reach?" Taika asked her.

"Between a hundred and fifty and two hundred paces. The closer the being is the higher chance of succeeding."

"If I understand correctly, could you make an enemy soldier stop fighting?" Ivo asked.

"I can do better than that. I can make a soldier fight against their own comrades," Lily replied in a lethal tone.

"That would be worth seeing," Aiden said in an impressed tone.

"Very useful, no doubt," Taika nodded.

"A little evil, if you think about it..." Nahia commented.

"It's more evil for the soldier to kill you," Lily argued.

"Yeah, you're right there," Nahia agreed.

Chapter 38

Nahia went to the library, hoping to see Ana and Logan. She needed to know how they had fared during the mid-year test, since they hadn't been able to tell her yet. She sat at the far end table they always used, waiting. She saw the lamp with the wooden base on a ledge and realized it was through this that the chief librarian listened to them. Unobtrusively, she went to the lamp and pretended to fetch a book from the shelf beside it. She checked that no Exarbors were watching her—none were—and she quickly loosened the base of the lamp and took off the wooden ring. She put this in her pocket, tightened the base, and left the lamp as it was before but without the wood. Then she got rid of the wooden ring, leaving it on a shelf between books.

"Let's see how you listen to us now, Liburex," she muttered under her breath.

A while later, Logan appeared. Just seeing the handsome, dark-haired, light-eyed boy filled her with great joy, and butterflies fluttered in her stomach.

"Hi, I guessed you'd be here," he said.

"It's either here or at the gym," she replied, smiling.

"And that's where I was," he smiled back at her.

For a moment they were both quiet, gazing into one another's eyes, enjoying the moment and their joint company. When their eyes met, Nahia felt as if the whole world vanished and only the two of them existed. She wondered whether Logan felt the same way. She wanted to think so; that would be wonderful, it might mean there was something between them. But as soon as the thought formed in her mind, she had doubts. Surely Logan did not feel the same way she did. Surely nothing was fluttering in his stomach and his heart did not fill with joy at seeing her. No, of course not.

"Hi, you two," Ana greeted them.

"Hello, Ana," Logan greeted her, and the moment between them was gone.

"Hello," Nahia also replied.

Ana sat with them, and Nahia could not help but feel that she would have liked to have a little more time alone with Logan. An Exarbor passed by their table and Nahia returned to reality. The cause was the important issue, and that was what they were there to discuss.

"We have to talk about what happened in Tremia during the mid-year mission," Nahia said, voice low.

"Absolutely," Logan nodded. "You go first."

"Good," Nahia thought for a moment, organizing her ideas, and then she told them what had gone on in Norghana during their mission and their new encounter with their allies in the snow kingdom.

"White Foxes?" Logan asked.

"Yeah, it's another group of Rangers, like Egil's and Lasgol's Snow Panthers."

"And they let you leave?" Ana asked.

"Yes, they showed us what the dragons were searching for—a silver pearl—and afterwards they let us leave."

"I see that the bonds of trust are strengthening between the Rangers and us," Logan told her.

"Yes, they are completely trustworthy. Great fighters, and honorable. They are allies we are grateful to have," Nahia said reassuringly.

Logan nodded.

"We're going to need all the allies we can find."

"Allies sometimes end up betraying you," said Ana.

"I can promise that you can trust them fully. They seek the same thing we do: to free themselves from the dragons."

"Fine," Ana said, who still seemed to harbor some doubts.

"The matter of the silver pearl is interesting," Logan commented. "It must be very valuable to the dragons for your leader to protect it so fiercely."

"That's what I think too. It must have great power for the dragons to use," Nahia said.

"I wonder if we could use them…" Logan was thoughtful.

"I doubt it. They're made especially for dragons. We're not at their magical level," Ana shook her head.

"There's only one way to find out. We have to find one and see what we can do with it," said Nahia.

"Yeah, but that's only if we find one in the first place," Logan said. "It won't be easy."

"That's for sure," Ana added.

"Your turn, Logan. How's the center of Tremia doing? Are they holding up?" Nahia asked, very interested.

Logan became serious and shook his head.

"I'm afraid not. This time we went first to Zangria, escorting a convoy with over a thousand carts full of food and other supplies for the dragon army. We were also carrying a silver box, but we didn't have trouble like you. When we arrived at the capital, we found it razed to the ground. The dragons had defeated the defending forces—Zangria had fallen."

Nahia heaved a sigh.

"What about their armies? Completely destroyed?"

"Almost. They've withdrawn to secondary cities. But they were very battered and their numbers are fewer. They've lost thousands of soldiers defending the capital. The dragons are securing what remains of the capital and the adjacent areas. Then they'll finish taking the kingdom. In my opinion, since they don't have powerful magi, the Zangrians are doomed."

"I see," Nahia nodded, saddened.

"Now it's only a matter of time before the White Dragon King controls all of Zangria."

"And the Kingdom of Erenal?"

"Likewise. The capital has also fallen. It took longer, but the inevitable happened. The dragons are too powerful. The magi of Erenal couldn't withstand them. The armies, what's left of them, have retreated to other cities within the kingdom, but like in Zangria's case, it's only a matter of time before the whole kingdom falls."

"What about the pirates of the Central Sea?"

"They continue avoiding the dragons. Their island base has been taken and they are now at sea, fleeing the armies of the white dragon king."

"So, it's a total disaster."

Logan nodded heavily.

"It's what was expected. The kingdoms fought and resisted conquest, but in the end, they couldn't defeat the dragons and were forced to succumb."

"Yeah, I know. It makes me very sad." Nahia was shaking her

head.

"Without the golden weapons, I don't think any kingdom can withstand them," said Logan.

"Yeah, unfortunately we weren't able to speak to Lasgol and learn if he'd found them. I guess not, because Molak and Luca didn't mention them."

"Aren't there others?"

"Not that they know of, but he did say they believe it's not the weapons themselves that kill the dragons, but the magic in them."

"How does that work?" Ana asked.

"The magic is what really matters when it comes to those weapons," Nahia specified.

"Golden Magic," said Logan.

"That's right, Golden Magic. If we find that magic, we'll be able to use it against the dragons."

"And do we know where that kind of magic is?" Ana asked.

Nahia shook her head.

"Unfortunately, not."

"Well, we'll just have to look for it," said Logan. "It could be the key to our freedom."

"Yup, that's what I think too," Nahia said, nodding hard.

"Maybe we'll be lucky and find it," Ana said in an optimistic tone, although her eyes betrayed her statement. They looked dull.

"Tell me, Ana. How are things in the west of Tremia? Has the west fallen under the blue dragon king's control?"

"Well, you see… it's interesting… because, against all odds, they're holding strong."

"Are you serious?" Logan could not believe it.

"They're resisting? How's that possible?" Nahia was shocked.

"Rogdon is holding up. The capital, Rilentor, isn't falling," Ana confirmed.

"But the dragons' punishment must have been tremendous, it's bound to fall," Logan said.

"New magi have appeared who seem to be very powerful."

"How powerful?" Nahia wanted to know.

"Powerful enough to wound and kill dragons," said Ana.

"That's impossible!" Logan cried.

"It's true. The soldiers have removed several dead dragons, and there are several more wounded."

"What magi are those?" Nahia saw a chance, an incredible opportunity.

"From what the soldiers told me, at first there was only one powerful mage who, with the help of three others, defended the city. But these magi could not hurt the dragons. But then two new magi, a couple, featuring a dark-haired man and a blonde woman, came. They have a different magic, more powerful, and this is what's defeating the dragons."

"Do you think they might have Golden Magic?" Nahia asked.

"Maybe. That's the only kind of magic that can hurt a dragon," Logan speculated.

"I have no idea, but whatever type of magic it is, it's powerful and can kill dragons."

"That's amazing news!" Nahia said joyfully.

"It truly is," Logan joined her.

An Exarbor looked at them and put his twig finger to his lips.

Nahia contained her enthusiasm.

"What can you tell me about the Masig and the Usiks?"

"Their situation hasn't changed much. The Masig ride through their steppes and move around constantly. The dragons have nothing to conquer and the armies of the Blue King wander the prairies without direction. When they least expect it, the Masig attack by surprise and then flee. The dragons are so angry that they seek tribes to destroy, and when they find them that's what they do, but the Masig are intelligent and are never in the same place for more than a day. At dawn, they pick up their tents and leave."

"They sound smart," Logan nodded.

"And the Usiks?" Nahia asked.

"The savages of the fathomless forests are presenting great difficulties to the armies of the Blue King. The regiments that enter the forests vanish, but there's no record that they're killing savages. From what I've heard, the forests are so thick there's no way for them to spot a savage, and from the sky it's even harder."

"That's very good news, they're resisting," Nahia cheered up.

"Let's hope they do so for a long time," Logan said.

"Ana, you've made me incredibly happy," Nahia said.

"Me too," Logan said.

"Well, I'm telling you only what I heard, but yes, it is very good news,"

"Now if we have the golden weapons and those two magi—that couple, whoever they are—who can kill dragons," said Nahia.

"We need to get more information about them and their magic," Logan said.

"Yeah, to see whether it's Golden Magic or not," said Nahia.

"Let's hope the chance arises," Ana said.

"If it doesn't arise, we'll seek it out," Nahia said emphatically.

"That's the spirit," Logan cheered her.

The following day, for Weapons training, they had to go to the Weapons Building instead of The Arena. They were not happy since they would have to report to the dragon, Beldur-Gorri-Handi, and see what it wanted from them, which was not usually a good thing. They walked into the class together with the other two squads they met in the corridor. They greeted each other and exchanged smiles, not for their impending class but for seeing the others alive and without serious injuries.

I see that none of you have died during the mid-year test in Drameia. That pleases me. I am sure the teachings received here have much to do with the fact that you have all survived. You will continue under my tutelage until the end of the year. I am sure you all appreciate it and are proud and extremely grateful for it, Beldur-Gorri-Handi sent them in greeting.

Nahia could not believe how vain the dragons could be. Well, she could believe it because she witnessed it over and over again. Each of their dragon instructors believed that the pupils of the Academy were alive thanks to the teachings of their own class. That the pupils were intelligent and skilled had nothing to do with their survival, at least according to the dragons.

Today we begin training with the most noble and deadly of the Dragon Warlock weapons: the spear. This weapon is superior to all others, and you must learn to wield it like a true master. There is no adversary more fearsome than a Dragon Warlock wielding a combat spear. You will learn its use and it will become your greatest ally, even over the sword. That is mainly due to its reach being greater, as well as its sturdiness.

All Nahia heard when the dragon mentioned greater reach and sturdiness was how heavy it would be. It was as if her mind now had a sixth sense dedicated to identifying this aspect. From behind the dragon came the three weapons masters, each carrying a spear. Just by seeing it Nahia knew it weighed a ton. At least compared to what she could bear. It was metal, with a wide, double-edged tip, and it had to be about six feet long.

In order to accelerate and facilitate your learning, each squad will continue with the same weapons master. The training will take place in The Arena. It is a teaching system which is most productive. I expect you to soon wield this noble weapon as well as the dagger and sword. I expect nothing less.

Lily and Daphne were exchanging worried looks. They were both thinking the same thing as Nahia. How were they going to wield such a weapon? This was not for them: it was a weapon for Ivo or Aiden. But, like everything else in the Academy, they had no choice. They would simply have to adapt and make it work. There was no other option.

Weapons masters, gear up your squads and begin practicing. I will enjoy watching the first efforts of the pupils with the spear.

Urus came up to them.

"Tauruk, follow me," he told Ivo, pointing at him.

Ivo went with Urus to the back of the classroom where there were six training spears in the armory. They were dull, with snubbed tips to avoid hurting or killing one another by accident during training.

"Take half."

Ivo picked up half and Urus the other half. They came back and handed them to the rest of the squad.

As soon as Nahia had the spear in her hand and felt its sturdiness and weight, she felt like running away and never coming back. That spear weighed as much as the dagger and sword combined. Not that this surprised her—she had been expecting it—but confirming her suspicions depressed her. Beside her, Daphne and Lily were weighing their spears with the same miserable look Nahia had on her face. The weapons class had been a nightmare from the first day at the Academy and had only gotten worse with the passing of time and additional courses. The spear was the final torture that finished off the three of them.

Aiden was weighing his own with a triumphant look, as if they had handed him a spear of pure gold for being a loyal servant to the dragons. He was thrilled with his new weapon. Taika was weighing the weapon and studying it with eyes filled with curiosity. Ivo did not seem to care too much about the spear. In his hands it looked like a toy, and he was using it as a support while he was standing.

Start the practice. First, basic moves, the dragon ordered, and they received a feeling of impatience.

Urus addressed them.

"We'll begin the instruction. I will teach you how to hold the weapon with one or two hands. Then we'll practice the basic movements using both grips. The main difference between this weapon and the dagger or sword is that it's used for piercing attacks. You can also cut and skewer with this weapon, but it's a little more complicated than using the dagger or sword. In any case, you'll all learn its use and the different attacks and defenses you can carry out. The spear is the most honorable weapon, and those who master it will gain special respect."

Nahia knew she was never going to master such a heavy weapon, so she would not earn anything special. Not that she wanted to. She contemplated the weapon and felt increasingly desperate. They were really going to suffer.

The first three weeks of training with the spear at The Arena was torment for Nahia, Daphne, and Lily, although the Scarlatum bore it better. There was no way of getting away from it: the spear was heavy, and there was nothing she could do about it other than hold up and suffer. The offensive and defensive movements Urus was teaching them were not very complicated. In fact, they were easier with the spear than with the sword. This was a relief, albeit a small one.

By the fourth week, Nahia waited with horror for the day when the duels began at the end of each class and Urus punished them with his skill and physical power. But these did not come, at least for the time being. They did the training in pairs, shifting partners after a certain number of offensive and defensive repetitions, but they did not fight Urus, for which they were all grateful.

After the Weapons, Talent, and Magic classes, if they did not need to go to the library to study, Nahia, together with Daphne and Lily, went to the gym to keep working on their strength. This left them exhausted at the end of the day, but they had no other option. Without going to the gym, they would never pass the weapons class. Nahia knew that she had to graduate, not only so she would not die at the Academy, but to pursue her destiny.

Every day that went by, she was more convinced that her destiny was to rise against the dragons and fight them. The weapons class was going to be a stumbling block, one she would have to overcome any way she could. She was confident she was going to learn the technique, that did not worry her. They did so many repetitions that it would not pose a problem. Whether she liked it or not, repeating the exercises so many times was engraving them in her mind so that afterward they came out unconsciously. Besides, Urus corrected the slightest error. The problem was the weight of the spear. She had to build more muscle.

Chapter 39

Just seeing Buru-Beira-Gogoa, Nahia had the feeling there would be pain and suffering that day, like almost every day they had Magic class. She hoped she would be wrong and things would take a turn for the better, but she doubted it. Her classmates, just like her, had the same fear and low spirits. The arrival of winter was always hard at that height, and the one they were having now was the worst they had experienced since coming to the Academy.

Today, you will split into two groups. Those who haven't been able to master the mental attacks on one side, and those who have on the other. Those who have not will work with Membor and perhaps the unimaginable will happen, and one of you will succeed, although I doubt it at this time of the year. Go now, you are not worthy of being in my presence.

Ivo and Taika left with their heads down and heavy steps. The other unlucky students followed behind them. Membor took them to an adjacent classroom so they would not upset the crystalline dragoness.

Today you will learn how to get rid of your enemies, and at the same time, stop them from getting rid of you. Get ready: it will be a painful experience, for it cannot be any other way. But the power you will possess once you master my teachings will be enviable. Many would kill to have it. Luckily, you will be able to prevent that with your minds.

Nahia swallowed and looked at Lily and Daphne. They both looked stressed. They were expecting another horrible class of suffering. It had said "get rid of." Did that mean kill or just knock out their enemies? She hoped it meant the latter. The idea greatly upset her, and her stomach turned.

The Mental Attacks you have been using cause intense pain in the mind of your enemy. The more energy you add to the attack, the more powerful this will be. The attack's ultimate power depends on how powerful you are. The more energy you can use in an attack, the greater the effect on the enemy, leaving them aching and stunned. But this is not enough. You must be able to completely disable them, and then kill them.

There it was, just what Nahia had feared. She did not want to learn how to kill others with a Mental Attack. She thought it was an aberration. It was one thing to throw a ball of fire at someone who could see it coming and avoid it, and a very different thing to directly attack the mind without possible defenses.

Only the most powerful dragons can kill with a Mental Attack. You inferior beings cannot. If it crossed your mind that you could, keep dreaming. Of course you cannot. You do not have enough power inside of you to accomplish such a feat and are not intelligent enough to achieve something like that. Only a thousand-year-old dragon, of high lineage and very powerful, is capable of such a feat. And it can finish off not only inferior beings like you, but also other dragons. You can only dream of such power. You will never reach it. Therefore, I will teach you the closest thing to killing, which is knocking out your rival. Then you can finish them off with your knife, sword, or spear.

Nahia felt a bit foolish for having thought that perhaps it was possible. But right then, rage surged in her stomach from the dragon's insults and demeaning comments. Only the all-powerful dragons could. This thought lit her up. Perhaps it was like that now, but one day that would change. One day a being with magic, maybe not from this world, perhaps from another, would do it. They would kill a dragon with a mental attack even more powerful than that of a thousand-year-old dragon. Why could that not be the case? Why was it an impossible task? They also claimed to be invincible, indestructible, and now they knew this was not true. Dragons could be killed with golden weapons or Golden Magic. In the same way, one day someone would kill a dragon with a mental attack. Absolutely. Nahia hoped she lived long enough to witness it.

Let us begin with the exercise. The moment you feel me reach your mind, I want you to try and reject the attack. You will not be able to, but let us see how long you can bear it. The way to resist is to create a defensive ring around your mind's aura and send energy to repel the attack. If you concentrate hard enough, you will see the invading light with a stronger color and a specific form of attack. In my case it will be light, since that is my elemental energy. In any case, it will feel alien, like an invasion. You will not find it difficult to detect it.

They did not have time to think about the impending attack. Nahia felt the mental attack at once. A force was trying to enter her mind, and was doing it with overwhelming power. She had to resist it. The problem was, the force it was using to enter her mind was tremendous. Nahia shut her eyes and focused on the light energy surrounding her mental aura, which was red and orange with multiples shade of both colors. The invader was light, bright and very

326

powerful. She saw it surrounding her aura and trying to enter. Almost instinctively, she raised a barrier shaped like a ring that enveloped her mental aura and sheltered her mind.

The dragon's light energy attacked her defensive ring. Nahia saw it like a great dragon maw trying to devour her mind. She felt an acute pain. She frowned and fought back. She sent more inner energy to fight against the dragon's maw of light. She could feel how the energy of her ring fought against the maw of light. It was as if a dragon's maw of intense light was trying to swallow her defensive orange-red ring. She felt pain, but the ring was holding up. It was trying to reject the attack, and that was what caused the pain. Both forces crashing against each other was what brought on the pain. But that did not discourage her. She was not going to give up that easily. She would fight and resist. She would not let the dragoness defeat her that easily.

She sent more energy to defend her mental aura. The dragon's invading energy was consuming her defensive energy in the ring, devouring it. If she did not send more, a lot more, it would destroy her completely and the pain would come, and with it the suffering. Nahia sent a great amount of her inner energy to defend her mental aura. To her surprise, the bite weakened. The maw of light lost its light, becoming more translucent. That must mean she was winning the battle, because her defensive ring now looked thicker, almost solid. Besides, she no longer felt pain. Yes, she was managing to reject the attack. If she were not so focused, she would have smiled.

Suddenly, the maw of light returned to its original size and power. It shone with great intensity. The dragoness had sent more energy to strengthen the attack. Nahia cursed under her breath. The attack intensified and the pain returned to her mind. Of course, that dragoness was not going to let her win, that was unthinkable. It was not going to let any of them reject its attack. The opposite would be a dishonor it would never accept. The rage in Nahia's stomach lit her inner flame. She sent more energy to defend her mental aura. She was going to lose and suffer, she knew it, but she would fight to the end and give it her all. She was not going to give that haughty, evil, heartless dragoness the satisfaction of defeating her so easily. No, no way. She would use all her energy to defend herself.

She clenched her fists and jaw and sent another massive amount of energy to fight the dragoness's. Once again, and to her surprise, she managed to reject the attack. The dragoness's maw of light weakened and became almost translucent, which indicated that she was rejecting the attack. Nahia was pleased again with her small, partial victory. No one would take away these small victories against the arrogant dragoness.

Suddenly, Nahia began to feel hotter and her body temperature began to rise.

"Oh no…" she muttered under her breath while trying to maintain her concentration.

She could feel her temperature rising rapidly. Her whole body began to burn, as if the flame she had inside her, lit up with rage, had created an intense fire in her guts. The flame became a fire that generated a tremendous amount of heat outward. Nahia recognized the symptoms. It was not only the flame that used to light up and which she had learned to control, it was her condition… her illness. It was attacking her.

"Not now… no…"

Her plea was not heeded. The great fire raged inside of her. The insufferable heat inside her spread to her skin. The palpitations began and grew at an accelerated rhythm. While Nahia was trying to defend her mind from the attack of the dragoness, sending more energy to her protective ring, her pulse raced so much that she felt her heart was going to burst. She was having one of her seizures, one of the strong ones. She did not know why. She had not had one in a long time. She had started to believe she had mastered her condition. She controlled the inner flame, but she had been hasty thinking she was cured.

She became dizzy and the nausea began. She lost her concentration and the dragoness entered her mind. She felt a terrible pain in her head which joined everything else she was already feeling. She lost her balance and fell on her side to the floor. She started to shake compulsively. Cramps lashed at her legs and arms and she held back a cry of pain while she convulsed on the floor.

Her comrades had already dropped down from the attack of the dragoness. She was the last one to fall. They were not convulsing, since that was caused by her condition. Nahia made a tremendous effort to dominate her right hand and lead it to her neck. There she carried the container with her grandmother's concoction. Perhaps because she was stronger, she managed to control her hand better than she had in the past. She reached the container and took the top off, gulping down the contents. A moment later, the cramps and convulsions ceased. Her temperature dropped until it was normal again. She was left lying on the floor, unable to move. Luckily, everyone else in the class was on the floor from the mental attack, and she thought that maybe the dragoness would not realize what had happened to her.

Very well. It appears that the one who resisted the most was the Flameborn, but she has paid for her resistance. Her body did not bear the effort well.

Nahia huffed on the floor. The dragoness was so arrogant it believed it had caused the attack Nahia had suffered. Thank goodness—that freed her from a punishment for being weak and sick.

Now that you know what you must do to protect yourselves from an attack, you will practice in pairs. In duels, of course. One attacks and the other defends him or herself. Whoever loses suffers. That is how you learn in life. Go ahead.

Nahia finished, completely worn out, but without punishment, and that was the important thing. What worried her was that her condition had manifested again, and that was not good. She had thought she had it under control and she had been wrong. This troubled her.

The following day, the three girls of the Igneous Squad headed to the gym to exercise after class.

"Time to build muscle…" Daphne said in a resigned tone.

"Well, look on the bright side, you yourself said that muscle is good for the body and health," Lily said with a grin.

Daphne nodded.

"That's true. The thing is, it's hard to get."

"It costs sweat and much effort," Nahia commented, also resigned.

"Yes, but at least it benefits *you* to go to the gym," Lily said with a mischievous smile.

"Me?" Nahia looked at her in surprise. "The one who gets the most benefit is you, who have more muscle than either of us."

"Oh, sweetie, you missed my meaning. It benefits you because it gladdens your heart a lot. And if muscle is important for a long life, a happy heart is even more so," Lily said, giggling.

Nahia still did not get it.

"I don't know…"

"She means Logan," Daphne stated directly.

"Oh… ah…" Nahia mumbled, blushing to the roots of her hair.

"Yeah, you go ahead and pretend, but the three of us know you love to go to the gym, and it's not because of the effort and sweat, but because of our handsome instructor," sad Lily, giggling more.

Nahia stumbled. This conversation was so uncomfortable, she nearly fell on her face in front of the gym door.

"Logan and I are just good friends, that's all."

"We know that," Daphne said. "What Lily is insinuating is that you are head over heels in love with him."

"Me? Noooo," Nahia shook her head and blushed even more, if possible.

"Not, not at all. That's why you turn as red as a flame," Lily accused her.

"You have to admit that when you see him, your face changes. It becomes a happy one," Daphne said.

"Because… we're friends, and I'm glad to see he's okay…"

"Yeah, keep on pretending. But we notice it. Your eyes sparkle."

"Me? Noooo!"

"Yes, they sparkle. You look as if you were going to have a seizure," Daphne told her.

"You don't need to pretend with us. We think it's great," Lily said. "The gorgeous, dark-haired boy with light eyes is very handsome, although a bit too serious for my taste. He almost never smiles."

"Physique isn't important," Daphne commented. "He's a very good person. He's been helping us since our first year, and he's always willing to lend a hand. Besides, he's intelligent. We need more people like him, that's what."

"I assure you I'm not pretending. We're only friends," Nahia insisted, overwhelmed with this conversation. Although they had hinted at something before, especially Lily, they had never spoken so openly about it.

"Perhaps she hasn't realized what's up yet," Daphne said to Lily.

"Oh, she realizes, that's for sure. It's another thing if she prefers to do nothing about it and keep her feelings repressed," Lily replied.

"Can we change the subject, please? It's making me very

nervous," Nahia told them.

"And why do you think that is?" Lily asked her with a naughty smile.

"Because I'm not used to…"

"Well, you'd better get used to it, and fast, or perhaps someone else might get ahead of you," Daphne told her and nodded toward the building. At the gym door, Logan was talking to Ana.

When she saw this, and especially after Daphne's comment, Nahia felt the rage of jealousy rising again. She realized what it was and extinguished the feeling. Ana was her friend. She had no reason to think ill of her. None.

"Yeah, that one's going to steal him from you. She's always hanging around him," Lily said.

Nahia felt the jealousy emerging in her stomach again. But she did not allow it to grow, dismissing it once more. Ana and Logan could talk all they wanted, and if there was anything between them, Nahia would be happy for them because they were her friends.

"No one can steal Logan from me because he's not mine," she replied.

"Well, you'd better catch him soon, or you're going to lose him," Lily advised her.

They ended the conversation and got to the gym door.

"Hello to the three of you," Ana greeted them with a smile.

"Hello, Ana," Nahia greeted her cheerfully. She was not going to let jealousy or her friends' comments set her against sweet Ana.

"Training?" Lily asked, raising an eyebrow.

"Yes, the spear class is too much for me. Luckily, Logan is helping me," Ana said.

"Logan is a blessing," said Daphne.

"I'm only trying to help everyone pass the weapons class," Logan replied, waving her comment aside.

"Well, your three pupils from the Igneous Squad are reporting for duty," Lily said,

Logan nodded.

"I've already finished, I'll go. Have a good session," Ana wished the three of them and left with a wave.

"Thanks, Ana" Nahia said.

Daphne gave her a nod. Lily watched her leave with narrowed eyes.

"Let's go inside. We have to help each of you pass Weapons class," Logan told them.

Nahia threw one last look over her shoulder and saw Ana watching them for an instant before she turned and left. She thought that if Ana and Logan ended up together, it was only natural. Then she looked at Logan, who was waiting for her at the door, and hoped that would not happen.

Chapter 40

In class that morning, Beldur-Gorri-Handi announced the next stage of Weapons training. Urus had told them to go to the Weapons Building. They guessed it would not be anything good, especially for the girls. The boys were not having as hard a time in class as the girls were. It had been like that since the first year, and the suffering continued. On the other hand, the boys suffered a lot in magic classes and the girls did not. The suffering equaled out. It was a fools' consolation, because in the end they all suffered in one class or another. No one was free, and suffering and pain reigned.

Winter is coming to an end and spring is arriving. That is something many of you are grateful for. It should be the same for you, except that it marks the end of one season and the beginning of another. We come to the final part of Weapons class of the Third-year. I am sure you will want to know the last thing you will learn this year. I will reveal it to you: combat with both the spear and shield.

The announcement felt like an iceberg falling on top of Nahia, Daphne, and Lily. If they could not handle just the spear, how were they going to manage both at the same time? It was crazy. They could not do it. It was too much. They could already guess what was coming. It was logical, it had already happened with the dagger and the sword. First, they had learned to use the weapons, and then how to use them in combination with the shield. But the three, even knowing this was coming, they had refused to believe it, or at least had fooled themselves into thinking it would not happen. The reason was obvious. The spear and shield weighed too much for them to fight with both at the same time. The boys could handle it, but not the three of them.

A Dragon Warlock armed with a spear and shield is a formidable fighter. A squad of Dragon Warlocks fighting with spears and shields are a force to reckon with on the battlefield. A squadron in the middle of a battle, armed with spears and shields and in perfect, synchronized formation, is unstoppable. They will destroy the enemy even when the numbers are against them. There is nothing more fearsome than a squadron of Dragon Warlocks in formation, armed with spears and shields. They are unbeatable, unstoppable. That is what you must become before the end of the year.

They all listened to Beldur-Gorri-Handi's message very attentively. It reached them with a feeling of great honor and truth. That dragon had seen formations like it was speaking of it in action, and what it was transmitting to them was true. Nahia did not doubt it for a moment, and neither did the rest of her comrades. What she was wondering was whether they would not be equally unbeatable and unstoppable using magic instead of weaponry that weighed as much as a mountain. She knew the answer the dragon would give her, since this was Weapons class. But if they asked Buru-Beira-Gogoa, who taught their Magic class, perhaps it would give them a different answer. In any case, they had to pass both classes. There was no escaping; they would not be allowed to take any shortcuts.

Luckily, they had Urus again as their weapons instructor. He had turned out to be better than they had initially thought, seeing as he was a beastly Tauruk. An exception to the rule in the world of dragons, where beastly was usually bad for everyone. Urus had proven to be valid and decent.

The first week they practiced in the classroom, in front of Beldur-Gorri-Handi. It was horrible. Not only did they fail to finish the classes from how tired they were, but they also had to endure the threats and humiliation from the enormous red dragon. It messaged them what it thought of them—all niceties. Nahia, Lily, and Daphne could only bow their heads and endure the insults.

As of tomorrow, you will go to The Arena to practice. I see there are some of you who cannot even manage to finish one class. That only shows how weak you are, the pathetic physical strength and will that inferior races like you have. You are a disgrace to your races. You better practice with everything you have in The Arena, or you will not pass this class. Whoever does not manage to pass the class, much to my chagrin, will be expelled. Let me tell you that being expelled at the last moment of the third year is something you will not enjoy.

With that cheerful message, Beldur-Gorri-Handi sent them to The Arena. Things did not improve once they got there. Urus made them repeat the basic exercises over and over. The problem was not the complexity, but the weight of the weapons. Nahia, Daphne, and Lily started the class in good spirits, but after half the class they began to lose energy, and by the third quarter they were completely shattered. They tried, but their bodies could not cope. They were not going to give up, so they kept trying during each class.

Weeks went by, and although the weather was great in The Arena because it was already spring, Nahia began to feel mopish. She found it very difficult to pass that class, not to say impossible.

"Keep practicing. Attack, twenty repetitions. Defense, ten more," Urus told them.

Nahia was partnered with Taika. Since they had not been in class for too long, she was holding up so far.

"You're doing very well," Taika praised her attack with her shield.

"Thanks, but soon I'll be doing so-so, and then awful," she replied, launching another spear attack. Her right arm already felt very heavy, although lighter than the left one, which was holding the shield.

"Don't get discouraged. It's only a matter of time before you gain the strength to finish the class."

"I'm seriously beginning to doubt I'll be able to make it," she said and attacked again.

Taika defended himself from the attack with agility.

"You'll make it, I'm positive."

Nahia made a grimace that she was not and they went on practicing.

"Good technique," Urus told Nahia. "Keep it up until the end of class."

As Urus went to see how Daphne and Ivo were doing, Nahia sighed deeply.

"By the end of class, I won't even be able to keep my head up,"

"The gym is the solution to that problem," Taika told her. "You're doing well, you just need a bit more muscle."

"I'm already going to the gym, but my muscles aren't growing."

"Don't misunderstand me, but go more. Every day until the end of the year," Taika advised her.

Nahia nodded.

"I understand, thank you for the advice. That's what I'll do."

"And push your body while you're there. That way you won't have any doubts that you've done everything a person can do."

"Alright," she nodded.

They kept practicing without pause, repeating the exercises over and over. As usual, the last part of class was too much and Nahia, Daphne, and Lily did not manage to finish. They ended up sitting on the sand, exhausted.

"I have decided after seeing how you are doing and the improvements you've achieved that it's time to change the end of each class," Urus announced.

They all looked at him, surprised and fearful.

"What's going to change?" Nahia muttered.

"We're going back to having duels at the end of class. I believe this will help you improve even more. We did so with the sword and shield, and now it's time to do so with the spear and shield. I wish you good luck, everyone."

Nahia's eyes opened wide.

"Oh no…" was all she was able to say.

The following day, Nahia left the gym by the north door. She had been working hard to gain muscle. She went to the fountain and freshened up her face. She was dead tired with exhaustion. It was already night and she had not noticed.

"Are you all right, Nahia?" Logan asked her, coming out after her. There was honest concern in his voice.

"Yeah, I'm fine. I just needed to stop for a moment."

"I understand. You've been working very hard today," he said, coming to the fountain to freshen up too.

"I have no choice. I'm doing very badly in weapons training."

"You're making a great effort."

Nahia nodded.

"Yeah, but it doesn't seem to be enough. I'm never going to pass that class."

"I'm a witness to how much you work and the effort you're making. Don't get downhearted. You'll get the reward you deserve for all you're doing."

"I'm not so sure. Right now, I don't see how I'm going to make it."

Logan looked at her with his light-blue eyes, and Nahia could see fear in them.

"You'll do it, I'm sure."

Nahia smiled.

"Your eyes don't say the same thing."

Logan looked surprised.

"You read eyes too, Flameborn?" he asked, and his always serious mouth curved into a tiny smile.

"Yup, it's one of the skills related to my Sorcery Talent, Stormson," she joked.

"That's much better. Keep your spirits up," he encouraged her.

Nahia looked at him and there, under the stars, she thought him the most attractive boy in the world. Her world and any other. Not only was he handsome, strong, and agile, he was also good, loyal, and honest, and he had a strong sense of honor and of good and evil. He was exceptional. She felt very fortunate to be there with him, to have him by her side.

"You are a blessing, helping me and also Daphne and Lily. We'll never be able to thank you enough."

Logan waved it off.

"I'm good at the gym, and I like to help. It's nothing."

"It's a lot, and we appreciate it."

"It's a pleasure to help you. If I'm good at something, my duty is to help others. I don't want anyone to die here."

Nahia nodded.

"Ah you, what are you not good at? You're a physical and magical prodigy."

"I've been fortunate in those aspects. But there are many others where I'm a disaster. I'm full of defects."

"Yeah, sure. I haven't seen a single one since I met you."

"Oh, I swear I have them, I just hide them well," he joked. Nahia, who had rarely seen him joke, felt her heart fill with a feeling she could only describe as happiness, mixed with nerves.

"You'll have to show them to me, that way I won't feel so bad."

"Consider it done. And you have no reason to feel bad. You're a strong person, determined, and a natural leader. Our leader," he said and looked around to make sure no one was listening. The night was already covering them and the stars were shining, dancing in the spring sky. They were alone. Two dragons were watching from their lookouts, but they were too far away to hear them.

"Do you really believe I'm strong and a good leader?"

"With all my heart."

"You saying so makes me feel better, because I'm having a bad day."

"I say it because I mean it."

"I appreciate it, from the bottom of my heart," Nahia said and put her hand on his arm.

Logan looked at her, and this time his eyes shone with determination.

"I will follow you to the end."

That sentence touched Nahia's heart.

"You will? Why me?"

Logan smiled at her softly.

"Because you're my leader."

"Is that the only reason?" Nahia asked, feeling there was something else in the air, between the two of them, and she wanted to make sure. Or at least that was what she wished.

"And something else." Logan put his hand on Nahia's.

"Really? What else?" Nahia's heart was racing with anticipation.

Logan put his head close to Nahia's, slowly, without taking his eyes off hers. Then his lips touched hers. An instant later, they shared a kiss filled with sweetness and overflowing with love. The kiss went on, both of them lost in the magic of that incredible moment, filled with feelings and sensations wonderful to the two of them.

They moved away after a long moment and remained looking into each other's eyes, neither saying a word. Nahia felt so happy and joyful, she thought her heart was going to overflow. She did not know how that had happened. She had not even imagined it happening, but here they were. They had kissed. A kiss that had been as soft as it had been deep. She felt like she was having a dream she did not want to wake up from. A flame lit up inside her, and this one was not rage. It was something different. She felt an immense need to embrace Logan, to kiss him, to keep him beside her.

She did not think twice and kissed him again, driven by that unstoppable impulse. This time filled with passion, the kiss went on. Neither of them wanted their lips to part.

A figure came out of the gym.

"Oops, sorry," a voice said.

Nahia's and Logan's lips parted, and they moved away and turned toward the figure.

It was Ana. She was staring at them with surprise and sadness in her eyes.

"Ana…" Logan began to greet her, but before he could finish, Ana turned around and ran away.

"Ana, don't leave..." Nahia said, but she had already vanished inside the gym.

Chapter 41

They went into Magic class in rather good spirits, since the day was beautiful. The sun was shining and the scents of spring reached them from every direction. For this reason, and because there was less time left to finish the year—something everyone was wishing for—they felt good. They would put an end to their days in that academy of suffering and get out of there. They would go and fight in Drameia most likely, but that was better than being at the Academy. They were very close to achieving this, but the stumbling block of the last Magic classes was an important one, especially for Aiden, Taika, and Ivo, who were doing worse in that subject.

"It's the final stretch of Magic class, stay strong." Naha tried to cheer them up, knowing the boys needed it.

"That's it. Cheer up, everyone, we're already nearly done with this," Lily joined in with her charming smile.

"We'll make it. We'll pass the class," Aiden said, but his usual confidence wasn't reflected in his tone.

Taika and Ivo exchanged looks of resignation. They did not seem at all convinced and did not cheer.

"With our help, you'll make it, don't worry," Daphne said reassuringly as she patted Taika and Ivo on the back.

"Whatever the dragons want it to be, will be," said Aiden, and he went into the building.

The class began with an announcement by Buru-Beira-Gogoa, the great crystalline dragoness. It stared at them for a moment and then spoke.

The moment has come for you to learn to defend yourselves from the magical attacks your enemies launch at you. You do not know this, but in the different worlds we have conquered, and in those we are conquering now, there are enemies with different kinds of magic. These hostile opponents are magi, sorcerers, shamans, warlocks, and the like. Apart from these enemies, there are creatures that possess elemental magic, of life and death. Even black magic, which is the darkest and most dangerous.

Hearing this seemed to impress the other squads, but for Nahia that was good news. Very good, in fact. Not because she wanted to face all these different kinds of enemies—that would be bad news, since they would try to kill her—but because they presented a possibility. She saw these beings with magic as potential allies and not as enemies. If she could persuade them to ally themselves against the dragons, then they could defeat them.

The enemies with magic are the most dangerous, since even the tiniest or most harmless looking might be very powerful magically. Never trust them. Not all magical enemies will look as formidable as we dragons do. That is why you must always be prepared and alert. Very few among you, if any, are capable of distinguishing a being with power from one who does not have it, so I will not bother teaching you how to do so.

Nahia wanted to learn to distinguish those with magic from those without. She thought it was a very valuable skill. Not only to prevent a possible attack, but to recognize possible allies. If she could recognize a being with magic, then she could ask him or her to join the fight against the dragons, the joint fight of all those who suffered their abuse across countless worlds. Victory would only be achieved if everyone united, all the aggrieved worlds. This idea came to her mind over and over on repeat, stronger every time. She was very aware that it was more a dream than a possible reality, but some dreams did come true. When she thought about it, it always seemed impossible because of how colossal the task was. But at the same time, something in her soul told her it was what had to happen. And for that to happen, she had to help. She had to fight with her whole being.

When you face a being with magical power, you can either attack at once and catch it unawares before they're able to raise defenses against you, or you can raise a defense and then attack. I recommend the first option, since you will have the surprise factor on your side, and many times it is crucial in magical combat. If you are quick enough and the enemy has no magical defenses, you will win. If they have them, you will be at a disadvantage, since a counterattack from the enemy can kill you if your defenses are not raised. Just as in a physical fight, in magical combat, the surprise factor is a great advantage, as is the preparation before combat.

Nahia wrinkled her nose. This sounded like the usual dragon strategy of "kill first, ask later." Once the rival was dead, there was no longer a problem. Since the dragons had innate magical defenses, they did not care about the preparation for combat and raising defenses. They always attacked first. It was their advantage. She thought of Camu and wondered whether he too would have natural magical defenses. She hoped so, so he could defend himself from the dragons. Thinking about Camu led her to think about Lasgol and she realized that, without meaning to, she had already started making alliances with beings of power from other worlds to fight the dragons. This cheered her up a lot, and she had to hide a smile. She only needed more allies in Tremia, and then she could find the other worlds and create new alliances with them. She found this a lot more complicated, but she refused to think it was impossible.

The first thing you will learn is the anti-magic defense. According to how powerful you are, and how good you are at magic, your defense will be stronger or weaker. You will be more or less capable of withstanding your enemy's attacks. But you must all be capable of raising a basic defense. You are going to create what is known as a field of magic scales. Its function is to repel the magical attacks that try to reach your body or mind. This cloak of defensive energy rejects any magical energy that is not yours. That is why it serves against all kind of attacks from any type of magical creature.

This interested Nahia greatly. She wondered whether this would let them defend themselves from the elemental attacks and even the mental attacks of the dragons. She guessed so, since it served to defend oneself from any kind of magic. This idea made her smile inwardly, a big smile from ear to ear, which her face did not show. They were not only learning to fight, but to defend themselves from any creature, and this included the dragons. But the dragons were so vain and trusting in their absolute dominion and supposed invulnerability, that they did not realize the creatures they were teaching to fight for them, might one day turn against them. Nahia would be present that day, leading the revolt against those evil creatures.

Concentrate and seek your dragon energy, then turn it into pure elemental energy. This is what you will find more difficult: you must send it over every scale on your uniform. Cover each scale of your cloak, hood, shirt, and breeches with energy. Do it one by one, beginning with the breeches and going upwards. Turn the hooded cloak around and put it on hanging in front and do the same, scale by scale. They must all be covered by energy.

Nahia saw Daphne's and Lily's faces, and they had the same look as hers. This was going to be a tedious nightmare. She had thought they would be raising a barrier: that would be best. A barrier around her, surrounding her like the sphere of the portals, or a square box that acted as a shelter would be ideal. Or a wall with a roof, which was a simpler structure. Anything but this concept with the scales.

Begin, and let me remind you that you must all succeed or you will not be able to take the end-of-term test, or graduate, which is the same thing. And since it is the end of the third year, it would be a real waste. But do not be mistaken. The fact that it is a waste does not mean I will not sacrifice you. I will without hesitation, since you have had every opportunity to succeed. Only the weak fail, and there is no place for the weak among us. Get going!

Nahia did as the dragon ordered and followed its every instruction. She had a good amount of elemental energy she had gathered from her inner dragon and was trying to turn it into defensive energy. This was what they were going to find more difficult, and so it was turning out to be. No matter how hard she tried, she could not do it.

You will know you have transformed your energy because there will be a silver flash. I want to see who succeeds first. Do not make me wait too long, my patience has limits.

Nahia did her best, but there was no way to transform her energy. The others were not having success either. The hours went by, and they were reaching the end of class when all of a sudden there was a silver flash. They all turned to see who it had been, Nahia included. It was none other than Daphne. The Fatum, her face red from the effort, frowning and with a wrinkled nose, had done it.

Success in the first class. I can hardly believe it. A Fatum. That does not surprise me, they are usually the best aligned, and in touch with their inner magic. Finish what remains of the class. I want a flash for every day of practice. If there is not one, there will be punishment.

Nahia looked at Daphne and understood why the Fatum had managed to transform the energy. She already knew how to do so to transform it into healing energy. That was the reason. She must have found it easier because of that. She was very glad for Daphne, who had saved all of them from suffering. At least this day there would be no punishment.

In the next Magic class, it was Lily who managed to transform the energy thanks to Daphne's advice and help, and thanks to the fact that she was also used to doing so for her spells as an Enchanter.

Nahia did it in the third class. Her friends helped her, and she finally succeeded. She also had her stubbornness to thank, since she felt she had to do it like them. In the end, she was successful and saved the class from punishment on that day.

The Fatum and Humans of the other squads achieved success in the fourth and fifth classes and everything seemed to be going well, except that the boys of the Igneous Squad had not been able to do it, despite all the help from their friends. Aiden could not believe it and was terribly disappointed. Taika took it as a challenge to beat, and Ivo took it philosophically, as was usual for him.

The classes of magic went by, and the day came when there was no silver flash and the punishments began to fall.

This was going too well. I was wondering. But here we are, and you must pay for your failure. In case you do not know, you must all pay, not only those who have not made it. The class is one, and the punishment is for the whole class.

Before anyone could react, Buru-Beira-Gogoa attacked them all with its mental maw of light. The whole class went down from the agony of the mental attack, which it maintained for a long time while they were on the floor. That dragoness was ruthless and Nahia also believed it enjoyed causing pain to others. It was a despicable being.

There were two more punishments in the next classes, and they all suffered the unspeakable. But on the third class, silver flashes began to appear. Aiden succeeded, and his joy was great. Then Taika did it, and finally Ivo.

As you see, my teaching method is infallible. A little painful, but infallible. The whole class has succeeded. You should all be thanking me.

Lying on the floor, Nahia thought about all the kinds of thanks she would like to give that evil dragoness.

The next thing they had to work on was sending energy to each scale of their clothing. Nahia was better at this, except that when she got to the cloak, she made a bit of a mess, especially with the hood. She found the way the energy stuck to each scale curious; it formed a protective layer over it. The first few times it took her forever and she missed scales, but she gradually improved, and every time it was easier, for her, and all of them. Suddenly, it became almost natural, and what had taken a long time to do, became not only a simple task, but a quick one.

Daphne, Lily, and herself, were soon capable of covering all their scales with energy in the blink of an eye. Nahia noticed that her mind knew what it had to do and did not need to be guided one by one through every scale, doing them all practically in one go. This astonished her. At first, she had thought they would not be able to use the defense because of how long it took to create. Now she had completely changed her mind about it. If they gave her the blink of an eye, she would be able to protect herself. Daphne was the fastest, Lily was close behind her, and then it was Nahia. Soon, she would be as fast as her friends.

The problem they had was that the boys could not do it. Aiden had made some progress and was already working on covering all his scales. Taika and Ivo were still not capable of covering theirs. They did not give up, but they were quite desperate. It was not something they had not suffered before. All the Magic classes went the same way for them, more or less. This one was no different.

After the class of Magic, Nahia went to the library. She sat at the same table at the back of the hall. She did not know whether Logan and Ana would be there, but she was hoping to see them. What had happened with Logan had left her with a feeling in the middle of her chest so intense and incredible that at times she forgot where she was. She felt happy, glad, alive, excited, joyful, and many more emotions all at the same time. But this academy was not the place for this kind of emotion, and she knew it.

She sighed deeply and thought of Ana. She hoped that the fact that Ana had left when she saw them kissing was nothing but surprise. It had to be that. It had been an uncomfortable moment, that was all. They would clear the air and everything would go on as always, surely. Well, not like always, because there was now what had happened between her and Logan, but it had happened and it could not be changed. She didn't want to even think about the future. The best thing was to go step by step prudently and naturally and let whatever happened between them happen.

She waited a long while, but neither of them appeared. They must be busy. A Drakonid came to her table. It was Draider, of the Ardent Squad.

"Hello there, Nahia, studying?" he asked her in a friendly tone.

"Hello, Draider. Yeah, there's never enough time for everything," she replied. She had fetched a tome of magic and she had it open in front of her to pretend.

"May I sit down for a moment?"

The question took Nahia by surprise.

"Of course, sit down," Nahia invited him with a wave of her hand.

Draider sat down in front of her.

"How do the burn scars look on me?" he asked, pointing at the ones he had on his face.

"They look very good, they give you character and make you look fierce," Nahia smiled. She knew Drakonids liked those things.

"Thanks, that's what I think too. Let me thank you again for your help."

"You would've done the same. There's nothing to thank me for."

Draider was thoughtful for a moment.

"I don't know whether I would've done the same thing back then. But I would now."

"I'm glad for your change of heart."

"And that's why I wanted to speak with you."

Nahia found that strange. She instinctively feared the worst.

"What do you want to talk about?" she asked warily.

"About the rumors running around the Academy."

Nahia raised one eyebrow.

"What rumors are those?"

Draider looked around. There was only one Exarbor in sight, and he was further away. He could not hear them.

"Rumors of freedom…"

"I have no idea what you're talking about," Nahia gestured with her hands to reinforce this.

"Don't worry, you have nothing to fear from me. On the contrary, you helped me and I want to help you, you and your people."

"I still don't know what you mean."

Draider nodded.

"Brendan and the rest of the squad are with you, I know. They talk about it in secret, but I know. They didn't want to include me, and I understand. After all, I'm a Drakonid."

"That you are," Nahia nodded.

"But they forget, and so do you, that not all Drakonids are the same. Not all of us think the same either."

"The ones I know do."

"Then you should meet more. You'd be surprised. There are many among us who don't want to keep serving the dragons. They want a future of freedom, with a Drakonid people that are strong and proud, led by the Drakonids, slaves to no one."

"I've never met anyone among you who thinks that way."

"Well, now you know one."

"This way of thinking is dangerous. It can lead to your death. Especially if you admit it as openly as you just did."

"True, but I believe I'm safe at this table talking to you."

"Maybe."

"What the other races have forgotten is that we also wanted freedom. We also fought in the Great Insurrection."

"And they blame you for its failure. And the thousands and thousands of deaths."

"Because they blame the leader of the insurrection for the failure."

"A leader who was a Drakonid."

"Yes, Dramkon Udreks, a Drakonid. He was the leader of the Great Insurrection. He was followed by many of our people. There you have evidence that not all Drakonids want to live under the dragons' rule."

"Unless it was all a great deceit on his part."

Draider nodded.

"Yes, they call it the Great Deceit, but it was no such thing. That's what is told, but it wasn't a deceit. Dramkon Udreks did not deceive his allies. He rose and failed, but he did not deceive anyone."

"Many believe he did. That's what I've been told, and it's hard to believe that's not true after the way everything ended."

"True. But we, his followers, know it wasn't like that."

"Followers?"

"There are those among us who follow his teachings. Those who don't want to continue under the yoke of the dragons. There are those who want freedom for the Drakonids the same way that many in the other races of Kraido do."

"I find what you're telling me hard to believe. What we know and what we've seen is that most of the Drakonids are on the side of the

347

dragons. They want to serve their lords."

Draider nodded.

"But not all of them. I am proof of that."

"Or so you say you are."

Draider smiled.

"I understand that you don't believe me. It doesn't matter. I only wanted to come over and let you know you have my support and that of my people who think like me."

Nahia was left wondering whether she should take the risk or not. She decided it was better not to, at least for now.

"I appreciate your sincerity. I don't know why you're telling me, but I advise you not to tell others. It will cost you your life."

Draider looked into Nahia's eyes for a moment and then rose slowly.

"Thank you again," he said and gave her a nod and left.

Nahia was left pondering on her conversation with Draider. He had surprised her. She had always assumed that all Drakonids were like Aiden. It seemed that was not the case. It could also be a trap though. Had the dragons sent Draider? Did they know what was going on? Did they suspect? Perhaps. Things were getting dangerous. Very dangerous.

Chapter 42

The dining hall was quieter than usual. The end of the year was almost upon them and they were all feeling it, from the first- to the third-years. For all of them, it was a time of great stress and pressure. They had to finish the year, and for this they had to pass the last classes, which were the worst.

The Igneous Squad was dining at their table. They needed to get their energy back after a whole day of training and practicing. Because of the accumulated effort and the extensive punishment to their bodies and minds, it was imperative that they feed themselves properly. They needed their energy for the next day, which would be similar.

"How did the Talent practice go? Today was the last class, do we have good news?" Taika asked his comrades in a cheerful tone.

"Well, I can say that in my case it went well," Nahia told them. "I passed the class," she said and raised one clenched fist, celebrating her triumph.

"Well, in your case we had no doubts, Flameborn," Daphne said. "The opposite would've been weird. You've been outstanding throughout Sorcery class."

"Our little explosive, walking flame is a jewel of Sorcery," said Lily in a joking tone with a big smile.

"I'm glad you made it. It's a great honor," Aiden told her very seriously.

"What did you have to do to pass the class?" Taika asked her.

Nahia nodded and began to explain.

"After mastering Elemental Thunderbolt, the last skill we learned and which I had to demonstrate today was the elite skill Multiple Thunderbolt."

"How many?" Daphne wanted to know.

"I can attack three enemies at once with Fire Thunderbolt."

"From two hundred paces?" Taika asked.

"Yes, all three. I did it today in class, finally. I'd been trying for weeks without success."

"Moments of crisis make us perform better," Ivo told her,

"Although they take a toll on us. They are moments of great unbalance."

"Congratulations, that's a deadly spell. My sincere congratulations," Aiden said, bowing his head to Nahia as a show of respect.

"Thank you. It wasn't easy, but it's done. I passed the class," Nahia huffed loudly and felt great relief running throughout her body.

The others smiled, seeing how she felt.

"And you, Aiden? How did you do?" Taika asked.

"I passed Talent training, of course," Aiden proclaimed as if the opposite were unconceivable.

"Of course," Lily said, mimicking the Drakonid.

"No one should have had any doubts that I would make it. I always manage to pass all the classes. I'm a Drakonid. Born to be the pride of our lords."

"You mean our masters," Daphne corrected him.

"Slave drivers," Lily added.

Aiden ignored them.

"I managed to finish the class with the elite skill of the Barbarian."

"And what is that skill?" Taika asked, interested.

"The elite skill is Wrath. First, we developed Unstoppable Frenzy, then Rage, and finally Wrath. It multiplies our aggressiveness, strength, speed, and attacks by ten. We're unstoppable. We destroy everything in our way."

"You already do that without the need of an elite skill when you have one of your seizures, you loon," Lily told him.

"I already control that skill."

"Are you sure you do?" Daphne asked him.

"Well, I control it quite well. Not completely, not yet, but I will."

"Wonderful, now our loon is going to go crazy at will and not only by accident. We're going to have a ball!"

"I'm no loon, and I will control my skill like I said I would. I always do what I say I will."

"Well, just in case, I'm going to stay a safe distance away," Lily said.

"Nothing would please me more than you staying away from me," Aiden replied.

"Hah! Wouldn't you like to have me real close. You haven't seen anything more precious and charming in your life," Lily told him as she ran her hand down her curvy body from head to foot.

Aiden shook his head and muttered something in his language. It was not pretty.

"Well, to sum it up, I achieved the elite Barbarian skill and passed the class," he announced.

"Very well done," Ivo congratulated him and patted his back. Aiden bore it, straightening his back as if he did not feel the strength of the Tauruk.

The others congratulated him too, except Lily, who stuck out her tongue at him.

"Let's keep going around the table," said Taika. "How about you, Ivo?"

"Well, it's been complicated, a total unbalance. As far as the theory goes, the studying part, I was great. In magic, like I guessed, it didn't go as well. I managed to master the Circle of Poisonous Creepers. It cost me a lot. You'll see when I show you. It's spectacular—well, spectacularly horrible—but good for us, if you know what I mean."

"Yeah, it traps and poisons enemies. Very useful," said Aiden.

"I find it quite horrendous, no way to escape, and being poisoned besides…" Lily made a horrified face.

"Well, I've mastered that one. The problem came with the elite skill Tree of Life."

"That one sounds good," Lily said.

"Yes, but it's terribly difficult. It's a skill that allows Druids to create a tree of life that emerges from the earth. It's translucent and radiates healing energy. It can cure all kinds of ailments: poisons, wounds by cut or stinger, illnesses, and the like. Everything that is not close to death. It also hydrates and regenerates the body. Thirst and exhaustion vanish. The body is like new as long as it's in effect."

"What a good skill," Daphne said cheerfully.

"It is, the problem is I wasn't able to do it…" Ivo sighed deeply.

"Wow, I'm so sorry," Nahia told him.

"What a pity…" said Daphne.

"Then you haven't passed the class?" Lily asked in a worried tone.

"I didn't manage to create the Tree of Life, but I did manage to create the Tree Scion. It's the initial version of the skill. It doesn't have the properties of the Tree of Life, but supposedly I'll eventually be able to master that skill. Because of that, the instructor Druid dragon let me pass the class."

"Thank goodness!" Lily cried, relieved.

"I'm so glad!" Nahia said, really happy for the great Tauruk.

They all congratulated him effusively. Then they had to control themselves, because one of the dragons glared at them for the noise they were making.

"Your turn, Lily," Taika told her.

"The most enchanting of Enchantresses, I mastered the elite skill and passed the class."

"I had no doubt," said Daphne.

"No surprises here," Nahia said, smiling happily at her friend. "I was sure you would achieve it."

"As you know, we were learning Enchant-Being, which I mastered to perfection," she looked at Aiden, and he made a face of "don't even think about it." Lily smiled broadly and continued explaining. "Similar to what Nahia told you, we've been working on the elite skill Group Enchantment, which affects not only one but several people."

"Can you enchant more than one person?" Nahia asked, thinking that was a great achievement if it was so.

"Up to three people, from up to two hundred paces, like you."

"That's great!" Nahia said.

"And you can make them do whatever you want them to?" Ivo asked.

"That's right. I can make them cry or kill one another. Whatever I choose."

"Anyone?" Taika asked, looking surprised.

"If they don't protect themselves against my magic, yes. There are exceptions with people who have powerful minds, but there aren't many of those around. Most of the people don't have much of a mind," Lily laughed.

"You're not that wrong. The world is full of fools," Daphne agreed.

"That's a very impressive skill," Taika told her.

"But it's not fast. It takes me a long time to cast it. But I hope to improve with time and do it much faster," said Lily.

"I bet you can do it," Nahia said confidently.

"I want to be the supreme enchantress, so yes, I'll get there," Lily said determinedly.

Taika looked at his comrades and then at himself.

"My turn. In my case, after mastering Dark Daggers, we've been working hard on the elite skill Form of Shadow."

"Yeah, the one that allows you to take the form of a shadow where you can't be seen by anyone, harmed by any weapon, or reached by any enchantment or spell," Daphne recalled.

"Unless there is light magic," Taika told her.

Daphne smiled.

"Don't worry. I won't mess with your elite skill."

"Did you get it?" Ivo asked him. "Because you've been trying to master it for an eternity without succeeding."

"And I thought I wasn't going to. I was about to give up. But today, the last day of class, perhaps from the pressure of failure, I did it, at the last moment."

"That's wonderful! Good for you!" Nahia cried.

"You're a prodigy!" Ivo told him.

"I'm very happy for you," Lily congratulated him.

"I want you to show me, it must be impressive," Aiden said.

"We'll see when I manage to do it again. I don't know if I'll be able to produce it without the pressure from trying to pass the class."

"Don't worry, you'll surely have a chance to use it when some huge beast wants to eat you," Ivo said, chuckling.

Taika laughed.

"Yeah, in that case, I hope I can call on it in time."

"And now it's only me left," Daphne said once Taika had finished.

"How did you do?" Nahia asked her, very interested to know whether she had done well.

"I managed to pass the class and master the elite skill Multiple Healing," she announced, and a smile lit up her face, something quite rare for her.

"Awesome!" Nahia cried.

"You're the best!" Lily told her.

Again, one of the two dragons glared at them, and they had to leave aside cries and hugs of joy for their achievements.

"It wasn't easy, as you can imagine, but in the end, I managed to cast Multiple Healing," Daphne told them. "It's an impressive skill.

I'll be able to heal all of you at the same time on the battlefield, as long as you don't go too far away from me."

"Really impressive," Ivo said.

"I was one of the few in class who made it, so you can imagine how difficult it is."

"And how incredible you are," Lily told her.

"Thanks, friend," Daphne gave her a nod.

"Remember, don't spread out in battle, or my healing magic won't reach you."

"I'll be close to you all the time," said Lily. "Well, as we're always in formation," she laughed.

"I'll also try to stay close," Nahia said.

"Then it seems we've all passed Talent training," Taika concluded.

"Yes indeed, some of us by the skin of our teeth, but all of us," Ivo said with a look of relief.

"One class passed. We're that much closer to graduation," Nahia said, clenching her fist and making an encouraging sign to her comrades.

"Now we have Magic and Weapons," Lily commented with a heavy sigh.

"The three of you will pass magic without problem, I'm sure," Ivo said.

"Yeah, but weapons…" Daphne looked at Nahia and Lily. The three of them knew they were doing very badly in this discipline.

"Don't lose courage. An achievement like this must push us to achieve the other two that are left," Taika told them.

"Yes, it gives us courage, but one of the remaining goals is like a mountain, and I feel like a tiny ant," said Lily.

"Well, I'm big, and I feel just like you when I'm in magic class. The mountain seems unreachable and immovable," said Ivo.

"Take it easy, all of you. We're going to make it. We're the Igneous Squad, and we're going to succeed because we're the best squad of the whole academy," Aiden said, fully convinced.

They all looked at him, surprised by his eloquence and power of persuasion.

"Well, if you say it so convinced…" Lily said, looking at him in surprise.

"Of course I'm convinced. And you know I'm never wrong. If I say I'll do something, I will. If I say we are the best squad and we'll overcome the two other classes, we will. We will achieve the three goals. Without a doubt."

They all stared at Aiden, not knowing what to say. They had never seen him like that. They did not even know he could think like this. But Aiden's message sank in. They were the best squad, and they would achieve the three goals.

Chapter 43

The end of spring was near. The days went by so fast they could not even count them. Every day was getting up in the morning at first light, working hard and suffering a lot in classes and at the gym or library, then dropping exhausted in bed at night to repeat the same nightmare the following day. They were so focused on their efforts to conquer the classes that the days slipped through their fingers. None of them wanted to fail the last stage of the year. They were so close to passing they could almost touch it with their fingertips. And they were not the only ones, all the squads worked hard every day beyond their own possibilities with the sole goal of reaching the end of the year.

That morning, they were heading to magic class feeling a little more cheerful than usual, especially the boys.

"Today the boys are going to class in a better mood, huh?" Lily commented with a knowing smile.

Ivo did not bother pretending. He let out a snort that came from deep inside his chest.

"We finally managed to create the field of magic scales. I can't believe it, honestly. It was killing me."

"Effort and perseverance usually lead to obtaining your aim," Taika said, also smiling. "Although this time I had my doubts too. When I saw I was getting there, I had to rub my eyes."

"I had no doubts. I knew you'd make it, it was only a matter of time," said Aiden.

"And effort," Nahia added.

"But you finally did it, and it does each of you great credit," Daphne congratulated them.

"Since it's us, I think it does," Taika said with a smile.

"It was easier for us, but only because we're spectacular, especially me," Lily laughed, making a charming pose.

The light joy they felt going into Magic class vanished rapidly with Buru-Beira-Gogoa's first announcement.

Today you will start the study of the second magical defense a Dragon Warlock has: Elemental Scales. This defense, although of magical origin, actually has a physical purpose. It will cover the scales of your clothing with physical scales of the element you are aligned with. These scales, unlike the magical ones, will be physical, and will defend you from attacks with weapons, whether steel, wood, or any other non-magical type.

Nahia found this very interesting. They already had a magical defense against magical attacks and now they were going to learn another magical defense that protected them from physical attacks. She not only liked the idea that they would be able to defend themselves, but this would make them even harder adversaries to defeat. Once again, she had doubts about whether this new defense could be used against the dragons. She wanted to believe so, even if it only partly helped. Anything that might help them against the dragons, no matter how small, was welcome.

Just as you have covered the scales of your clothes with energy to defend yourselves from magical attacks, you will now cover them with another cloak, this one of elemental energy. Each one with your particular element. For instance, you can create scales of ice if your elemental magic is water. Exarbor, tell them what the protection of each element is.

Membor stepped forward and, opening a tome of magic that looked almost as ancient as the Exarbor himself, he read.

"Scales of hard lava for fire… rock if your magic is of earth… whirlwinds for air…ice for water… diamond for light… and black diamond for darkness… all of which are hard… and difficult to destroy with physical attacks."

Nahia tried to visualize in her mind what they would be like. She could not really imagine what dry lava looked like, so she assumed she would have trouble creating it. Ivo's rock she could see clearly, chunks of hard rock covering the scales. She could not visualize the whirlwind scales at all. She turned unobtrusively toward Aiden. He noticed and looked back at her blankly. He did not have any idea how he was going to manage this whirlwind armor. Lily's ice defense was also easy to imagine as hard, solid ice drops. She could also imagine Daphne's. The scales on their clothes were a silver color, and in the sun, they sparkled, so changing them for bright diamonds was easy to visualize. Daphne was half-smiling. She could also visualize it and was pleased, which was not usual. Taika's black diamond Nahia could vaguely imagine, but she could not say how hard it would be.

You have received the explanation of each element. Now it is time to get to work. You must all achieve it, and it must be before the end-of-year test takes place, which is very soon. You do not have much time, so I advise you to each work hard. Remember that this protection will help you in battle against any physical attack, so it a very desirable addition to your skill set.

"Begin. If you need to consult... the tome on magical theory... let me know," Membor told them.

Once again, they found themselves having to cover the scales on their clothes. Nahia imagined it would not be too different from what they had already learned, so she got started. She concentrated, gathered energy from her inner dragon, and without turning it, she began to send it to one of the scales on her breeches. Something strange and unexpected happened. The scale began to burn. Nahia stopped because she started feeling the heat against her leg.

Beside her, one of Daphne's scales began to shine brightly, like a brilliant point of light. Daphne looked at her blankly. Lily had frozen half her thigh and was thumping it to remove the frost covering it. And if they were struggling, the boys were doing much worse. None of the three had managed to cover any of their scales with their elemental energy.

As you are finding out, it is not as easy as you thought it would be. This is because you are accustomed to using your elemental energy in a pure state. In this case, this is not required. You must manipulate your elemental energy so it takes on the shape you want it to have. You do not have to transform it into any other type of energy, just give it shape so it is not in its pure state. Learning to do this will take you some time, time you do not have, so I recommend going straight to the library as soon as class is over.

Membor showed them the open tome.

"Manipulation of elemental energy... study..." he told them.

Nahia began to understand what they had to do. What she did not see clearly was how to do it. They had never tried to manipulate their elemental energy. They had shaped it for their Elemental Claws or Elemental Maw, but that was pure elemental energy, like what they used for Elemental Balls. Turning that elemental energy into hard lava sounded complicated to her.

Think of what you must create first. Some lava, others rock, whirlwind, ice, diamond, or black diamond. Concentrate. Gather a large amount of elemental energy and start manipulating it as if you were handling it with your own hands. You must shape it. Think of the shape you want to achieve at all times. Manipulate it until you get it right. Then project it onto one of the scales of your clothing. Go ahead, time is of the essence.

They did not like being told to hurry, and it did not help at all. The more nervous they got, the worse they performed. The rush and the pressure for the nearing end-of-year test did not help either. Perhaps because of that, or because it was exceptionally difficult to manipulate elemental energy, no one succeeded in the first class. They all went to the library, defeated. Luckily, there was no punishment.

They kept trying during subsequent classes, but the result was the same. They could not do it. No one was able to manipulate their elemental energy and turn it into the desired element. Nahia was having nightmares where she fell into the lava of a burning volcano, brought on by thinking about lava all day. Her comrades had similar nightmares. Every time Ivo saw a rock, he stayed there staring at it for a while, as if he expected it to tell him its secrets. Daphne went to study the diamonds that were embedded in buildings and squares, but it did not help her much either. Aiden walked around disoriented, with a blank look on his face. For the first time ever, he was faced with an order from the dragons that made no sense to him. He did not understand how he was going to be able to create whirlwinds for his scales. It was crazy. Lily was a little more cheerful. She was used to creating ice. She only needed to control it so it took on the size of a scale. She had not been able to manage that yet, but she was trying. Taika was carrying a piece of black diamond with him everywhere.

Several weeks later, at last they had their first success. Lily managed to manipulate the ice until she made it the size of a scale and adhered the ice to her armor. Her face lit up so much from joy, that she felt like everyone noticed.

At last, someone has succeeded. I was beginning to think you were all failures. The Scarlatum has done it, now all of you do the same.

They did not succeed that day, but they did in the next class. This time it was Nahia who did it. It took her a lot of effort, but out of sheer stubbornness, she managed to manipulate her energy and shape it like hard lava. Then she shrunk it down to the size of a scale, following the advice Lily had given her. Nahia was so pleased, she nearly cried out. Luckily, she held back just in time. Two more succeeded in that same class, none from the Igneous Squad though, but at least they were beginning to master it.

After another class, it was Daphne who did it. She created a tiny diamond of light the size of a scale, and it was beautiful. It shone bright and was hard. Daphne was perspiring from the effort of creating it and felt exhausted, but she had done it.

They devoted the following classes to working on covering all the scales in their clothes, something they knew would take them a very long time, but it was easier than creating Elemental Scales. The boys, on their part, continued suffering because they could not create their scales. Everything they tried failed. They knew they could not despair—they had to succeed—but it was terribly frustrating. For the first time, Aiden was losing hope of doing it, which demoralized Taika and Ivo even more. But in spite of everything, they did not give up and kept trying class after class and in the library. They had to pass that class anyway, and they were not going to throw away everything they had already achieved because of some Elemental Scales. They could not fail now that they were so close, not only to finishing the third year, but to finishing all their training at the Academy and graduating.

They left every class defeated. Taika always tried to cheer them up.

"We're close to doing it," he told them every time.

"A baby step closer you mean," Ivo corrected him.

"We need to take a giant step, not an ant-sized one," Aiden replied.

"Every forward step we take, no matter how small, counts. It brings us closer to the goal," Taika insisted.

"The goal is very far away," Ivo repeated.

"And time is almost up," Aiden added.

Nahia, Daphne, and Lily felt their hearts sink as they noticed their comrades were unable to create Elemental Scales, no matter how hard they worked at it.

Spring was coming to an end and summer was already knocking on the door. They were out of time. In Magic class, everyone who had managed to create Elemental Scales were already capable of covering their whole body with them—with the exception of their face and hands, which they left uncovered. The head and back were covered by the hooded cloak, which they could already completely cover without trouble.

Nahia could now do it pretty fast, in a single breath, after devoting the last few classes to working on her speed. She had also noticed that when she covered her clothes with the solidified lava scales, she could create additional ones besides those already on her clothes. She was experimenting with this during class. First, she covered all the silver scales on her clothes, and then she added others where there was space in between scales. She looked at her legs and touched the solid lava scales, a dull red-black color. They were hard as rock. No doubt they would protect her from enemy steel, perhaps claws too…

Daphne was working on creating her "armor of sparkling diamonds," as she called it, as fast as she could. When she covered her body with the diamond scales, she shone so brightly that everyone was forced to close their eyes. It was beautiful armor, and it left everyone numb. She looked like a battle goddess shining with blinding light. She loved it, but she was worried she would be seen from a thousand paces away with such bright armor. No matter how much she tried to make then shine less, she could not do it. They were diamonds of light, and there was no way to dim them. Certainly, for a night mission, or an undercover one, it was not appropriate. To awe allies and blind enemies, it was perfect.

Lily was already capable of creating ice-scale armor in the blink of an eye. Her mastery over ice and frost was amazing. She covered all her scales with "others" layers? of ice as hard as rock before anyone could even realize she was going to do so. She was now practicing how to harden the ice even further by giving it an additional layer of solid frost. As she said, she could not allow herself to get hurt and lose her irresistible figure.

You have one last chance in today's class to create Elemental Scales. Whoever does not succeed today will not pass the class, will not take part in the end-of-year test, and will not graduate from this illustrious academy.

Buru-Beira-Gogoa's message left them all frozen. They knew time was running out, but they did not know they had already run out. They always held onto the hope that there was still enough time. Now they knew, and it made everyone quake. The boys because they only had one final chance to succeed, and the girls because they feared for their comrades.

"Do… your best… last class…" Membor told them.

Nahia swallowed. She looked at Ivo, Taika, and Aiden and tried to cheer them with a small signal of strength by clenching her fist. Daphne and Lily made similar gestures, also trying to help them succeed. The scene was repeated with the other two squads. Those who had already succeeded were encouraging those who had not with gestures.

Taika nodded and started trying at once. Aiden cheered himself by clenching both fists and doing his best. Ivo shrugged resignedly and braced himself for the attempt. Nahia knew they would keep trying until they fell over from exhaustion. They had done so many times. But this was their last chance. They either did it today, or they were done.

The day went by slowly. Nahia, Daphne, and Lily were working on their improvements, but without too much concentration, since they were paying attention to what their friends were doing. Taika was keeping calm, trying not to be hasty as he worked quietly. Aiden seemed to be fighting himself. His look and gestures were those you would find on the battlefield. Ivo looked relaxed, as he always was. They could see no signs of anxiety, although he was likely experiencing it and trying to keep it under control.

They say that magic and other life skills develop in moments of great need or tension. I believe this is precisely one of those moments, and it might help you achieve what you're missing. It is today or never. Your fate rests in your own hands.

The mental message left Nahia even more restless. But that was not Aiden's case. His body flashed in a mixture of silver and white and one whirlwind scale formed on his left sleeve. They all stared at it in astonishment. It was as if a tiny tornado spinning on itself at great speed had formed over the scale. It was really odd and at the same time captivating. It looked alive as it spun, unlike the girls' scales, which were hard and solid, lifeless. Aiden put his finger on the tornado and pressed in. He could not reach the scale. The tornado was spinning with such force that it was impossible to press inward. Aiden looked at the others with large eyes. He also did not understand how this was possible. He tried to press down with his claw-like hand but could not manage to crush the tornado. He watched the strong, tiny whirlwind of white air blankly for quite a while.

That Aiden had succeeded gave Taika and Ivo courage, and they made signs of victory as they tried with even more effort. Half the class had already passed and time was running out. In the other two squads, they also had one success each. There was hope. They had to make it.

With three quarters of the class gone, Taika flashed silver and black. He had done it. On his chest there appeared a bright black diamond scale. He was so happy that the usually calm, pensive white tiger jumped in place.

"No celebrations…" Membor scolded.

Taika nodded at the Exarbor and touched the black diamond scale. He squeezed hard but was unable to damage it. It was incredibly tough. Nahia, who did not miss a single detail, thought that for a black diamond it shone too much.

Now there was only Ivo. The class went on and was coming to an end. Nahia and her comrades did not even bother pretending to work on their scales. They all had their eyes fixed on Ivo. The Tauruk was sweating profusely, perspiration running down his forehead and neck. His torso was soaked. With eyes closed, he kept trying without giving in to frustration or lack of hope.

Nahia was positive that just at the last moment he was going to succeed, she and all her comrades. And the final moment came. The class was coming to an end. Nahia held her breath, hoping to see the brown flash that would mark the appearance of a rock scale on Ivo's clothes. They were all staring at Ivo, filled with apprehension. And then the class finished.

End of class. Those who have made it pass the class. Those who have not, and I see there is more than one who has not, do not pass the class…

"Oh no… no, no…" Nahia muttered in despair with clenched teeth.

And at that moment, Ivo gave off a brown flash and in the center of his powerful torso a rock scale appeared.

… the Tauruk passes. In extremis, but he passes. Go, everyone. Practice. It will save your life. Fight well and earn us glory on the battlefield.

Ivo snorted so hard he nearly knocked down old Membor, who was right in front of him.

They all lunged at him and gave him a bear hug, breaking protocol, incapable of holding back after all the tension.

Buru-Beira-Gogoa turned and left, ignoring this last

363

misdemeanor.

Chapter 44

At the end of the day, Nahia went to the library in good spirits from passing magic class. She had been so busy during the last few classes that she had not seen Logan other than at the gym, and always in the company of Daphne and Lily, so she had not been able to enjoy a moment alone with him. It was something she was looking forward to a lot, but she also knew that first she, Daphne, and Lily had to pass all the other classes, so she did not mind not having the privacy and intimacy she desired, in order to continue what had begun. Logan threw her glances which Nahia interpreted as significant. They were not mere glances of concern, there was something more to them. A special glow she noticed, and which she liked.

As for Ana, Nahia had not seen her again since the day of the kiss. At first, she thought it was just a coincidence, but soon she began to suspect it was not by chance. And now she had no doubts. It had been too long since the two events had coincided, and that could only be on purpose. Ana no longer went to the gym or spent time with Logan like she used to. She avoided both of them. There could only be one reason: she had feelings for Logan. Nahia was now sure, and she felt very bad for her friend. She wanted to speak to her and explain, but Ana did not give her a chance and continued to avoid her.

She heaved a sigh and walked up to the nearest lamp.

"I want to speak to you, Liburex," she whispered to the lamp. Then she waited patiently.

After a long moment, a librarian Exarbor came over to her.

"Follow me… please," he asked her.

Naha smiled at the Exarbor and followed him. They went up to the fifth floor and the Exarbor walked her to the office of the Chief Librarian.

"Come in," the voice said, and Naha did so. The Exarbor stayed outside, waiting.

"To what do I… owe the honor?" Liburex received her, comfortably seated behind his desk.

"Are you always listening?"

"It's entertaining… and as you know… entertainment here is scarce."

"Apart from the fact that you want to know each and every one of my movements."

"That too," Liburex admitted with a nod.

Nahia looked at him for a moment. She had been thinking about this for quite a while, and although she knew it was risky, she did not have many other choices.

"I need a favor." Liburex looked at her with interest on his face of bark.

"I understand… it'll be something that implies risk."

"That's right. Otherwise, I wouldn't be here."

"I see… go ahead. What favor is that?"

"I need to have access to the dungeons."

Liburex leaned back in his armchair with a sound of creaking wood, as if his back split.

"This is a request that is… certainly risky."

"One I am sure that the Chief Librarian, with his contacts throughout the Academy, can organize."

"Who says I have… contacts… throughout the Academy?"

"I do. I've been thinking, and I've come to the conclusion that you lead all the other Exarbor from here."

"Not all… the Exarbor," Liburex pointed out.

"Those with progressive ideas," said Nahia

Liburex nodded.

"Those with old-fashioned ideas… will die under the yoke of their masters."

"And if there's an Exarbor like you, there must be a Tergnomus with ideas, and an organization similar to yours in the Academy."

"I have always said… that you are not only a brave girl… but smart."

"Therefore, if that Tergnomus wanted to, he could grant me access to the dungeons."

"This request is very dangerous… the risk is very high… the dungeons are watched and… we don't have control over them."

"I understand that. I also imagine it's possible to organize something."

Liburex was silent, and he shut his eyes.

"I will see… what can be done… that's all I can promise."

"You said you'd help me."

"That… I'd try to help you…"

"Well then, try until you succeed."

Liburex smiled.

"It will take… time"

"All right," Nahia said and turned to leave.

"One more thing…"

"What is it?"

"Try… not to get killed… during the end-of-year test…. This place would be very boring without you."

Nahia smiled.

"I'll try with all my being."

And the day came for the last Weapons class. If in the class of Magic, Taika, Ivo, and Aiden had suffered until the last moment, it was now Nahia's, Daphne's, and Lily's turn. They had to do very well on their last day with Urus in The Arena and show him they had mastered the spear and shield so he would let them pass the class and take the end-of-year test.

They were arriving at the entrance to The Arena, and Nahia's skin crawled just seeing the building.

"You're going to make it, I'm sure," Aiden told them in a bout of camaraderie.

The three looked at him blankly.

"What's with this new behavior of yours?" Daphne asked him.

"I've always had team spirit. For me, it's very important that the whole squad graduates."

"Aha, so that you don't look bad, what else," Lily replied, looking unimpressed.

Aiden looked offended.

"Not just that. Of course I want us all to graduate."

"I'm not so sure of that," Daphne said, making a grimace of disbelief.

"Is it possible that inside that dragon shell there's a being with a little heart after all?" Lily asked sarcastically.

"I have a warrior's heart, I am a Drakonid."

"Yeah, sure, meaning that we might all fall into an abyss and he would keep fighting for his masters," said Daphne.

"If you fall into an abyss, it would be a clumsy act unworthy of a

Dragon Witch," Aiden retorted with a look that said he hoped it would not happen.

"Don't be mean to Aiden. I'm sure he cares about us," Nahia intervened, patting the Drakonid's back. It was true that Aiden, although he was often obnoxious or constantly talking about his masters, was not bad either. He had always been good to all of them. Very good in fact, honorably so. It was a completely different matter that his opinions and way of thinking were contrary to those of the group.

"Nahia is right. Aiden is a good comrade, and he only wants what's best for the whole squad," Taika said in his defense.

"You always defend him," Daphne said accusingly to Taika.

"And you, Flameborn, don't defend him. You know how rock-head he is," said Lily.

"I don't need anyone to defend me. Think whatever you want. I don't care. I'll do the right thing," Aiden snapped, lifting his chin and entering the building.

"Yeah, you'll do whatever your masters tell you to!" Daphne shouted at him.

"And on your knees!" Lily added.

"You two really are terrible," Nahia chided them.

"He deserves it, for being such a granite-head," the two said in unison.

"Let me remind the three of you that this class is crucial. You'd better stay calm, relaxed, and focused," Ivo suggested in a transcendental tone.

"Ivo's right," Nahia tried to calm down.

They walked in and Urus was already waiting for them at the north side of The Arena like he always did. They went over to him and lined up respectfully. They were all carrying all their gear on them as the weapons master had demanded. They carried the dagger on one side of their waist and the sword on the other. In one hand they held the shield and in the other the spear. This was how the Dragon Warlocks were armed, which is why they had to practice their weapons this way. Nahia found it excessive. They were only going to practice with the shield and spear; there was no need to carry the rest of the weapons. But that was not Beldur-Gorri-Handi's opinion or Urus's.

It was true that with the passing of the season, the gear weighed less. She did not know whether she had gotten used to carrying it or if she was getting stronger from all her training in weapons class and the gym. Most likely it was a combination of both.

"Today you will only do the basic movements for half the day, since it's the last class. Then we'll have our last duels."

They were all surprised but grateful not to have to exercise all day, especially because they would be less tired for the final duel.

"This last duel not only signals the end of class, but it will determine whether or not you pass."

This announcement made them nervous. One last combat with the weapons master would determine whether they passed the class or not. They had worked a lot and done their very best. They were gambling everything on one single combat, since if they did not pass the class, they would not go on to the end-of-year test and would not graduate. The problem was that the duels they had been fighting this last month had all ended badly for Nahia, Daphne, and Lily. The boys were doing better every time, and they had held their ground during the last duels pretty well.

"Start with the basic exercises, in pairs," Urus ordered.

They worked on the exercises and Nahia tried to use as little energy as possible, saving her strength for the confrontation with Urus. Daphne and Lily did the same. They hit with a little less intensity and moved more lightly, without straining themselves. Urus noticed—he saw everything—but he did not say anything. He seemed to want to give them a chance.

When they had been at it for half the class, Urus called a halt.

"The moment has come for the final duels," he announced.

Nahia could not help looking terrified.

"In a circle around me," he ordered.

They did as he told them. Nahia, Daphne, and Lily knelt on one knee and stuck the heel of the spear on the ground while they rested the edge of the shield on the ground and leaned the rest against their bodies. It was a resting pose Urus himself had taught them and which they always used when possible, because they did not have to bear the weight of the spear and shield that way.

The first one called was Ivo. Seeing the two armed, one in front of the other, with such muscular bodies, was impressive. Urus gave the signal and they started the fight. Ivo had improved his technique a lot. He had plenty of strength, although Urus had more of both.

They exchanged offensive and defensive moves about fifteen times, and the next time Urus managed to break Ivo's defenses and thrust his spear at Ivo's wide neck. Ivo began to cough and had trouble breathing. It took him a moment to recover and everyone was worried about him, but he was all right.

"Your technique is acceptable. Your strength and endurance are remarkable. You pass the training."

Ivo saluted Urus with a respectful bow.

"Thank you, master."

They were all very happy for Ivo. Aiden went next. The Drakonid was not as strong as Ivo, but his technique was better. He endured a dozen attacks and defensive moves until Urus caught him in the stomach with a swift attack Aiden could not avoid. He doubled down in pain.

"Your technique is good. Your strength and endurance are good. You pass the training."

Aiden stiffened, bearing the pain. Then he saluted with respect.

The sound of metal against metal echoed in The Arena, since the other two squads were also having their final duels. Nahia suddenly found herself wondering if any dragons were enjoying the spectacle, like a premonition. She looked upward. The round walls that enveloped The Arena were very high, and on top of them she did spot two dragons, two huge creatures whose presence was foreboding. They were the Colonel and the Commander of the Academy. She knew why they were there—to enjoy the spectacle and see whether the weapons master had taught them all a lesson. And it would surely be so.

It was Taika's turn. It was a very close fight. Taika was a wonderful fighter, no matter what the weapon was. His great feline agility gave him an advantage in movements and skill with the weapon. He was slightly less strong than Ivo and Aiden, but he was strong enough. This duel went on for twenty attacks and defenses. Urus had difficulty reaching Taika, who never stopped sliding fast and with enviable skill. At last, he hit him on one leg and then the other, which slowed him down, and Urus finished him off with a blow of the shield to the face.

"Your technique is remarkable. Your strength and endurance acceptable. You pass the training."

Taika, still stunned from the blow, saluted Urus, and withdrew.

Urus called Lily and she stood up. She walked up to the master with a determined look. Out of the three of them, it was Lily who had the most strength and endurance, so Nahia trusted that if any of the girls could pass, it was the Scarlatum. The duel began and Lily did well. She had good technique and seemed to be doing well strength-wise. Judging by her eyes, and the intensity of her attacks, it was obvious she was going to give everything she had to succeed, and she did. She withstood ten exchanges until Urus knocked her down with a sweep of his spear and finished her off on the ground with a blow to the chest. Lily was left lying on her back on The Arena with a look of pain on her face.

"Your technique is good. Your strength and endurance are enough. You pass the training."

Lily opened her eyes wide and nodded.

"Thank you… master." Then she crawled back to her place.

The next one called up was Nahia. She looked up to where the two enormous dragons were watching the spectacle. She promised herself not to make a fool of herself. She was not going to let those two cruel, abominable creatures laugh at her. Urus gave the signal and the duel began. Nahia waited attentively for Urus's attacks. She was not as tired as other times; she found herself with enough strength to hold her ground. She just needed to stop him from reaching her too easily. Urus began with a series of swift attacks they had studied, and Nahia defended herself well. Every defense with the shield hammered her left arm, but she was holding up. She countered with three accurate attacks, but Urus deflected them all without trouble. They kept exchanging attacks and defenses. Nahia had never lasted so long, and she was very pleased. She was doing better than ever. And then exhaustion struck. Suddenly, her arms and legs seemed to lose all their strength. She found she could barely stand. She withstood two more attacks, and on the third one she received a blow to the stomach that made her double over with pain. She could not defend herself anymore. She had no more strength. She fell to the ground, defeated.

"Your technique is good. Your strength and endurance are barely passable, but I will consider them enough. You pass the training."

Nahia looked at Urus, unable to believe him.

"Thank you… master… honestly." Urus motioned with his spear for her to return to her place.

Daphne was the last one. The Fatum wrinkled her nose and braced herself. She would draw on her surly character and nerve, because she knew she had no resistance. Of the three girls, she was the one with the least muscle. Not because she trained less: she practiced as much as her two friends. It must be something to do with her Fatum physiology. Urus started the duel and Daphne attacked three times with measured movements and accurate spear blows. Her technique was as good as Nahia's and Lily's, and she proved it. But when it came to her defenses, she soon found herself in trouble. If Nahia had held up quite a bit before her strength left her, this was not Daphne's case. Her shield dropped and her spear did not attack with the same precision. Exhaustion struck. Daphne wrinkled her nose and frowned. She cried out and kept attacking out of sheer rage. This granted her a few more attacks, until Urus disarmed her shield and spear with two powerful blows. Then he knocked her down with a kick to the chest.

"Your technique is good. Your strength and endurance are not enough, but your rage made up for them, and I consider that enough. You pass the training."

"Daphne, on her back on the ground, cried out with joy.

"Yes, sir! Thank you, master!"

Urus looked at them all for a long moment, and then he heaved a deep sigh.

"I have prepared you as well as I could. Fight with your head and the technique I've taught you. And your passion and rage. Fight and never give up. May death not find you. Fight and avoid it. Good luck to you all," he said and took his leave with a nod.

They all returned the nod and thanked him for his teachings. Nahia felt that Urus was a good person, fighting his own way in order to survive. His teachings would save their lives. Of that she had no doubt. She looked up to see if the two monsters were still watching, but they had already become bored with the spectacle and left.

Nahia sighed. The important thing was that they had managed to pass all the classes. Now they only had the end-of-year test. A shiver ran down her spine. They had to survive it.

Chapter 45

Three days later, Nahia woke up with a considerable headache, one she was already familiar with. This was the kind of headache caused by crossing the great portal between worlds. It took her a moment for her eyes to focus and realize where she was. She recognized the canvas of the military tent and half-rose in her camping cot.

"We're back in Tremia, aren't we?" she asked, although she already knew the answer.

"Yeah, we're in Drameia," Aiden replied, with his body half in and half out of the tent.

"We're in the end-of-year test," Daphne told her, grabbing her head in her hands.

"The good thing about this headache is that I can't really remember the Colonel's grandiloquent, arrogant farewell speech," Lily said.

"You mean the honor and pride we should feel being here serving the dragons as third-year Dragon Warlocks, our chance for glory and conquest and how grateful we should be? Is that what you're referring to?" said Daphne.

"It was too good not to remember…" Nahia said ruefully as the test ceremony started coming back to her mind.

"You'd better remember quickly, it's less traumatic," Ivo said, smiling.

"I don't understand why you mock. Of course, it's an honor and a privilege to be here for the third-year end-of-year test, and you should all feel it," Aiden said, very serious.

"Whether you like it or not, marble-head, I'm going to enchant you so you do exactly what I say. You'll be hopeless," said Lily.

"Yes, please, he's making my headache worse," Daphne said hopefully.

"Don't you dare use your magic on me," Aiden said, and just in case he rushed out of the tent.

"Do we know anything else about the mission?" Nahia asked.

"So far, nothing," Taika said, coming into the tent, "only that the

373

mission is in enemy territory and it'll be dangerous."

"Well, and also if we don't fulfill the mission that we won't graduate, of course," Daphne added in a tone of irony.

Taika nodded.

"Yeah, that too."

"Hasn't our leader spoken?" Lily asked.

"No, he's not present. I don't see any of the other leaders either," Taika said, going outside again to check.

"That's a good start. Going on a dangerous mission without information." Daphne was already wrinkling her nose.

"As usual, you mean," Lily made a comical face.

"What's important is that we're here, and we're still together and well," said Ivo, bending over so his horns would fit under the canvas door as he left the tent.

"Let's see if we can finish the mission the same way," Nahia hoped.

"We will, you'll see," Lily said cheerfully.

They rested for a while, and since Irakas-Gorri-Gaizt had still not shown up, Nahia decided to take a stroll around the camp. The part with the military tents and the carts with supplies did not interest her. But the immense glacier did, which looked like a half-ruined fortress and housed the Pearl they used to travel between worlds. She headed there.

She went to the entrance. About twenty human soldiers were on watch duty, distributed on either side of the glacier. The guards looked at her, but after seeing she was a Dragon Witch, they did not stop her and let her through. She walked inside the colossal ice structure.

The place was immense and captivating. The glacier was as big as it was beautiful. Nahia stared at the high walls of blue and white ice and her jaw dropped. It was an awesome place. The incoming light bounced off the walls as it sparkled and made it look almost magical. She went over to the large central chamber, and there she was struck dumb.

In the middle of the colossal cavern was the Pearl, which was also of a colossal size, a hundred times larger than the others. It was giving off a silver pulse. Nahia did not know whether it had begun to activate or was de-activating. The silver flashes reflected on the walls of ice, generating a most singular lighting. But what was really impressive was the Pearl itself.

In front of the giant Pearl was a silver dragon even larger than Irakas-Gorri-Gaizt. It had to be nearly nine hundred years old. Seeing herself close to that powerful being, Nahia felt tiny. She wondered how Lasgol and his comrades could have fought and killed an even greater one than the one standing in front of her in that same spot. Egil had killed the Immortal Dragon here before falling into the portal that had taken him to Kraido. She imagined herself fighting against that dragon; it felt like an impossible feat. What Egil had achieved with his friends' help was an amazing achievement. And yet it had happened here right, where she was currently standing. And they had done it.

She looked at the silver dragon, which noticed she was there but ignored her. Nahia stepped closer to the enormous creature. That did require honor, courage, and valor. Many had fallen here that day, but in the end, they had achieved their purpose. Unfortunately, their success did not keep the dragons out of Tremia. But for Nahia that did not make the deed less worthy. You had to do the best you could for good, even if in the end, you could not free the people of Tremia from the evil that was lurking. When you gave it your all, you had nothing to regret. She believed this with all her heart. For her, Egil, Lasgol, Camu, and the Snow Panthers were heroes who had given their all, just as she would give everything to free her people from being slaves to the dragons. If she did not achieve this, at least she would give everything like they had done. She would also pay the consequences, like Egil, who had lost everything and had been a prisoner for so many years. Like Lasgol, who had been robbed of his memory and magic, and was only now beginning to recover both.

Suddenly, she felt the scale on her neck growing hot. Something was happening, something that had to do with her destiny. Not knowing why, her head turned to the left. On one side of the wall of ice, she saw several entrances that looked like adjacent caverns. Nahia closed her eyes and let herself be led by this strange feeling. Suddenly, she felt her head growing cloudy. A silver mist was beginning to form around her head and she began to feel something she already knew, as if she were in a dream and the world around her was not real, but part of the dream.

She felt her head as if in a cloud and a need to walk east, as if there was something there, a power drawing her to it. She did not resist. It was a very odd feeling, but one she was already familiar with. It was caused by Garran-Zilar-Denbo's scale on her nape and it had something to do with her destiny, so she wanted to see what it was.

She kept walking as if lost in a silver cloud. She opened her eyes and found herself in a large cavern on one of the sides of the glacier. She could not see anything inside the cave. It was empty. But the scale on her nape was still burning. She looked in every direction: all she could see was ice. There was nothing here.

She closed her eyes again and let the silver cloud envelope her mind once more. Again, she felt as if an invisible force drew her. She let herself be led, or rather she let her body follow that magical, mystical attraction. She found what was happening very strange, but that silver cloud in her mind had already shown her a vision of her and Egil, so she was ready for anything. Her existence was anything but normal, and it was becoming more singular day by day. Suddenly, she felt something cold and solid, so she stopped. She opened her eyes and found she was a handspan from the wall of ice on the north side of the cavern.

"That's weird… there's nothing here…" she muttered to herself.

She reached out and touched the glacier's ice wall. As she expected, it was frozen. She could not detect anything but cold. She took a few steps back to see the wall better. She stared at it closely. It emitted blue and white flashes, like the rest of the glacier. She could not see what might be calling her. She thought it might be some object of power, like a silver pearl, but she could not see it. She looked in every direction but saw nothing but the glacier's walls of ice. Nothing else. And yet, for some reason the scale was still burning against her neck.

"There's nothing here…" she muttered, annoyed as she reached back to touch the scale and check that it was still burning.

She closed her eyes in case she was going to have a vision and had to be at this specific place to receive it. She felt her head clouding again. The silver mist was coming back to her. Again, she felt like she was in a dream, as if that cave of ice, that glacier, was not real. A blurry image began to form in the middle of the fog in her mind. Little by little, the mist gave way to an image that formed in the middle. She saw it in a large round mirror with silver edges. She had already seen this before, in the vision of Egil, so she guessed another vision was taking shape. It finished forming, and in it she saw a figure that gradually became defined. It was a man. Nahia did not recognize him, but she did recognize his clothes. They were those of a Ranger. In his hands he carried two golden knives. His hair and eyes were dark and his gaze was lethal. Suddenly, he took a leap and got onto the back of a dragon, climbing from the tail with astonishing speed and agility. The image began to grow blurry as the Ranger climbed up the back of the dragon toward its head. A moment later, the image faded and Nahia could not pick up anything else.

She opened her eyes, and the wall of ice in front of her brought her back to reality.

"Who are you?" she muttered. "Why have I seen you?"

She was thoughtful, not knowing what was going on until a voice came from behind her.

"Nahia, we have to go back. Irakas-Gorri-Gaizt is calling us to line up," Daphne's voice reached her.

Nahia turned to her friend.

"Line up? Coming."

"What were you doing here?" Daphne asked her when Nahia reached her side.

Nahia sighed.

"Not sure. I had another vision."

"Of Egil and you?" Daphne looked interested.

"No, this time I saw a dark-haired Ranger with two golden knives."

"Molak or Luca?"

Nahia shook her head.

"No, I don't know who he was. But I felt something distinct."

"What was that?"

"He was special, lethal."

"Then I hope we're allies and that he's not coming after us."

"Yeah, me too."

"Didn't you hear the call to line up?"

"No, I didn't. Maybe because I was in here?"

"Or because you were having a vision?"

"Yeah, that might be it," Nahia smiled.

"Come, let's run, or our leader will roast us on a grill."

"He can't roast me," Nahia smile.

"True," said Daphne, giggling.

They both ran out of the cave. Irakas-Gorri-Gaizt was already waiting with the rest of the squadron, which was all lined up. They sprinted to their positions in the line-up of the Igneous Squad. Their comrades eyed them with unrest for the delay.

Irakas-Gorri-Gaizt glared at them with fire in its eyes.

I have received orders. Our mission is to help take a fortified city of great strategic importance due to location. It is a city you all know: Olstran. The Norghanians are receiving reinforcements from their allies in the Frozen Continent there. We must take the city and prevent them from receiving reinforcements. It will be a complicated mission. I trust you will be up to the task. Not just your graduation or passing the mission are at stake here. In this mission, you risk your life, so follow my orders without hesitation at all times. I do not like to have casualties in my squadron. And this is a mission where there might be more than one. I hope my warning will be heeded.

They all understood the warning. They had seen the city under siege and the high casualties among the troops of the red dragon, so they knew where they were going. Nahia had a bad feeling. Taking this city was going to be a nightmare, and they would be risking their lives. She did not like this at all. The looks of her comrades were troubled. She looked at Brendan and Logar in the other two squads; they had the same looks on their faces. They all understood their lives were at stake on this final mission for the Academy.

Grab your gear and we will meet at the Pearl of the Reborn Continent, to the south. From there, we will go to the Pearl in Norghana. The rest of the way will be on foot, like last time. We will accompany an infantry regiment of two thousand soldiers. This time without a supply cart, so we will reach our destination in half the time. There will not be a guerrilla ambush, since there are no supplies. I am not expecting any trouble until we arrive at the siege. Anyway, keep your eyes open on the way.

Nahia thought their leader was being very optimistic after what had happened the last time. Although it was true that they were not carrying anything the White Foxes or Molak and Luca might want. Risking killing a column of over a thousand soldiers without anything to gain did not seem like a good option. Perhaps Irakas-Gorri-Gaizt was right.

Move on! Glory and conquest await!

Nahia sighed. She did not want glory or conquest.

Chapter 46

Irakas-Gorri-Gaizt was right. They had no armed incidents on the way to Olstran. They arrived at the city in half the time it had taken them the first time. The two-thousand soldier column was in a hurry to reach the walled city, and the officers set a punishing pace.

One of the main reasons for the imposed rhythm was the winter storms. In the north of Norghana they were deadly, and they hung around them the whole way. They had to dodge several of the stronger storms. Even avoiding them, over a hundred soldiers died, frozen when two storms fell too close. Luckily, Nahia could now warm up the whole squad without any trouble, even in the middle of an icy storm, although with some problems in that case. She had managed, but such bad weather made that region highly dangerous.

What Nahia could not do was reduce the weight of the spear and shield they had to carry the whole way. It was not a pleasant experience. The whole journey had turned out to be a lot tougher than they expected. Marching for so many days in the middle of winter to the north of Norghana, with heavy war equipment and winter storms that sought to kill them, was not something she wished on anyone.

When they arrived at the war camp of Erre-Gor-Mau, the Red Dragon, they could clearly tell a great attack on the city of Olstran was being prepared. The city refused to fall to the siege. It was a curious image, since the whole city—the houses, the towers, the walls, and the surroundings—were completely covered in snow and ice. They could not see a soul, just a landscape covered with snow, and a city buried under it. Being on a high plain, it looked like a dream. The forests north and east were a league away.

"How many troops do you count?" Ivo asked Taika as they waited at a camp access control post north of the city. They could see it in front of them, and behind, in the distance, was the great walled city.

Nahia strained her neck and stood on tiptoe to see better. There were nearly three thousand camping tents all along the snow-covered northern side of the city. As was usual, hundreds of soldiers and camp personnel were moving from one side to another, hurrying as they carried out countless tasks. Behind the tents were the supply carts. She counted over a thousand, and about a hundred were leaving the camp in search of more supplies.

"I count about ten thousand soldiers marching toward the north wall in front of the camp," Taika said with narrowed eyes.

"I see more than six dragons flying over the camp and six others over the city," Aiden added as he watched the flight of his lords with interest.

"Yeah, they keep punishing it without pause," Daphne commented as she watched the dragons flying low and sending their elemental breaths against walls, buildings, and towers. With their roars, they shattered the idyllic image of the snowy city.

"That way they'll ruin the enemy's morale and they'll have to surrender," said Aiden.

"I highly doubt it. Those Norghanians won't surrender, even if they have a dragon in front of them about to eat them. They would attack them with axes and shields among cries of war, the brutes," said Lily.

"Well, they'll die," Aiden replied.

"Yeah, but surrender? No way!" Lily snapped back.

"How many soldiers surround the city?" Ivo asked as he looked with his hands above his eyes as if the sun bothered him. There was no sun though, and it was beginning to snow again quite heavily.

"A thousand east, a thousand west, and two thousand to the south," calculated Taika.

"The enemy has no escape. They are surrounded and under siege, they will perish," Aiden said energetically.

"In case you didn't realize, little marble-head, we don't celebrate the fact that they're laying siege and killing Norghanians."

"Speak for yourself. I'm here to fulfill the mission we've been entrusted with and graduate from the Academy."

"He speaks for all of us," Daphne said, indicating them all, herself included.

"Well, I speak for myself, and I'll become a Dragon Warlock, despite all of you. The mission is taking the city, and that's what we're going to do. The fact that there are Norghanians inside is irrelevant. Orders are to be followed, and there's nothing else to do about it," Aiden told them angrily.

"See how he gets, the little Berserker. He's going to have one of his seizures," Lily said.

"I'm not going to have a seizure!" Aiden cried, and a glow appeared in his eyes that bordered on crazy.

"Ooooo!... there he goes...." Lily muttered.

Aiden made an effort to calm down, and after breathing three times through the nose, he looked toward the war camp and said nothing more.

"The city is similar to the capital, robust and made of rock. It's holding up well," Taika commented.

"These Norghanians build cities of granite and rock to bear these deadly winter storms they suffer. What they didn't expect was that it was going to help them resist a dragon invasion," Ivo commented.

"I'm sure it's already helped them against other enemies before now. Seeing how they fight and endure," said Taika.

Nahia looked around and saw that Irakas-Gorri-Gaizt was flying over the area. She spoke in low tones.

"Lasgol told me the Norghanians have had confrontations with several kingdoms, like Zangria, Erenal, and Rogdon. Even with the peoples of the Frozen Continent. Their cities have always withstood sieges."

"Aren't the people of the Frozen Continent and the Norghanians allies?" Lily asked blankly.

"They are now, but in the past, they've been enemies. Irreconcilable enemies," Nahia explained.

"But when an even bigger and worse enemy comes, even the most irreconcilable enemies make peace to ally themselves against the new one," reasoned Lily.

"I think they were already allies before the invasion, but surely the threat of the dragons has united them even more," Nahia said.

"And that's why we're here, right?" Lily said. "To stop the reinforcements from the Frozen Continent from arriving."

"It appears they cross the northern sea, much further up, behind the great mountains, and then come down to this city to restock and fight," Taika said. "That's what the soldiers told me when we were here during the mid-year test."

You have leave to enter the war camp. The officers will assign you your tents. Await my orders, Irakas-Gorri-Gaizt sent them from the heights.

"Thank goodness, it's beginning to snow heavily," Daphne said, shaking the snow off her cloak and hood.

"Thank goodness they've given us winter gear," Nahia said, gratefully wrapping herself in the thick hooded cloak.

"Does anyone know what material our clothes are made of?" Lily asked.

"No idea, but it protects us from the cold and weighs very little," said Ivo.

"What I don't understand is why it has to be winter here when at the Academy it's almost summer," Lily complained.

"We're in another world," Taika said, smiling.

"And in this world, we're in a region where it's currently winter," Ivo shrugged.

"Yeah, yeah, well, I think it's wrong. It should be summer, especially if we have to come here to fight," Lily said.

"You're not wrong," Taika said. "It's not the best time to lay siege and take walled cities in the north of a continent."

"True. The winter storms and the low temperatures are against us," said Ivo.

"They're only obstacles we must overcome," Aiden said.

"When you end up frozen alive, you'll see how easy this 'little obstacle' is," Lily told him.

"It's not the best time at all. They should wait for spring to attack," said Daphne.

"That would be the most sensible, but I don't think dragons are very sensible," Nahia shook her head.

"The soldiers have received the order that the city must fall now to cut off the reinforcements' route from the Frozen Continent. The dragons don't want to wait longer," Taika told them.

"It's a terrible strategy, not well thought out," Ivo said. "Very unbalanced. The risk is great and the reward is small."

"Not from our point of view, but a victory like this is very important for the dragon lords," Aiden said.

"It's just one more victory," Daphne waved it aside.

"Which might leave the capital without options, forcing the Norghanians to surrender," Aiden argued.

"Do we know if there is any other important city resisting in Norghana?" Nahia asked.

"Estocos. They call it the capital of the West. It's resisting too."

"That's Egil's city," Nahia recalled. "I'm glad it's resisting."

"If the people are like Egil, it will resist for a very long time," Daphne said.

"I think there are some more, but I'm not entirely sure," Taika shrugged.

"Like I said, they're all sensible," Daphne looked toward the dragons, shaking her head.

"I hope the dragons feel the rigor of the weather and reconsider," said Lily, already shivering.

"They should. They're not immune to heat or cold," Taika guessed.

"That's what I was wondering too," Nahia said. "It's one thing to have defenses against magic and tough scales, but they're still creatures like any other. The heat and cold must affect them."

"It's only natural. No creature is immune to nature," Ivo said.

"Well, then I hope they freeze alive, for being so smart," Lily cried.

"Lower your voice or they'll hear you…" Aiden warned her, looking around.

"The soldiers? They think the same thing I do," Lily waved her hand in a gesture that made it clear she did not care if she was heard.

"I'm hungry. So much walking always leaves me famished," Ivo commented.

"You were born with a famished spirit, which is very different," Lily told him, laughing.

They went into the war camp and the soldiers, mostly humans, stepped aside when they saw them coming. They did so with respect, not fear. They knew they were skilled Dragon Warlocks. They reached the officers' tents and two captains attended them. They were quickly assigned three tents, one for each squad. Nahia noticed they were being given officers' tents, which was a treat.

They went into theirs and lay down to rest after leaving all their gear in two armories the tent had at the back. The journey had been long and the weather so icy that their exhaustion was significant. Ivo did not waste a moment and finished his last ration. Then he left the tent, seeking the camp kitchen to ask for more food. He came back with several rations. The Tauruk did not seem to be affected by the winter cold and the low temperatures.

"Does anyone want some? I brought enough," he offered.

Lily and Daphne were already asleep from exhaustion.

"I'll take a ration," Aiden said.

"So will I," said Taika.

"Great." Ivo handed them the food.

The three ate avidly. Nahia watched them for a moment; she had just finished her own ration and was full. What she had was extreme weariness, and she lay down and shut her eyes while she listened to the wind whipping their tent. Luckily, they had good blankets and winter garments to keep them from freezing, but even so, it was cold. She wondered how Lasgol and the Rangers survived in this freezing environment. In all that region—and Norghana still had a lot more territory to the north—it was terribly cold, and further north it would be even worse. Somehow, she had the feeling that the Rangers were used to this climate, to the constant snow, freezing ice, and wind that froze the heart, soul, and body. With these thoughts, Nahia fell asleep.

They woke up to the sound of the dragons' roars.

"It's already daylight," said Aiden as he shot out of the tent like an arrow.

"Our charming leader hasn't called, has it?" Lily asked, still buried under two bearskin blankets, and looking like she did not want to come out.

"No, not yet," Ivo told her. "I'll see about getting some breakfast."

"But you just woke up," Lily told him.

"And my stomach demands energy to keep this body in balance," Ivo replied.

"Yeah, in balance…" Lily waved her hand but did not come out from under the blankets.

Daphne and Nahia were the same and did not seem to be willing to get up unless it was absolutely necessary. The wear and tear of the journey had been greater than they had initially guessed, and they were still exhausted. Besides, outside it was snowing heavily, and although it was very pretty to see the snow fall, it was not that nice outside.

They were left to rest until noon, which they were grateful for. They got up, and Ivo courteously brought them their rations so they could eat.

"You're a dear, Ivo," Nahia told him.

"He's a rascal, that's what he is. I bet that with the excuse of getting our rations, he fetched an extra one for himself."

Ivo blushed.

"Ah, you know me too well, little Scarlatum," he laughed.

The three laughed together. They ate their rations and drank from the water-skins. Then they went outside and found the camp bustling with activity. There were soldiers and support personnel running everywhere.

"What's going on?" Nahia asked Taika.

"Are we going to attack the city?" Lily asked.

"No. News has arrived that there's an enemy column coming from the north," Taika explained.

"Reinforcements for the Norghanians?" asked Daphne.

"It would seem so. From the Frozen Continent," Taika informed them.

"The dragons are deciding their plan of action." Aiden pointed at a rectangle where the dragons were camped, apart from the rest of the army.

"So, let the dragons fly over and destroy them, right?" Lily suggested.

"It seems they're moving under the shelter of the storm…" Taika said.

"What are you saying?" Daphne asked blankly.

Nahia also gave him a blank look.

"You mean to say they're traveling under a storm?" she asked.

Taika nodded.

"That's right. We don't know how, but there's a great winter storm coming from the north. The reinforcements are traveling with the storm," Taika explained.

"That can't be." Lily made a face of absolute disbelief.

"That's what I said," Aiden joined her with a grimace.

"Nothing can travel in a winter storm here. They're mortal. They would freeze alive, the winds and lighting would kill them," said Nahia.

"Nothing can hold up in a winter storm here, in this region. We've already seen how bad they can get," Daphne insisted.

"And we've run to escape them," Lily pointed out.

"Well, somehow it seems that the peoples of the Frozen Continent can travel with the winter storms," Taika said.

"And of course, our brave dragons don't like these storms," Lily said, eyeing Aiden from the corner of her eyes.

"Our dragon lords can cross those storms without trouble," Aiden declared.

"Yeah, I can see them all flying to the north, unconcerned. Oh, they're arguing on land? I wonder what that could be about," Lily said, full of irony.

"It's what we were commenting on yesterday. It does seem that the cold and storms affect the dragons," said Taika. "Or that's what the soldiers I've spoken with are saying. They don't go into the storms of this region."

"It's as I was saying. Steel and magic can do little, but nature is a very different beast," said Ivo. "A dragon, no matter how powerful and big it is, will not emerge unscathed if a tornado catches it, or a volcanic eruption, an icy storm, a giant wave, hurricane, or similar," Ivo said.

"I bet they could survive them," Aiden assured them, not wanting to lose ground.

"Well then, there's no problem. They'll go and solve it," Lily said and looked at Aiden with an ironic smile.

They waited to see what would happen, and while they waited, the weather began to get worse. The snow gave way to icy wind and rain. They had no option but to get back inside the tent. The temperature was dropping. The storm they had been talking about was arriving from the north, at the back side of the camp. The nearby forest offered some shelter to the camp, but when the storm came upon the city, there would be no place to seek cover.

Squadron, be alert! Line up in front of your tents, Irakas-Gorri-Gaizt's mental message reached them.

And that was the end of their peace and rest. It was time to take action.

Chapter 47

They came out of the tent and lined up. Beside them were the Ardent and the Searing Squads. Irakas-Gorri-Gaizt flew over the camp without landing.

We set out. Direction: north. We must locate the enemy forces arriving to strengthen the city. Arm yourselves. Fast.

Lily threw a glance at Aiden that clearly said, "I was right."

Aiden lifted his chin with pride and ignored her.

They went back into the tent to fetch their weapons and other gear, and a moment later they were out again.

Let's go. I will lead the way by air. The Igneous Squad will march first, then the Ardent, and the Searing will bring up the rear.

"Great, we have to go first," Lily made a horrified face.

"It's in recognition of our excellent work," Aiden told her, who felt very proud.

"Keep your eyes wide open," Taika told them.

"And your ears too," Ivo added.

They started out toward the north. Nahia looked up and did not like what she saw. Large, dark clouds filled the sky in that direction. They were scary. Luckily, they were still far away. The storm would take a while to reach, and this cheered her up a little. They left the war camp. The first league was on open land and there was not too much snow, so they traveled pretty fast. The weather was cold but not freezing, and the land was not too abrupt.

Things became more complicated once they entered the forest and headed north. The forest was buried in snow and the temperature was noticeably lower, although still bearable. Their clothes were holding up well, which was a relief. What they did not know was how long they would hold out if the temperatures continued plummeting. The trees sheltered them for now, but they were moving toward the storm. If the dragons did not want to go into it, it was crazy for her and her companions to do so. They would all freeze to death. And if there were enemies in those forests who were acclimated to those winter conditions, they would not have many chances of defeating them if they found them.

"I don't like this at all," Daphne said, frowning.

"You've read my mind," said Nahia.

"And mine. The snow is up to my knees and the cold wind is cutting my face," Lily joined in.

Keep going, we must reach the storm, Irakas-Gorri-Gaizt sent as it flew over them.

Nahia, Daphne, and Lily exchanged looks of worry. They went on until they crossed the forest and then veered west and again north, crossing a clearing covered in snow. It started snowing lightly, which was not bad news, because if it snowed, the temperatures would stay stable and they would be able to cope. What they feared were the storm's icy winds.

The Ardent and Searing Squads followed them in silence. Nahia was sure they were just as worried as they were. It was one thing to fight the enemies of the north from Norghana or the Frozen Continent, and another to fight a killer winter storm. They could face the former and survive; the latter they could not. But they could not disobey an order with Irakas-Gorri-Gaizt above them, so their only option was going headlong into the storm.

Suddenly, they heard dragon roars. These were followed by war horns from their army. They were coming from the war camp. They all turned their heads to the south to see what was happening.

"What is it?" Daphne asked blankly.

"It sounds like our army is getting ready to attack," Taika guessed.

"Attack now? But the storm is heading this way." Lily looked shocked.

"Our armies will take the city before the storm arrives," Aiden boasted.

"Yeah, sure, that's why they've been laying siege for months," Daphne said.

"Perhaps Aiden's not completely wrong," said Taika. "I think it's an all-or-nothing attack before the storm arrives with reinforcements."

"That must've been what the dragons were planning at their meeting," Ivo guessed.

"It's a wild idea," Nahia said, shaking her head.

"Staying and maintaining the siege once it receives reinforcements in the middle of a harsh winter is even crazier. The human soldiers will freeze to death before the winter's over," Taika argued.

"And all because they didn't want to wait until spring…" Daphne huffed in frustration.

Don't stop. The attack on the city has begun. Keep moving north, Irakas-Gorri-Gaizt sent them.

"It seems you were right, Taika," Daphne said.

"I wish I wasn't," he replied with a sad face.

Nahia looked toward the city in the south and saw a dozen dragons flying over it. They started punishing it. Then the assault on the walls would begin. She was sorry, not only for the Norghanians who would suffer death and destruction, but for the human soldiers of Kraido who would die too. Unfortunately, she still did not have a way to help them. Thousands of them were doomed to die, and this broke her heart.

They went on north and had to cross two other forests covered in snow. It was hard to walk, but their leader wanted them to continue going in that direction, and so they did until noon. There was not a soul in sight. Some elk and wolves were following them, and all kinds of regional birds they did not recognize. They saw a beautiful white fox, and Nahia thought of Molak and his group. She wondered whether they would be around, camouflaged. If they were, they were sure to see them.

They went on until mid-afternoon. The snow on the ground increased. Nahia guessed that the further north they went, the more snow they would find. Thus were these lands. When the wind blew from the south, and it changed directions often, they heard the roars, shouts, horns, and the din of battle. They were already attacking the walls and gates of the city. On the other hand, the storm was arriving, and the first freezing winds started to make themselves known. The sky was turning dark.

Be on the alert. The storm is a little further on. The enemy is hiding within it. You must locate them and follow them.

"This is getting weirder. Follow the enemy?" Lily looked blank.

"What do you think, Taika?" Nahia asked.

"The dragons want to know how the reinforcements get to the capital."

"Do you think they don't know?" Nahia asked.

"I don't think so. I suspect they're not going through one of the gates of the city, since it's under siege and they'd be stopped."

"Then how?"

"I have no idea, but I believe we're here to find out."

"I see. They have a secret way to enter the city," Nahia guessed.

"That's what I think," Taika nodded.

"Traveling within a lethal storm seems impressive to me," Ivo said, looking at the dark clouds and the lightning they could already see in the black horizon.

"I don't know how they'll do it, but it won't be in the middle," Taika guessed.

"At the front or the back, or through the sides," Ivo said.

"But that's a whole lot of terrain to cover," said Nahia.

Igneous Squad, to the front of the storm. Ardent to the east and Searing to the west. I will go to the end of the storm. Find out where the enemy forces are traveling and follow them. We must find out how they enter the city. As soon as you do, I will warn the dragons and we will destroy them before they strengthen the city, Irakas-Gorri-Gaizt ordered them from the sky and rose to go around the storm and reach its tail end.

"It seems our leader has it all planned out," said Daphne.

"It's going to take it a while to get to the end, it's a huge storm," Ivo commented.

"In case you haven't realized, we have to go straight into it," Lily said with a horrified look.

"Take it easy. The important thing is that it doesn't swallow us," said Daphne.

The Ardent and Searing Squads went by on their left and right and greeted them.

"Good luck!" Brendan wished them.

"See you!" Logar greeted them.

"Good luck, comrades!" Nahia wished them.

They went their separate ways and continued north through a plain where the snow came past their knees. Moving like that with a shield and spear was torture. To make things more difficult, the winds began to arrive, stronger and colder.

"Let's go to the forest. It will protect us," Taika pointed to his right.

"Yeah, it's almost upon us," Nahia said.

They reached the forest and walked toward the middle. It protected them from the icy winds. They heard thunder and lightning falling more to the east.

"It makes no sense to keep moving. We should wait here until the

390

storm arrives," said Taika.

"Yeah, there's no reason to walk into the dragon's mouth," said Lily.

"We'll use this time to rest a little," Daphne said and stuck her spear and shield in the snow.

The front of the storm covered them and they suddenly felt a terrible cold. Winds and freezing water began whipping them hard.

"This is getting ugly!" Daphne commented, looking up at the black sky that covered them, above the trees.

"Does anyone see any enemies?" Ivo asked as he looked north, his face soaked and his eyes narrowed.

"I don't see anyone, only wind and freezing water," said Lily.

They waited a little longer and things got worse.

"This is a very bad idea," Daphne said.

"Yeah, we should move away out of the storm's path before it's too late."

"I'm not buying all this about the enemy traveling under the storm," Lily said as the freezing winds pushed her around.

"It doesn't seem likely," Ivo agreed.

"Let's go to the right and get out of its path," said Taika.

They moved in a line, sheltering from the winds with their shields. Their clothes were holding up, but if they got any wetter and the temperature kept dropping, they would not and they would freeze to death.

"I love this kingdom. The weather is spectacular," Lily said sarcastically.

Suddenly, in front of them in the snow, a patrol of Tundra Dwellers from the Frozen Continent appeared. They were unmistakable: tall and athletic, their skin a crystal white as if covered with snow and ice, their hair of frozen snow. There was no doubt they were from the Frozen Continent. They were armed with javelins they carried on their backs, and long knives at their waists.

"Watch out! Shield up!" Taika said,

Instinctively, they all raised their shields and readied their spears.

The Tundra Dwellers attacked them without a word. A dozen javelins fell on the squad. They all hit the shields.

"Form up in two lines! Magic behind!" Taika called.

In an instant, in spite of the snow and being in the middle of a forest, they placed themselves and maneuvered in perfect formation.

They faced the group of twelve Dwellers—Aiden, Taika, and Ivo in the first line and behind them Nahia, Daphne, and Lily. Another dozen javelins sought their chests and faces. They hid behind their shields. One of the javelins brushed Ivo's horns. Another grazed Aiden's face, giving him a cut.

"Watch out, they're good with those javelins!" Aiden warned them.

"Let's move toward them. They're all carrying several javelins and they're not getting closer!

Nahia nodded in agreement.

Taika set the pace and they took five steps forward. Javelins were thrown again, and one cut Taika's spear arm.

"They're moving back to attack again from a distance!" Aiden said.

"Attack with magic, they're fifteen paces away!" said Taika.

A moment later, Nahia, Lily, and Daphne had their Elemental Balls ready.

"They're going to throw again!" Taika warned, and the three balls headed at the group of Dwellers. They hit them full on as they were throwing. Nahia's fireball exploded, creating a great flame and burning the four on the left where they were. Lily's ice ball exploded on the right and froze another four. The center ones were hit by Daphne's ball of light, which blinded them.

"Move forward," said Taika.

They reached the Dwellers. The ones in the middle who were still alive tried to spear them with their javelins, despite being blind. They had no choice but to finish them off. Ivo and Aiden did so with their spears.

"Do you see anyone else?" Taika asked.

"No, there's no one else around," Ivo replied.

"The fact that these were here is bad news," said Daphne.

"Yeah, it means the army is actually traveling under the storm," Nahia said.

"But where are they?" Aiden asked.

"Let's go east," Taika suggested.

They all nodded and set off. The winds were whipping them hard, and an increasing cold began to make its presence felt. They crossed the forest, and before them a plain opened. It was now thundering heavily, tremendous lightning striking everywhere.

"Let's cross the plain to the other forest," Taika said as he watched the storm above them. It was heading south; they were going east so it would not crush them with its power.

On the plain, the winds and the heavy, freezing rain punished them in earnest. Ivo had to grab Daphne by the arm so she would not be blown away. They reached the forest and took cover from the winds. But they did not have time to recover.

"Watch out, Wild Ones of the Ice!" Nahia cried, recognizing the strong, brutish, fierce savages. They had blue skin, their hair and beards as white as ice. They carried double-edged axes in their hands. The large muscular bodies and their brutish faces were scary. They were right there, ten paces away.

They were a dozen. Another patrol. They did not seem affected by the storm in the least. They were used to the icy cold of their continent. They attacked with cries of war, armed with huge axes that looked rustic but fearsome.

"Form a line of five to one!" Taika said.

They formed the line at once and prepared for the onslaught— Aiden and Taika at the ends, with Ivo in the center and Daphne and Lily on either side of the Tauruk. Nahia was behind Ivo to use her magic. They had no time for anything else. With their shields in front, spears ready, and legs flexed, they were in a defensive stance like Urus had taught them. They were about to find out whether his teachings, and all the duels at The Arena, would be useful or not. If they were not, they were about to die.

The first Wild Ones arrived at a run through the trees and the snow. An enormous one struck Taika with his axe. The tiger slid to the right swiftly and the axe struck the ground where he had just been standing. Next, he plunged his spear into the neck of the Wild One with a quick, dull blow. At the other end, Aiden blocked the axe strike with his shield. The blow was brutal, but Aiden stood firm. Next, he attacked with his spear and plunged it into the savage's groin. In the center, Ivo responded to the strength with even more strength. His opponent was as strong and big as he was. He liked this—a real opponent. The axe struck his shield and Ivo delivered a tremendous kick at the savage. He caught him in the stomach and left him breathless. He bent over, and as he did, Ivo hit him with a knee to the face which made him fly backward. The enemy fell on his back in the snow.

Daphne and Lily were defending themselves skillfully, deflecting the axe blows to one side without making too much effort to block. They were more focused on deflecting like they did with Urus so their arms would suffer less. Their rivals were enormous and very strong. But they had no technique, only brute force. Daphne plunged her spear into a savage's armpit and the Wild One lost his weapon. He lunged to strangle her and Daphne cut him with her spear in the neck from the waist up, and the savage stumbled backward with his hands to his throat, where he was bleeding profusely. He would die in moments. Lily opted to plunge her spear three consecutive times into the heart of the Wild One she had in front of her. The first two did not stop him from delivering axe blows, but the third one did.

The other six Wild Ones were already arriving when Nahia's maximized fireball exploded behind them. The flame was so large, and the explosion so great, that five were carbonized on the snow, and the sixth one reached Ivo in flames. The Tauruk finished him off with a terrible blow, smashing his face with his shield.

"Good fireball, our little explosive flame," Lily congratulated her.

"Thanks. I do need a moment to create it, but it's pretty good."

"It's devastating," Aiden said. "Great job."

"I think I can already see them," Taika said, squinting inside the storm.

"The enemy?" Aiden asked.

"Look, they're at the front of the storm, as if they're preceding it," Ivo commented as she saw it.

"Hide well so they don't see us," Nahia told them.

They crouched and hid behind the trees. What they saw left them speechless. Several thousand Wild Ones of the Ice and Tundra Dwellers were moving nonchalantly under the storm, getting ahead of its center, immune to the icy cold and cutting winds. Their skins and conditioning to the Frozen Continent, where the temperature was still more freezing than Norghana in the winter, must act as protection. They were far enough from the storm vortex that it would not swallow them and kill them. But if this was impressive, what they saw next was even more so.

Nahia rubbed her eyes to make sure she was seeing properly. In the middle of the strong, icy rain and the cutting, blowing winds, she saw about a hundred Arcanes of the Glaciers. Egil had explained to her that they were a race from the Frozen Continent who had powerful magic, magic that controlled the mind and their natural environment. They walked with their arms raised, and they seemed to be casting some kind of magic. Nahia narrowed her eyes and saw that out of their hands, threads of blue magic went up and into the storm clouds. Several threads of blue energy emerged from each hand. She counted hundreds of them. She did not know what they were for, but the Arcanes made them go up to the storm clouds.

What on earth are those magi doing?" Lily asked.

"They're Shamans, not magi," Nahia corrected her. "And they're using magic for something.

"To protect themselves from the storm?" Daphne suggested.

"Maybe," Taika said.

"They were all looking when suddenly the Arcanes of the Glaciers, as one, moved their arms to the left. As if they were pulling on the clouds, the storm followed the Shamans' arms.

"By all the stormy skies in nature!" Ivo cried, unable to believe what he was seeing.

"They're directing the storm!" Lily realized.

"They are doing it, you're right," Nahia nodded, unable to believe it.

"Where are they leading it?" Aiden asked.

"To that depression there, between the woods," Taika pointed out.

They watched for a moment, and indeed they were going that way. They had escaped the storm with the change of direction and were not suffering from the cold and winds so much.

"Thank goodness it didn't come on us," said Lily.

"Yeah, a much better temperature now, although I'm still frozen to the bone," Daphne said, "This is not weather for a Fatum."

"Well, for a Scarlatum even less. We're made for the sun and heat!"

"We must follow them or we'll lose them," Aiden told them, pointing with his finger.

"Yeah, let's go, but around the storm," said Taika and started moving.

They followed the head of the storm from about five hundred paces to one side, and they saw that it was now passing over the depression between the two forests.

"We have to go into the forest," said Aiden.

They did so, and after crossing the forest they remained in hiding without revealing themselves. Then they went out to the depression. They had entered the storm again, and the winds and cold attacked them.

"Where are they?" Aiden asked blankly.

"I don't see them," Nahia said.

"The storm is breaking over us, and it's not the head, it's the center!" Daphne cried in the midst of the strong winds and icy rain.

"Does anyone see them?" Ivo asked, looking at the depression covered in snow but without a soul in sight.

"They have to be here!" said Taika. The wind was so strong that it forced them to shout in order to hear each other.

"The snow has swallowed them!" Lily said.

The situation was getting very ugly. They could not stay there—the storm was going to swallow them.

"Follow me, I have an idea!" Nahia told them as she went out of the snow between the forests.

"Where are you going?" They'll see us!" Daphne shouted.

"They won't see us! Come with me!" Nahia headed to the end of the depression and the others followed her. The storm was about to swallow them from the back.

"There it is!" Nahia cried and pointed.

Where the depression ended to the south and another forest began, they found the entrance to a tunnel.

Chapter 48

"That's where they went!" cried Aiden.

"That tunnel is invisible from a distance!" Lily realized as she protected her face from the icy wind and rain with her forearm.

"And impossible to spot from the sky. It's a cut in the ground, inwards, toward the forest!" said Taika.

"It's not natural. They've dug it out so it can't be seen!" Ivo said.

"We have to get inside, the storm is going to swallow us!" Nahia told them. She could barely stand from the strength of the gusts of wind pushing against them.

They looked over their shoulders and saw that the deadly part of the storm was upon them. They had no time to run away. They had to go underground, or else they would die.

"Run!" Taika cried.

They all ran toward the entrance of the tunnel under the forest. A few paces away, they saw they were going to block the entrance from the inside.

"They're blocking the entrance!" Daphne warned.

"I'll see to it!" Ivo shouted, and lowering his head, horns to the front, shield and spear in hand, he charged the entrance.

The others followed the assault of the great Tauruk.

Ivo charged into the camouflaged door they were trying to hide the tunnel with. He also ran down four Wild Ones of the Ice who were moving it. Two others at the corners turned, caught off guard by the attack. Taika and Aiden went for them at a run before they could react. Taika plunged his spear into the heart of the Wild One as soon as he turned to face him. Aiden launched an attack to the neck of the other Wild One, but he saw the Drakonid and deflected the spear with his great axe. Aiden reacted and struck him in the face with his shield. The Wild One took a step back, dizzy, but he did not fall.

Ivo recovered his weapon and got up. He plunged his spear into the neck of one of the Wild Ones he had knocked down. The others came out from under the round wooden door and got up slowly, stunned by the tremendous blow they had received and the weight of the camouflaged door. Nahia, Daphne, and Lily came running and did not hesitate for an instant. Despite how enormous and brutal the Wild Ones of the Ice were, the girls attacked them with their spears. The fight was brief. Before the Wild Ones could recover, they already had several deadly wounds from the precise attacks of the three comrades. The good part about attacking with a spear was that you did not need to get too close to the enemy. Sharp attack, retreat behind the shield, and repeat.

Aiden and Taika came to them once they had finished off the other two Wild Ones, but they had already dealt with their rivals.

"Good work, Ivo," Nahia told him, smiling.

"Nothing like using your head," he replied with a chuckle.

"Very good," Lily said and laughed.

"I see lights in the distance, in the tunnel," said Aiden, who had gone on ahead to see if there were any other enemies.

"It must be the troops we're following. They use this tunnel to get into the city," Taika said.

"Do you think this tunnel ends at Olstran?" Daphne asked.

"It's practically guaranteed. That's how they've been bringing reinforcements and supplies to the besieged city," Taika explained.

Suddenly, a tremendous gust of wind came in through the mouth of the tunnel and threw the six up in the air. They hit the ground hard, several paces ahead.

"What a blow," Lily complained while she picked up her spear and stood up.

"A hard one," Daphne said, retrieving her shield from the ground.

Through the mouth of the tunnel, more icy winds came in, and they noticed that the temperature dropped to dangerous levels, invoking freezing and death.

"The storm is right on top of us," Ivo said.

"I was going to ask whether we were going back, but I believe this rules it out," said Daphne.

"If we go back out, we won't survive," said Ivo. "The temperature at the center of the storm is very low, the kind that causes instant death."

"Then all we can do is follow the troops," said Lily.

"Which is what we've been ordered to do," Aiden added, as if any other option were not valid.

"You do realize that if they turn back and see us, we're dead, don't you?" Lily told him, pointing at the lights at the end of passage and then the entrance of the tunnel.

"Well … yeah… but we'll manage." Aiden was looking in both directions, worried.

"I'm not very confident about following a few thousand natives of the Frozen Continent into a city full of Norghanian soldiers… but it seems to be our only choice," said Taika.

"We can stay here and wait for the storm to pass, or the siege," said Daphne.

"That's a bad idea," said Lily.

"We have to follow the enemy." Aiden's face was pure disbelief.

"We'll have to go," said Ivo.

"And why's that?" Nahia asked him,

"More reinforcements from the Frozen Continent are coming," Ivo said, narrowing his eyes to see outside.

Nahia went over to the door to look.

"They're coming, indeed. They still haven't seen us, but they're running, so we'd better run too."

"Let's go!" Taika said, and they started running.

The tunnel was wide and dark, but they could not create light—which Daphne could do almost without thinking—because they could not risk either the enemies behind or ahead noticing. Nahia ran, careful not to trip. The ground was quite flat and firm. But it was earth, and it had potholes which might make them trip and fall or twist an ankle, which was even worse. She looked back and saw that the group behind them were lighting torches to move along the tunnel, like the one ahead had done. Luckily, they went between the two groups in total darkness, and neither the ones ahead nor those behind could see them. Nahia could not believe the situation they were in. Getting out of this mess alive was going to be very difficult.

They walked as fast as they could. The tunnel was long and wide, and it seemed to have no end. Suddenly, Ivo tripped and fell on his face. There was a loud noise when he hit the ground with his shield and spear and his enormous body. They all stopped, looking behind and ahead of them to see if they had been discovered. Everyone kept silent, holding their breath, but when there was no reaction from either group, they calmed down. Ivo picked himself up, as well as his spear and shield.

"I'm okay," he whispered.

"Let's keep going, carefully. We're coming to the end of the tunnel," Taika whispered,

Nahia noticed there was more light ahead, like Taika had guessed. She was grateful. That long tunnel, although wide and high, was not at all to her liking. And it was too long. She wondered how many workers it had taken, and how long they had worked to create such an underground passage. She calculated that from where they were, at the end of the tunnel to the city, it was about two leagues.

They came to the end of the tunnel. The reinforcements ahead of them had all gone out and had not left anyone on watch. Most likely because another group was coming after them. The tunnel opened onto a great room, a cellar. Part of it was in shadow and part of it was illuminated from the outside light, which is what they saw.

"We have to leave the tunnel," Taika said, looking back. "I see far too many torches following us."

"But if we go out there, we might come out in the middle of the enemy," said Daphne.

"I could try my Form of Shadow skill," Taika suggested.

"Try it," Ivo encouraged him.

"All right." Taika bent down by the end of the tunnel, shut his tiger eyes, and concentrated.

For a moment that seemed like an eternity, they waited, but nothing happened. Taika was not succeeding. Nahia looked behind them and saw the torches drawing closer. She started to grow uneasy. She looked at Taika; she could only see half of his crouched body and saw he was not succeeding. They would soon be discovered. They had no choice but to go out into the open. At that moment, Taika became a shadow, and a moment later he vanished into the gloom.

"Wow, he did it. Wonderful," Aiden whispered, very pleased with his comrade.

"This gives me an idea…" Ivo said, turning.

"What are you going to do?" Nahia asked.

"I'm going to leave a gift to those coming. In the dark, I doubt they'll see it."

"What gift?" Nahia asked.

"A couple of circles of poisonous creepers. It will slow them down and give us some more time."

"That's a great idea," Daphne congratulated him.

Ivo got started. It would also take him a moment. These skills were difficult to call on and took time to create.

They waited another long moment in tense silence. Suddenly, Taika appeared before them. Well, not Taika, but a moving shadow. They only noticed him when he stepped into the light.

"Follow me, I'll tell you where to go," he whispered.

"You know we can't see you, right?" Lily told him.

"I'll try to remember," shadow Taika whispered back.

There we go, I've left them a couple cozy surprises," Ivo murmured.

"Come on." Taika passed into the hall, striding along the part with no light. The others followed. It was an enormous stone cellar, not designed to store anything, but built as the exit of the tunnel. Three sets of wide stone stairs went up, one ahead, and the others to either side.

"Up the right one," Taika whispered.

They went up the stairs, and before they reached the top, they saw three guards. They were Tundra Dwellers. They were not looking toward them but outside, drawn to the clamor outside. A tremendous battle was taking place in the city. They heard dragon roars; rocks exploding from their elemental attacks or claws; the shouts of the soldiers of the red army taking the walls, and those of the defenders stopping them and throwing them down the walls; the sound of steel against steel; the cries of the wounded and dying; and the endless cacophony of brutal battle.

"We have to eliminate the guards," Taika said.

"I'll do it," said Nahia, who pointed her spear at them to aid her aim. She concentrated on the three, gathered energy from her inner dragon, and called on her Multiple Fire Thunderbolt skill. It took her a moment, but she managed to conjure it. Three bolts of fire fell upon the guards as if they had come down from the sky, and they burned alive in an instant. They were incinerated on the spot.

"Wow, remind me not to make you angry," Aiden said, impressed.

"What a spell," Lily congratulated her.

Nahia was pleased that the spell had been successful on her first try. She had doubted she would succeed.

They went up to the end of the stairs at a crouch, and what they saw when they looked out left them dumbstruck. The city was being attacked from every direction, and people were fighting to the death in every tower, battement, stair, and in the center of the city. At the top of the eastern, southern, and western walls, the soldiers of the Red Dragon King were fighting against Norghanian soldiers, trying to gain control of the walls. The fighting was fierce and terrible. The shouts of the attackers met those of the defenders, and death hit soldiers on both sides. The soldiers of the Red Dragon King attacked with spears and shields and the Norghanians defended with axes and shields. The attackers were more numerous, but the Norghanian soldiers were as fierce as they were brutal. They were holding the three walls with shouting and strong axe blows. The soldiers of Kraido fell, hacked to pieces before the Norghanian brutality. Only at the battlements were they holding up because of their numeric superiority and the support of the dragons from the air.

The north wall was a totally different situation. It had fallen into the hands of the Kraido soldiers and the dragons. The gate was destroyed, and through it two large dragons had come in, one of fire and the other of air. They had taken it. The ten thousand soldiers Nahia and the others had seen lining up in front of the camp were now fighting in the north area of the city against the Norghanian soldiers and the reinforcements they had just received from the Frozen Continent.

The battle was brutal in the north of the city. Nearly all the forces on both sides were fighting there. The soldiers from Kraido were facing the Norghanian soldiers, who were brutal but did not reach the beastly levels of the Wild Ones of the Ice or the Tundra Dwellers. The soldiers of Kraido looked diminutive compared to the latter, who destroyed them either with brutal axe strikes with their double-headed axes or ran them through with their javelins. The snow that covered the whole city was now stained red with blood all along the walled city.

Above the stone buildings and towers, the dragons flew and came down to attack when they saw there were not too many of their own troops located there. Two dragons came down upon each of the walls that were still under the enemies' control. When they landed on the wall, they crushed enemies and their own soldiers equally, without any consideration, roaring and proving they would leave no one alive. They used their elemental breaths of fire, earth, water, and air against the Norghanian soldiers, who fell dead without any defense.

Nahia saw that they had come out on the north side of the city, surrounded by the fighting filling the city. The north gate with the two dragons defending it was right in front of them. But between their position and that of the dragons, ten thousand soldiers of Kraido were fighting against another ten thousand soldiers of Norghana, plus their allies from the Frozen Continent. It was a sea of heads, swords, axes, and spears in constant movement amid the deafening sound of battle. The shouts of both sides and the roars of the dragons were chilling.

"It would appear we have arrived in time for the real battle," Aiden said, ready to fight.

"And we've come out at the hottest place," Lily commented with a shocked face.

Taika's spell faded and he returned to his natural form.

"We have to move. Soon the rest of the reinforcements will come out of that tunnel."

"Yeah, they will have finished with my traps by now," Ivo nodded.

"Watch out, they've seen us!" Aiden warned.

A Norghanian officer had turned around and was pointing at them. He was barking orders to his soldiers, about fifty of them, who turned to attack them.

"There are too many of them!" Daphne shouted.

"We have to find a defensible position!" said Aiden.

"To that tower, quickly!" Taika indicated.

They ran to the tower. It stood in front of them, in the middle of a small square and surrounded by a low wall. It must be some sort of military post. It would provide them with shelter. The top of the tower did not have a roof, but a battlement, and it was rectangular. At the top of the tower were several Norghanian soldiers with short bows releasing at the soldiers of Kraido.

When they reached the wall, Ivo lifted the others over it. Then from the top of the wall, Taika and Aiden lifted Ivo and they all passed into the little square and ran to the door of the tower, which was defended by four Norghanian soldiers. Lily stopped and enchanted them while the others ran toward them. Aiden reached them first and was about to attack them until he saw they were absolutely terrified, as if they were in the middle of a horrible nightmare. They were screaming and pulling on their blond hair and beards. Suddenly, they ran off, terrified. Aiden turned and looked at Lily, who smiled at him. The Drakonid shook his head and lunged at the door.

"I'll deal with it," Ivo told him, and he charged like a bull, knocking down the wooden door.

Inside the tower, they ran up the stairs and finished off four soldiers on the floors in between. They arrived at the top and Ivo and Aiden toppled down the archers, who fell to the little square and did not get back up. A moment later, they were all at the top. Ivo stayed on the stairs and set a few of his poisonous creeper circles. The Norghanian soldiers following them reached the square and started climbing the wall. But Nahia pointed to the battle in front of them.

"Look!"

They saw how the Arcanes of the Ice came to stand behind their warriors. At once, the Tundra Dwellers withdrew to surround and cover them. The Arcanes began to cast spells with their strange staves, moving them in circles while they conjured, ancient chanting or a litany of the depths of the ice.

After a long moment of conjuring, a blue mist began to form under the feet of the soldiers of Kraido, who were fighting with all their might before the more powerful Norghanians and their allies of the ice. The mist rose while the fight went on. Nahia noticed that it only rose in the area of the soldiers of Kraido. This made her suspect that something bad was going to happen. The blue fog completely covered the troops of Kraido in the north area. They vanished within it. Nahia could see all the Arcanes of the Glaciers conjuring at once, moving their staves. It had to be some great spell they were all casting at once. She found it exceptional.

Suddenly, the soldiers of Kraido in the middle of the blue mist stopped fighting. Their gazes became lost. They all had blue pupils and irises. They were under the influence of the great spell the Arcanes of the Glaciers had cast.

"I think I know what's going to happen now," said Lily, who was looking down at the foot of the tower from the battlement. She had just conjured against three Norghanian soldiers at the base of the tower and had left them enchanted, horrified and scared to death.

"What?" Nahia asked as she discharged a tremendous fireball against six Norghanian soldiers who were trying to enter the tower through the door Ivo and Aiden had blocked with a couple of fallen cupboards from the first floor. The powerful flame caught them all and they burned as they ran, terrified until they died.

"End your life," Lily told another enchanted soldier who had climbed up to the first-floor window. He took out a knife and plunged it into his own heart. "Something like that," she told Nahia.

"I see," Nahia said, changing sides on the tower since three soldiers were climbing up the windows. She concentrated and called on her Fire Thunderbolt, striking the first soldier who fell down. She threw a ball of fire at the second one, which incinerated him. She did not have to do anything to the third soldier because Taika threw Dark Daggers his way and killed him. On the other side, Aiden and Ivo were throwing balls of storm and earth at those who tried to climb the tower. The twin explosions finished off their attackers. They both had a bit of trouble conjuring them, but the tower was high and gave them plenty of time. It was that or wait until the soldiers reached the battlement of the tower, because they did not have long-distance weapons.

"Watch out, it's already beginning!" Lily told them, and she pointed at the soldiers of Kraido in the middle of the blue mist. They stopped fighting and began to turn. They faced the two dragons at the northern gate and started heading toward them.

"They're not going to attack them, are they?" Aiden asked, shocked.

"Of course they are. They're all enchanted. The Arcanes control them now," Lily told them.

"That's amazing," Ivo watched, numb.

"It is," Nahia nodded.

The soldiers headed toward the two dragons, that watched them for a moment. They must be ordering them to turn around, but the soldiers enveloped in the blue mist kept walking toward the dragons, impassive.

The two dragons did not wait any longer. They opened their mouths, and from them came their terrible elemental breath. A great flow of fire, and another of stormy lightning fell on the soldiers, who died without a cry or moving away.

"They're enchanted, they can't feel or suffer," said Lily,

"The dragons will kill them all," Ivo said in horror. Then he turned around and delivered a blow with his shield to the face of a Norghanian soldier who had managed to reach the battlement. He fell to the square.

"They won't be capable of killing their own army," said Daphne, and she conjured Multiple Healing to heal the whole squad now that she had a moment.

"They're very capable," Nahia said as she threw another fireball at the base of the tower by the door, incinerating another half dozen soldiers.

And at that moment, the battle became even more complicated. From the same place they had come out, Nahia saw the second group of reinforcements arriving. A couple of thousand Wild Ones of the Ice and the same number of Arcanes of the Glaciers headed to take the south, east, and west walls.

Nahia immediately recognized the last group that came at the rear of the reinforcements.

It was Lasgol, Gerd, and Camu. They were accompanied by Ona, the snow panther, and Argi, the giant wolf.

Chapter 49

Nahia leaned over the battlement and called out to Lasgol.

"Lasgol, over here!" she shouted. She dropped her shield and spear on the floor and waved her arms so he would see her.

But in the midst of the noisy battle, it was impossible to hear anything. The battle cries came from all sides. She tried again, but without luck. Lasgol and his companions launched into their attack, against a dragon no less. They faced a red dragon that came down from the sky to attack the new reinforcements that had entered the city. The dragon used its fiery breath and roasted a group of Wild Ones of the Ice who attacked it. They died amid war cries.

Lasgol used his golden bow. Nahia saw a golden flash come out of the weapon. It was the Golden Magic the weapon possessed. An arrow flew true and plunged deep into the right eye of the dragon. The beast roared, furious. Gerd, the Ranger who was almost as big as Ivo, released at the dragon's head with earth arrows that exploded upon impact with a loud noise, creating a cloud of smoke and blinding and stunning substances right in the dragon's face. The beast shook its head to get rid of the noxious effect and roared with rage.

Lasgol released again at the same eye and made another bull's eye. Nahia had no doubt he was using some skill that kept him from missing. With that skill, plus the Golden Magic, he left the dragon one-eyed and roaring again with rage and pain. Gerd released again quickly and hit it full in the mouth. Once more, he used an earth arrow, and when the arrow exploded it released a blinding, stunning cloud that enveloped the dragon's head. It shook its head again, but in an intelligent and unexpected movement, the dragon covered its head with its right wing and the next arrows from Lasgol and Gerd hit the wing. Lasgol's wounded it, but Gerd's could not reach its head. The dragon counterattacked at once with its breath of fire. A tremendous flame came out of its mouth and aimed directly at Lasgol's group.

"Oh no!" cried Nahia, horrified.

The flame reached the group, which was staying close to Camu in the middle, Lasgol and Ona on one side and Gerd and Argi on the other. But the flame did not reach them. Nahia could make out a dome of protective energy around them. The flaming breath was striking the dome, unable to pass through. That was Camu's magic, she was sure of it. A most impressive magic. The dragon was unable to penetrate it, and Nahia was sure it was sending all its energy in order to do so. Camu, on his part, would be sending energy to maintain the raised defense. Taking advantage of the magical defenses, Lasgol and Gerd released again while the dragon kept trying to bring down Camu's protecting dome. Lasgol's arrow plunged deep into the left eye and Gerd's also reached it with a fire arrow.

The red dragon roared in rage. It shut its mouth, putting out its breath of fire as it moved its head as if trying to see. It took a step and stumbled. Nahia realized it was blinded. It could not see. It roared in rage and frustration and tried to escape, beating its wings. Ona and Argi ran to attack the wings of the dragon. The panther and the giant wolf bit the dragon's wings and hung from them with their own weight. The dragon felt it, but it could not see them in order to kill them. It shook its wings to get rid of them, but both of their grips were spectacular and they did not let go with their teeth.

Lasgol gave some orders and about fifty Wild Ones of the Ice ran and split into two groups, throwing ropes with balls and hooks at the wings to stop it from flying. They had clearly already done this before—it was some kind of maneuver they were familiar with. The dragon with all that weight on its wings could not take off, but it was trying to free them amid roars. Lasgol, Gerd, and Camu hurried, getting very close to the blind dragon. Lasgol and Gerd riddled the monster's open mouth with arrows. Unable to escape or stop roaring, it received many volleys of arrows in its mouth that reached its brain, killing it. The great red dragon collapsed on its snout, dead.

"Did you see that?" Nahia asked her comrades.

"I saw it, and can't believe it," said Daphne.

"Me neither," said Lily.

"They've killed a dragon…. That's… that's… not possible…" Aiden was in shock.

"An impressive display of magic and skill," Taika nodded.

Ivo threw two Norghanian soldiers over the battlement and turned.

"I missed it!"

"Don't worry, I think there'll be more," Nahia told him as she saw Lasgol and his group heading toward another dragon, this one a white beast that had landed on a building and was discharging its storm breath on the Norghanian soldiers in the center of the city.

"Yeah, look east," Taika told him.

Nahia looked and saw a group of six Rangers wearing snow-white clothes attacking a brown dragon in the middle of a wide square. They were using the same tactic as Lasgol. They released at the eyes of the dragon with elemental arrows of earth and fire. The dragon, half blinded, was trying to get them with its elemental storm breath, but the Rangers did not stop running and releasing, hiding between the houses around the square before coming back out and releasing again. Nahia recognized them.

"Those are Molak, Luca, and the White Foxes," she told her comrades.

"They're risking a lot..." Daphne said, concerned.

"They have no choice, facing a dragon without golden weapons," said Nahia.

Suddenly, about a hundred Wild Ones of the Ice appeared behind the dragon with enormous nets they were all carrying. They threw them on the dragon while the White Foxes kept it busy with their attacks. The beast, half blinded, did not realize until it was too late. The nets fell on its body and imprisoned its wings. The dragon roared furiously and tried to free its wings while arrows kept bursting in its face. The hundred Wild Ones of the Ice pulled down hard and the dragon was unable to free its wings and take off. A moment later, two dozen Tundra Dwellers appeared. They threw ropes at the head of the dragon, and once they were wrapped around its neck, they pulled on them until they managed to bring the head down to the ground. They kept it like that, and the White Foxes hastened to finish binding the dragon. They hacked at both eyes multiple times and then went for another dragon.

"Impressive, these Norghanian Rangers," said Ivo.

"They certainly are," Taika agreed.

Nahia watched the north wall where the two dragons were killing Kraido soldiers possessed by the Arcanes of the Glaciers. They were no longer doing that. The dragons themselves were surrounded by the blue cloud that was swallowing them. Nahia knew that the natural defenses of the dragons would defend them from the enchantment. But since the Arcanes continued conjuring all as one, the blue mist was very thick and high. It did not allow her to see anything. The two dragons as well, unable to see and fight, took off and escaped to the heights, shaking their heads to get rid of the blue mist.

The possessed soldiers went out through the north gate and left the city, as if they were living dead, nothing more than mindless bodies. They simply headed north.

"They've been enchanted to keep walking north," Daphne guessed.

"For how long?" Nahia asked Lily.

"Judging from the number of Arcanes conjuring and all that mist covering the whole northern part of the city, I'd say they're going to keep walking until tomorrow."

"They're going to go beyond the war camp."

"Yes, and a lot farther than that," Lily said, nodding.

Taika, Aiden, and Ivo rejected the last Norghanians trying to reach the battlements of the tower they were in.

"Clear," Taika said.

Nahia felt a terrible cold at her back. She turned, and the freezing winds of the winter storm hit her face with their icy breath.

"The storm!" she cried.

They all turned toward it. It came from the northeast.

"It looks like the center of the storm will pass without hitting the city," said Daphne.

"Thank goodness," Lily huffed.

"Or the war camp," said Aiden.

At that moment, four dragons came down from the sky and threw their elemental breaths against the enemy forces in the center, and north of the city. The four walls had fallen, or rather the dragons had not left anyone alive on them, regardless of the side they were on. Now they were going to focus on the inside of the city.

"They're changing strategies. They're going to destroy the city from the air," Nahia realized.

"If they come down, Lasgol and the Rangers will kill them. It's logical," said Taika.

"And the soldiers of Kraido are heading north by the thousands," Lily added.

The breaths of fire caused flaming explosions, those of earth burst with stone and rock, those of air discharged tremendous lightning, and those of water froze whoever they caught until they froze to death. The Norghanian soldiers and their allies of the Frozen Continent were in trouble. The dragons began to fly low, punishing the city and killing hundreds of people in every pass.

Suddenly, the blue mist began to turn darker and covered everything: Norghanian soldiers, Wild Ones of the ice, Tundra Dwellers, Arcanes of the Glaciers, buildings, squares, the whole center, and north of the city.

"The Arcanes are covering everything with the mist so the dragons can't see their prey," Taika said.

"I see the soldiers are taking cover in houses and other buildings," said Ivo.

"They're smart," Lily admitted.

"Yeah, but that only delays the inevitable," said Aiden. "The dragons will take a thousand passes if necessary."

"You know he's right," Lily said.

Suddenly, a fire dragon flew past, throwing its flaming breath near them.

"Lay low!" Taika warned.

They threw themselves on the floor away from the passing stream of fire. But it only missed them by a hair's breadth.

"Hey! We're Dragon Warlocks, you idiot!" Lily shouted at the dragon as it flew away to return with another lethal pass.

"They don't care. They're going to destroy everything, no matter who's in the city," Nahia said, who could see the dragons' intentions.

The red dragon was coming from the opposite direction, and this time its breath was going to hit the center of the tower.

"We have to get out of here!" Taika shouted at them.

"Downstairs!" Daphne cried. They ran downstairs, and the dragon reached the tower with its breath of fire. It hit the structure and everything burned. It passed right over the tower. If they had still been at the top, it would have incinerated them. Below, on the stairs, the fire managed to get in, but not too far.

"My hair!" Lily cried as it caught fire.

Aiden put it out by slapping it as his arms caught on fire.

In the middle of the stairs, Taika and Ivo were hurting from burns on their feet, and their cloaks were burning. They took them off and threw them out the window.

"How are you?" Daphne asked the Scarlatum. She was the only one the flames had not touched somehow, besides Nahia.

411

"Burns on my arms and feet…" said Lily, looking around at her comrades. She had a nasty-looking burn on her right arm.

"Take it easy, all of you. Give me a moment, I can heal you." Daphne concentrated, and a moment later her Healing Energy was running over each of their burns. It took her a long moment, but she was able to heal all their injuries.

"You're the best in the whole world!" Lily said, delighted.

"They weren't serious wounds, thank goodness," Daphne snorted.

"You're worth a thousand rations," Ivo told her.

"That's the best compliment I've ever received," the Fatum smiled at him.

"We have to get out of this city before the dragons kill us," said Taika.

"Okay, let's clear the door." Ivo and Aiden set to open the door, and once they finished, they prepared to come out.

"We need protection against their Elemental Breaths," said Nahia. "We have to use our scale protection."

"Do you think they'll hold?" Daphne asked.

"They should, at least if it's not a sustained attack," said Nahia.

"Yeah, that's a very good idea," Lily agreed.

"Come on then, let's get started," Nahia said, and in a moment she had called on both levels of scale protection: the energy one and the hard lava.

Daphne and Lily did not have any trouble creating the field of magic scales, which provided protective anti-magic energy. Or their Elemental Scales, of diamond and ice respectively.

Unfortunately, the boys did not have the same results. The three had their eyes shut. They were concentrating, trying to create them, but without luck. They were failing.

"Come on, boys, I'm sure you can do it," Lily said encouragingly.

It did not seem like they were going to be successful. Outside, the low flights increased and the explosions and cries of agony grew. Suddenly, Aiden succeeded. His scales of energy and whirlwind protection covered his body.

"Wonderful!" Lily cried.

A moment later, Taika did it. His scales of energy and black diamonds appeared all over his body.

Ivo wanted to give up. "We'd better drop it, let's go."

"No way. We're not leaving until you're protected," Daphne said, very seriously.

Ivo snorted and tried again. A moment later, out of sheer stubbornness, he did it. His great body covered with scales of energy and then of rock.

"Very good. Remember that you have to send energy to the scales in order to keep them active," Nahia said.

"All right," Ivo nodded.

"Let's go!" Taika cried and went out of the tower into the square. They all followed. Like a bad omen coming true, a white dragon flew past them, discharging its storm breath. A stream of lightning bolts reached them, hitting them with great intensity. A dozen bolts hit each one of them, and those that fell around them raised a storm of stones from the ground that also hit them. They all stopped where they were.

"Any injured?" Daphne asked.

"No… I'm not injured…" Ivo said, unable to believe it.

"Me… neither…" Aiden was feeling his chest where he had been hit by two lightning bolts.

"My scales are almost destroyed," Nahia said, "but they held up. Send more energy before you lose them."

They all did what Nahia said, and they managed to maintain their two protective scale spells.

"Well, I think this answers your question," Nahia told Daphne.

"The next time I'd rather find out some other way," she joked, wrinkling her nose.

Nahia shrugged.

They left the square and realized that if they went toward the center of the city, they would enter the great blue mist.

"I don't think that mist will be good for us," said Lily.

"We'd better avoid it."

Suddenly, a dragon roared above them. It was a brown dragon, and it had several arrows stuck in its head.

"Watch out!" Taika warned.

"That dragon is fleeing," Daphne said.

"From who?" Lily asked.

Then, from between some houses about twenty-five paces away, the group of pursuers appeared. It was Lasgol, Gerd, Camu, and his friends.

"Lasgol!" Nahia called him with a loud shout.

This time, Lasgol heard her. He turned toward her and aimed his bow at her. Gerd did the same.

It's me, Nahia!" Just in case, she dropped her weapons on the ground and took off her hood so he could see her.

"Nahia!" Lasgol recognized her. Then he pointed his bow at the rest of the squad.

"Friends!" Nahia shouted in Norghanian.

Lasgol watched them for an instant. Then he nodded and came closer. The rest of the group followed him. When he was level with them, Lasgol motioned them to follow him inside a large rock house. Once inside and under cover, he greeted them.

"Hello, Nahia," he said and gave her a nod.

We very happy find you, Camu sent to everyone.

Daphne, Lily, Aiden, Ivo, and Taika were surprised to receive Camu's mental message.

"I'm happy to see you too."

You no worry, I translate to message with my Transmute Message skill.

"Thank you, Camu, you're a star."

I much star, yes. Intelligent too. Much.

Nahia could not help smiling.

"Camu is going to take what we say and transform it into a mental message he will send to each of you. That way we'll all understand one another. You will hear everything with an echo," she told her squad.

"How's Egil?" Lasgol asked her.

"He's all right. He sends you greetings. He's still a prisoner in the dungeons. We haven't been able to free him yet."

"But he's all right?" Gerd asked, worried.

"Yes, he's well of health and spirit. He says we must keep fighting and that we'll find a way to free him."

"About freeing me… thank you very much, all of you," Gerd told them.

"Here, let me introduce my squad. This is Daphne, Lily, Aiden, Ivo, and Taika."

Much pleasure meeting you all, Camu sent them, smiling.

"A pleasure," Lasgol said.

The squad greeted them with brief nods.

Roars sounded outside and a dragon gave a fiery pass that fell near them.

"There's not much time, you have to get out of here," Lasgol told them.

"What's going on?" Nahia noticed Lasgol's tone of voice.

"The Arcanes of the Glaciers are going to lead the winter storm over to the city. Then to the war camp. No one will survive."

"Oh, wow…"

"We're all going back to the tunnel for protection," Lasgol said.

"I see."

"You could stay with me…"

"Hmmm, that's very risky. We're the enemy," Taika said.

"I think I'd be able to protect you…" Lasgol replied.

"That's a lot of people to persuade…" Gerd was not so sure.

"The Norghanians will hang us," Aiden assured. "Or the blue savages will."

"Yes, it's very risky. I appreciate it, Lasgol, but it's better that we leave. Besides, we have to go back to Kraido. Otherwise we won't be able to help Egil," Nahia said.

"That's true. In that case, go now. The storm is about to arrive."

"Okay. We'll leave. I hope we can meet again with more time to talk," Nahia told him.

"Yeah, same here," Lasgol replied.

"Good luck! Nahia wished him.

"Good luck," Lasgol said.

Lasgol's group left the building, and a moment later Nahia and her squad did too. No sooner had they left their shelter that the winds of the storm shook them. The temperature was freezing. They looked up at the sky and did not see any dragons, only a dark, threatening mass of black clouds heading toward them. In the middle of the city everyone was running to find shelter, some in the houses, but most were going to the tunnel they had come through.

"We have to get out of here!" said Aiden, and he ran toward the north gate that was free of soldiers and blue mist.

"Let's go!" They all ran toward the gate, aware that they had to win the race with the storm.

They ran as if death itself was chasing them.

Suddenly, they encountered a group of Norghanian soldiers running in the opposite direction along the street they were on. They were about a dozen of them.

"I'll deal with it!" Aiden cried as he called on his elite skill, Wrath. He yelled as if possessed and lunged headlong at the Norghanian soldiers. He hit with extraordinary fury, delivering sword thrusts hither and thither, and as he struck, there came storm lightning bolts from his body which fell upon the soldiers. In the blink of an eye, he had killed them all and the passage was clear.

"I'll cure him, he's wounded," Daphne said, and she used her magic. Aiden came to, coming out of his state of Wrath.

"You really are a crazy little thing, aren't you," Lily told him, shaking her head.

"Let's get out of here!" Aiden yelled and ran to the gate.

As they were crossing it, the storm at their heels, Nahia noticed that the dragons were also withdrawing like them, fleeing the storm.

They arrived at the war camp, and there the saw that the order to evacuate had been given. They ran west, escaping the storm. They ran for hours, but at last they managed to reach safety.

Worn out with exhaustion, they sat in the snow beside a forest.

"What a peaceful mission," said Lily.

"Yeah, we've lost the squadron, our leader, and half the army," said Daphne.

"Well, we're alive, which is what matters," said Nahia.

"That's the truth," Ivo nodded.

"It was horrible. We've been defeated," said Aiden.

"That was chaos, not defeat," said Lily.

"In any case, we've fulfilled our mission," said Daphne.

"That's true," Taika agreed.

"Even so, I bet we'll be punished for this," Nahia said.

No one replied, but they were all thinking the same thing.

Chapter 50

Nahia came out of the tent in the invasion camp situated on the Reborn Continent. They had arrived the day before after a long journey from Olstran to the Pearl in the south of Norghana, the one Lasgol and his friends knew as the Pearl above the Lair at the Shelter. Irakas-Gorri-Gaizt had opened a portal to the Reborn Continent, and now they were all resting and recovering. The mission had been total chaos, but they had not received a reprimand from their leader. So far.

"How are you?" Ivo asked her as he sat on a box in front of the tent, eating a ration which was surely not his first.

"Well… tired but well. I feel weak for some reason," Nahia told him, frowning.

"It's natural. We've done a lot of fighting and a lightning journey back here," Ivo told her. "Eat something, you'll feel much better."

"Yeah, I think I'll go and fetch a ration."

"Do you want me to go for it?" Ivo asked her.

"No, don't worry. It'll do me good to stretch my legs."

Ivo nodded and kept eating.

"How are Lily and Daphne?" Aiden asked as he approached them.

"Asleep. They're worn out," Nahia looked toward the tent.

"It'll do them good to rest. It's been a difficult mission," Aiden nodded.

"What news?" Nahia asked Taika, coming to stand beside him. The Felidae-Tiger was watching the camp with narrowed eyes.

"Not much. Our leader and other dragons have flown north, behind the great glacier. They must be conferring there. About what, I have no idea. I think we're waiting for the other missions to return. I guess they won't open the great portal to Kraido until we're all here."

"It's not efficient. It requires a lot of power to be able to open it. They'll wait until we're all here, I'm sure," Aiden declared, looking toward the great glacier.

"Who's back?" Nahia asked with interest.

"The Brown, Blue, White Squadron, and us," Taika told her.

"Oh, in that case I'll go see how they are."

"Don't forget to eat something," Taika told her.

Nahia nodded and left her comrades. She wanted to make sure Ana and Logan had come back and were all right. She headed to the tent of the White Squadron and instantly recognized Logan standing beside the armory. Her heart leapt with joy. He was here and seemed to be fine. Nahia sighed with relief and happiness.

Logan was talking with two people: someone from his squad, and someone else she could not see. Nahia went around some tents and saw that Logan's comrade was heading to the kitchens, revealing the other person. It was Ana. Nahia was very glad to see her safe and sound. Ana looked like she usually did, worried and anxious, which meant she was okay. She and Logan were talking. Seeing them together, Nahia thought things had been fixed. Logan must have talked to Ana and everything was all right. She reached them.

"Hello, Ana, Logan! I'm so happy to see you!" she greeted them joyfully.

The two turned toward her. Logan's face lit up and his seriousness vanished. His eyes shone and a smile appeared on his face. Ana looked at him, and her face showed surprise. An instant later, her face shadowed, and there was no smile on her lips.

"Nahia, you're all right!" Logan welcomed her with joy in his voice.

"How nice to have you back," Ana told her, but there was no feeling of warmth or affection in her tone, and Nahia noticed.

"You're not hurt, are you?" Nahia asked, examining them from head to toe.

"We're all right," Logan said reassuringly as he checked her in turn.

"It's wonderful that we're all well," Nahia said, genuinely happy.

"Did your mission go well?" Logan asked her.

"Well, what you'd call well, no. I'd say it didn't. It was a surprising, messy mission. But we did what we were ordered to do, so I guess that's good. Our leader hasn't yelled at us, so…"

"Similar to mine then," Logan said.

"And you, Ana?" Nahia asked her, looking straight at her.

"Mine was awful. Death and destruction everywhere," she said, looking down. "The dragons have destroyed everything in their way.

Nothing can stop them. You can only flee from them or bend the knee…"

"Don't say that. No matter how bad things get, we'll defeat them in the end," Nahia told her.

"Tell that to the thousands of Rogdonians, Massig, and Usik they've killed without mercy," Ana shook her head. "I'm going to lie down for a while. It's been days since I last slept."

"What's the matter with her?" Nahia asked Logan.

"She's witnessed the horrors of war, and it's affected her greatly," Logan said.

"Is it only that, or is there something else?" Nahia asked him.

"Something else?"

"Because of… you know…"

"Oh, no, I don't think so," Logan said, shaking his head.

Nahia nodded.

"War is terrible. Horrific things happen."

"Very true," Logan nodded again.

Suddenly, two members of his squad came out of the tent.

"Are you coming, Logan?"

"Sure, coming. Sorry Nahia."

"What is it?'" she asked.

"We're going to the infirmary. We have two wounded, one very serious."

"Oh, I'm sorry."

Logan nodded, "I hope they both recover."

"Me too," Nahia said wistfully.

"See you," he said, and in his eyes, there was a special glow Nahia could detect, surely the same as hers.

She watched Logan leave, her heart beating fast. She sighed and headed to fetch some food. That would make her feel better. She arrived at the kitchens and they gave her a ration, which she gulped down right there. Indeed, she was hungrier than she thought. She asked for a second serving, and she nearly finished that too. It made her feel much better. She left the area of the kitchens and went to her tent, crossing the camp.

But when she was already close, she veered off unwittingly, her mind lost in a thousand thoughts: Logan, Ana, her squad comrades, the wounded, war casualties, dragons and the need to finish them. Without realizing it, she found herself in front of the entrance of the great glacier instead of her tent.

"What… why…?" she muttered, not knowing how she had got there.

She decided to go in and take a look at the great Pearl to see whether it was being prepared to open the great portal back to Kraido. The soldiers on watch duty let her pass. She was expecting to find several silver dragons working on the Pearl, but she was wrong. The great Pearl was there in the middle of the immense glacier, but there was no dragon in sight. The great central chamber was deserted. This meant they were not going to go back right away. The idea did not displease her. She was in no hurry to return to the Academy.

"Nahia?" a voice asked behind her.

She turned. It was Logan.

"Hi, Logan."

"I thought it was you. I saw you as I was coming back from the infirmary."

"How are your comrades?"

"They'll both live," Logan sighed, and his face showed great relief.

"That's very good news."

Suddenly, Nahia felt the scale on her nape heating up.

"Oh… oh…"

"What is it?"

"I might start acting weird, don't worry."

"What?" Logan looked at her blankly.

Nahia felt her mind clouding and the silver mist beginning to form around her mind.

"It's starting, stay calm," she told Logan.

"I feel power. It's coming from you, from your… neck?" Logan said, worried as he reached out his hand to her.

Nahia began to walk to the east. She was in a dream again and the strange power was drawing her. She went into the side cavern adjacent to the main chamber of the glacier where the Pearl was.

Logan followed, worried.

The scale on Nahia's nape was burning, and the mist and that power were drawing her forward. She walked the whole cavern until she reached the wall of ice on the north side. She touched the wall of ice with her hand.

"I might have a vision now," she warned Logan.

"What makes you think so?"

"I had one a short time ago. This place has something to do with my destiny."

"There's nothing here, only a wall of ice."

Nahia began to feel very strange. Now it was not only the scale on her neck, the mist in her head, or the dreamy feeling. She felt heat, a burning heat that was beginning to climb up her whole body. Her inner flame had lit, but not from rage. It was her condition, her illness.

"Something's happening... I'm going to have a seizure," she warned Logan.

"What can I do?" he asked her with wide, anxious eyes.

Nahia felt the flame creating a tremendous fire inside her. All of her was burning. The fire was spreading, the heat expanding through her skin.

"Nothing. Don't touch me. You might get burned, or something worse."

"But there has to be something I can do. How can I help you?"

Nahia shook her head. The palpitations began and grew to a heavy rhythm. Now the dizziness and the nausea would appear. Her heart was beating like a wild horse. But something strange happened. This time was different—she did not get dizzy or nauseous. She realized that her head was still in the middle of that dreamy mist and that the scale was still burning. Her condition was combining with the power of her destiny. Now she should fall to the ground, amid tremendous cramps and end up convulsing on the ground. But it did not happen. She felt like the terrible fire inside her wanted to come out, that she was going to explode outward. She felt it would be with great strength and power.

"Logan, move back, I'm going to explode!" she shouted in warning.

Logan took several steps back.

Nahia lifted her arms up without knowing why she did so and the fire inside her burst. A tremendous flame came out of her body, upward, guided by her raised arms. The powerful flame rose and reached the upper part of the cavern. The terrible power of her flame melted the ice and continued rising. It made a round hole in the ice as it went up through it with incredible force and power. It went on rising and piercing the layers of ice until all the fire left her body.

Nahia felt very weak, empty. She remained standing but was about to drop off.

"Nahia!" Logan cried and ran to catch her in his arms.

There was a dull crack and Logan looked up. A block of ice fell on top of them. Logan jumped aside, carrying Nahia with him. The block of ice hit the ground right where they had just been standing and broke into a thousand pieces.

"What…?" Logan was looking at the broken block and the pieces of ice everywhere. In front of him he saw a large, whitish pearl that shone with power. A little beyond that was another like it. Between the two was a dark-haired human.

Nahia pointed her finger at him.

"Those clothes…"

Logan helped her get up.

"What is it?" he asked her.

"Those clothes are… Rangers' clothes."

"Is that a Norghanian Ranger?"

"He's more than that. He's one of the Snow Panthers. That's Viggo, the Assassin who disappeared here in the glacier."

"Oh wow… is he alive?"

"He has to be, otherwise he wouldn't be part of my destiny. Bring Daphne, we have to revive him."

"But what about you?" Logan worried.

"Don't worry, I'm fine. Weak, but fine. Bring Daphne, hurry."

"Sure?"

"Go, please."

"All right," Logan started to leave.

"And get some soldiers clothes."

Logan stopped, looked at her, and then nodded.

A while later, Nahia and Daphne were trying to revive the human. Lily and Logan were with them.

"Watch the entrance, we don't want prying eyes," Nahia told them.

"I'll take care of that," Logan said and went to cover it.

"Give him some more heat, he's frozen solid," Daphne told Nahia.

"Nahia nodded. She used her Fire Hands skill but with a small flame, just to generate heat. She passed them all over the human's body.

"I can't believe they had him in a block of ice up there," Lily shook her head at the idea.

"It must have been some evil torture brought on by the Immortal Dragon," Nahia guessed.

"It kept him alive. Those two pearls have vital power," said Daphne, who was beside them.

"Alive, yes," said Lily, putting her fingers on his neck, "frozen, but alive. He's attractive, this Assassin. He has a roguish face."

"Lily, he's half dead, please focus," Daphne told her.

"Knowing water magic, if they froze him alive, he'll live. You can use water magic to freeze someone to death or to freeze them alive. A small but remarkable distinction," Lily explained.

"Then I'll be able to heal him," Daphne nodded.

"I think it's done," Nahia said and sat on the ground. She was about to faint from how tired and weak she felt. But she wanted to save him before losing consciousness.

"Right, now it's my turn," Daphne laid her hands on the chest of the young man and began to send her healing energy to his body.

Nahia and Lily, sitting on either side, watched for a long while as Daphne worked her magic using her healing energy. Finally, she was empty.

"I don't have any more energy. I'm not picking up anything wrong in him. He should be perfectly well after all the energy I've sent him."

"But he's not waking up," Nahia said. worried.

"I have an idea," Lily said, and she slapped him hard on both cheeks.

"Lily!" Nahia protested.

Suddenly, he opened his eyes.

"Blasted dragon without a heart!" he yelled and half rose. He was looking ahead, his gaze lost.

The three girls stood up.

"Viggo, are you all right?" Nahia asked.

Viggo did not seem to hear her. He was looking ahead with his gaze fixed somewhere beyond them.

"I'm going to try again with my technique," Lily said and went to slap Viggo again. As her hand was about to reach Viggo's face, his left hand moved like lightning and grabbed her wrist, stopping her blow. Then, leaning on her, he rose in a swift leap and stood up. He turned to them and studied the three from head to toe.

"Is this a dream? Or am I dead and I've ended up in a place full of pretty, strange girls?" said Viggo in Norghanian while he stared at Daphne and Lily, very intrigued.

Nahia, Lily, and Daphne were unable to understand him.

"I Nahia. Friend, Egil, Lasgol, Camu," she told him in what little Norghanian she knew.

"The know-it-all, the weirdo, and the bug? Where are they? And where's my bellicose blondie?"

Nahia did not understand a word he said.

"We have to go, dragons are coming," Logan warned them.

They heard several powerful roars, and Viggo crouched.

Nahia put her finger to her lips and then pointed at the soldier clothes on the ground in front of Viggo.

He understood, nodded, and began to undress in front of her without the least embarrassment.

Nahia, Daphne, and Lily turned their backs. Lily was smiling.

A moment later, they left.

Chapter 51

They came out of the glacier in two groups: Lily, Daphne, and Logan first, and then Nahia with Viggo. When Viggo saw the war camp, he stopped. Then he saw three enormous silver dragons landing behind them to enter the glacier and started walking again quickly. Nahia could see by his look and wide eyes that this all seemed crazy to him. She could not blame him. For him, time had not passed. It was the day after the Immortal Dragon had imprisoned him in the ice.

"I friend," Nahia repeated over and over to calm him. She would have given anything to be able to tell him everything. But she only knew a few words in Norghanian. It was impossible.

Viggo looked everywhere. As they passed by an armory, with great speed and skill, he grabbed two knives and put them in his belt. There were over a thousand Human soldiers, and Viggo looked like any other soldier, so he did not draw any attention. They took him to the tent of the Igneous Squad, but it would be suspicious to have him there with them, so they hid him in an empty tent behind theirs.

Taika, Ivo, and Aiden saw them. They said nothing but guessed that something was afoot.

"Not a word," Lily told the Drakonid and pointed her finger at him.

The Drakonid looked the other way.

"Come inside and I'll explain," Daphne told the others as they followed her into the tent.

Nahia went with Viggo. She did not go into the tent with him because it would look suspicious. She indicated for him to wait there. The problem was, they had to get him out of their camp as soon as possible. Nahia realized it had to be quick. The next day the rest of the squadrons might return and they would be sent back to Kraido. She went to see Logan. They had to think of something.

For a long while, Nahia and Logan thought.

"Isn't there a way you could warn Lasgol and Camu so they could come for him?"

"No, we don't have a way to reach them, at least for now."

"In that case, I think the best option is to do it secretly," Logan said.

"Secretly?"

"Yeah. You see, if we help him leave the camp, he'll have to wander the continent, unable to leave it. No ships come near here because of the war, and he can't use the portal on his own. Besides, there are always dragons watching it."

"Yeah… besides, if he wanders around, the dragons might see him on one of their scouting flights."

"That too. That's why I think the carts are the best idea," Logan pointed to a convoy being prepared.

"Hiding him in a convoy to Norghana?" Nahia guessed Logan's intention.

"That's right," he nodded.

"That way he'll go through the portal and appear in his own land."

"And being a Ranger, he can vanish into the forests."

"That's a very good idea," Nahia replied, cheered, and without meaning to, happy to have a solution, she leaned in and kissed him.

Logan smiled.

"I'll try and have more good ideas," he joked.

Nahia blushed.

"All the time," she said and kissed him again.

Then they pretended. They were in front of Logan's squad's tent and his comrades acted like if they had not seen anything, but they were grinning.

The following day, they put Logan's plan into action. A convoy was setting out for Norghana that evening. Taika had found out after chatting with the soldiers. They got ready to put Viggo in the convoy. Only the Black Squadron had not come back yet. Once it did, they would have to leave. Nahia was worried; she wished they would delay to the next day, or they would not be able to get Viggo out of there. Her wishes seemed to be granted. Night came, and the Black Squadron still had not appeared. They still had until dawn at least.

Nahia heaved a sigh of relief. She set the plan into motion.

"We have to act now."

"Ready," said Lily.

"Are you sure you can do this?"

"I can do this and a lot more," she reassured her.

Nahia nodded.

"The others?"

"We're with you," said Daphne.

"Are you sure you want to be involved?"

"Absolutely," Taika told her.

"You too, Aiden? You can stay out of it."

"If you all go, I go too. You're my squad."

"As you wish," Nahia said. She was not very convinced, but it was better to have him close than leaving him at the camp and having him betray them by warning the dragons.

"Let's go then," said Nahia.

They picked Viggo up at his tent. Nahia had tried to explain the plan to him as best as she could. She was not sure how much the Ranger had understood, but she hoped it would be enough. In any case, she was sure he was someone special so he would manage.

Logan joined them at edge of the camp in an area with few guards.

"Taika, it's your turn," Nahia said once they were ready.

"I have this," Taika said, and a moment later he created a darkness that enveloped him completely. Then he sent more and more energy and made it big enough to cover the whole group.

A moment later they were leaving the camp, enveloped in the blackness that made them invisible in the middle of the darkness of night. They headed to the Pearl of the Reborn Continent. When they arrived, they saw two dragons watching it, so they waited at a prudent distance. They hid behind some boulders. Now they just had to wait.

The convoy of carts arrived a few hours later. There were about a hundred carts, one lined behind the other. They were loaded with supplies for Norghana. They stopped in front of the Pearl and waited. The two dragons began opening the portal.

"The moment has come."

"I'll handle it," said Lily, and she approached the last cart at a crouch. Two soldiers were at the back. Lily cast a spell on them. She spent a long time conjuring and then returned to her friends. "That's it. They'll think Viggo is their best friend."

"Right. For how long?" Nahia asked her.

"I don't know. I've enchanted them with all my energy. It should last until dawn at least."

"That's more than enough time. Once at the Shelter, Viggo will be able to slip away without any trouble. He knows the place well," Nahia said.

"The Shelter suits me perfectly," Viggo said in Norghanian. He had understood the name and made a sign of agreement.

Nahia nodded.

"Get on the cart." She mimicked running and jumping onto the cart. The convoy was already getting under way. The first carts were entering the portal up the ramp.

"Thank you, all of you," Viggo told them. "I won't forget this. I owe you big time." he ran off, reached the last cart, and jumped onto it. The two soldiers welcomed him with open arms. He sat behind them and hid among the crates of supplies.

"See? I'm the best Enchanter," Lily said proudly.

"That was very good, indeed," Daphne said.

What does this betrayal mean? How dare you betray the dragons? Betray me, your leader? Irakas-Gorri-Gaizt's message reached them, filled with fury.

Nahia's eyes opened wide. They had been discovered.

They all froze where they were.

From the darkness Irakas-Gorri-Gaizt appeared, walking toward them, enormous and powerful, eyes red with fury.

At that moment, they all knew they were going to die.

You really believed you could fool me? Do you really believe it is possible to rebel against the dragons? Who do you think you are?

Nahia's heart sank. They were all going to die. She looked at Logan. She had doomed him. She looked at her comrades. They were all going to die because of her, because of her dream to reach freedom. She did not mind dying, but she could not bear the idea that they should die because of her.

"I'm the one responsible!" she said.

Oh, I know. You are the leader of this revolt. The one who leads the cause, Irakas-Gorri-Gaizt glared at her with eyes of fire.

Nahia realized that Irakas-Gorri-Gaizt knew everything. They were all lost.

Lily turned to Aiden.

"You betrayed us!" she accused him, tears in her eyes.

"You had to do it, you had to be a faithful slave!" Daphne

accused him, also filled with rage.

The Drakonid remained erect.

"I haven't betrayed you. It hurts that you'd believe that."

It was not the Drakonid. He has remained loyal to you.

Lily was stunned. Daphne had a look of total disbelief on her face.

Show yourself so they know who has betrayed them.

A figure began to grow visible behind the dragon, coming out of the darkness of the night. Nahia recognized her and felt like she was being stabbed in the chest.

"Ana! No!" Logan cried.

Ana stood beside the huge red dragon.

"Why, Ana?" Nahia asked with moist eyes and a broken heart.

"Because the dream is just that, a dream. We'll never be free. We'll never defeat the dragons."

"But you believed in the dream!" Logan told her.

Ana shook her head.

"No, I never did. When Maika died, I knew it. I saw it clearly. The dragons are going to rule forever. Whoever opposes them is going to die. It's serving and living, or opposing and dying. I choose to live. I don't want to die for a dream that's impossible. I want to keep on living, and if it's under them, so be it."

"But all the meetings, our plans, the message?" Logan still could not believe it.

"I did all that for you. To be with you. To spend time with you… because I loved you. But you preferred her," Ana said, pointing her finger at Nahia. "You always loved her, not me. No matter how hard I tried, it was in vain."

"And that's why you've betrayed us?" Logan felt sick.

"Because of that, and because I want to live. At first there was not much risk with your little revolution. But now the risk has become enormous. The whole Academy knows. The dragons were going to find out, and when they did, I would fall too, as one of the leaders. I chose to live. When you told me of this plan today, my sweet Logan, I knew it was my chance, so I went to your leader and told it everything about your plan to help a Norghanian, an enemy, escape. That's treason, and you've been caught in the act."

"I can't believe it. I don't understand," Logan kept saying, shaking his head.

Nahia felt like Logan. She was devastated by the betrayal.

"We were friends," she told Ana. "I trusted you."

"I only wanted to be with Logan. You were always an obstacle, nothing else."

Nahia felt those words like a knife in her stomach. She had always believed Ana to be a good person. How could she have been so wrong? She had fooled Nahia completely.

Treason is paid for with death, Irakas-Gorri-Gaizt sentenced.

"The die is cast," said Ivo.

The Tauruk is right. The die is cast and I decide your fate, right here and now.

"If we're going to die, let's do so fighting!" Logan said and prepared to do so.

"I'm with you!" Taika said, unsheathing his sword.

"We'll die fighting!" said Daphne.

"It's time to fight." Lily got ready.

Nahia knew they were going to die. They could not beat such a powerful dragon. It was far mightier than them, but her comrades were right.

"For freedom!" she cried.

I like your spirit. I knew you would not disappoint me." Irakas-Gorri-Gaizt opened its mouth and out came its breath of fire. It was so fast they had no time to react.

But it was not directed at them. It hit Ana consuming her in an instant. She died, incinerated before she had time to realize.

They all froze. They did not know what to think or do.

As I said, treason is paid with death. She has paid.

Nahia wanted to react, but she was completely unable to. She was in shock, and her comrades were the same.

As for you... nothing has happened here tonight. Understood?

Now they were all staring at Irakas-Gorri-Gaizt blankly. Was it pardoning their lives? Were they not going to fight? They did not understand.

If you want to live you will tell me one by one that nothing has happened here tonight.

"Nothing… has happened…" said Aiden.

The Drakonid is intelligent and honorable. I want to hear it from all of you!

"Nothing has happened," said Taika.

"Tonight? Nothing," said Ivo.

"Nothing at all," Lily said.

"Nothing," said Logan.

"Nothing has happened," Nahia said,

That is what I thought. Remember that if you want to live, the great red dragon messaged them, and then it turned its back on them. It spread its huge wings and took off.

Nahia watched it vanishing into the sky. Then she looked toward the portal and saw the last cart, the one carrying Viggo, entering the portal and vanishing.

Chapter 52

Nahia was lining up with the Red Squadron in front of the castle. Beside them, the rest of squadrons were also lined up. Further back, in the middle of the square, the pupils of the First- and Second- years were lined up in two rows behind their squadron leaders. It was Graduation Day for the Third-years. A day Nahia never thought she would live to see. She had always believed she would not be capable of graduating from the Martial Academy of Drakoros, that she would die before, and yet here she was, against all odds, lining up with her squadmates to graduate.

She looked at Daphne and Lily beside her. She could not be happier, or more proud of them. They had been amazing comrades, the best. They were brilliant in every aspect. She looked back and saw Taika and Ivo. The Felidae-Tiger and the Tauruk had turned out to be not only intelligent, but also people with great hearts and courage. Then she looked at Aiden right behind her. They had misjudged him. The Drakonid had turned out to be honorable and loyal to his squad and his comrades. He had not betrayed them and had supported them in his own way.

Nahia heaved a sigh. Having her comrades around her always soothed her and gave her a feeling of safety, which she cherished in her heart. They had spent the three regulatory days of rest since the return from their end-of-the-year mission in Drameia and it was time to graduate from the Academy. Nahia's head was full of thoughts of every kind, and her heart with mixed feelings. She had barely been able to sleep during the days they had been back. She felt she had to accept and digest everything that had happened and put her thoughts in order. There was too much at stake for her not to have a clear mind.

What she had still not been able to process was Ana's betrayal. It was something so unthinkable and brutal that no matter how hard she tried to accept it, she could not. Her heart was broken, and it hurt. She tried to reason with it, to find some excuse for Ana, a way to understand why she had done it, but Nahia could not find any. It seemed impossible that it had happened. The betrayal was so painful that she felt as if a part of her heart had been cut out.

She shook her head, unable to believe what had happened. They had been friends ever since the first day they had met when they were sent to the Academy. They had lived through Maika's death, and a thousand other hardships here. All the suffering lived during those three agonizing years in order to survive, all for it to end this way. She did not understand it. She could not understand it, and least of all digest it. Perhaps that was what had defeated her: all the deaths and the lack of hope in this place. That, and the situation with Logan. She did not want to think about how much her relationship with Logan had affected Ana's decision to betray them. She hoped it was not because of that. In any case, she had died. And this could not be changed. It was terrible, but so was the world of the dragons.

She looked at their leader as it stood firm in front of them beside the banner of fire, as great and powerful as it was. What had happened with it had her still in sheer disbelief. She could not get used to the idea. She had thought about it a lot and had reached the conclusion that Irakas-Gorri-Gaizt had to be on Garran-Zilar-Denbo's side. It had to be one of the dragons that belonged to the Faction of the New Tomorrow. She would never have imagined it. She still could not believe it, although it was right in front of them. But she could not think of any other explanation. On the other hand, that dragon had always been terrible to them and the whole squadron. It was cruel and ruthless. The only explanation she could think of was that it had acted thus to avoid raising suspicion among the other dragons in the Academy. This was a dragon with a very good reputation among its own, and that could only be achieved by acting brutal and achieving major success.

What was unarguably true was that, out of all the squadrons, Irakas-Gorri-Gaizt's had the fewest casualties. Nahia had noticed that. Now that she guessed that he belonged to Garran-Zilar-Denbo's faction, she saw this as an effort to keep them safe. And it did so very well; it had not raised suspicions within the squadron or among the other dragon leaders. In any case, it had saved them from Ana's betrayal, and that was undeniable. Just in case, she would try to find a way to make sure it belonged to the faction and could be trusted. She needed to ask Garran-Zilar-Denbo. She had to find a way.

This led her to think that at least she had profited from these three days of rest to finish weaving alliances within the Academy. She needed to tie up all her loose ends before leaving. She had gone to the library to talk to Liburex and had told him what had happened in Tremia, as well as her plans to continue with the cause. The Chief Librarian was pleased and had shown himself to be collaborative. He seemed to trust her more, as well as her purpose, and had been happy to help with whatever she needed, except for taking unacceptable risks. The Exarbors were as intelligent as they were prudent. Nahia had tried to make him reveal who his equal was among the Tergnomus, because such a person had to exist in the Academy. Liburex had not denied this existence of such a being but had refused to reveal his name. He argued reasons of security, and Nahia understood and accepted it. She would find out who it was sooner or later.

Her gaze went unwittingly, to where Logan was lined up with his squad. She was more than happy that he had survived and was graduating with her. She had always known he would. For some reason, Logan seemed indestructible, a warrior who overcame any obstacle in his path. He knew he might die, like all of them, but his mind and heart refused to believe in such a possibility. They had not been able to talk about everything that had happened; there had not been a chance. They had seen each other and talked, but without the intimacy necessary to deal with those matters and their feelings. They would have to do so with time and quiet, somewhere else.

She kept looking his way in the hope that he would look at her. Logan seemed to feel her gaze and turned his head to her. Or maybe he simply wanted to look at her too. She smiled sweetly and her heart flooded with joy, just like every time the handsome, dark-haired young man looked at her with those sky-blue eyes she lost herself in. He returned the smile, and putting his hand over his heart, he gave her a slight nod. Nahia felt happiness flood her whole being.

All of a sudden, the six dragons roared in unison.

Attention! All firm! Irakas-Gorri-Gaizt sent them.

Colonel Lehen-Gorri-Gogor and Commander Bigaen-Zuri-Indar came out of the castle through the great door and stood looking toward the bailey to address the squadrons.

The Colonel, powerful and fearsome, roared.

Today is a glorious day for the Academy, and for you. Today is Graduation Day. The day when you become Dragon Warlocks and Witches on your own merits. Today, the Third-years who have finished the year alive, graduate. It is an expected, dreamed-of day, one of extreme glory and honor for the six squadrons lined up before me. My congratulations first to the squadron leaders. They have done their duty once more. Some have managed to have more graduating pupils than others, as is usually the norm, but they always perform impeccable work.

The six dragon leaders roared in response to the congratulations.

The Academy is grateful to you for the good work, discipline, service, and loyalty of the six dragon leaders, Commander Bigaen-Zuri-Indar thanked them.

Again, the six dragons roared as one.

My congratulations as well to all of the third-years before me who have managed to complete the training. You graduate from the distinguished Drakoros Academy. You ought to feel great pride and honor, since many started the first year and not even half are finishing this last one. But you have done it. You have passed the whole training: Weapons, Magic, and Talent. Today is a day of celebration and pride, because you leave this academy with the rank and skills of Dragon Warlocks, Lehen-Gorri-Gogor sent them, along with a feeling of pride mixed with glory.

Honor all of the third-years graduating this year. Perhaps one day you will do so too, ordered Bigaen-Zuri-Indar.

The pupils from the first- and second- years lined up behind them with their squadron leaders and let out cheers to the sky.

"Blood and Glory!"

"Conquest and Power!"

It is time to proceed with handing out the graduation badges, Bigaen-Zuri-Indar announced.

Nahia had been waiting for this moment. Not for the badges, which she did not care about, but for those who brought them and left her speechless every year. This, her last year, would not be different. She raised her gaze and saw them coming.

Six powerful dragons flew down, one of each elemental color. That was not what impressed Nahia, but the fact that they each bore a rider. She watched them. There was a Human, a Tauruk, a Drakonid, a Fatum, a Scarlatum, and a Felidae, each wearing heavy armor. They carried a spear and shield. They landed in the great square, between those who were graduating and the first-and second-years who were watching, spellbound. They put away their spears and shields and got off their dragons with ease, approaching the six Third-year leaders. In their hands, they carried the silver chests with

435

the graduation badges.

Nahia watched without missing a detail. She did not even pretend she was not interested, and she was not the only one. Her squadmates were watching too.

They went to stand beside the banner of each squadron. They saluted each leader with a solemn nod and then turned to the pupils who were graduating.

Nahia could not help but ask herself why the dragons allowed those riders to ride them. It did not make sense. She had not managed to find out, but she would keep investigating. There had to be a reason, and it had to be important, or otherwise no dragon would ever allow an inferior creature, a slave, to ride it.

It is time to hand out the graduation badges of the Drakoros Academy, Bigaen-Zuri-Indar announced.

Each leader called the members of their squadron. The dragon rider gave each of them a silver badge with an engraved dragon, and a number 3 under it. Nahia took hers and went back to her place. Daphne, Lily, Taika, Ivo, and Aiden took theirs after. Out of the corner of her eye, she watched them each take theirs. She felt very proud of her friends; they were the best. Thanks to them, she had survived and managed to graduate. She could never thank them enough.

Once they all had their badges, the dragon riders closed the chests, went back to their dragons, and got on them. Nahia watched them, waiting for them to take off.

Lehen-Gorri-Gogor roared loud.

My congratulations to all who have graduated from the Drakoros Academy as Dragon Warlocks. Tomorrow morning, you will leave the Academy. You have been destined to serve in the war in Drameia. It is an important post, and I am sure you will bring honor and glory to this academy with your performance in the war.

The first- and second-years cheered again in honor of the third-years at the order of their leaders.

"Blood and Glory!"

"Conquest and Power!"

Nahia looked at her comrades. They all exchanged worried gazes. They had been expecting that would be their destination, it was the most logical. They had been sent to that war several times already, so it surprised no one when the colonel announced it. Going to the war in Tremia was not good news, but at least they would leave the Academy and their suffering there would end.

She felt well. She realized she had survived the academy. She had just graduated; she had the badge, but it was more that filled her with pride. She was no longer the weak girl without magic, or strength, unable to defend herself who had arrived there. Now she was strong in body, mind, and magic. She could fight with a dagger, sword, spear, and shield. She could use her elemental magic and she was a powerful Sorceress, an impressive Dragon Witch. The dragons did not know what they had done. They would pay for making her who she was. Everything she had learned there, how powerful she had become, she was going to use against them. She now had no doubt of her destiny: achieving freedom for the slave peoples of Kraido. She would fight to succeed with everything the dragons had taught her, and they would pay.

The Colonel roared.

There is one last announcement of great importance. This is a special year. It is not usually the case, since this happens very few times, but this year it has. We have a candidate to become a Dragon Rider, an incredible honor only bestowed on the best.

The announcement took everyone by surprise. There were muffled cries and blank looks among the third-years and also surprise among the first- and second-years who were attending the graduation ceremony.

Commander, name the candidate to become a Dragon Rider, it called.

The commander roared.

Of the Red Squadron, Igneous Squad, the Human Nahia, it announced.

Nahia's head was thrown back and her eyes opened wide with surprise.

"What…?" she muttered, unable to understand what was happening.

Daphne and Lily turned to her with troubled looks.

"It's an amazing honor," Aiden whispered in her ear.

Taika and Ivo also looked at her, worried.

Suddenly, the Commander roared again.

From the White Squadron, Whirlwind Squad, the Human Logan, it announced.

Still stunned, Nahia looked at Logan. He shook his head; he had not been expecting this either, and the announcement had left him as

437

numbed as her.

Let those nominated approach me, Lehen-Gorri-Gogor ordered.

Nahia and Logan looked at each other, then at the great red dragon, and they walked up to it. They stood before its gigantic presence at a prudent distance, over fifty paces. Beside the Colonel, a little further back, Commander Bigaen-Zuri-Indar looked at them fixedly. The colossal white dragon seemed to be analyzing them. Commander and Colonel looked at each other and seemed to exchange private messages.

Colonel Lehen-Gorri-Gogor spoke, *Interesting. It makes perfect sense. A Flameborn and a Stormson. You certainly have much potential. I trust you will not waste it. You have a different destination than your comrades. You will not go to serve in Drameia. Tomorrow morning you will go to Jadrakos, where you will train to become Dragon Riders. It is the highest honor a Dragon Warlock can receive, do not waste it. Kneel and accept the honor you have been granted.*

Nahia and Logan knelt and bowed until their foreheads touched the ground.

The selected have accepted this honor. The Third-Year graduation ceremony ends now. Go and prepare yourselves to serve your dragon lords, Colonel Lehen-Gorri-Gogor sent as an unappealable order.

The Dragon Riders took off, and a moment later they vanished in the sky. The Colonel and the Commander withdrew inside the castle.

Break ranks! They received the order from their leaders, as a moment later they also took off.

Nahia rose slowly. She was very confused by this turn of events. She had counted on going to Tremia with her squad. What awaited her in Jadrakos? Why her? Why Logan? As she was wondering, she felt a tingle in the nape, one that grew warm. She knew it was Garran-Zilar-Denbo's scale. An instant later, it was burning. This meant that going to Jadrakos and becoming a Dragon Rider was part of her destiny. This is what the scale indicated as it let off a silver flash. She was startled because of where she was. She looked around, but there were no longer any dragons there. They had all withdrawn.

Logan looked at her, concerned. She realized this, and made a sign of encouragement with her fist. She suddenly felt strong. Knowing that this was part of her destiny, gave her strength. She could cope with any obstacle that came their way, no matter how difficult and dangerous it might be. This was an uncertain, strange turn of events, but they would overcome it.

"We'll make it," she told Logan, convinced, fire in her eyes.

Logan looked at her and nodded.

"I'm with you. Always."

Nahia went over to him and kissed him.

"Together we'll conquer all."

Chapter 53

Nahia went to the dungeon door that evening after graduation. It was the last night. At dawn, she would leave the Academy and begin an uncertain future as a Dragon Rider. But she did not want to leave without one last visit. What she intended was very risky. Her squadmates did not agree and had tried to get the idea out of her head, but Nahia had not listened to them. She did not want to leave that place without finishing two important tasks.

She sighed deeply while she watched the two black dragons guarding the door out of the corner of her eye. She already knew that what she was going to do was dangerous, that it was crazy to risk dying after graduating on their last night at the Academy. But even so, Nahia was determined.

The door opened and an old acquaintance came out to receive her.

"I can't believe it. I see it but I don't believe it," Tarcel, the Chief Tergnomus of the Dungeons, shook his head.

"You know I love to visit," Nahia joked, knowing Tarcel would have a fit of bad temper.

"You're the worst pupil the Academy has ever had!"

"Coming from you, I'll take that as a compliment," Nahia smiled.

Tarcel cursed in the language of the Tergnomus. Then he switched to the language of Kraido.

"How could you manage to get punished on the last night? That's a new milestone never before reached in this academy."

Nahia shrugged.

"You know my leader hates me, and it has punished me one last time. I think it doesn't want me to leave the Academy alive."

"I'm sure your punishment is well deserved. You must have done something, I haven't the slightest doubt. Follow me inside."

Nahia went with Tarcel. As she went in, she felt an unpleasant sensation, a mix of danger and anxiety. They went to where Jaibor, Chief Exarbor of the Dungeon Registrar was waiting with his open tomes.

He raised his gaze from the tomes and looked at Nahia.

"Nahia… of the Igneous Squad…. Red Squadron…" he recognized her.

"Hello, Jaibor, once again," Nahia greeted him.

"You're registered… you have a one-night punishment … from your leader."

"What level?" asked Tarcel.

"Underground level three…"

"The third one again? But what have you done to be sent to the third level on your last night?" Tarcel could not believe it.

"Something ugly," Nahia shrugged.

"Unheard of," Tarcel gestured, annoyed. "Come on, I'll take you down."

"There's no need, I know the way well."

"I'm the Chief Tergnomus of the Dungeons, and you'll do what I say without opposing me!"

Nahia had already expected Tarcel to get angry when he saw her there again, so it did not surprise her. She did not insist, not wanting to force the situation. She was already taking enough risks.

"Of course, Tarcel. Lead on, I'll follow."

Tarcel led the way. He gave her the bracelet to go down and Nahia put it on without a word.

They went down toward the depths of the dungeons. It felt normal for Nahia. Not even glimpsing the dark watchers scared her now, she was so used to doing this route.

They got to the third level and Tarcel opened the door with his heavy keys. They went in and met Utrek. The Tergnomus responsible for this underground level opened his eyes wide.

"Nahia? But what…?"

"She's been punished on her last night. Her squad leader," Tarcel shook his head.

"What could you have done to be punished on your last night at the Academy?" Utrek made a face of disbelief.

"It seems I have a tendency to infuriate my leader."

"You don't say. I hope I never see you around ever again," Tarcel said. "Well, it's practically guaranteed that I never see you again. You either die tonight or you leave the Academy tomorrow morning, so I won't see you again."

"I'm very happy to have met you too," Naha said with a smile.

Tarcel made a gesture of extreme frustration and left.

"Tarcel only hopes you don't end up dead. He's a good Tergnomus," Utrek said.

Nahia nodded.

"I know. I'll miss him."

"And here we are again."

Nahia had the situation under control up to this moment. But now was when things might go awry. She needed to do one specific route, and if Utrek sent her on another, she would not achieve her purpose.

"Ready to work, as always," she told him.

"Before you insist on a route, because I know you, let me tell you that tonight will be different."

Nahia did not like this in the least. She had prepared several arguments so that Utrek would let her do the route she wanted.

"Different how?"

"Tonight, since it's your last night, I'll let you choose the route you want," Utrek told her.

Nahia's eyes opened wide.

"Can I choose?"

"You can, but only one."

Nahia was thoughtful. She would have liked to do two routes. But she had already guessed it would not be possible.

"Thank you for letting me choose."

"Consider it a parting gift. Route one, your favorite?"

Nahia thought about it. Route one was that of Garran-Zilar-Denbo. It was her favorite, indeed, and the least dangerous because she had the protection of the great silver dragon. Besides, it would allow her to talk to the great dragon before she left, something she would not be able to do otherwise. She thought hard and then decided.

"Route four."

Utrek stared at her, opening his eyes very wide.

"Are you sure?"

Nahia nodded.

"Yup, four."

"Very well. Four it is, then. Your favorite partner will come with you."

"Couldn't I go alone? I know the tunnels well and can deal with the carts with no trouble."

Utrek shook his head firmly.

"It's forbidden. A Tergnomus of the level always has to go with the delivery. Burgor! You'll go with Nahia! Route four!" he called.

Burgor appear from behind a door, and when he saw Nahia, his eyes nearly popped out of their sockets.

"What the heck!" he cried, coming into the room.

"What a joy to see you again, Burgor," Nahia told him in a sarcastic tone.

"I'm not happy to see you. Not at all."

"Route four, off you go," Utrek said.

Burgor muttered curses and went to get ready. Nahia followed him. She took the repulsor belt and the hat. They came out and went to the carts. They got on and started the route. Burgor threw her furious glances out of the corner of his eye.

"You have to hassle me, even on your last day," he told her after a long while.

"It's so that you don't miss me too much when I'm not around anymore," Nahia replied in a cheerful tone.

"I don't want to die on this your last night, so no chatting," Burgor warned her.

"Of course. You know I'm very quiet and formal."

"Oh, sure!"

They did the route without incident and without speaking. They arrived at the final part where the caves with the fires were. They started to unload, and Nahia did not miss a single detail of the prisoners. They unloaded in front of the Humans, then the Fatum, then the Scarlatum, followed by the Felidae, Tauruk-Kapro, and finally the Drakonid. Nahia did not try to speak to any of the groups. She knew they would not answer her. Except one. The Drakonid who had spoken to her the last time. She wanted to speak to him specifically, which is why she had organized this last incursion into the dungeons. They unloaded the pieces for the Drakonid, and when they finished Nahia addressed Burgor.

"You can go on now, I'm staying here for a moment," she told him.

"No and no! No staying! No speaking!" he shouted at her, furious.

Nahia gave him a serious look and showed him the palm of her hand.

"Go on with the carts, I'll see you inside."

"It's forbidden to speak to them!"

On Nahia's right hand there appeared a burning ball of fire.

"You keep going with the carts, let's not have a work accident."

Burgor opened his eyes wide and raised both hands.

"You wouldn't dare!"

"I leave tomorrow, of course I would dare. Besides, if you trip and fall on a torch, it's just a work hazard that might happen to anyone. I'll tell it very persuasively. I'll even shed tears."

Burgor eyed the torch a few paces from him.

"You will pay for this…."

"I don't think so, because you're not going to say anything. If you do, I'll make sure you have a very unpleasant visit."

"I don't want to see you ever again," he cried and got on the cart.

"The feeling's mutual. Get out and forget about me."

"Consider yourself forgotten!" Burgor shouted at her as he left with the carts.

"That was very reckless on your part," the Drakonid she had spoken with the last time said.

"Sometimes we have to do reckless things. I've come to speak with you," Nahia said, pointing at him.

The Drakonid looked at her and tilted his head.

"You shouldn't, it's dangerous."

"I know, but I had to do it."

"Why?"

Nahia looked at both sides of the silver path. She saw no one, so she stepped over to the Drakonid, leaving the safety of the path. She reached him and looked into his eyes.

"Because I'm following your footsteps, Dramkon Udreks, leader of the Great Insurrection."

The Drakonid shook his head.

"This is something I wasn't expecting. How do you know who I am? Who told you?"

"No one. I guessed. I wish I had done so earlier, when I met you the first time, but for some reason I didn't see it then. Later on, I realized. I had a very revealing conversation with a Drakonid from another squad of my squadron and he opened my eyes. Then I understood. I understood why there were Drakonids down here, locked up. And not only Drakonids, but Humans, Fatum, Scarlatum,

Felidae, and Tauruk-Kapro. The dragons have the leaders of the Great Insurrection locked up here."

"You're intelligent, and also clever, which isn't the same."

"Thank you. I'd like to be even more so."

"You say you're following my footsteps. Explain, please."

"I'm trying to free the slave peoples of Kraido."

Dramkon Udreks shook his head.

"You shouldn't. Look at what happened to me. Look at what happened to us," he said, and with his arms open he encompassed the Drakonids behind him, and then the other caves. If you follow our footsteps, you'll end up like us. Dead, or here, which is pretty much the same thing."

"If we don't do anything we'll die as slaves, fighting for the dragons in strange worlds."

"But at least you'll live longer than if you rise up against them. We rose by the thousands. And there's only a few of us locked up here. All the others died. That's what awaits you and those you manage to persuade to follow you."

Nahia shook her head. That was not what she had hoped to hear.

"But you, all of you and those who followed you, had the same dream I have, and that my people have: reaching freedom."

"We all had it, yes. But we failed. It's an unreachable dream. One that will doom thousands to death once again."

"I wasn't expecting such a negative message. I thought you'd encourage me, that you'd help me."

"And I am helping you. Not to make the same mistake I made, and for which thousands from all the races of Kraido died."

"Was it a mistake, or a deceit?"

Dramkon Udreks heaved a deep sigh.

"Not only was I defeated, they sank my name and my credibility. I expected as much. The dragons are beastly. But they're also very intelligent. Pretending it was all a hoax eliminates the possibility of new risings. If you make people believe there's no way to defeat them, no one will rise against them."

"Then it wasn't a hoax? Did you find a way to defeat them?"

"It wasn't a hoax, no. I did have a way to defeat them. Otherwise I wouldn't have attempted an uprising, and the leaders of the other races wouldn't have followed me," he said, indicating the other caves.

"I understand that you proved it, that you killed several dragons before the leaders and persuaded them."

Dramkon Udreks nodded.

"That's right, I killed three dragons. And I convinced them."

Nahia looked at the other caverns with the fires lit and the leaders around them.

"They joined you because of that, and you prepared the great uprising. They told the others races you had a way to kill the dragons and that, if they all joined together, they would bring them down."

"That's what happened, yes," Dramkon Udreks said and sighed deeply.

"Then what happened? Why did the uprising fail, and so many thousands died?" Nahia asked, not understanding.

"The dragons are very powerful, not only because of their incredible strength and elemental magic, but because they also possess divination magic. They discovered our plan. They saw it before it happened. The Great Oracle had a vision and saw it. They stopped us right as the uprising began."

"The Great Oracle saw what was going to happen?"

"That's right. It consulted the threads of destiny and discovered that something of great magnitude, and contrary to the dragons was going to happen. It continued following the threads until it found us and destroyed us."

This was terrible news. Nahia knew from what she had seen Garran-Zilar-Denbo do that it was totally possible to glimpse destiny. She did not know whether changing it was possible, but it looked that way.

"Did it change the destiny that was about to take place?"

"It did. Or to be precise, another, different destiny occurred after its intervention. Perhaps it would've happened no matter what. Destinies have a strange way of occurring. Or not."

"But if you had the way to defeat the dragons, even if the Great Oracle saw it, it shouldn't have been able to stop you... unless... it took away your ability to defeat them."

Dramkon Udreks smiled.

"You really are smart. That's exactly what happened."

"What did the Great Oracle take away from you?"

"You want to know how I defeated the dragons."

"Yes, I need to know what it was."

Dramkon Udreks nodded.

"I'll tell you. The Sphaera Aurea."

"The Sphaera Aurea? What's that?"

"It's a creation of the Aureans, the Golden Gods. A devastating weapon that can kill dragons. It knocks them out of the sky."

"It can do that?" Nahia made a gesture of disbelief.

"I've done it myself."

"But how…?"

"The Sphaera Aurea radiates Golden Magic. The Golden Magic of the Golden Gods, the only magic capable of getting past the dragons' anti-magic protections. If you know how to use it, it can emit an enormous magical pulse which, if it hits a dragon, brings it down. If it's on land, it knocks it out."

"Unbelievable."

"It's a very powerful weapon. Against dragons, that is. That Golden Magic, in that form, has no effect whatsoever on other creatures."

"That's awesome. And who are the Aureans? The ones who created it and have that magic?"

"The Aureans are the deadly enemies of the dragons. Golden beings, with a magic capable of killing dragons. They've been fighting for thousands of years."

"Where are they?"

"No one knows. They have vanished with the passing of time. No one knows how many are left or where they are."

"How did you find the Sphaera Aurea?"

"You wouldn't believe me if I told you."

"Oh, I'll believe you. I've seen many strange things in my short life."

"I stumbled upon it, literally."

"In Kraido, in the country of the Drakonids?"

Dramkon Udreks shook his head.

"I was like you, a Dragon Warlock. They sent me to fight on a far-away world. One the dragons had conquered and where they now reign. Fighting in that world is how I stumbled upon the Sphaera Aurea. In the battlefield, I picked it up without knowing what it was. I felt its powerful magic, and I kept it to study it. That's what I did as soon as I returned to Kraido. Here I spent a long time trying to interact with the magic of the sphere but didn't succeed. It was a different magic from ours, from the dragons'. It took me years, but in the end I did it. When I discovered it was Golden Magic, I knew I had a weapon we could defeat the dragons with in my hands."

"And you organized the Great Insurrection."

"That's what happened, yes. The feelings of rebellion were strong in me. I had passed through the Academy, I had conquered worlds for the dragons, I had seen all their evil and the destiny that awaited us all. I decided to rebel, to fight for freedom."

"And you showed the Sphaera Aurea to the other leaders and persuaded them."

"I did, yes. I used it and killed three dragons. They were all convinced, and they joined in the Great Insurrection."

"What happened then?"

"The day we rose, that ill-fated day, they took the Sphaera Aurea from my hands as we were leaving to fight."

"But it couldn't have been the dragons. You could have killed them with that weapon."

"It wasn't the dragons. It was six squadrons of Dragon Warlocks. Their leaders sent them to my home to capture me. I was with five hundred loyal Drakonids. The squadrons massacred them, and then they captured me and took away the weapon."

"Because its magic doesn't affect the races of Kraido."

"Only the dragons. It's a weapon created to kill them, not other creatures."

Nahia nodded. It was like the weapons Egil had told her about; like Lasgol's bow, only more powerful still.

"Then it wasn't a hoax. It was all real. It just went terribly wrong."

"Horribly wrong. Thousands died, and the few the dragons didn't kill are here, awaiting our deaths. That's why I beg you not to follow in my footsteps. Don't try what I tried to do, or you'll end up the same way."

Nahia sighed deeply.

"Maybe. But my destiny might be different."

"The Great Oracle will see that destiny and intervene. It will stop you, you can be sure of that."

"I'm not saying it won't. But I also have allies who can see the future. And although I don't have the Sphaera Aurea, I have weapons of Golden Magic and allies who are trying to get more."

"Even so, you'll fail. You won't be able to fight against them, against the five dragon kings supported by the Great Oracle. It's suicide, believe me."

"Who has the Sphaera Aurea?"

"One of the five kings or the Great Oracle I guess."

Nahia nodded.

"Thank you for telling me all this."

"I haven't persuaded you not to do it, have I?" Dramkon Udreks asked with sadness in his voice and face.

Nahia shook her head.

"I'm going to free the slave peoples. I'll defeat the dragons. Now more than ever, I know it wasn't a hoax and is in fact possible."

Dramkon Udreks sighed.

"I wish you luck. You're going to need it."

Nahia turned and began to head toward the silver path. She stopped and turned toward Dramkon Udreks.

"When we first met, you recognized me."

The Drakonid nodded.

"You're the spitting image of your mother."

"So, you met my parents."

"Yes, they were two of the leaders of the Humans. Wonderful people, idealists, with great dreams for your people. I'm sorry they died."

Nahia nodded.

"Me too. But I'll finish what they started. For them, and for all of us." She turned around and left.

Chapter 54

Just before dawn, Nahia returned to the surface. She had waited until that moment to come up. Utrek had not given her any trouble; he was glad to see her alive. Luckily, Burgor had already gone to rest. She passed by the door to underground level two and went on up the stairs. She reached the door to underground level one and stopped in front of it.

She waited.

She heard how the lock opened from inside. A moment later, the door opened.

A Tergnomus appeared. It was Ufrem, the Tergnomus responsible for the south area.

"Come in, quietly. They've all gone to rest already," he told her in a whisper.

Nahia nodded. She went inside.

"I'll come with you, that way there won't be any suspicions."

"All right, thank you."

"Don't thank me, I'm with you. Others like me, of my race, are too," the Tergnomus assured her.

"Framus, the cleaning manager of this level?"

"No, not my boss," Ufrem told her. "Neither is Tarcel."

"Yeah, I imagined as much. He's the Chief Tergnomus of the Dungeons. He must be loyal to the dragons."

"That's right, but we have someone on every level," Ufrem told her as he walked briskly and opened the door to the cells.

"That's very reassuring."

"Unfortunately, in lesser posts, for now."

"That's enough," Nahia said and put her hand on his shoulder.

"I'm sorry I haven't been kinder to you. I didn't know who you were…"

"Don't worry. It's better this way. We haven't raised any suspicions."

"Yes, that's true."

"May I ask whether Hiputz, the Chief Supplies Manager, is the leader of the Tergnomus?"

"You may ask, but I'm not going to answer."

"All right, I understand. Do you have the information I asked for from the third level?"

Ufrem nodded.

"The answer is yes."

Nahia huffed, very relieved. She had sent a question to Garran-Zilar-Denbo. *Red leader, yes or no?* The answer had been positive, which meant Irakas-Gorri-Gaizt was with her. A tremendous weight lifted off her shoulders. She had been almost certain it was so, but she preferred not to take risks. Now she knew, and she understood why it had not killed them.

"Let's go quickly, we don't have more than a moment." Ufrem rushed her forward and they headed to the south sector.

Nahia recognized Egil's cell from a distance and hastened to reach it and slide the peephole open.

"Egil, it's Nahia."

Egil came to the peephole.

"I'm happy to see you."

"I'm happy to see you. Are you all right?"

"Yes, no worry. I'm well."

"I'm glad. We don't have much time. I'll quickly tell you what's happened here at the Academy, in Tremia, and Norghana."

"Alright, I listen."

Nahia told him as much as she could, quickly and without stopping. She could feel Ufrem behind her getting nervous. When she finished telling him, she looked at Egil, although with the mask on she could not see the look on his face.

"I understand everything. Viggo well?"

"Yes, we found your friend Viggo. We healed him and got him to Norghana."

"I very happy. Viggo be special."

"Special like Lasgol and Camu?"

"Another kind of special. You will see."

"Understood. Now I have to give you the bad news."

"Igneous Squad graduate and leave."

"That's right. I'm sorry. You have no idea how much it breaks my heart to leave you here. Daphne and Lily are also inconsolable."

"Not worry. It is not my time. It will come."

"But you've been locked up so long. It's horrible!"

451

"Now be less so. I have hope. For you, I work with you to get freedom for all. That give me hope."

"You're one of a kind. You have no idea how much I'd like to find a way to free you. We've talked about it and looked for ways, but we always come across a problem we can't solve."

"Get out of realm in the air."

"That's right. We thought we might be able to get you out of here, but we can't open a portal for you to leave. Least of all to Tremia."

"Not worry. You free me when the time comes."

"You're a brave one. I promise we'll get you out of here. You have my word. We'll find a way, between us all."

"I know. You person of word. The day will come, not worry. I have time. One day you and I laugh out of here."

Nahia smiled, although her eyes were moist and she had a lump in her throat.

"Yes, we'll smile because we'll finally be free. You, me, and everyone else."

"We'll triumph. You see," Egil promised.

"We have devised a plan to be able to identify those who are with us. It consists of a question and an answer."

"What be?"

"Ufrem?"

The Tergnomus came to the open peephole.

"Higher Drakonian?" he asked.

"Camu," Egil replied.

"That's it. Ufrem is with us. There are more all throughout the Academy. We're already organized. There's an Exarbor leader and a Tergnomus leader who's in charge of coordinating the efforts here and passing information within the Academy and from there outside."

"Be organizing net of spies."

"That's right. Now we want to do it below, on land. Among the leaders of the races, each in their own nation. Those who are with us, I mean."

"Be careful, game of spies always very dangerous."

"You have experience?"

Egil nodded.

"Much experience," he said, and he could not help chuckling.

"That's very interesting, because we don't. Perhaps we can organize it so you direct a network of spies from down here. I'm sure no one will suspect you, being a prisoner."

"Be good idea. I do. Get me information."

Nahia turned to Ufrem.

"I'll speak to my leader."

"Good."

"We must leave now," Ufrem urged her.

Nahia nodded.

"Take good care of yourself, Egil. If you need anything, Ufrem will take care of it."

"You take good care too."

"For freedom." Nahia put her hand through the peephole and Egil gave it a firm shake.

"For freedom. We'll succeed."

The adventure continues in the next book:

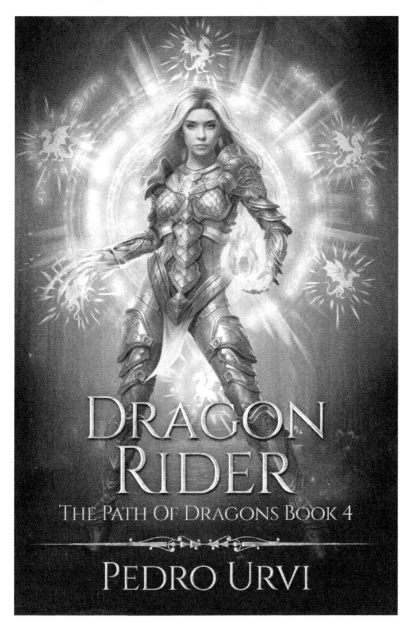

Note from the author:
I really hope you enjoyed my book. If you did, I would appreciate it if you could write a quick review. It helps me tremendously as it is one of the main factors readers consider when buying a book. As an Indie author I really need of your support.
Just go to Amazon and support me.
Thank you so very much.
Pedro.

Other Series by Pedro Urvi

THE SECRET OF THE GOLDEN GODS

A world ruled by merciless Gods. An enslaved people. A young slave-hunter at the service of the Gods. Will he be able to save his sister when they take her?
This series takes place three thousand years before the events of Path of the Ranger Series.
Different protagonists, same world, one destiny.

PATH OF THE RANGER

A kingdom in danger, a great betrayal, a boy seeking to redeem his father's honor. Will he succeed in exonerating him and saving the realm from an enemy in the shadows before it is too late for the whole North?
The beginning of the legendary story of the Snow Panthers of the Norghanian Rangers.

THE ILENIAN ENIGMA

A powerful evil. A deadly destiny. Will a young warrior fulfill his calling or doom millions of lives?
This series takes place after the events of Path of the Ranger Series. It has different protagonists, but one of the Snow Panthers joins the adventure in the second book. He is a secondary character in this series, but he plays an important role, and he is alone…

SERIES READING ORDER

This is the reading order, top to bottom, following the main story of this fantasy universe. All series are related and tell a part of the overall epic story.

Acknowledgements

I'm lucky enough to have very good friends and a wonderful family, and it's thanks to them that this book is now a reality. I can't express the incredible help they have given me during this epic journey.

I wish to thank my great friend Guiller C. for all his support, tireless encouragement and invaluable advice. This saga, not just this book, would never have come to exist without him.

Mon, master-strategist and exceptional plot-twister. Apart from acting as editor and always having a whip ready for deadlines to be met. A million thanks.

To Luis R. for helping me with the re-writes and for all the hours we spent talking about the books and how to make them more enjoyable for the readers.

Roser M., for all the readings, comments, criticisms, for what she has taught me and all her help in a thousand and one ways. And in addition, for being delightful.

The Bro, who as he always does, has supported me and helped me in his very own way.

Guiller B, for all your great advice, ideas, help and, above all, support.

My parents, who are the best in the world and have helped and supported me unbelievably in this, as in all my projects.

Olaya Martínez, for being an exceptional editor, a tireless worker, a great professional and above all for her encouragement and hope. And for everything she has taught me along the way.

Sarima, for being an artist with exquisite taste, and for drawing like an angel.

Special thanks to my wonderful collaborators: Christy Cox, Mallory Brandon Bingham and Peter Gauld for caring so much about my books and for always going above and beyond. Thank you so very much.

To my latest collaborator James Bryan, thank you for your splendid work on the books and your excellent input.

And finally: thank you very much, reader, for supporting this author. I hope you've enjoyed it; if so I'd appreciate it if you could write a comment and recommend it to your family and friends.

Thank you very much, and with warmest regards.
Pedro

Author

Pedro Urvi

I would love to hear from you.
You can find me at:
Mail: pedrourvi@hotmail.com
Twitter: https://twitter.com/PedroUrvi
Facebook: https://www.facebook.com/PedroUrviAuthor/
My Website: https://pedrourvi.com

Join my mailing list to receive the latest news about my books:

Mailing List:
http://pedrourvi.com/mailing-list/

Thank you for reading my books!